# A Reckoning of
# Angels

# A Reckoning of
# Angels

## Stuart James Whitley

**GREAT PLAINS FICTION**

Great Plains Publications
3 - 161 Stafford Street
Winnipeg, Manitoba
R3M 2X9

The publisher acknowledges the financial assistance of the Canada Council
and the Manitoba Arts Council in the production of this book.

Design & Typography by Taylor George Design.

Printed in Canada by Friesens

CANADIAN CATALOGUING IN PUBLICATION DATA

Whitley, Stuart James, 1947 -
A reckoning of angels
ISBN  1-894283-06-6

1  Northwest, Canadian—History—1870-1905—Fiction.
2.  Frontier and pioneer life—Canada, Western-Fiction.
I.  Title

PS8595.H4935  R43  1999    C813'.54    C99-920164-6
PR9199.3.W4575  R43  1999

*For Christie,*

*you in chief, my love,*
*My peaceful Haven,*
*and my Beauteous Feast...*

*to employ Shevchenko's*
*fulgent verse.*

# Contents

# PROLOGUE

A fine mess, this. There was no longer any doubt. The two men he had noticed earlier were following him, and had been for some time. Though they were trying to be inconspicuous, they were clumsy, starting and stumbling over one another whenever he stopped and turned. God's eyes! This was the drawback to carrying everything he owned upon his back. Jan decided to make his way back to the immigration sheds at the railway depot next to the forks of the two muddy rivers. At least there were plenty of policemen to be found, because the Winnipeg authorities considered suspicious newcomers like Jan, who spoke poor English, dressed queerly, and had fearfully strange customs. He turned a corner sharply, and picked up his pace. No need for confrontation if it could be avoided. The clatter of nailed boots hurrying on wooden cobbles behind him confirmed what he already suspected: it would not be easy to shake determined men.

It was a peculiar sensation, being hunted. Close to exhilaration. He allowed the percipience to flood his body, feeling it drift like smoke through empty rooms, sensing its grip. It affected him each time he had been the subject of other men's predatory attentions. The prickliness started in the nape of his neck, spreading to the pit of his guts in a slow burn like a cave fire. His fingers twitched. Spit dried at the back of his mouth as his body brought itself to a state of bellicose readiness. He swallowed involuntarily, feeling his breathing deepen.

He was a big man, barrel-chested and standing six feet and four inches. With a high forehead, sharp aquiline nose, and thinning hair already at twenty years of age, Jan Dalmynyshyn could have been an imposing figure. But in his filthy clothing and tattered, lousy sheepskin overcoat, together with the shouldered jumble of boxes, tins and sacks bound up in grubby burlap and twine, he looked more the vagrant peddler.

Sidestepping quickly into an alley, he slipped his burden to the muddy ground. It was spring, but snow still lay like heaps of soiled bedding in the shade, though the thaw was well underway. Jan looked about him at the unpainted rear walls of the buildings, and the overspilling bins of rubbish lining the back lane. He shook his head imperceptibly, and wondered for the thousandth time whether the decision to come to the Canadian Northwest — Manitoba — from Pennsylvania was the right one. Perhaps he should have stayed in Galicia. The streets here, he decided with a inward sigh, were surely not paved with gold. Shrinking back into the shadows cast by a brace of leaning timbers, he could hear the hoarse whispering of the approaching strangers: "Where'd 'e go? 'E can't be far! Shaddup!"

Jan remembered the night his father and he had nearly been caught poaching by the patrolling groundskeepers of the *pahn*, or Polish landlord. Squirming down in the deep grass, three snared hares in a sack between them, Jan had felt the hairs prickling under his collar, and the blood had pounded in his ears then as it did now. Poaching was a serious matter. Prior to 1848, his father had told him, the forests were free for the harvesting of wildlife and fruit and fuel. But with the abolition of *pahnshchyna*, the compulsory free labour each man was expected to supply to the *pahn*, the nobility, had taken unto themselves the vast common pasturages and forests. Fees were extracted for each activity, whether gathering berries or twigs for the hearth. This was but *pahnshchyna* in more onerous form. And it was fiercely policed. The wardens were armed with pistols, and they were known to have killed men on mere suspicion of theft. The shooting of trespassing peasant thieves was considered no more serious than the killing of wolves in the sheep pen.

Jan's father, Pawlo Dalmynyshyn, had held his hand-axe firmly at his side. He was a devout man, regularly resorting to prayer both in matters of hope and forgiveness. But he loved a good fight, and his skills with his fists were a minor legend in the district. He stood away from no one, though he did not seek out quarrel. When the wardens wandered off without noticing them, and father and son were making their way back to their village, Jan asked: "Father, would you have struck at them?"

"That I would. Never fear. We were lucky that they had no dogs with them this time. Perhaps the luck was theirs." He spoke softly, the menace thereby amplified. Jan said nothing for several moments, for the tension had not left his body. His father had showed him how to fight, and he too loved a good tussle. But there was more at stake here than a quart of vodka, or someone getting improper with one of Pawlo's daughters. Jan spoke again: "But the punishment for raising a hand against the landlord is death; that is, death after flogging in some cases?"

His father trudged on in silence, for he appeared deep in thought, finally replying: "It is a serious matter to harm a man; take his life. But if the act preserves your own, or intercedes in the matter of your family's hunger, it may be necessary. Once having reached your decision, act. And act decisively, for a half-measure will surely seal your own fate. Make up your mind, and stick to it. Hmmm... it seems to me this is good advice in all matters." He put his hand on his son's shoulder.

The boy was not so sure, but he was certain that had they been caught, both of them would have been imprisoned, and that would have been the best they could have hoped for.

These thoughts dissipated as the two men pursuing him stood frowning at the entrance to the laneway. The sun had almost set, and its slanting rays were directly in their eyes. One of them hissed: "It's the only place he coulda gone, less'n he had wings! Shit! It's dark in there!"

He flattened against the wall; he could feel each chink, each nailhead against his back. His hand closed on a length of rough paling. The two stalkers started in, walking slowly, squinting. Across from Jan, in a pile of broken crates, a rat scuttled noisily, and the men stepped forward eagerly.

"E's in there!" cried the shorter of the two, as the other reached for the planking. "Come out ya scummy bohunk!"

Jan struck him behind the ear, putting all of his considerable strength behind the blow, breaking the board in two. The man fell headlong into trash, and did not move. His confederate turned with a cry, lashing out as Jan drove the splintered board into his throat. Eyes bulging and gurgling, he fell to his knees, dropping the knife he had been holding. It rang thinly against a pallet of bricks. Jan kicked his face as hard as he could, and the thief fell back in the mud and lay still, his legs folded like cast rags beneath him. Jan picked up the knife with its ornate, harlequin handle, fingered the blade, and stuffed it under his coat without further considering the two bodies. Picking up his bundles, he strode out of the lane. It did not occur to him to glance back; only fools wasted time looking over their shoulders.

He walked back to the immigration sheds, shrugging off thoughts of the violence like a brief, annoying rain shower. He stopped at the last outfitter, Bloode & Bell, at the foot of Bannatyne Street, next to other prosperous merchants such as the Botterill Bag Company, J.J. McDiarmid, and Ashdown's. He had been browsing all day in the shops and warehouses of agricultural equipment. It had been a depressing business, for the prices were all close, and all he had was twenty-four dollars in a folded bag, tied to his belly under his clothes. He chose not to enter the B&B warehouse. One glimpse of the gleaming implements, mowers and ploughs and rakes, convinced him that he would be wasting his time. He could ill afford more discouragements or diversions. But there in the compound behind the building was the wreckage of a Democrat. Looked like it must have been dropped from a gantry during unloading, he thought. The front end was stoved in, both wheels beyond repair. But the rear wheels, high and handsome under dainty mudguards sat true on their axle. He studied it at length, then turned to go back to the immigration sheds.

As he did so, an elderly man hailed him: "Wasn't she a handsome vehicle?"

Jan turned to appraise the newcomer; the man looked frail, but he walked with a spring in his step, aided by a cane in his left hand. His hair was white, unfashionably long, over the ears. Jan had noticed that men of means these days wore their hair cropped short at the sides, longer above. The old man had bright, friendly eyes, and the lines around them crinkled as he extended his right hand:

"David Bloode, sir, at your service."

Jan regarded him suspiciously. Each time someone had addressed him – an obvious immigrant — with courtesy, it meant that dishonesty was not far behind. He did not let go his bundles, and the other withdrew his hand, not seeming to notice.

Pointing at the wreck with his cane, he said: "Had it custom-made in Chicago. Look at them wheels! Fifty inches! She would've pulled like a dream. But some idiot unloading the steamer *Selkirk* let a brace of planed timber fall on her, and now look." He shook his head. "My customer was as mad as hell, but there was insurance."

Jan spoke without looking at him: "How much are you wanting?"

Bloode looked at him with some surprise: "I hadn't thought to — well, I was going to salvage the nickel fitments — the whip bracket and chair rails. You could have the hulk for three dollars; the wheels alone are worth more." There was no restraining the salesman in him, even though he had not expected to sell anything to this tatterdemalion.

"Agreed," said Jan. "Can keep it three or four days in yard to make it ready?"

"Ready?" The old man was puzzled. "Sure thing. Ready? You think you can salvage something out this? Those wheels are a bit high-set for a trap. Might be cheaper in the long run ..." he trailed off as it was obvious the big man was absorbed in his new purchase. He took the three dollars and dropped the silver coins, American, into a vest pocket.

"Good luck to you, and take your time here. I've no need of the yard until the week after next. If I can be of further help ..." He watched the young man stride off in a powerful, swinging step. How many settlers, miners, fur men, traders, freighters, hard cases, fools and hopefuls had he seen since he'd started business back in the seventies? These Galicians were a strange, suspicious lot. Well, the land was big enough to embrace them all, and it had its own way of spitting back the unworthy. A simple businessman could only give the benefit of the doubt, for he had decided a long time ago that most men were decent, if only given half a chance and a fair shake.

Back at the immigration sheds, Jan settled into the narrow bunk he had been allotted. There was no privacy, other than segregation between men and women on opposite sides of the building. A woman who chose to stay with her husband could do so, but she stayed with the men, and makeshift attempts to partition the space with suspended blankets limited what little air circulation there was. Fortunately, it was unusually cool in May. Though the breeze was stopped, sound was not, and the sheds clamoured with a mélange of languages: Scots brogues, American drawls, guttural German, and overwhelmingly, the slurring consonants of Slavic tongues. It was hard, waiting. But there were too few agents, and too many immigrants.

Jan turned to the wall and took out his purse. Recounting his meagre funds, dirty folded bills, and a small pile of silver and copper, he arrived at a figure that had not changed since he had arrived, save for the three dollars just paid to the merchant Bloode. The ten dollars for the land registration permit stitched inside his waistband was not to be touched. He stared. Not enough for implements, seed, food supplies and winter clothing, to say nothing of the fare to his homestead, for the Dominion government would pay only to the nearest rail stop. All the choice properties nearest to such points had long been snapped up by British, American and Canadian settlers. But until he got word as to where he was to get his land allotment, he could do nothing.

Tucking his money away, he rolled on his back, clasped his hands behind his head, and stared at the rough-timbered ceiling with its tufts of straw insulation starting from uneven seams, and thought about the two men who had accosted him earlier. They were but two of dozens of parasites who had shadowed him and his countrymen since he had left; he gave them no more consideration than he might had he pulled a bloated tick from a dog's neck. But unexpectedly, and despite himself, he thought again of home.

*Book One*

# UKRAINE

# i

Kameneta-Podolak was a sun-washed village in Ukraine, close to the Galician border. Most mornings, as he straightened during his work in the fields, a man might catch the morning sun glinting off the Carpathian Mountains. But there was not much time for pastoral reflection, for most of the men who were indebted to the landowners, moneylenders and others who thrived on the sweat of the peasantry were paid by quota: so much to till, so much to seed, so much to gather, according to the season. A man with a family would benefit by bringing all his children old enough to work out to the fields. But he who could not meet his quota was heavily penalized, and was without recourse. The courts were appointed and controlled by the privileged, which meant that decisions rarely went in favour of the worker. In fact, as recently as 1881, out of thirty-two thousand claims, not more than two thousand had been decided against the landowners.

Jan was the sixth brother in a family of fourteen. There had been four other siblings, but they had died of various illnesses which were a function of extreme poverty. Pawlo Dalmynyshyn worked like the slave he was to keep his modest plot of land. It was his fervent wish to be able to buy land for his sons, perhaps even add to his own tiny holding, but such dreams proved elusive. In addition to the taxes owed to the *pahn*, there were levies assessed by the local *viit*, head of council, or by the more well-to-do landowners, who extracted charges for pasturing, gleaning, and harvesting hay.

Then there was the fat village priest who sat beneath his onion-shaped spire with his apron held open for his share of tithings. Burial fees, christenings, services and blessings all contributed to funds in excess of his salary paid by the church, to say nothing of his own vast holdings which brought in a generous income. Pawlo felt that all of these and more had their hands in his pocket. There was never any end of it. The only respite for him was a tip of *horilka*, the strong vodka of the region, at the nearby tavern. But even here, Gallitzien, the dour old Jew who owned the rights to distill and sell drink, charged a heavy toll for his product. The only good thing one might have said about Gallitzien was that he was as harsh with any of his customers, including the *kaptsonim*, the poor Jews. "One chops the wood; the other does the grunting," he would intone in response to protest.

When the eldest of Pawlo's two daughters announced their intention to marry, worry was mixed generously with relief for Pawlo. He needed their labour, but they were mouths to feed. He could draw upon his new family, but there was the matter of dowries. Pawlo made a little extra with his skill in carpentry, but he was paid miserably below what his woodcraft was worth. He passed on his love of tools and wood to Jan, who would often help him with repairs. Even so, there was never enough.

In 1886, as soon as the fall harvest was in, and the hay put up for the family's two gaunt cows, he had set off for the oil fields at Drohobych in Galicia, about one hundred and eighty miles west, toward Krakow. There was always work to be had in Drohobych and Boryslav, for there was increasing demand for oil and ozokerite, or mineral wax. All the major countries had investments in the business. From as far away as America, John D. Rockefeller's Standard Oil Company was setting up business, for the lax legal regime permitted a free-for-all approach to extracting oil. Shafts were permitted to be sunk within arm's reach of one another, to work the same deposit. The only rule was that the product belonged to he who could draw it out the fastest. There was quick money to be made, and it drew capitalist, labourer, and rogue alike.

Drohobych was a village that had been inhabited since the days of Taras Bulba, and probably before. The primitive huts of cattle-herders and subsistence farmers had all but disappeared under the onslaught of foreign invaders come to spade and bail the greasy treasure from the soft shale underbelly of terraces lying in the shadow of the Carpathian Mountains. All of Ukraine, as this part of the world was shortly to be known, knew it for a befouled sewer of a place, but with a smile from lady fortune, a man could get in and get out with his pockets full, after only a short stint in the pits. This last thought Pawlo solemnly related to the family. Jan was to continue the woodworking that came in, so that there would be a little extra on the table over the winter.

It was not more than two months later that news came that Pawlo had no such grant of luck; he had been killed in a collapse. Pawlo's mother had taken the official-looking note to the fat village priest, for she could not read. She shook as she handed it to him, for nothing good ever came in official-looking documents. The priest demanded a fee of one *shistka* for the reading; this "small fee" would be sufficient for as "many repetitions as was necessary".

Pawlo's body, the note read, along with four of his co-workers, was irretrievably lost underground. No wages accompanied the note; there was merely a terse sentence explaining that Pawlo's debts to the company for room and board and 'extras' equaled what had been earned to date. Amid much grief, the family held a service outside the church yard, and interred Pawlo's old hat which he had left behind. There was nothing else. But a Christian burial for a hat? The cleric wouldn't hear of it, and suggested that Jan and his family arrange for a mass to be said at the mouth of the cave-in at Drohobych. The fees for such a service would be quite reasonable. As was often said: before one found God, one was eaten by the priests.

It was agreed that the land would be worked by a close friend of the family, Stefan Pivtorak, whom all the children including Jan called *vuyko*, uncle. Jan had always been unsure what the actual relationship was, but Uncle Stefan was liked and trusted. But he had his own worries, for his own holding was barely enough to feed him and his wife Katya. Though he took on the responsibilities of managing the small Dalmynyshyn place willingly enough, the future for all of them was uncertain. At fourteen, the future for Jan looked as dim as it had for his father.

Stefan Pivtorak was old. How old, no one was certain. But his age seemed to impart wisdom, of a sort. He knew about magical things. Above all else, he was a *kobzar*, minstrel, holding the secrets of some of the old *dumy*, or epic ballads. "The *duma*," he would say to those who protested that he often did not sing the same words each time, "is not a song but an expression of thought. It must make you think, remember, and above else — feel."

The instrument he played, and which was of great interest to Jan, was the *bandoura*, a fourteen-stringed instrument which resembled a large mandolin.

"This is not the instrument of our ancestors," said Stefan with more than a trace of sadness. "The *kobza* was very old. It had twenty-three strings. I heard it was the sound to which angels sang. But I never knew it. Those who have enslaved us over the centuries smashed every one they could find, but the *dumy* lived on in the hearts of our people; though it is true many songs have been forgotten."

To teach Jan the chord and melody arrangements necessary to link together the couplets, Stefan had to unstring and restring the instrument in opposite order, for Jan was left-handed. Stefan never complained about this, saying only with a grin that he should have taught Jan the *skazka*, stories usually told rather than sung.

Stefan's voice was low, with a raspy quality to it, though not unpleasant when raised in song. Jan had a higher, fuller voice, and they often took alternate verses as Jan began to commit them to memory. He preferred the humorous, ironical stories and fables, while Stefan had a fondness for the political *duma*, or the tales of sadness, such as *The Dying Kobzar*, which his gravelly tones made even more unbearably sad:

*...maybe some wandering Cossacks, a-gallop, will ride near.*
*And piteous music, perchance they will hear -*
*Turn them to this mound,*
*And bury me.*

Out of respect for the death of Pawlo Dalmynyshyn, the weddings of the two elder sisters were delayed. This had them both in a frightful state of worry, for without dowries and means to stage even a modest pair of celebrations, it was possible that their suitors might look elsewhere. All of the reassurances and reflection upon their physical beauty, and skill in the fields as well as the home were of small consolation to them. They would not be comforted.

This frustrated Jan. He felt keenly for his sisters. None of this was any of their doing. But how could a man's affection be suspended by the promise of gifts? Dowries in Kameneta-Podolak were hardly princes' ransoms. Only a fool could fail to see his sisters' charms; their dark brows and high, full breasts were the ideal hallmarks of *kunitzia*, Slavic beauty. In the beet patch one day, pulling weeds alongside Uncle Stefan, he raised the issue, showing some indignation at the possibility his sisters might be discarded for want of dowries. It wasn't fair, he argued, as the two of them, inched their way like crabs between the beet shoots. Stefan listened patiently, then straightened, both hands on his hips. Jan could hear his bones crunching and popping.

"So how would you feel, if you were to marry, but for one reason or another — forget the reason — you were to receive no dowry, and no proper ceremony. How would this make you feel?"

"I would feel unworthy, I suppose, but if the reason was good — "

"Why unworthy?"

Jan pursed his lips: "Well, it is always done. I mean, among people of equal ranking. As we all are," he added hastily. He felt uncomfortable as it began to dawn on him.

"So you see," said Stefan slowly, "the matter of marriage is more than a well-turned hip, or a comely face and *karmaziny*, fine clothes. It is a serious business, involving as much the union of families, as it is of man and woman. By poor Pawlo's death," and here he crossed himself, "I'm afraid your family has been diminished beyond the loss of head of household. But do not underestimate the importance of the *posah*, dowry. It must be observed. These are our signposts: they show us the way."

Jan turned away, ostensibly to mop his brow, but he did not want to show his discomfiture to Stefan. Deep within him, he felt the powerful, insidious undertow of unthinking convention.

One significant difference in Jan's life as the result of Stefan's influence, was that the older man insisted that Jan accompany him to the fortnightly meetings of the reading circle, the Mykhailo Kachkovsky Society, which had been established in 1874. The group, about thirty in all from the surrounding area, was chaired by an itinerant Jesuit, *popá* Kudryk, who was as different from the greedy village friar as a fart from a kiss, the saying went.

Those in attendance were a motley lot. Some could read; others did not understand the written word being read aloud. Some were deferential, respectful; others were argumentative to the point of being blasphemous. But the cleric was patient with each. His responses, though heavily reliant upon faith, nevertheless were compelling and respectful. He divided his classes into two parts: he would teach from three worn texts, the Bible, a book of sums, and a tattered volume of poetry by Taras Shevchenko, bound in well-worn leather, limp from handling. The second half of the lesson consisted of readings by the literate ones present, debate and discussion, and readings of the few letters that had been received by those who could not read them. It was the poetry recitations which stirred Jan, for they evoked powerful images of both past and future as yet unimaginable. There was a miller from a neighbouring village who went to all the reading clubs in the region, whose rich baritone delivery added a thrilling resonance to the recitation.

As the book of verse was passed about, each one who could chose a passage, and read aloud:

*when I die, then make my grave*
*high on an ancient mound*
*in my own beloved Ukraine,*
*in steppeland without bound*
*whence one may see wide-skirted wheatland,*
*Dnipro's steep-cliff'd shore,*
*there whence one may hear the blustering*
*river wildly roar*

Familiar images gave way to stanzas decrying oppression as well as the cruel privations to which the peasantry were subjected. Yet Taras Shevchenko, poet prince of the Ukraine, had written those words some fifty years earlier. Would matters ever change? Was there reason to hope? Often the poetry readings would yield to fierce debate over what the future held. Were the cries of poets any more worthy than the anguish of the toiling farmer?

"Remember what the Polish Prince Czartoryski said once?" one called out, " 'We don't need Peruvian gold mines. The skin of the peasant — that's the best Peru!' The bastard's been dead more than thirty years, and we are still thought of as no more than the carcass upon which the privileged feed! Nothing has changed. Nothing will."

When Jan was called upon to speak, for it was the priest's practice to include all present, he asked: "To be called 'selyahnen' peasant — is this not a form of condemnation? Is not the path we follow fixed by the conditions into which we are born?"

Kudryk shook his head slowly: "Words. Many men sneer when they use this word. But what does it actually mean? The word comes from the root word meaning 'country'. That is all it means. But if you choose to allow it to have more meaning ..."

A whiskered, pot-bellied man removed his pipe and spat: "All well and good. A fine discourse in language. But to the *pahn* we are nothing more than serfs to do his bidding. Things are worse now than they ever were before emancipation ... what, more than fifty years ago? The boy's right: our path in life is fixed, right enough."

There was a pause, some shuffling. Jan thought he could sense agreement; was it resignation? Things were bad for everyone. It was undeniable, this. Never was there enough to eat. As growing families necessitated the subdividing of lots, land was becoming scarce if not barren. And debts and taxes were a grinding, unrelenting burden. Would *popá* Kudryk have an answer? Indeed, was there an answer?

The priest seemed tired. He gazed at the group arranged about him, some standing, others sitting, and still more who were sprawled at his feet.

"Tonight's discussion," he said gently, "puts me in mind of a custom said to be observed by the Romans: once each year, they sponsored a feast for their slaves, following which each slave had liberty to speak as he wished. The idea was that it would act as a release. Once finished, they would return to servitude of varying degrees of severity. Is one day enough? Can it be possible for a man to travel the path of freedom once, and not long in his heart to make it a permanent condition? I think not.

"I'll warrant you that your lot seems not much changed from the time of enslavement of our grandfathers. But there is a fundamental difference. Every man in this room is free." He held his hand up, uncharacteristically, as if to forestall premature debate. "And that makes each man here, and his neighbour, a monarch."

There was more shuffling and small noises of dubiety. But it was clear Kudryk was about to say more.

"Serf or free man, we are all able to make choices, because God granted that we should have independent minds, capable of free thought. He allows even the heretic to choose a path away from Him. Oh yes. We are all free to ignore the signposts. We are free to leave the map in our pocket. A man chooses the breadth of his grasp, and so he will choose what will guide him. The smallest mind is preoccupied with others: why does my neighbour have so much, and I so little? Did you hear what old so-and-so did with such-and-such? These are the blamers and the nay-sayers. Those who bemoan their lot, but find time to sneer at the efforts of others."

He spoke passionately, and it was clear that he had some experience which underscored his remarks. He continued:

"The next class of people is the majority. These are those who think of nothing other than things. How many *gulden* can I stash under the loose brick in the hearth? What a fine coat I have! Look at the whiteness of my best shirt! How brilliantly has my wife embroidered it! How happy I would be if I could only live in a fine house. Fools. Blaming others. Blinded by greed; imprisoned by anger, distracted by helplessness. Such people have their needs - their happiness - defined by others. Or more precisely, what others seem to have.

"Then there are those — like most of you here — who are concerned with ideas. Yes. An idea can change what ten thousand armed soldiers could never do. But you must commit to it; believe in it, follow it."

One man shook his head. "These are grand words, *popá*. But they do not change the condition of our miserable lives! How will they put food on our tables?"

The cleric smiled without humour. "The sweat of your brow will always put food on the table. But to have enough, and to work so that there is time to contemplate; to be treated fairly — this is the problem. But the first step in the journey is emancipation, and that has already occurred. The second step is direction, and third, commitment, and so on. It is not complicated, only difficult." Smiling, he thought for a moment, and added. "We are not all graced with the courage and talents of a brilliant poet. Sometimes it is important to choose the battles we fight, if that is open to us."

Jan spoke up: "But there are no choices. If the landowners and moneylenders cut off all our hope, what chance is there? We are still nothing more than serfs, as Vasil Drydych just said."

Kudryk turned to him sharply: "Boy, you seem not to be listening." There was a shade of hardness in his voice, as if he had expected more. Jan cringed a little, inwardly; he felt his cheeks flame.

"Shevchenko, the light of our people, was a serf. Did he resign himself to whatever lot befell him as the result of his birth? No. But his central, driving idea was that we are all equal, on earth as in God's eyes.

*all on this earth - no matter*
*be they czars' or beggars' children*
*are the sons of Adam!*

"Old Ha Daschko, stand and read to us *The Dream*." He handed over his tattered volume to be passed hand to hand to the old man in flowing mustaches who was struggling to his feet. "Read well. To recite good verse is to experience another man's tears, or his joy. It is as good for the soul as the writing of it."

Clearing his throat, and gesturing broadly with his left hand, the elder read in a worn voice that still reverberated with the strength he once had:

*to every man his destiny.*
*his path before him lies,*
*one man builds; one pulls to ruins,*
*one, with greedy eyes*
*looks far out, past the horizon,*
*whether there remains*
*some thing he can seize and bear*
*with him to his grave ...*

And so it went, giving Jan so much to ponder that he fought sleep at night following each meeting of the reading club. Did a man truly have choice which path to follow?

# ii

There was not much time, however, to consider abstract thoughts, for the needs of the moment consumed the daylight hours as well as the short time before bed. The matter of the dowries still pressed upon the household, as there were signs that at least one of the suitors was becoming less ardent in his attentions.

Finally, Jan announced that he was inclined to spend the winter at Buryslavka, as his father had tried two years ago. There was considerable debate amongst his mother, sisters and younger brothers, but it was decided that Stefan would accompany him, and return in the spring. Manoly, at twelve years of age, would remain as head of the household until they came back.

The distance was not inconsiderable, for the path they would need to follow was well over two hundred miles. There was nothing for it but to walk, carrying their possessions. No money was available for an animal, or to hire one.

"Well," said Stefan cheerily to the assembly of relatives, "we'll see a bit of the countryside, and we'll find work to keep ourselves in food, with perhaps a roof should the weather turn nasty. No need to worry."

But worry they did, for though unbidden and unacknowledged, the spectre of Pawlo and his faded dream sat with them. That anxiety was thinly veiled as the families bade farewell to the two, one a man well into his maturity, and the other, a strapping young boy who knew nothing of life beyond the horizon of Kameneta-Podolak.

As they walked along barefooted to save the leather on their boots, Stefan kept up a steady discussion on a variety of subjects, insisting the normally taciturn boy reply. "See there," he pointed to three men dancing on the treadmill of a chaff cutter. "Landless peasants working like draft animals! Only cheaper!" he laughed. "For the few *shistkas* they will earn for that torture, they will have riding on their backs the landowner, the tax-collector, the money-lender, the priest, the tavern-owner and God knows who else. So it will be with us, do you think?"

Then, as often happened, Jan was at a loss for words.

"Speak to me boy, speak to me. Use your head for more than a place to hang your boots; think. We may be poor as mice, but God gave us a brain. Consider what you have learned from *popá* Kudryk. After all, you can read and write a little. And do your sums. Do not be afraid to exercise your brain, for it is no different than a muscle that may grow fat if not in use."

It was late fall, and the countryside was resplendent in autumn foliage. The land was a patchwork of manorial estates, peasant farms, and the dwarf holdings of the poor. In the distance, the purple sentinels that were the Carpathians formed a steady line to the northeast. The sky was a pale blue, and though it was tolerable enough during the day, by nightfall it would become quite cool. There was a constant tang of smoke in the air, as straw and chaff were being burnt off. Jan's heart swelled, for this was a glorious land, and he felt that he was setting off on the grand adventure of his life. He could not want a finer tutor, mentor, or companion than Stefan, he thought, for Stefan spoke to him as an equal. He did tend to push him in his thinking, Jan noted; but that was good. Yes. A good thing, this.

They talked about many subjects, but a pervasive theme was the possibility for escape from the crushing poverty both had known all their lives, by the ownership of land. They talked about emigration, as many were starting to do.

"The stories we hear of America sound almost too good to be true," said Jan.

Stefan shifted his pack to the other shoulder. "Yes. If anything sounds too good to be true, it usually is. There's the story of Vanko Koralia, from Svoboda. He left his land, small as it was — but adequate for himself and his wife and two children. Lured by tales of fantastic riches, he left for America, settling in a place called Jersey.

"He married another woman there; a Ruthenian who had emigrated before him. Later, he dropped her and moved to some other place, I don't know. And he married another woman."

Jan stared at him in amazement: "This confirms it! Only a rich man could afford to maintain so many women! But he must be a fool!"

The other man laughed, stopping to tamp his *barunka*, a bell-shaped pipe. "I doubt whether he ever maintained more than one at a time. He was a man who, like many, thinks only with his *chooi*, cock."

"In any event, wife number two found out about wife number three, in some accident by which such knaveries are inevitably discovered, and he was sent to an American prison. When he got out, no one would trust him or hire him, so he returned to Svoboda, with no greater wealth in his pockets than he had when he left, several years before. He found everything in order. There was his house, his property and his wife; all was in order." He broke into a grin.

"However, unhappily, his children had now increased in number from two to four!"

They chuckled mightily for several minutes, their laughter echoing in the still evening. Holding each other's hand to steady themselves, they walked for a time so, the residue of merriment yielding to a deeper fondness. It was getting dark, and time to get off the road.

There were many travellers, and each waved or had a greeting as they passed. There was a bond between honest men, Jan thought. It was courteous and reassuring to acknowledge a passerby. Too many thieves and cutthroats lived in the shadows, and no chicken's neck was too skinny to wring, as the saying went. It was well to get away from the roadway and snugged down in the woods, if a barn was not made available to them. There, they would be safe, and Stefan might play a song on his *bandoura*. Softly, of course, with pauses to listen for sounds in the darkness. Occasionally, they heard the passage of rough men, curses and muttered threats rending the night's gentle fabric. One evening, they heard plaintive cries in the distance, just before dawn. One, a man, imploring; the other, a female shrieking, then silence. Jan shivered under his thin blanket.

"Should we not go to see what is the matter? They cannot be far off," he whispered to Stefan. "Go for help from the authorities?"

Stefan turned on his side, facing away from Jan. "Pah!" he spat. "For all we may know, the trouble is being caused by the authorities! Besides, if you are going to pelt every barking dog, you will need to pick up a lot of stones." After a long silence he spoke again. "An old man and a boy will not add much to the night's festivities, I do not think. It would be foolish to intervene. Besides, it may only be the *russalki*, water sprites who were maidens who had drowned themselves, and entice men to their deaths in a watery grave."

Jan did not agree with this, but said nothing. His mind seethed with the horrible possibilities the night noises promised, and he felt impotent. He thought about the stories he had heard from his mother as a young boy about evil in the form of *chorts*, little devils, *nichki,* the shadow people, and *russalki*, witches. Jan glanced at Stefan. Everyone knew that witches abhorred aspen; perhaps that was why the old man chose such a grove each time they bedded down in the open. After all, he knew about magic, it was said. With a nervous scan of the surrounding gloom, Jan pulled the edge of his blanket over his head, exposing his feet, and fell asleep.

Some nights later, they had settled once again under their blankets, hands clasped behind heads, gazing at brilliant canopy of stars coruscating above them. The nearly full moon was at its apogee: "A waxing moon or a waning one?" asked Jan.

"The cusps point to the left; it is a waxing moon. The weather will change in the next few days, but I think we shall be there by then."

Jan suddenly thought that he did not want this journey to end. The silence hung between them as if speech were unnecessary. "I was thinking," said Jan quietly, "that this moss-covered bank is as soft as the finest feather bed."

"And a steel-sprung one, at that," replied Stefan, his pipe glowing redly in the dark. "Such a bed, I am told, inspires the sweetest dreams ... mmm, the fairest women, the choicest meats, sweetbreads, riches ..." he trailed off sleepily.

"And there is no window to see upon waking," added Jan, referring to the folk belief that should one first lay eyes upon a window at awakening, the dreams of the night will be instantly forgotten. "So such images can be savored the following day!"

After a moment, Jan spoke again in a sigh: "How did we all come to be so poor? Why are there so few who can realize their dreams?"

Stefan answered in a distant voice, though by the tone of Jan's voice, he was not really seeking an answer.

"Our fathers were serfs. They traveled a fixed path without deviation or relief. Born unto the land, they died on it. If for some reason they were able to leave - to serve in the army, perhaps - they returned to it only after permission from the *pahn*. Freed in 1848 - the very year I was born - we hoped for great things. A chance to share in the wealth of this beautiful country, perhaps. For some of us.

Stafan rolled over. "But then they imposed a law which prevents immigration. They will not pay us to keep ourselves alive, but they do not want us to leave. Bah!" Gone was the light mood of only moments earlier. "A country of such beauty, possessed of a plundered heart."

Neither spoke while the moon settled, casting a gentle silvered lumination over the wooded valley. Fireflies flickered in the thick underbrush nearby, and far off, they could hear the thumping of grouse, and the sharp yap of a hunting fox.

Stefan recited softly:
*peaceful land, beloved country*
*o my dear Ukraine!*
*why, my mother have they robbed you?*
*why do you thus wane?*

Jan managed a smile: "That's *The Plundered Grave* isn't it? Ah, *Tarasdissime!* The conscience of our land! Do I have it right?"

But he was answered only with a gentle snore; Stefan had gone to sleep, hands still clasped under his neck, pipe still clenched in troubled jaws.

## iii

For another four days they marched steadily, taking work where they could for a bowl of soup or an onion. They poached the occasional partridge, and found hospitality rarely, for few had much to share. In a hilly stretch along the Carpathians, the *Pidkarpattia*, they rested with warm, generous people who called themselves the *Pidhiryany*, the hill-folk. These were fiercely independent souls whose claim to this inhospitable terrain reached back to their retreat from the Tatar invasions. In these mountains there had once roamed the fabulous Dobush and his band of followers, who robbed the rich in order to aid the poor. Here were the *truskarvets*, warm, sulphurous mineral baths that soothed aching joints and leached weariness from tired limbs. How wonderful it was, Jan thought, to linger with those whose generosity asked nothing in return save good manners. It took more than poverty to demean the spirit: was it despair, the absence of hope?

Upon their departure, they were presented with an egg. No *halunka*, single coloured egg, this, but an exquisite *pisanka*, multi-hued, decorated object. Legend had it that the peasant who laid his basket of eggs down to help the stumbled Christ lift his cross, turned back to discover them changed into glorious *pisanky.* Such a gift was a measure of high esteem, and portended good fortune. Jan wrapped it in a bit of cloth, and put it inside his hat.

On their way again, they stopped at the village of Voroblevychi, where they prayed at a curious chapel created by hewing out the centre of an oak tree that must have been all of seven arm spans in diameter. This was the last survivor of many such trees that covered this land in his great-grandfather's time, Stefan had observed. To pray in such a place was considered good luck, and no traveller would pass without stopping to request the kind graces of the saints, and leave at least a *shistka* in the collection box. "We can ill-afford not to invoke the protection of the heavens," said Stefan. "Never be so foolish as to think you can do without divine providence."

Bypassing the town of Drobhobych, they followed the river Tysmenytsia south to Boryslav, the major site of oil extraction for twenty years or more. They needed no milestone to know they were getting close. The smoke over the city hung like an ominous pall, and the cloying stench of petroleum was evident many miles out. The countryside was yielding to a tree-stripped, bad smelling place, and there was a constant sound, a murmuring insinuation, which continued even after night fell; Jan was unnerved. They stopped before entering the city itself. "We'll have to pay for lodging, once in town," Stefan had said, and had bedded down under a tree. That night, they had nothing to eat, and Jan's stomach rumbled, so he directed his energies to speaking with Stefan, so as to avoid thinking about food. He asked about the work they were about to do; the subject had not been raised since they had set off.

"Make no mistake about it. The labour will be hard. I have no direct experience of it, of course, but I have heard from others without exception, that it is grim work." Sensing Jan 's anxiety, he added quickly: "But what is hard work to a peasant?" He laughed.

Then serious again, he spoke more about the matter: "I heard once that the oil oozed from the ground like sweat. All that was needed was to dip a mare's tail into it, and squeeze the goo into a bucket.

"Then shallow wells were dug, and overnight the oil seeped into the hole, filling it, whereupon it could be easily scooped out. But now I think they go much deeper to get the stuff. This is the work we will do, if we are lucky enough to secure positions. Pick and spade work. The only difference from what we're used to will be that we avoid the sun's heat and the wind's breath."

But now that they had arrived, Jan had serious misgivings about working at the bottom of a great pit, where neither light or birdsong penetrated. He shivered; it was not a pleasant thing to contemplate, and he wondered how soon they would be able to return to Kameneta-Podolak.

After an uncomfortable night, they were off before sunup, reaching the outskirts of the sprawling town just as dawn broke. Boryslav lay in the centre of a saucer-shaped valley, which had been entirely taken over by the petroleum industry. The headframes of the deeper wells sprouted like alien beings from the treeless landscape, some as high as eighty feet, with two supports extending from their box-shaped crowns, like thin, trailing arms. Buildings were of the poorest construction, with roofing being of oil-streaked rolled tin in most cases. The stench of oil was oppressive. As they started down the gravelled road, they were accosted by two policemen in high boots, tunics nipped at the waist, wearing large pistols dangling in front. One held a short, thick staff with a turned knob at the end. He wore a high, peaked hat with the cresting of a senior officer; the other was shirtless, and even from a distance they could smell the raw reek of vodka.

"*Ne tak svdko, chomak!* Not so fast, wagon-master! You are obliged to report in for questioning. There is a small matter of the passing-by tax!"

Stefan snatched off his cap, and assumed a posture of total deference. "Good sirs, we are not passing through; we are here to work."

"Ah!" said shirtless, while his smirking partner looked on "Then there is the matter of the arrival tax!"

Stefan looked at Jan. There was bewilderment in his expression as he turned back to the policemen. "To be sure, there are more taxes in this land than the imagination of man, but I have never heard of such levies. This cannot be right."

The senior policeman stepped forward, a cold face now colder. "This is serious. You not only display a peasant's ignorance, but you insult my officer. This undermines authority, and encourages disrespect for the law. I may have you up for insubordination!"

"Forgive me, *hetman*, chief." Stefan dropped to his knees. "Pray, what is the toll?"

"That's better. The fee for both is two *shistkas*. I'm prepared to overlook your poor attitude this time." He extended his hand, palm upward, as Stefan fumbled in his sash for the coins. Shirtless looked on greedily, and seemed almost ready to make further demands, but the other waved him off with his baton.

"Now be off with you, but be warned. If you come to my attention for even so much as the slightest infraction, I'll strip you, lock you up, and drop the key in the nearest mine shaft. Away!"

His companion kicked Jan in the seat of his trousers, as he walked by. Jan did not look at him, but kept his gaze on his uncle, walking with bowed head in front of him. We starve ourselves so thieves like these can prosper! The guffaws of the two policemen stung like a switch. Jan's jaw worked, and he resolved that if Boryslav was a hard place, then he would be harder yet.

# iv

Jan lifted his toolbox and placed it in front of him. It was a beautiful thing, the corners neatly dovetailed and reinforced top and bottom with brass fittings. He smoothed his chapped, leathery hands across its gently scarred surface, worn smooth with the unguents of oil and sweat and care. Opening the lid carefully, reverentially, he studied the oiled tools, each on its peg; one separated from the other. They were old, but of the best quality. Such tools enabled cleaner, stronger joinery; people were willing to pay more for such work. These dully glowing implements were not just things, they were an extension of his eyes and limbs, and they could mould wood like clay under a potter's fingers. He looked up, studying the smashed vehicle he had just purchased, drawing mental lines where it would be reshaped to his particular needs. The wreck drew his thoughts back to Drohobych, and another wrecked cart.

They had found work at the first place they applied. Ten *shistkas* a day for work at the windlasses, and thirteen for underground pay. While they debated this between themselves — Stefan wanted Jan to work above ground — they heard a crash, followed by a storm of curses, then a man wailing. Rushing outside, they saw that a hand cart that had been bearing two barrels full of raw petroleum had slipped off a ramp, rolled over and spilled its load. The cart was ruined; oil was everywhere. The overseer was livid, thrashing the hapless labourer with a walking stick.

"*Soó kin sin!* Son of a bitch! *Schlah to bi trafith!* May curses befall you!" The object of his fury rolled about, trying to avoid the blows.

"I'd fire you, you piece of shit! But you'll pay back every *shistka*, with interest!"

Jan and Stefan looked at each other dubiously. Stefan shrugged. "Let's sign on. We can try it for a week, and then we'll see. In the place of your father, I must insist that you work at the windlasses, at least until I can get some first hand idea of the work below. At least I'll know that you're safe."

Reluctantly, Jan agreed. To their surprise, they were put to work immediately. The dormitory was not far away, they were told, and they could move in when the shift was done. Jan walked with Stefan to the pit's edge, inside a crude framework which housed the cables. Stepping into a large wooden tub with another man whose features were barely distinguishable under a coating of grime, he nodded at Jan with a wink and was lowered away. In a trice, he disappeared from view as the hole swallowed him. Straining his eyes, Jan could not see a thing; suddenly his name was called in a harsh voice: "Dalmynyshyn!"

Hurriedly fastening his identification slip to a buttonhole, for there was considerable secrecy about the direction of digging, and the productivity of mines at any given time, he scrambled to the windlass shed, where he was shown to a horizontal wheel with five men between the spokes. He took his place, resting his buttocks as the others were doing. The basket was descending; this was relatively easy. One of the others grunted his appreciation: raising was back breaking work, for the baskets were filled with clay from which the ozerkerite was broken out. It took six strong men to wind the cable, and there was a quota to meet, or the crew was docked a portion of their wages.

All that day, until dark, the routine was the same: wind, pause, lower, pause, and repeat. The muscles in Jan's back screamed with the labour, and when the shift bell sounded, he could not straighten up. Together, he and Stefan followed the mob of silent men to the long, ramshackle building that served as the worker's hall. Inside, there were long tiers of shelves as high as a man's head which served as sleeping benches, and equally crude trestle tables set around a large stove.

Jan was ravenous, but he was surprised to see that most men headed for their stash of vodka. It was not long before the two of them were singled out as the newcomers, as the spirits seemed to slough off the day's fatigue.

"Petro-virgins!" cried one man. "We cannot break bread with those who have not savoured the sweet wetness of our goddess!" The mob of workers surrounded Stefan and Jan, forcing them roughly to their knees.

"Now bow your heads and close your eyes while we intone a prayer to the black queen!"

The two did as they were told. There was violence in the way they were handled, but no real menace. The chant began:

*O deep in the bowels of the darken'd earth*
*far from love or joy or mirth*
*we toil on our knees - no room for standing*
*still the o'erseer shouts and threats, demanding*
*till at last her greasy kiss embraces*
*with sooty lips upon our faces!*

At this, ladles of oil were poured over the heads two kneeling men. The thick, foul-smelling liquid matted Jan's hair and rolled down his neck under his blouse. He leapt to his feet, outraged.

"This is my best shirt! I only have two! This is a crime!"

The crowd laughed heartily: "How long do you think your precious shirt would last in the pits?"

Stefan reached out to steady Jan, but he shook his arm off, looking around antagonistically at the chortling, sneering men.

"And now," said another, "it's customary for the newcomer to stand us to a round of drink; Kaspar has plenty on hand ..."

Jan was incredulous. But before he could utter the curse which was forming on his lips, Stefan cut him off. "Then a drink it is for everyone!"

There was loud cheering, and the workers swarmed to the bent old man at the door, who was happily unpacking clear, shining bottles from a box on a handcart. Stefan approached Jan, and with an edge to his voice, he said, "Be still, boy! We need the good graces of these clods, or our life here will be far more miserable than it need be. It'll be hard enough as it is. No more of your petulance, and show some cheer, even if you do not feel it."

They sat on the floor, and passed a bottle of *horilka*, vodka, one to the other. One grinned at the newcomers: "How do you like Kaspar's *samohon*?" he cackled, using the slang expression for 'self-propelled'.

Jan felt its numbing bite at the back of his throat, then the giddy sensation at the back of his neck, forcing out all other thoughts for the moment. He took another swig, and wiped his sleeve on the back of his shirt, passing the bottle back to his uncle.

"Perhaps there'll be some compensations," he nodded. Funny thing was, he didn't feel a bit hungry now; he had his hand back on the bottle before Stefan had finished swallowing.

Jan hated the work at the windlasses. It was as crushing to the back as it was to the mind. The men, stooped like beasts of burden, walked in an endless circle until the lading bell rang. Then the pawl on the winding gear was flipped over, and the basket was lowered, the men using their bodies as a brake. The silence was broken only by the rhythmic clicking of the windlass gear, and the grunts of the workers. Each was alone with his own thoughts until they came off their shift, and had reached for the bottle. Then hopes and dreams, disappointments and rage spilled out in a torrent.

The toilet was a particularly dangerous place. The dormitory butted up against an abandoned headframe, and the waste was expelled into the shaft which had been boarded with a crude platform, into which had been cut a row of draughty holes. It fascinated Jan to think of his shit whirling more than eighty feet to the bottom, though no sound could be heard from the depths of the fouled mine. He looked across the concatenation of bowed and grunting men; the rough food meant that constipation was a frequent ailment.

"What're you staring at, boy?" snarled an oil-stained miner who was working at his buttocks with grimy fingers. "Never seen a man passing a length of timber before? Avert your prying eyes, unless you have a mind to come over here and help withdraw it!" There was a rattle of chortles from the others. "Wasyl, be careful. It may be that you're passing the last head you bit off, and who knows what it will bite off on the way by!" More sniggers now, but wary. Wasyl Shepticky had a foul temper, and was quick to put his fists up.

Shepticky growled and stood up, and his place was hurriedly taken by another. Jan could see the black handprints on his white buttocks as he pulled his threadbare *kholoshni*, winter trousers, to his waist. He turned and glared at the others, all of whom looked down and leaned more earnestly into their exertions, except Jan, who made ready to leave his seat.

"That's the thing about me, even my shit won't leave me. Nothing like loyalty, I say. What say you?" His small, red-rimmed eyes stared under heavy lids at Jan

Stefan was right: rough work begat rough men. Be careful. He sized up Shepticky. Shorter than Jan by a head, he was nonetheless powerfully built, with thick arms and legs made for heavy work, and the cunning, suspicious face of a rain-soaked dog at the door. His fingers worked at his sides. No doubt: he was spoiling for a fight, looking for an opportunity.

"I have the same problem," replied Jan slowly. "Shit, unlike money, is slow to leave me."

The other man took a step closer; the odour of menace as tangible as that from the petroleum pit over which they stood. "Perhaps I can help. Maybe I should kick the shit out of you." He said this quietly, in a parody of a grin. Jan said nothing, but turned slightly sideways, and gently limbered his left elbow, tucking his jaw in. His right arm hung at his side. Keep the target small, protect the nuts and throat, and watch the eyes, his father had explained. When you strike, strike to finish. Fighting is not lovemaking. No half-measures, now; a dirty business, this.

On came Shepticky, head down, fists like dirty carriage lamps. Jan side-stepped quickly, and the older man's flailings passed by harmlessly. The row of seated spectators turned their heads to follow his charge as he thumped by in his heavy boots. Jan could see he relied on brute strength to destroy his opponent, and his quick glances gave away where he wished his blows to land. As Shepticky charged again, Jan suddenly dropped to the ground, and the other stumbled over him. Quickly, Jan jumped as high as he was able, coming down with his knees on either side of the man's spine, knocking the breath from him. Then with all possible strength in it, he kicked the prone body in the head. It was a vicious blow, tearing open the scalp and rendering Shepticky nearly unconscious. It was necessary to make an example.

Seizing the groaning man by the hair, he dragged him to a vacated hole, and stuffed his head into it. It was too narrow to permit Shepticky's shoulders to pass through, but Jan pushed at him all the same, cursing the man through gritted teeth. He relented only when he felt Stefan's hand on his arm, and his gentle voice.

"Such bad language. Your father would not approve. Come. You have made your point with this worthless ox - and with anyone else who would try you."

There was not much to show for the first month of labour. A fight, very little money after the deductions, and not much prospect for improvement. At the end of the first week, they had been shocked to learn that the paymaster took his own tithe from the earnings, but were cautioned not to protest for fear of firing. That was why there was a spare spoke at the winches, Jan was told. A winchman foolishly protested. And the retribution did not end with the firing, for there were dozens of new arrivals each day to take the place of the dismissed employee; it was the blacklist that cut deep. There was no mistaking an oil worker, and he had to produce his tag in order to work at the next pit. There were many ways that the owners kept their greasy grip on the workers, and the blacklist was as good as any.

The work at the winches became worse by reason of the fall in temperature with the onset of winter. The winch room was unheated, and the men sweat during the raising, and shivered at the lowering. Their breath hung like a pall in the rough plank shack, and condensed and froze on the underside of the tin roof. It resembled an ornamented ballroom where the men daily danced their slow version of the tarantella. Jan asked for the right to go underground, and this was granted, but that for the first month he was to work at the same rate as winching, for it was a "common trick" to get underneath for warmth. Angry, Jan was, but helpless to do anything about it. Angrier still was Stefan, who felt that this was both disobedience and work unfit for a boy not yet sixteen. But Jan was determined, and the following day, he shouldered a pick and rode down the shaft with his silent, sullen uncle. As they climbed into the bucket, Jan saw the skinny, red-nosed replacement at the winches being ushered into the winch room. He'll not last long, Jan thought. They could hear the lad coughing as they disappeared into the gloom of the shaft.

The circular entrance to the shaft was a shrinking paleness above them as they lowered slowly. After a few minutes, Jan could make out in the feeble glow of the storm lanterns they carried with them, the irregular cribbing timbers about six feet away on either side. These were trees with the bark and many branches left on, so that their passage seemed through a sunken forest on the pathway to hell. Stefan was silent yet, and Jan could see that he was not looking at him. His head was down, and Jan felt his sadness, though he could not see his face. Lower still they went, and the closeness of the dark was like an eyeless mask, close over the face. There was no sound. But the smell of the earth's bowels was overpowering. Jan was used to the petroleum smell, for the cable and winch drums were covered with the stuff. But this was different. Jan could almost feel the miasma invade his lungs with each breath, and he hurriedly tugged a rag over his mouth and nostrils, as Stefan had done several moments ago.

By and by, more than seventy feet of cable had paid off the drum, and the winchmen saw the tattered bit of rag rove through the twist which marked the bucket reaching the bottom, and they halted. As the cable had a certain elasticity to it, according to the load, this was not an exact indicator, and the bucket stopped suddenly with a bump on the platform rigged over the sump. Beneath them, under the loose-fitting planking, the two men could see their lamplight reflected back in the oily ooze, not more than five feet away. Off to one side yawned the drift, and as they got out, they could see men arriving with a fresh load of mineral wax for hauling to the top in the vacated bucket.

As they moved past the silent men, Jan turned to Stefan: "Whew, the air is poisonous down here! Aren't these lamps dangerous? Might they not set off a fire in the oil?"

Stefan took a long look at him. "Dangerous? Now you are asking if it is dangerous?" He shook his head. "If your father is watching, he will have his famous fists ready for me at the gate of St. Peter." He pointed at the bird cages suspended every twenty paces or so. "Sparrows, they are. And they're the first ones to go, with their tiny lungs. You've got to learn to keep an eye on them, for when they fall from their perch, the time left to escape is measured in heartbeats. There is a line at the shaft hooked to a warning bell at the top. One tug, and the bucket will descend quickly." They walked to the face of the drift, where others were working, loading the wax-laden clods into a small tram. In the dim reflected light, men moved like ghosts, stooped, for the ceiling at this point in the drift was low.

The foreman, a thickset Pole named Jackyno approached them. He looked over Jan the way a butcher might appraise a side of spoiled pork. A miserable customer, this, Jan thought morosely. He pulled aside the cloth over his mouth.

"You are big enough to get some proper work from. You will break out the wax from the earth, and load the trams. Watch the others, and learn. Lay your tools down only at my signal."

He took his leather cap off, and combed his fingers through lank hair. "You must get to know the earth as if she were your mistress. Listen for her sigh as you caress her private parts with your pick and your shovel, for that will signal that she will shortly open herself to you. There is no escape from her dirty embrace. Should you feel a tremour, watch the birds closely, for when her Ladyship belches, her breath will not be sweet. Get to work, for we're well behind today's quota, what with all this socializing."

Stefan followed Jan, whispering: "And never follow a seam higher than your shoulders without proper cribbing, regardless how badly you may want to make your quota. No matter how insistent the foreman may get."

Jackyno stopped and spun on his heel, almost as if he had heard. "One more thing," he cautioned. "For the first four shifts, you, boy, will work alone. Make a mess of it, and you're done. Mess badly, and some accident or another will finish you off. Accidents are God's way of protecting us from fools. Better you should kill only yourself, than to take other valuable labour with you." He stared intently at Jan in the gloom, greasy water dripping in slow, cold punctuation from the ceiling of the drift behind him. Then he spun and was gone.

The tunneling and excavations had no plan more complicated than the following of promising clay deposits. This meant that rival companies could tunnel at cross-purposes, for the treasure belonged to he who could first extract it. Among other unpleasant possibilities, this meant that tunnelling could be going on mere feet or even inches from the drift in which one was working. This explained why working men would stop at the cry of the foreman, each holding breath while listening for the shuffle and thump of nearby excavations. The well in which Jan worked had long ago given up its oil, though there was always hope that another pool would be discovered. A blow of the pick could bring the greasy black flow oozing into the drift, flooding the sump, where it could be brought out in open barrels. Of course, the possibility existed that the flooding could occur suddenly, like a tear in a rotten bladder. Then there was no chance that anyone could get out alive. Bodies of hapless men were recovered as the oil itself was ladled into tubs like so much paraffin, the corpses oil-saturated and dissolving. Each swing of the pick was a lottery.

All of the labour was manual. Beyond the windlass and block-and-tackle, everything was done by hand, so cheap and plentiful was the supply of hungry men and boys. Even women whose appearance had fooled the foremen had gone into the pits. And some whose appearance had not. A few of the operations, most notably those owned by the Americans, were flirting with steam engines, which offered a huge advantage in production, for they could be operated with no interruption. But the majority of owners laughed at such pretensions. They too could operate without pause, and without the fantastic capital investment necessary for engines and the expense of trained mechanics. And there was a further advantage: should production fall, or prices tumble, wages were simply reduced. There were still plenty of starving *komornyky*, landless peasants, stumbling in from the interior to take their place.

"*Hey, gazda!* farm-master!" the Polish foreman Jackyno called to Jan one cold morning in February. "Why do you Galicians enjoy fucking sheep so close to the mine shaft?" He snickered mirthlessly.

Jan hated the attentions of the overseer. He was sarcastic, nasty, and he held their jobs over their heads like a cudgel. "I don't know," he mumbled.

" Because they push back that much harder!" More snickers; he watched Jan slyly for a reaction.

"That's a good one, *namiestnik*, governor," replied Jan without a smile, using the Polish word in apparent deference. "Here's another riddle: what's the definition of frustration in Poland?" This time it was the foreman's turn to be silent. Then he spoke:

"What? Working with dullards like you?"

"No," replied Jan "The cow moving after the stones get piled!" And he laughed in spite of himself, Stefan and the others joining in. Jackyno was flushed and tight-lipped. No one told jokes at his expense, and he flashed Jan a murderous look.

"*Wstaway, drabie!* Get out, bum!" he said in Polish, shaking his finger at Jan As the labourers turned to leave for the tavern, one of them muttered that Jackyno had lifted too many stones as a boy, and now his brain was addled.

"*Co to jest?* What's that?" the man was clearly becoming unhinged. "*Ah, Idz do !karczmy!* Oh, go to the tavern!" He showed his yellow teeth and spat in Polish: "*A zaraz tam wychodz do roboty!* And better be at work on time!"

The threat was plain enough, and the men were subdued as the men shuffled from the dormitory, and made their way to the commercial district.

In 1890, Boryslava had all of the aspects of a wide-open frontier town. It no longer bore any resemblance to the sleepy, bucolic village it had been only twenty years prior. Every enterprise was committed to the pursuit of profit, which meant that the ends of enrichment were to be accomplished by the most minimal means. Buildings were thrown up in a hurry, and leaned against one another like squat, stolid drunkards. Roofs leaked, doors would not close, and chimneys leaked smoke. Roads were muddied tracks of convenience, no public lighting existed, save for the flares from the mines, and refuse was piled everywhere, for its removal was a private responsibility. Large grey rats scampered everywhere, and it was believed with good reason that more than the occasional rodent found its way into the *kulbassa*, sausage, that was sold in the company store.

In addition to the capitalists, hordes of parasites followed in their wake: money-lenders, liquor-purveyors, prostitutes, gamblers and thieves, quacks, fortune-tellers and charlatans of all kinds lived off the simple peasants who managed to save a few *kreuzers* from the owner's clutches. To Jan's consideration, this seemed no different than the situation at home. True, there was more cash to be made, but there were more hands in the pocket. And the sheer brutality of the work demanded respite, and the options were few. Cigars and *keishka*, blood sausage, those sweet braised loaves, *kolachyky*, were fine treats to look forward to, but a man needed more than tasties to get away from the black bitch that ruled their lives underground. The *chytalnia*, reading club, supplied the necessary commodities in abundance.

The *chytalnia* was in fact a whorehouse afloat on a sea of vodka. It was grimly observed that the only things read at the reading club were the last rites for those dying from fighting, from alcohol poisoning, or from some disease picked up from the slatterns who serviced customers while standing in the shadows. It was no secret that the establishment was owned by the same Pole who owned the mine they worked.

The road to the *chytalnia* wound through the rigs which were tightly packed together like grim spectators at a funeral. The law in Galicia required only the purchase or lease of sufficient sod upon which to erect the necessary headframe and excavated clay heaps, and tunneling or extraction could proceed in any direction at any depth without limitation. The shack which housed the prostitutes and vodka barrels was an unnamed warehouse, furnished with the most elemental fixtures. The roof was in such disrepair that rain or snow passed freely into the interior. In winter, as now, a thick, gleaming rime of ice lined the inner roofing planks, as the warmth from the sweating men condensed above them. It yielded a steady patter of cold droplets without end, a *slohta*. The term was the equivalent of those who made dreary company, or an unending, mind-numbing task. It was a popular expression.

The door opened on a scene of near-bedlam. The raucous swirl of voices made ordinary conversation impossible. Glass smashed, furniture rattled and tipped, harlots shrieked at their customers, and the grunting curses of struggling, intoxicated miners formed a pandemonium, as indeed the grinning, toothless miner in front of them turned and shouted over the cacaphony: "Welcome to the Capital of Hell!"

The slaking scald of vodka at the back of his throat calmed Jan, as it always did. There was an open hearth, over which a cauldron simmered, giving off the heavy scent of pork stew. Two *kreuzers* was entitlement to all one could eat, black bread included. Men coming off double and even triple shifts with nothing more during that time than an onion and a dry slab of bread, kept this crusted black pot firmly in their mind's eye, as a mariner might steer by the pole-star.

Jan nursed his jar of spirits contentedly, feeling the pleasant blunting of his aching muscles. All around him, men tussled and elbowed, but he moved with them like a wheatstalk. He found himself staring at a pair of blue eyes, quick, vulpine. They stared back, widening ever so slightly. Entranced, he held his jar to his lip, motionless, dirty thumb hooked into his belt. The noise around them seemed to fall away; it was as if the two had stumbled upon one another in a forest glade. A grimy hand slithered around her waist, groping at her bodice. She jabbed it with what must have been a hair pin, and with an anonymous yelp, the hand was hastily withdrawn. She moved forward, and slid her arm under his free elbow, and looked up at him with a smile. Tucking a loose frond of glossy black hair in place with the pin, she said:

"Hello, *holub*, sweetheart. Are you wanting friendship tonight, or is it loving you have in mind?"

Jan blushed furiously. He stood frozen, still holding his raised drink. She laughed and gently eased his arm down. Jan stammered, speaking so low that his mutterings were inaudible. She responded gaily, as if every word was clearly understood. Tugging at his arm, she began to draw him through the crowd. He followed, a foundering barge in tow by a yacht. Threading her way up a swaying staircase, ignoring the drunken catcalls from onlookers recumbent on the steps, she coaxed him into a warren of small rooms, each behind a forlorn rag of a curtain.

Drawing aside a curtain as they passed, Jan was startled to be confronted by a man wearing only an open shirt, his soft white belly hanging in folds above his nib of manhood. No miner, this. Beyond him, naked as an egg, a woman sprawled indifferently on a pallet, her legs shamelessly open. The fat man's angry bellow broke the momentary spell, and Jan's new companion turned and yanked on his elbow, laughing.

"Naughty boy! Shouldn't peek where you're not invited! We're only entitled to the cubicles that have the drapes drawn open."

So saying, she led him into one, and sat him down by easing him backwards, he still the puppet; she the master. As she lighted a candle with a sulphurous match, he asked: "What is your name?"

She giggled as she loosened and removed her bodice in a single, practiced motion: "Next you'll be asking to meet my father!"

Jan stared helplessly at the gloom above him, unsure what to say next. This was the first woman he had ever seen undressing, and the sight of her was as a hammer blow to already addled senses. When he looked back at her, she was stepping naked and without apparent modesty out of her shift, kicking it aside with an almost dainty sweep of her toe. Straddling his legs, she put her arms around his neck, kissing him hard on his lips. He could taste the vodka in her mouth. He suddenly realized that he still held the jar from the tavern. She pulled back and contemplated his face, her palms cradling his jaws.

"A couple of *kreuzers* I'll need for an aging mother who's barely survived the cholera. You wouldn't begrudge me such a small favour, would you?"

He shuffled in his pockets, awkwardly, for she still sat on his lap. Looking down, he could see the mysterious darkness of her disappearing between his thighs. There was a breathless feeling to him now, and he was sure this wasn't the vodka. As he handed her the coins, she looked greedily at the change. Springing up suddenly, so that her small pointed breasts trembled, she tucked the money in a stocking toe slung from a thong. Kneeling, she briskly pulled off his trousers and opened his shirt.

Jan could not speak. His heart slammed at his ribs. She stepped over him again, and slithered against him until she was seated over his legs. Jan leaned back on his arms. He could feel the heat in him rising, and he groaned, closing his eyes. Deftly, she reached between their bodies, grasped him firmly, and guided him into her with a slight shrug of her hips. His eyes opened, his mouth flopped, and a sigh was cut off by her wet mouth. She shuddered against him, rocking so that he moved deep within her. Very quickly, it was over with three sharp spasms of release. He cried out and fell back.

"Mary, Mother of God!" he cried. "Again!"

"That was quick, sure enough, *holub*, but that's all for two *kreuzers*. Now, for another two ..."

Later, when Jan returned to the lower level, his head was spinning. Not a bad way to spend a little cash, this. Most of the coins in his pocket were gone, and he realized that he had only enough for another half-quart of vodka. Well, one more it would be, then he would find Stefan and get back to the bunkhouse. The morning shift was at six, and it must be well past the middle of night.

He made for a clutch of familiar faces at the serving counter. They were in the boisterous throes of denouncing Jackyno, a regular pastime:

"May he be cursed, his seed be cursed, and the product of his seed be cursed!"

"May Jackyno be cursed in his comings and goings!"

"Oh that he roast on the white-hot grids of hell for eternity, and then some!"

"Amen!" they all cried, as others tried to outdo the previous condemnation.

Jan took the remaining coins from his pocket, and was about to call on the tap-man, when a shout came in Polish:

"*Co to jest, chamie?*" What was that, you scum? A powerfully-built man was moving through the crowd like a steam-plow. "No one insults my country-man! Insult him; you insult me!" He began to push men aside more vigorously; some fell, others protested. Suddenly, the room erupted into chaos, as men attacked other men, for the addled wits of the revelers perceived threats at every gesture. Jan was struck heavily on the temple, and he was sent headlong into a squirming mass of antagonists. His tightly-pinched coins were knocked from his fingers. He was hit again, and he staggered against the wall where his slumped to the floor. It was cold here, and a bit out of the way, but Jan felt nothing. It was as a dream. The brawl played out in front of him, and he slid over onto his back.

Looking up, he could see the brilliant array of stars through a missing plank in the roof. What were their secrets? This was surely where the angels dwelt. How beautiful things were from a distance! What promise! Like Boryslava, would the promise fail to match the mind's assurance? A blurred face swam above him, luminous, beautiful. Blue eyes hooded, dreamy. *Behold, I send an angel before thee, to bring thee into the place which I have prepared!* Unbelievably, the face lowered over him, red lips parted. He became lost in the sensation of a warm, moist mouth over his own, and he did not notice nimble, soiled fingers tugging and searching his pockets.

# V

Winter was nearly passed in a routine as predictable as it was brutal. The talk among the miners increasingly was of America. Emigration had started in earnest, and many tales of success and ruin were finding their way back to the old country. But most intoxicating of all were the rumours of free land. Rich, treed, and as much for the taking as a man and his family could work. Nearly every man in the pits was there because he had been put off the land, or was trying this last resort to save what little was left. The idea of land for the asking seemed limited only by the fact that it was very far away. Real as a dream upon waking, but no less intangible.

Stefan and Jan spoke of little else. A Polish recruiter, then another, had been through, leaving elaborately illustrated flyers showing bucolic scenes of plenty in the American West. That these men were commission-paid salesmen for the shipping authorities, little better than thieves and mounte-bancs who preyed upon the gullible and the desperate, was lost on the hoardes of men who gathered around to hear them speak. The advertisements they had brought from their masters, passage brokers for Cunard, White Star, Black Ball and others, were sold, so eagerly were they sought. In some cases, it was reported, such otherwise worthless pamphlets had been peddled as if they were the actual bill of passage.

One evening, a tall, scholarly man by the name of Josef Oleskiw held a meeting in the open space at the back of the reading club. The crowd of oil-stained workers filled the room to overflowing. Many were men whose desperate need of sleep from the long hours of toil showed on their faces. But these were men in need of hope more than rest. Everywhere Jan looked, anxious faces strained to hear the handsome stranger's soft voice. Well-dressed and deliberate, his black suit gave him the aura of an academic, which indeed he was.

He held up two pamphlets, like playing cards. "I have written two booklets which can assist you. *O emigratsii*, about immigration, and *Pro Vilni Zemli*, about free land. The first was written after I returned from America and Canada." He pointed to a map of the world, indicating the two countries with a determined finger, then pointing to their own country. "Those of you who can't read should have someone read them to you, for they contain all you need to know about obtaining your own land."

There was an animated murmuring; men looked at one another and their eyes shone. Here was news that confirmed what they had been hearing from the agents. He talked not so much of the land to be had, but of the pitfalls that faced them, should they decide to go. He related tales of unscrupulous agents, and shipboard conditions worse than any sty of diseased pigs. He spoke of resentment and even hatred among some of those who would be their new neighbours. He at one point seemed to be so discouraging, that the initial excitement died away. He seemed to sense the moment, and changed course.

"But America and Canada await the toil and sweat of some Ruthenian men and women. I have been to both countries. I suggest to you that Canada is the wiser choice. There is more land for the taking, and it is a more peaceful place. A more empty place. In the year 1895, when I was there, I was able to convince the Canadian government to appoint my good friend Kryrolo Genyk as immigration officer in Winnipeg. This means you are welcome, and the person who will greet you will be a countryman."

Suddenly, a harsh voice challenged Oleskiw. "Why do you mislead our people? Is it for profit? How much for each poor head that you deliver up?"

Another voice: "Yes, what is this fraud you attempt upon us?"

Oleskiw blinked. An inherently courteous man who pursued his concerns for his people out of altruism, he was not accustomed to confrontation. Lately,

however, he had become aware of the opposition of the landowners to immigration, and the objections of the Austrians who counted on poor Ukrainian
boys to fill out the ranks of their military.

"I am paid nothing but my expenses. The Canadian government ... "

"Pah," said the man who had interrupted. One of the Polish overseers.
"What do you take us for? Fools? It is a land colder and more inhospitable than
Siberia. Everyone knows that."

And another: "How do you expect us to buy the passage for such a vast
journey? We are simple workers, not rich men." He looked around for approval.
There were several who nodded their heads, for the tide of opinion began to
falter.

"Who appointed you as the watchman?"

Oleskiw cleared his throat, and spoke softly; those at the edge of the group
could barely hear him. "I care not whether any of you go. But if you do, there
are things you must watch for. Others have gone before, and you can learn from
their mistakes. I am here to sell you nothing, to take nothing from you. I have
something precious to impart, and that is information. That is all."

Then the owner stood up and threw aside his hood. Instinctively, the crowd
immediately around him opened up, and deferred to him. His Ukranian was
fluent. There was no mistaking the anger in his voice, upon his brow.

"You would send these hard-working men off to a place so far away, so
bitterly cold, that they would surely die, if not from cold, then loneliness, then
the heartbreak. I charge you with being in the pay of foreign governments who
need slaves to work their barren soil. Is that not true?"

Oleskiw fixed him with a steady eye and replied calmly. "I know it is true
that you need the men you work to death here. I know it is true that every man
has a wish to have a piece of land to call his own. I know it is true that every
man needs hope, which is not to be found at the bottom of your filthy pits."

The owner looked as if he would explode. With a gesture that clearly had
been pre-arranged, others stood up and made for the chair upon which Oleskiw
was standing.

"Get off my property!" the owner bellowed. "Off! No more lies and insults!"

Now others stood up, Jan among them, uncertain. This Oleskiw seemed
like a good man to him, and he should not be mistreated. He moved, as did
others, to place himself between the guest and the owner's goons. Soon there
was mayhem, with shouting and pushing, and Jan found himself up against
Oleskiw. He took hold of his sleeve.

"This way, sir. Come quickly. Things can get out of hand."

The other man crouched to avoid an object that was flung at no one in
particular. "Lead on," he said. "I shall pass over the usual glass of rum after my
presentation." He smiled thinly, for the uproar seemed to be increasing.

Quickly, Jan lead him outside; the night was cool, and the stars were resplendent overhead. The two walked in silence to Oleskiw's carriage. Jan had

many questions to ask, but they all tumbled in his head at once. The other man glanced at him.

"Thank you for your intervention. These meetings don't usually get so rough. Emigration has barely begun. Only the most astute landowners and pit-bosses realize what it means, potentially, for their profits. Word gets around fast. So I am starting to experience more and more of this ... frustration."

He spoke softly, in an even tone. Like *popá* Kudryk, he was obviously not a man given to extremes in language or gesture, though he was committed to great causes. There were mythic qualities about such men, Jan thought, that made him feel shabby and irrelevant. Was it possible to become great? Was it only the pursuit of noble ideals that produced such a man? That was a part of it, to be sure, but men like this had something which set them aside from ordinary folk. It was as if ... as if men of such stature had been touched by an angel. How else could they think and act with such divine confidence?

It was as if the other man was reading his thoughts. "You are thinking perhaps that I am not what I appear? That there is some other motive for my presentation, as some of the others suggest?" He smiled, softening the question.

Jan looked at him, wondering why indeed a man would otherwise risk such displeasure from powerful men, but he was afraid to ask. Instead he asked, "Is it true? I mean, about the land?"

"There is land aplenty for those with sufficient courage to leave and find it. It costs not only the money for the passage, but the strength to withstand terrible adversity. And part of that is forsaking the old country, this tortured land of ours."

"And this land - ?"

"In America, in the Canadian Dominions. I have seen it with my own eyes. Rich, black and fruitful. Wooded sufficient to last a man a lifetime, to cut and dry as he pleases."

Jan's eyes were wide, and Oleskiw took notice. "There are many evil men between here and there. Some will try and restrain you; others ... many others will steal from you. Some will hurt you; some will hate you for no other reason than you are not of them. I know, I have felt it myself."

"This cannot be true, sir. You?"

Olsekiw managed a thin smile as he stepped on the spoke of his pony cart, and swung himself up. "Had I but time to talk to you all, I would have warned you. No one is free from hatred and ridicule.

"But this place, our fair land, has too many people competing for the same diminishing sum of soil. There is starvation and *beehta*, misery, upon the land. Something must be done. If this is the way I can assist my countrymen, then so be it. We are all God's servants in one way or another."

He clucked at the sturdy pony, which swung its head and lurched into a walk. Jan sauntered beside it, his hand upon the mud guard, as if his evanescent tie with this stranger could be maintained for a moment longer

"Should I go?" he asked. "Do you think that I should go?"

Oleskiw tightened the reins, and the animal stopped. He looked down at Jan. Though his face seemed impassive, there was a warmth in his eyes that suggested to Jan that he accepted the question with the enormous trust it carried. What he said next could have the effect of changing a person's life forever. Hold out promise, or condemn. The choice was his, he knew. As did Jan. There was a pause, which surprised the man, for he had been asked this question many times. Yet for the first time, he had a sense of how much hung in the balance, and he addressed the young, oil-stained man firmly.

"Only you can decide. To make a decision, you must gather as much information about the subject matter as you possibly can. Weigh the consequences of each choice. Be honest. Consider which decision is the best. Seek help, advice. Pray. But also know this. That your mind's choice must also be that of your heart, otherwise you will not find the true path." He took up the reins again, and the pony started in anticipation.

"And mark you this: live with your choices in life. If you have selected as I have advised, then at that place, for that moment, the decision will be the right one. Good night my boy." And the darkness swallowed him.

# vi

For a time, Oleskiw seemed forgotten, for no longer did talk of free land animate the conversations of weary men. The drear routine of the pit was a narcotic; it made the pursuit of thought an impossible task. Stefan and Jan now worked the same shifts, in the same part of the stope. Stefan had promised Pawlo his son would be looked after, and a man who failed his word was without honour. There was little time for chatter when a man was bent over a shovel. But Jan could not entirely remove Oleskiw's images of rich soil in the new world, empty, untilled, waiting.

"You never said what you thought of this man, Oleskiw?"

"I did not."

Jan smiled. Stefan had a way that lacked subtlety when there was a subject he did not wish to pursue. "Well, tell me now." There was a pause in the work, as the huge copper drum filled with thick, tarry fluid was being maneuvered for the hoist to the top. "Did he impress you, as he did me?"

"I saw you stealing away with him, I did. Perhaps a good thing too, for many were in a good appetite for a tussle."

"Why do you avoid my question?" It was a puzzling thing, this.

Stefan turned to consider his young charge, though the boy was nearly half a head taller. In the gloom of the pit, his blue eyes sparkled with the reflected glow of the safety lamps. He opened his mouth to say something, appeared to reconsider, sighed, then said, "You are grown. It is for you to make up your own mind about the man and what he has to say. In truth, I was afraid to encourage you. There are many perils associated with such a trip, as he quite fairly warned - or at least, tried to warn, before the managers' puppets got into the act.

"I am too old for such a journey. I would not consider it in any event. This is my land; I could not imagine leaving her. I fear for you for these same reasons. There was a time when such a trip would entrance me, however ... "

"But once a fortune is made, it would be an easy matter to return home, perhaps to live out our days in ease." The warming in the boy's voice was apparent, and Stefan smiled wearily.

"I tell you this: Oleskiw seems a good man to me, and seems to speak the truth. Unlike so many we have seen here, sticking papers under our noses, selling impossible dreams, taking the scratched marks of poor men who cannot read or write, pocketing their paltry funds ... it sickens me. But Oleskiw: different, I grant you that. An honest man. But I say again, what seems too good to be true ... "

A stern shout from the overseer cut off the low chatter among the crew. They went back to the face of the tunnel, and began their tentative explorations, picking and digging and listening.

It was Smyla, the short man with the terrible scar across his forehead who heard it first. "Hist!" he shouted, and the other men froze, knowing that a rumble had sounded somewhere. They stood in the near-dark, a tableau of tormented forms, unmoving, silent. Smyla's grubby finger in the air a silent warning: be still. As each man reached the end of his breath, they collectively exhaled, each conscious of the beating of their own hearts. There it was again, this time a tentative shake of the clay beneath them. In the distant darkness, a piece of wood splintered, then popped.

"Run!" screamed one, then another, as tools were dropped, and men rushed as one for the shaft. The shaking became more rhythmic, it seemed to Jan, then suddenly he was shoved forward in a shower of filthy soil, and he sprawled on his hands and knees. Behind him, there were muffled clumps of earthen material tumbling from the shaft ceiling, punctuated by the rending and cracking of green timbers pushed past the point of their resilience. Then silence. Dazed men picked themselves up from the floor. Then a shout: "She floods!"

A thick stream of heavy oil moved silently and sluggishly between the heaps of timber and collapsed shale and clay, like a thick, venomous serpent. By now the cage had fallen, so that the first shift of men were already being winched to the top. The run of oil was torpid but steady, and there was no telling whether it would remain constant, dwindle, or inundate them suddenly and without warning. There was a clamour at the shaft as each man vied to be taken next. Some in desperation had started to climb the rough cribbing that framed the open shaft. Jan was dazed, for the fall had caused him to strike his head against a shovel blade. The sludge had now formed a puddle over the toes of his boots. He looked around for Stefan. He was not at the shaft; it was impossible to believe that he would have left in the first shift; even now, the cage had returned, and a second load of miners struggled to get aboard. Their shouts and curses were swallowed up by the cavern's close walls and the black ooze that now spilled without a sound into the sump below them.

"Stefan!" he called. "Stefan!" But his voice had no greater potency than those whose thin cries seemed distant, even though they were not more than two dozen paces from where he stood.

He sloshed through the muck back along to the point where they were working, a sense of dread mounting in him that had nothing to do with his fear for himself. He continued to call, but it was nearly impossible to see anything more than murky forms. On all fours, the slime making for near impossible purchase along the way, the stench in his nostrils seeming to force the air from his straining lungs, he put his hand upon what was unmistakably a human body. His hand drew away involuntarily, and he gasped.

"Not Stefan, dear God. Let it not be Stefan," he prayed.

It was not. Smyla. He let the man's head drop back into the muck. There was a groan, and his heart fell as he saw Stefan, buried except for head and left arm, in a tangle of broken beams and clay. The oil rippled by him, and just beyond, Jan could see where a large seam had opened up, and through this wound the glistening blackness drained steadily.

"Stefan," said Jan. "I am here. I will have you out in no time." He began to paw at the debris that covered the old man. It was apparent that the task was hopeless without men and tools. "Help!" he cried. "Help! Help us!"

There was no response. The remaining men at the shaft were nervously eyeing the rising level of oil in the sump, and many were beginning the climb up the shaft itself. This was a dangerous proposition, for the footholds were greasy and the timbers of the most inferior grades of wood, much of it salvaged from other pits, fires, or other such sources. Already, one man had fallen into the bottom of the shaft, and had drowned in the tarry mess without the remotest possibility of being saved. Not that any man paid him the least attention in their panic.

He shouted again, then cursed them. Pleaded. He turned back to Stefan, who was barely conscious. "It won't be long," he said desperately. "We'll have you out and away in no time, you'll see."

There was a faint movement of the other man's head. "It is finished. Go. Save yourself." It was almost inaudible.

Jan shook his head furiously. "Never! We go together!" He began to scratch at the material around Stefan's head. He strained at a balk of timber, ceasing only when Stefan groaned in pain.

"Leave me, boy," he moaned. "I am broken inside, for there is no feeling." The oil lapped at the side of his face, and it would be a matter of an hour perhaps, at most, before it covered his nostrils. Unless they were suddenly flooded, as others had told had happened in other pits. He seized the man's hand, tears streaming down his face at the impotence he felt. There was nothing he could do, and the was no hope of assistance from the others, for they had gone.

He squeezed the callused hand, and felt a feeble response. Or thought he did. Stefan was trying to say something. Jan lowered his head, until his ear was nearly against the man's mouth. There was a flecking of blood on his lips.

"You must go, Jan. Go and find the land that awaits you. You cannot stay here any longer, for you ... you will end like this. I will join your father soon, and ... when I beg his forgiveness for leading you here, I would diminish my guilt by securing your promise that you will leave."

Jan wept, holding onto the man with both hands, that he might by sheer will extricate him from the soil's grip. "I will not leave you."

"It is almost ... time. Promise you will ... seek a new beginning; find the land that awaits you. Promise."

Jan pressed his lips against the back of the man's hand. "I promise," he cried. "It will be."

There was no answer. For a very long time in the silence of that foul hole, the boy held the hand of the uncle, and the fire of life passed from one to the other. He remembered *popá* Kudry's tale of the Greek myth, how they believed that only upon the death of the gods can human beings have interior fire, for the death of a powerful spirit ignites the flame in another: it must be true, he felt, for Stefan lived on now within him. When the oil rose above his nostrils, the old man did not move; it was clear, mercifully, that he was gone. Jan reluctantly let go, removed his filthy wool cap, and recited:

*the kobzar ceased, in sorrow plunged*
*his hands no more can play*
*young men and women round him pause*
*to wipe his tears away*

He stood up, and slipping, falteringly, he made his way to the shaft, and began to climb. The tears flowed freely, and he briefly considered that he should fling himself to the bottom of the pit. But he remembered his promise to Stefan. He remembered Stefan's earlier injunction, one made many times. "A man who fails his word is without honour; a man who fails his heart is without faith."

# vii

The journey by train across Austria and Germany to the point of departure at Bremen, was long and costly. There were others on the train like Jan, hundreds of them, who had been pushed to the point of giving up their homeland, to try for the New World and a fresh start. The promise of these things could not be seen in these weathered faces. Even the children seemed sullen and remote. There was no place to sleep beyond where they sat, and the stench from the tightly-packed bodies overwhelmed all else. Here and there, a fight would break out, as a man returning from the tiny toilet cubicle which opened out onto the tracks found his seat taken by someone whose numbness from sitting on the floor required reprieve.

There was no grace, no generosity between people whose ability to endure privation had seemed unlimited. It irritated Jan, without his understanding it. He could not plumb the vast gulf of fear which underlay the abandonment of home, family, and country. True, hope lay in the expectation of a better life, but this was nothing more than chance. This for a people whose life was bounded by the shout of the overseer, the times for planting and harvest, and the rituals and icons of worship. These moorings were being left behind. For many, the fear showed itself as anger. This was exacerbated by the depredations of the swarms of parasites that flocked to relieve the unworldly, mostly illiterate travelers of their funds. Phony visas were extracted, unnecessary medical examinations by 'doctors' demanding a fee, poor food, lice-ridden blankets; there was no limit to the ingenuity of the charlatans brought by this swelling tide of fleeing humanity.

Jan kept to himself. The pain he felt over the loss of Stefan was not yet scarred over. The indifference of the owners and overseers was difficult to comprehend; it was as if Stefan was not a man, merely a number, and one easily removed from the roster so that another might take his place. Daily such men had been arriving, as the two of them had, not yet a year ago, hungry for work. So many, that wages had begun to shrink, and the threat of job loss was a constant spur to do more, to work harder, longer. It was his promise to the dying man that propelled him, and yet, as each mile rattled beneath him in this wondrous conveyance, the vision of a place of his own, of riches, of a future that would be solely dependent upon the fruits of his labours, began to take hold like a beacon. It is not what prompts action that is important, he thought, it is the belief which sustains it. That is what they all shared: this fragile belief that the rumours and testimonials spread by letters of those that had gone before, the hucksters and swindlers, and men like Oleskiw, were true. A better life lay ahead, it was certain, but ... would the path be so difficult that the prize be too costly?

Of the three hundred and twelve persons who lay packed into steerage class of the *SS Kaiser*, eighteen of them - all but one, children - died in the storms that wracked the North Atlantic, that autumn of 1896. In each case, a brief service was held in the ship's stern, and the body, wrapped in a blanket and weighted by a fathom of chain, was consigned to the gray water. It was bitterly cold on deck, and people did not linger at these dreary punctuations of a dreadful passage. But Jan stayed. He imagined the body as it silently slipped beneath the troubled, thrashing waves, to a place of calm and peace.

*the water groaned, as pained,*
*then parted and enfolded him*
*and not a trace remained*

Why did one man die, and another live? One suffers and the neighbour thrives. To some, things came easy; for others, blistered hands and an early grave. If this ... this randomness was God's will, then it truly was a strange thing indeed. Did not each man possess within him something extraordinary, even the brute? That was how *popá* Kudryk might have put it. Even Stefan would have grudgingly conceded the point, while asserting how some people sometimes unintentionally hurl us into the pain of grief and loss. Jan struggled with these matters, and it daunted his faith. What was the use of the try, if the gifts God provided were to be covered over by hatred and cruelty or simple misfortune? Each man is alone, he decided. And success was a matter of chance. But without the try there was nothing.

The landing at New York was without ceremony. Like beasts, they were herded into vast immigration sheds on Staten Island, from where they could see a dim outline of the city, now shrouded by rain and fog. The noise was frightful and unceasing. Officials barked names from lists; their underlings shouted orders. People came and went in groups according to numbered rosters and dates of arrival. Lineups for food, medical examinations, toilets, bedding, information, translation, embarkation, interviews, even haircuts - which were mandatory as a means to limit the omnipresent flea infestations - were continuous and unending. Each man, woman and child was assigned a number, to ease difficulties with the range of languages and dialects. As a single man, Jan was given a card with the number 'seven-hundred-thirty-seven' to hang around his neck by a loop of string. The cord itself was grimy, for it had graced the throats of many before Jan. Had there been a family with him, they might be '737-1' and '737-2' and so on. It was efficient but devoid of humanity.

Once landed a fortnight later at the docks, the change from this regimented society to one of indifference was something of a shock. For a long time, Jan stood near the top of the gangway from the ferry dock, uncertain where to go. The clatter of men and equipment, the clamour of a dozen different languages around him, the swirl of people and goods had a hypnotic effect. Bumped from behind, he moved to one side, but no one heeded the few attempts he made to ask the way.

At length, he was hailed in his own language: "*Ho chomak!*"

He swiveled, delighted to hear a countryman's voice.

A sturdy young man, perhaps twenty-five, strode toward him, arm outstretched. "Welcome to America, land of the plenty; home of the brave. Your new country. Now your home."

Jan shook his hand eagerly, admiring the man's fine clothes. He was immediately aware how shabby and dirty his own were.

"I am Poitras Kerasevitch, recruiter for the Darlingford Coal Company of Bethlehem, Pennsylvania. Are you in need of a job?"

Jan nodded vigorously. "Oh yes. Yes. I will be a very hard worker."

"I have no doubt of that. You are a well-built man. Have you experience in mines?"

Jan looked at his hands. The mark of the oil was still with him. The heels of his palms, and the linings of his fingernails were black etchings. He had not seen a looking-glass in some days, but he knew there were similar stains on his face where the petroleum had entered a cut. Of course, the recruiter understood this.

"Another refugee from the Boryslava caves!" he cried, slapping the newcomer on the shoulder. "Well, there will be no slopping around in tar pits here. Coal, hard coal, is what we take from the ground. And there are laws to protect workers, and we take great care to ensure safety." Seeing the deepening interest in Jan's eyes, he hurried on in a presentation well-greased by hundreds of such speeches. He had not yet yielded Jan's hand.

"We offer the cost of your trip by rail to Bethlehem, provisions, and an outfit for work, including boots." He cast a barely concealed look of disdain at Jan's cheap footwear. "Real leather boots, properly hob-nailed and paraffin-treated. These will be charged against your pay in six equal payments. You will receive eight dollars a week, based on ten hour shifts, six days a week. Pay packets every two weeks. A bonus of fifty cents a shift if you work a double shift."

He shrugged. "It is up to you. You work hard; you make more money. There are many others like you at our place. You will see. Are you satisfied? Will you come with us?"

Jan was delighted. From a deepening sense of worry just moments ago, this man had arrived like an angel to sweep him up into heavenly wealth. He tightened his grip on the other man's hand. "Yes, by Saint Michael. I'll come."

## viii

The elevator car carrying the shift boss floated up on steel cables and vanished in the gloom. Jan watched it go, then turned back to the drift where he would return to work. Like the lower bowel of some diseased beast, it glistened with the water that was everywhere dripping and trickling. No stench, like the pits he had worked in Boryslava, but the black dust and the water formed an ink that smudged everything it came into contact with. Here, only a single electric light pierced the silent tunnel, other than the yellow glow cast from the top of his helmet. Was he forever condemned to work in the blackness of the earth's gut? What sins in past lives of his forefathers had earned him this? The stain of the oil had been traded for the coal tattoo.

Leaning on his pick handle, Jan rubbed at his forehead, where the rim of his helmet liner irritated him. Each night he noticed that the black line of coal dust was becoming harder to remove. Though there was coarse soap and water aplenty, the water was nevertheless hard, and the cleanser did not lather well. Eight months of experience had told him that these marks, the 'touch of Lord Coal' as the other men put it, would become indelible in time. Even the phlegm he hawked up and spat was flecked with sooty deposits, and he was convinced that his innards resembled his outer appearance. He shuffled forward, stooped, and adjusted the large felt pads on his knees. The tunnel at the coal face was rarely more than five feet in height. In consequence, it was necessary to work on his knees most of the time. Still, compared to the hell that was Boryslava, this was an improvement. He had a fine metal helmet, to which was attached an electric light. On his wide belt hung a heavy battery. Leather-trimmed goggles with glass lenses protected his eyes from flying splinters of coal. And on his feet were the finest pair of boots he had ever owned, though it was clear that the heavy labour would soon finish them.

He had been in increasing demand to help with the steam engines which raised the ore from the base of the shafts. Once, he had helped repair a flat-bed tram upon which the tiny, rugged and blind ponies drew the broken coal to the lifts. This had caught the eye of a foreman, for mechanical skills employed at a hewer's wage avoided the kinds of expenses that made the accountants mutter to the dark-suited, frowning men they worked for. In an abandoned drift, there were workshops for metal work, harness repair, and carpentry. Emperor of this stygian kingdom was an old man whose cancerous lip was so far advanced that most avoided him. He had taken to remaining in the shops, even when his shift did not require it, living underground like a troll.

"Dmitro Vishnivetski," he had said to Jan in rich Ukrainian as he wiped a thatch of white hair from his forehead. "Welcome to the world of the *nichki*, the shadow people. I am their patron." He coughed furiously, slapping his chest.

Jan had eyed him with a trace of nervousness. *Popá* Kudryk was a man to scoff at the prevalent superstitions of the time, but Jan had been subject to his mother's warnings as long as he could remember. The clergyman might be right, but why tempt the fates? And down here in the abandoned drift, with its winking lights and dancing shadows, there may very well be *chorts*, little devils, or *domoviks*, stable gremlins, over there where the little blind ponies shuffled and whickered in their wretched stalls.

"Dmitro Vishnivetski? That is a very famous name," Jan had said.

"It should be," Vishnivetski had responded, coughing again, curling his hideous lip in what passed for a smile. "I have been living in this mine for five years." He spat, a glob of red and black-flecked slime glistening under the lamps.

Jan had laughed. They both knew that the name belonged to a fabulous Ukrainian prince, known for his attacks on the Turks. "But I heard you were captured by the Sultan of Constantinople, and ordered to be hung on the city walls by great iron hooks through your ribs?"

"Mmm. Much overstated, I'm afraid. God has saved me for a worse fate." He was suddenly morose. "He has decided to take my face by degrees. All things considered, I think I should have preferred the iron hooks."

Jan too had fallen silent. The man's initial good humour had fallen away like a stone, and his face, shrouded in the mystery of the work-lamps, was as forlorn as an unloved child. He had raised his head. He was truly hideous; he had a habit of running a soothing, spittle-laden tongue across his bloated, lesion-ridden lip, in a way that looked sinister. Jan had suppressed a shudder. But as quickly as his mood had plunged, it righted itself, for clearly the man was happy to have a visitor. Jan had noticed that those who came to fetch the horses, or pick up or leave repair work, steered clear of him. It was as if they believed that his affliction could be passed on. Of course, Vishnivetski did not help matters. He called out to those who sought to avoid him: "Hey, *zazula*, cuckoo (woman), come and give me a kiss! Ho, *yahida*! Sweet ripe berry! Come share my cup of *vishnevka*, cherry liquor!" Loud smacking noises from those awful lips. But angry mutterings from those who looked away and hurried off.

Jan admired his nimble work with wood and machinery. "A fool believes that things constructed of metal are without life. But listen: study them carefully, and they will share their secrets. Come to an engine believing that you will not understand it will guarantee such a result. Like a dog, it smells fear," Vishnivetski said, grinning in his grotesque way.

"Be patient, contemplate, use all your senses, and all will be revealed to you. Choose the right tool: don't use the *topir*, battle axe, when a fine instrument will do. It is not necessary to be a *chaklunka*, one who casts spells, to repair what the hand of man has wrought.

Vishnivetski's eyes were not good, but he had been fitted with small, round spectacles which enabled him to continue with the fitment of small parts. Jan seemed to have an intuitive understanding of machinery and what was required to restore it to good working order. He followed the older man's instructions carefully, and it seemed for him that the old man's dreadful affliction passed from sight. Jan had experienced this before: Stefan was wizened and bent from heavy toil, but Jan had never seen him as other than straight and tall. Without really comprehending it, he understood that there was the inner person to whom it was necessary to be awakened. This was at the heart of interpersonal attraction. But knowing this, and allowing it to flourish notwithstanding the fears and prejudices that plague daily life was a continual struggle for him. For now, his relationship with Vishnivitski had evolved as easily and as naturally as it was possible to do, and it was clear that the other man understood that Jan saw past the ugliness. And he was grateful for this beyond the simple expedient of having an apprentice, showing it in his patience of instruction, and the attention to detail.

"It is a pleasure to converse with a countryman who is not as dull as a pig's arse. Most of these men," he waved at the silent walls, "are good only for digging Lord Coal. Or shovelling shit. Do you know, until you, no one knew the significance of my name?"

Jan felt a spasm of smugness; then he put down the tremble of pride. Nice compliment, this. "But surely it is not their fault? I mean ... "

"Pah! All of them, to a man, came for land. But what do they do? The only land they work is the filth of these pits. Each day, they cough harder and spew the blackness from their throat. Every month one or more dies from the black lung disease, but no thought is ever given to the reason they came here in the first place.

"Just a few more dollars. As soon as I have enough ... and so it goes. Fools." He shook his head.

"Forgive me, Dmitro Vishnivetski: how else is a man to make his way? Everything takes money. Everything. And it is worse here than in our country, for there is no stopping in for an onion or a twist of bread from a countryman. Money. It is necessary."

"Hold this." Vishnivetski took Jan's hand and placed it on a wrench set to a nut on a valve held in a grimy steel vise. He picked up a similar tool and applied it to the opposite end of a bolt. "These men - you included - give suck to the owners' coin. In return, the owners allow them to die here, their dreams as distant and nearly forgotten as the *stariny*, old epic songs of the past."

Jan was offended. "I have not forgotten my dreams. No. But I shall work here until - "

"Hah! See? You speak the same language as these other *vovkulaks*, were-wolves, sneaking about down here in the dark, pretending to be men."

" ... until the end of the month of May of next year, then I shall leave for the free lands in the west."

Vishnivetski rolled his eyes. "We shall see. I wager you that ... that ... " He looked around his cave. "That tool box and its contents. It is a fine thing I made myself. You are good with such things - but, I need not worry myself. You will still be here a year from the end of May. Just a few more dollars, you will say. Oh, I have heard it all before."

"I will match your wager." Jan walked over to the chest. It was well-made, with finely-scarfed joints, reinforced with brass corners. Inside, each tool fit in its own place, chisels, planes, hammer and saws. "I will yield all I have saved by then if I am not on my way to the western territories by the time I have set for myself."

Vishnivetski waved him off in a fit of coughing. "Save your money. I have no need of it. You will still die here. Which is good, since until then, I have need of your capable hands."

The old man laid down the steel wrench he was holding. He looked over to Jan who had knelt at the tool box, and was cradling a spoke shave, a thumb running gingerly over the keenness. "But in the event you do not completely succumb to the idea of money in your pocket and a pitcher of rum in the evening, you should go to the Canadian territories. There is land aplenty for the asking. Not much left in America that is fit for growing things." Then a sigh; a note of, what, regret?

"I, myself, waited too long. Now it is too late." Jan looked at him sharply, but the old man had turned away.

# Book Two

MANITOBA

# i

Byron Bloode's return from the British Isles to Western Canada affected him in a way that he found curious. After four years in England, including travel on the Continent, he was half expecting to be blasé, even disappointed. But as the rail bed through the rugged shield country made way to canopied parklands, he leaned against the windows excitedly. It had been more than four years since he had been sent by his father to school in Oxford. All the well-to-do families sent their sons away. The greater the distance, the greater the prestige. But his stay, extended for two years in post graduate reading was at an end, and his father expected him home.

Home. What a mélange of emotions that expression contained. The familiar and the friendly and the known. A leaving and a coming back. Reading his father's letter, he found it hard to conceive that he would be content returning to a sprawling frontier town after London, Paris and Rome. Yet here he was craning his neck for a glimpse around the next bend, and it puzzled him. The letter in his hand undeniably had a warmth to it, for it represented welcome and attachment, and whatever was meant by the ephemeral term: love. Home.

All along the railway right-of-way, the woods had been pushed back, and small farms were taking shape. Rough homesteads and outbuildings of log and plaster were but promises of things to come. But here along the right-of-way, there were few poor properties. Most had the appearance of well-established agricultural ventures. Clattering across the Whitemouth River, larger holdings came into view, with crops already showing well. Here and there, the homes of more prosperous farmers were storied, built of hewn stone, and ornamented with gingerbread fretwork at the eaves and over the verandah. And still the train rolled on. It occurred to Byron that this country — his country — was impossibly vast, and yet in this year of 1897, it was still sparsely settled. Looking back at the rear of the train as it snaked around a graded curve, squealing and shuddering, he could see the three 'Colonist Cars'. Furnished with minimum fittings, they were jammed with staring hopefuls, they and their families dressed in the shabby, shapeless clothes of the poor. Walking past them on the platform back east, Byron could see that the aisles and overhead racks were jammed with bags, trunks, sacks and bedrolls, even babies.

Here in the first class coach, such unseemliness seemed a world away. Byron had his own comfortable seat, and the seat facing him was vacant. A steward attended to his requirements in the way of refreshments and newspapers, and at night, a soft bed was made up in the overhead berth. He sighed and settled back into the plush upholstery, loading his pipe, and regarding for a moment his faint reflection in the window glass.

At twenty-one, he was as thin as a whippet. A long, thick mane of coppery hair was swept back from a well-proportioned face. Handsome, well-dressed, and genial, he was a man who attracted a second look and he was aware of it. Complacently, he pulled out his father's last letter, trying to get an image of the old man in his mind. It was written in a stiff, formal, almost florid style. The old fellow seemed to be given to putting on airs lately, if his correspondence were any indication. Byron shook the letter open with one hand, holding his pipe with the other. He read the note again.

The letter was dated Dominion Day, 1896, written on company stationary: Bloode & Bell, Wholesalers, Merchants & Forwarding Agents, 119 Lombard, City of Winnipeg, Manitoba; est. 1869, was inscribed in a scrolled semi-circle around an engraving of the company warehouse. It was prosperous-looking stationary, but seemed odd that his father would use it for a personal letter. Byron lifted his eyes. Perhaps it reflected the amount of time his father was putting in at work. Letters were often like that: codes in which the inner person was revealed, not necessarily in the particular choice of language, but in the manner in which it was employed. Sometimes the selection of materials upon which one chose to write suggested further clues. One read letters, he thought, at several levels, including the emotional. Letters could bring huge pleasure. Or stir other feelings, which sometimes had little do with the sender's intentions. He looked at the paper again.

*I have not written in some time,* it began. Was it a reproach to Byron that he had not corresponded? Or a simple statement of fact. Probably the latter, he decided. The old man was not inclined to whine about such things.

*How long has it been, now, that you have been away? Four years? Five years? I think that your mother wonders if you will ever come home. It is important for you to see something of the world's offerings, for it gives a man perspective. The world looks different to a squirrel in a pine tree, than it does to a snake in a wagon rut, someone once said to me. I have always believed in education, and I think that you are getting the very best available at Oxford. But it may be time for you to consider what you will be doing with the rest of your life.*

*The present accommodations of Bloode & Bell are inadequate. When we built it during the boom of '81, to match the projections of immigration given to us by the Canadian Pacific Railway, we could not have expected that even their own robust estimates would fall short. Though Point Douglas Common has become quite congested, there are still a few prime lots available convenient to rail and steamship, and I have had preliminary talks with Charles Wheeler, who designed Holy Trinity Church in '84. He has told me that Sir Hugh John MacDonald wishes to commission him to build a substantial home for him shortly, to be called 'Dalnavert', so I must act fast if he is to be the architect.*

*This brings me to the main point of my letter. As you know, Edwin, my long-time friend and partner, has not been well. Lately this has meant that he has been spending most of his time in the dry southern states. He has recently advised me he wishes to become inactive entirely in the business. He has assured me that our St. Paul connections are well established, so there is no cause for concern there. So you see, we are at a bit of a crossroads. We need to expand, but I am not getting any younger. I can still get around well enough, but the demands of the trade are large. It would seem that if you are to join me in the firm, the time is now. I need your youth, your energy, and your education.*

*I have not much else to report. I think you'll find that much has changed in the half-decade. A little while ago, the North-West Bone Company took a last haul of buffalo bones out of the territories through here. One thousand railway cars, can you imagine? You never saw the herds as I did, and there is something infinitely sad about their passing, though it seems now it was inevitable. I confess that I went down to the yards, and pulled an old skull off. I have it in my office here even now, though goodness knows why. I should throw the thing out, one of these days.*

*Well, I must sign off. I have a group from the Salvation Army waiting to see me. They set up the Rescue Home and Children's Shelter in Winnipeg last year, for un-wed mothers, deserted children, and prostitutes. Demands for its services are so high that I and others are regularly petitioned for funds. It is yet another dimension of 'civilization' which I think you will find has changed the face of the city in which we live. Your mother sends her fondest affections. She is longing to see you. We have one of her cousins, Emma Daniel, living with us after the sudden death of her mother. Emma is thirteen years old, pretty as a picture, and a delightful child. You will like her very much. Christine still lives in St. Paul, still married to that lawyer. I think she would very much like a postcard from London, or one of those other exotic places you visit.*

*Best regards, Father*

Byron folded the letter along well-worn seams, and placed it with others he kept in a small bundle in his purse. He stretched and stood up, steadying himself against the sway of the car as it beat its ineluctable tattoo. It had been his father's idea to go away for his schooling. Mary, his mother, had initially been opposed, but she had yielded to arguments of opportunity and "broadening". He was glad of his experience, and for a time thought that he might not return. But he wondered how long he could live on his father's money. There was a bad year in '86, after Louis Riel's ill-fated rebellion on the upper Saskatchewan, when immigration had slowed markedly. People were drawn to American free homesteads because of the rumours of hard times on the plains of the North West Territories. Other possible downturns, drought, grasshoppers, perhaps even cholera, could put the old man out of business. And with that, the termination of the allowance which allowed Byron to live comfortably in the student's quarters at Oxford. He had always felt close to his father. It was not a difficult decision. Home it would be, and he would see about taking over the family business.

But an anxiety remained that his flair in college showed only for literature, languages and philosophy. Attempts at arithmetic, economics or law, subjects which might have had some application in business, were disastrous. He felt unsuited, but he was determined to give it a try. He owed it to the old man. Stooping to look out the window again, for he was a tall man at six foot three inches, he could see the dirty thumbprint of industry on the horizon. Inside of an hour, he reckoned, he would be at the station, and in the arms of his kin.

The whole family was there on the crowded platform. His mother wept openly, and Byron was embarrassed. It had been a shock to see his father, for the man had aged noticeably. Those letters which Byron read and re-read had maintained a vigorous image in his thoughts; it was obvious that David's mind was as alert as ever, but its vessel had deteriorated. The aging of the parent was a constant reminder of the mortality of the child, he thought. But Byron had learned manners at Oxford: "Haven't changed a bit, either of you!"

At the station, they had introduced him to Emma. He had difficulty taking his eyes off her since he had met her gaze as he embraced his mother. She was tall for her age, and startlingly beautiful, a miniature of what his mother probably looked like when she was young. Their skin was the same tawny hue. Black hair hung to her shoulders, and dark eyes smoldered in an expression of something between mischief and innocence. She smiled at him, white teeth flashing behind heavy, parted lips. This was the thirteen-year-old child mentioned in the letter? It couldn't be. His expression must have given him away, for his father spoke.

"So this is our Emma. You'll agree I did not exaggerate. Emma, this is my son Byron. I hope you two'll get along ..."

Byron was mesmerized. Emma addressed him in formal French. " *J'espere que vous avez a une belle journee?*"

"*Bien, merci, Mademoiselle. Je suis trés contente pour avoir arrivée chez moi ...*"

David stepped forward as Byron took her hand. "We don't speak much French at home any more. Only at the shop, now, when it's needed."

Her hand was small with long, tapered fingers, and cool. She met his gaze directly, and held his hand with firmness, closing their grasp with her other hand. "I am delighted to meet the mysterious Byron, whose mother never stops speaking of. She reads each bit of poetry you send, to us all."

Byron felt himself blushing. This girl — this *child* — was so self assured. It seemed impossible that she was thirteen years of age. "Ah, oh, my poetry ..." he stammered, "well, I hope you liked it."

"I *loved* it," she said enthusiastically. "I loved it. We all did. I hope you've brought some more for us to listen to."

His family crowded around him, offering other small bits of welcoming noises, herding him off the platform to the waiting carriage. Byron could not stop smiling; he was home. What mysterious resonance that expression had during the moments in one's life when it was not taken for granted.

# ii

The next day, his father took him on a tour of the city. "When you left," his father commented, "the town had, what, twenty thousand people? Now we're more than double that. And I think that we've seen nothing yet. This is a gateway city. Our location as practical head of navigation, and the rail bottleneck for the country, means that everything flowing north and west must pass through here. And to top it off, there's more unsettled good land out here than you can shake a stick at. Even here in the 'Far-Famed Red River Valley', as the land agents call it, though a lot of it's been tied up by speculators."

Byron half listened to his father. It was true that the place had changed, and was continuing to change. His father's house on Armstrong's Point had been completed, and he now lived on the Assiniboine River with the some of the best families in brick homes with graveled carriage drives and spacious, park-like settings. Log booms were thick on the river, near the busy saw mills. Spur lines were being laid to meet the demands of merchants and manufacturers. The noise and activity in the warehouse district was overwhelming, and the nearby immigration sheds teemed with recent arrivals.

David halted the matched team with a tug on the polished leather reins, and jerked his thumb at the long, low buildings near the rail yards. "Perhaps right there is the main reason that this town is going to grow. They're starting to come by the thousands. Land that's sat idle since the Creation will soon be worked, and that's going to be very good for business. 'Course, not everyone's happy with the new arrivals."

"Why do you say that?"

"Clifford Sifton, lead man for the federal Liberals, got it into his head to fill up the land with anyone who'd come and work the soil — anyone, that is, who was white. But when the Galicians started to come, as you can see over there, there's plenty enough of them. 'Social sewage', some call them; 'scum of Europe', 'vermin' and the like. Pretty strong feelings against 'em, I'd say."

A faint look of surprise at the depth of the antipathy his father described flitted across Byron's face. His father noticed. "Believe me. I'm not given to exaggeration. If anything, those expressions which you can read most days in any newspapers, are mild, compared to what a body hears on the streets."

"There were quite a number of them on the train. Raised a powerful smell, somewhere between garlic and horse piss." Byron laughed, but his father did not smile.

"It was many a time on the brigades that I smelled far worse. It's not every man that's lucky enough to have a bar of lavender soap at his disposal. These men and women are as poor as I once was, but with hard work, they may yet be properly civilized."

It was a faint reproach, but Byron coloured. He had not thought of himself as a snob, but here he was, all but sneering. He rebuked himself: when words are in the mouth one is their master; once out, one is their slave. He changed the subject.

"The city has sprawled since I've been away. Let's drive past Colony Creek."

"If it's the bordellos you have a curiosity about, they've been put out of business there." David smiled at his son. "But they've sprung up again not all that far from here. Out west, on Thomas Street, are some pretty fancy places that have sprung up. It was hoped that, out of sight, out of mind, but the housing has started to get built up out there, and with a school just up, there's bound to be problems. The city even stretched the streetcar service out there, which of course led to the construction of more homes along the way - "

Byron interrupted his father's travelogue, crying, "Emma! There's Emma!"

David looked to where Byron pointed. Standing outside a shop window was the girl and his mother. They both turned as the team drew abreast, and they were called.

Mary approached the carriage, eyes twinkling, her step firm. Her head was uncovered, her gray hair shone like polished slate. After an exchange, it was decided that David would accompany his wife on foot for the rest of her shopping trip, and Byron would drive Emma back to the house. Byron could barely contain his enthusiasm; for her part, the girl could not stop smiling.

Byron self-consciously took the long way around, cutting back along Main Street south to the river, then slowly along Assiniboine, past the point where his father had landed on the *Anson Northup*, in '59. The spot had been pointed out to him, at the foot of Graham Street, many times by the old man. As they passed, he mentioned it to his passenger. She laughed, a peal of small bells, as she reminded him that she too had been made aware of the location many times over. He kept glancing at her. When their eyes met, they both looked quickly away. At each witticism, she laid a gloved hand on his arm, and the feeling to him was delicious. As he drove the horses at a slow walk, he could feel her eyes on him even when there was a pause in the conversation. It was warm, but the faint discomfort he felt had nothing to do with the climate. He had the suspicion that she knew the effect she was having on him.

He grimaced. This was a thirteen-year-old girl. He looked away, frowning, wondering at the depths of foolishness a man could plumb without effort.

"Goodness. Whatever is wrong?" she asked, putting her hand lightly on his knee. It felt as heavy as a balk of timber, yet a part of him did not want it removed. "What's the matter?"

His emotions struggled with one another, as he strove to keep his expression neutral. "Oh, nothing." Offhanded. "It's damnably warm, and I daresay this jacket will be the end of me yet."

"Then take it off, you silly," she cried, sliding over on the narrow seat to take his jacket by the collar, helping him off with it. The horses strolled along, indifferent.

She was close to him now, against him, and her dark hair brushed his face. The warmth of her along his shoulder; hint of thigh against thigh. The smell of her. Heavens Above! It was a whiff of lilac, or some other gentle fragrance. This was no child, this was something else: powerful, enveloping, and as she tugged at his sleeves, he closed his eyes, giving in to the moment.

That night, as he lay abed, his thoughts were utterly beyond his ability to master. She was a graven image whose medium was the desire of a callow man. He spoke aloud in the dark: she is a child. This through gritted teeth, as if the effort to repress his infatuation, his lust, was a task monumentally beyond him. He was alarmed at his inability to think of other matters, and his thoughts became increasingly carnal. This continued every evening. One night, after a roiling dream left him soiling his bedclothes, he decided to ask his father for more of the agency work in St. Paul, Brandon and Regina, and other centres where the Bloode & Bell trade was carried on.

His father, pleased by his interest, agreed. This enforced separation gave Byron some relief, though not entirely. At the moments of the day when he was the least guarded, she would creep back into his thoughts softly, unbidden, like a shadow when the sun reappears.

For a time, Byron threw himself into his work, and for several months he went at it with the zeal of a probationary parson. But the truth of it was that he had no head for sums. Poetry, yes. Languages, writing, or the reduction of land-scape to watercolour, by all means. But his heart lay not with the instincts necessary for a merchant's trade. By degrees he became bored, then sloppy. One evening in St. Paul, he received a telegram from his father to return at once. There was no explanation, but Byron was happy to turn over the affairs of Bloode & Bell to their local agents.

The trip by rail was overnight; a far cry from his father's day, when the same journey took a week by riverboat, and a month by ox cart. In the first-class Pullman, he had plenty of time to read, or take in the countryside as it rolled by. But his thoughts were preoccupied by Emma and whether she would be at the station. It was a delicious image, and as he held it in his mind, he was conscious that his breathing had become increasingly shallow. He got up from his com-fortable seat, and went out to the swaying landing between the coaches for air. Gripping the railing, he shook his head as he leaned out into the evening breeze. What he was feeling was wrong, but it had become an all-consuming obsession. He decided that he would recommend that father send the girl away to finishing school. At least then, he would be removed from temptation. Comforted by this small appeasement of his conscience, he went back to his novel, and read until he dozed.

The next morning, as he alighted from the coach, he saw his father, grim-faced, at the end of the platform. For a moment, a faint tremor of panic passed through him, as he thought that perhaps something had happened to mother. Perhaps Emma. But of course not: that would have been in the telegram. But as the old man reached for one of the bags from the porter, there was none of the customary small chatter, or inquiries after the trip. He had something on his mind, there was no doubt. Byron decided to wait, rather than to prompt. His father would not be rushed in any event.

David had brought the dog-cart. There was barely enough room for the two of them as well as the two pieces of luggage, and the brightly-wrapped gift he had brought for Emma. But the pony drew it without effort, and it was highly maneuverable in the heavy traffic.

"So your trip was without event?" asked David, without looking at his son.

"Nothing out of the ordinary. Quite boring, actually."

"Ah. Boring." There was silence as they threaded their way along Broadway. The commercial traffic was dense, even though the street itself was enormously wide, a legacy of the west-bound cart trains, their wheels staggered to avoid carving deep ruts into the soil. "Boring, you say." The old man was annoyed, obviously. Well, out with it.

Byron nodded, rolling his eyes while facing across the street. Barrels had spilled, and a great shouting match was taking place between owner and accused. David took no notice.

"Do you recall the Prestwick Company order. The linens, silks, and worsted goods?"

Byron thought. Prestwick was a wholesaler, like Bloode & Bell. But they had increasingly leaned toward importing exotic fabrics which were all the rage in Winnipeg society. He remembered the manager, a flamboyant, florid-faced chap named Twyler with a brace of gold fillings in his teeth. Dressed quite beautifully, if one discounted his rather fat torso. But the order? Hmmm. No recollection of it whatsoever. It was hard to recall what one had no interest in, but that explanation would hardly satisfy his father. He looked at him questioningly.

"Do you know what we sell imported oriental silk for, by the yard?"

Byron opened his eyes wide, then furrowed his brow. "I should know this. Ah, is it ... I think it's around eighty cents a yard, is it not?"

His father nodded, pulling up the pony to allow a group of school children to pass in front. He turned to his son. "Very good. And do you recall what you've committed the company to in St. Paul?"

Byron shrugged, not sure where this was leading.

"Eighty-cents a yard. We buy for eighty-one cents; we sell for eighty cents, if we're lucky. How long do you think we'll be in business at that rate? Whatever were you thinking of? I mean, Harry Twyler must be laughing his face off at us."

His son opened his mouth to protest, but David shouted curtly at the horse. "Get up there!" He turned to Byron. "There's more. Do you recall the Massey-implement order, that you took care of, personally? Do you have any idea of the delivery dates you agreed to? What in blazing hell will I do with seeders in summer, and mowers in the dead of winter? What were you thinking of?" His voice had escalated in tension and volume. Byron was uncomfortable and embarrassed. He could not recall the precise arrangements, and the details were of stunning indifference to him.

"A company where just anything goes will soon be one where nothing goes."

"I don't think you give a damn about the company, Byron. You've cost us a lot of money by sheer carelessness. Where's your head, boy? Up your ass?" It was unusual for the old man to resort to rough language, but he was upset. Byron suspected that he was upset at his son's indifference far more than the money.

"I'm sorry, father. Truly. I don't know if I'm cut out for business, you see."

"Well, there's more than a grain of truth there, I'd say. Another month or two on the payroll, and we'd be out of business at this rate." He pushed his hat back and scratched his perspiring forehead with a free hand. "I don't know what's to become of you, my boy. You need to seize hold of your life, and make something of it."

They were rounding their street in Armstrong's Point. Among the young trees, the mansion loomed like the monument to wealth it was. There was a gravelled drive in a semi-circle in front of the house, and David pulled up in front of the massive steps to the formal doorway.

"I'm going down to the warehouse, as there's a number of things that need immediate attention, if we are to eat next week."

Byron got down without a word, and lifted his bags out of the rear of the cart. He stood looking up at his father, not sure of what to say.

"Mother's away at the Ashdown's for the morning, planning a charity ball. She should be back soon. We will need to pursue this conversation when I get home tonight. So give it some thought. I cannot abide the thought of a layabout in my house, and I will not have it. Think about it." And he abruptly drove off.

Wearily, Byron mounted the steps and entered the house. Inside, it was cool and dark, for during the summer, the drapes remained drawn on the south side until sunset. He placed the gift on the twist-leg table in the hallway. In the silence, he climbed the wide staircase, turning at the landing by the large stained-glass window depicting Saint George and the dragon, and setting his luggage down. They were rather more heavy than he recalled. He was tired from the trip. Picking them up, he mounted the rest of the stairs, and as he drew close to the top, the bathroom door opened and Emma stepped out, a brushed linen towel wrapped and bunched by her fists in front of her at the collarbone. Her long, thick hair was turned in a towel of identical size and colour, and the trailing end fell behind her shoulders.

He stopped short, astonished. She too, seemed surprised, and for a very long moment, they stared at one another without a word. Then slowly, and as he would later reconstruct it many times over, she lowered her arms so that her breasts were exposed to him. They were small but full. Her small brown nipples were hard in the coolness. Below, the parted toweling cast the lower parts of her body in mysterious shadows.

The blood hammered in his ears. He swayed on the steps, and he thought he might fall. Her expression changed ever so slightly, there, at the corners of her mouth, as if she knew the effect this was having on him. She was enjoying this: the power over him, the way in which he was transfixed by her beauty. How much time had passed while she held him so? It seemed as a dream. The bag in each hand grew heavier, and they slipped from his hands unnoticed, thumping down the stairs to the landing with a crash. The claw that wrenched and clutched in his groin left him breathless. His lower lip trembled with the effort to speak, but there was no sound.

Below them, the front door opened, and they heard his mother's voice cry out, "Oh, hellooo. Is anybody home?"

Emma quickly drew up the towel and ran lightly in bare feet to her room by the stairs to the third floor. Byron took the two remaining steps and sat in a chair facing the top of the stairs. He was intensely aroused. His pulse felt as if he had just run up the staircase in front of him, and he was sweating.

"Yes, mother, " he called weakly. "I'm home."

# iii

Byron slept fitfully that afternoon. He could not get the event out of his mind, and his earlier resolve was completely extinguished. His craving for the girl was past defiance, and he had relieved himself like a prurient boy, his hand becoming hers. At length, he fell asleep, and did not arise until the following morning. When at length he did leave his bed, his father had left for work, and there was no sign of Emma, which eased his anxiety somewhat.

His mother puttered about the kitchen preparing his breakfast while Byron sat on a tall stool beside the kitchen counter.

"Mother," he began, hesitating. "Father is quite cross with me - "

She looked up from the cupboard she had been rummaging the pots and pans about, and straightened. "I know. He was still upset when he left this morning. He's quite worried about you. He wonders what will become of you."

"I don't know why he should be, really." Byron knew this sounded more petulant than he intended. "It was only a few book-keeping entries that - "

"Oh, come now, Byron. A few book-keeping entries? Not from what your father told me. I don't think you really have a head for business — well, you have a brain, but you won't put it to anything that doesn't capture your fancy. Now that's the truth of it, isn't it?"

His mother was a tough old lady; always saw right through him to the heart, failings and all. He looked sheepish, and played with a pair of spoons lying on the counter.

"Your father thinks perhaps the time abroad has spoiled you." She was not smiling. She loved her son, but she could never be described as indulgent. "I'm afraid that the two of us did that long before you left. Your father particularly."

He looked hurt. "Spoiled? I would hardly have thought - "

"That's just it," she broke in. "You hardly think, Byron. Where is your head these days? You seem so ... so preoccupied. How you could let those mistakes happen is beyond me. Your father said that not even his most junior clerks have done what you have. And they would have been released immediately. Now he has to suffer the silent speculation about what he will do with you. It's a difficult position for him to be in. You know how proud he is." She bent over again to draw out the pan to prepare the eggs.

"That's easily solved. I'll withdraw from the position. I don't have to work there."

She walked out to the summer kitchen, where the coal stove was still warm from the morning's meal. Over her shoulder, she called to him. "Shall I poach one egg for you, or two?" Upon his reply, she continued. "That's hardly the answer. You know he wants someone to take over the business. He wants his son there, that's what. Surely you understand that; the place is his whole life. He's worked very hard to build it up."

She came to the doorway, a large spoon in her hand. Her brow was damp with the warmth of the stove. "But I told him, 'you can't make a silk purse out of a sow's ear'."

"Oh good grief, mother. Pile the coals on a blaze already high, why not? And couldn't you have chosen a better metaphor?"

At that moment, Emma swept in. She smiled innocently at Byron.

"Hello Emma," said Mary. "Where had you got to?"

"Visiting." She turned to Byron: "I spoke to Father last night. We want you to give a reading of your poetry this evening. The Baileys and the Quintons are coming after dinner. For sherry and sweetcakes."

Byron looked with dismay to his mother. "Oh yes," she said. "I forgot to mention it. Emma's got it all planned." She went back out to the summer kitchen, speaking as she did so: "I think it's a very good idea, especially today. I think your father should be reminded of your other talents."

As his mother went into the other room, Emma came very close to Byron, her eyes dancing. She laid a hand upon his thigh in a bold manner, saying, "You startled me. I had no idea you were waiting for me out there."

He thought that her palm would blaze its way to the bone. His cheeks reddened. "I was not waiting for you," he said in a low voice. "Be careful, Mother may hear."

She put her hand up to his cheek. She was incredibly forward with him. He relished her touch, though he fought with the inner contradictions of physical contact, her age, and the nearby presence of his mother. Sitting on the stool, he was at eye level with her. She leaned over and kissed him quickly on the mouth, then left. It was a fleeting pass, but the warmth of her lips lingered long after she was gone. Her last words had been gay: "You worry too much. I'm looking forward to tonight. Very much."

"What are you two chatting about?" asked Mary as she came back with the poached eggs in a bowl. "Oh. She's gone off again. What a child."

Byron took a deep breath. He moved over to the tiny table in the kitchen, as his mother set the eggs before him.

"You had better be careful, you know," she said, handing him a plate of sliced bread.

He started. "Whatever do you mean?"

"I think our little Emma has a schoolgirl's crush on you."

# iv

Byron's afternoon was no better than the day previous. He retired to his room, and fretted over the readings he might give. The state he was in was distracting beyond anything he had ever experienced. He worried about the matters hanging unresolved between him and his father. His mother had not been judgmental, he thought, but matter-of-fact, as was usual for her. And then back to the readings: it was one thing to read before his friends at university; it was quite another to perform before strangers.

Well, not quite strangers. Both families were well-to-do members of Winnipeg society, and he had known them for most of his childhood. Still, it had been more than four years, during which he had grown to manhood, and he was self-conscious. Old man Bailey was a grain merchant, and had made a fortune trading in Red Fife and the new Number One Northern. Hard as nails and ruthless, he had little time for fools.

And Emma. How would he react to her gaze? That worried him more than anything else. Yet, in the inner swirl of emotions, he anticipated it. He looked forward to reading from what he considered to be sensual prose. Reading poetry was second only to having it read to him. There was nothing, well, nearly nothing, quite so arousing as well-articulated recitation of good verse. It was after all, quite a popular parlour pastime, quite the rage in Victorian England. It was not surprising that it had caught on here, for from what he could see, the speech, clothes, mannerisms, the gadgets — everything Victorian, was enthusiastically emulated here in 'the Colonies', as the Brits liked to say.

Later that evening, after the company had been settled in the spacious front room, David picked up his pipe. Byron was nervous; he could feel the knot in his stomach tighten as the moment approached. Deep in his inner self he knew the powerful need he had to be approved, to be validated. Raised as a child whose every indulgence was met without much thought, he had found it rougher sledding out in the world. His experiences with women were limited. He had a difficult time with the elaborate courting ceremonies at Oxford. His sexual encounters were confined to prostitutes, all three of whom were brusque, and made him feel incompetent. One, he had tried reading some of his poetry to, and she had rolled her eyes.

The recollection of it brought the humiliation back again, and his anxiety increased. He resolved to avoid looking at the girl, as he had done all evening. At length, his father stood up.

"You all know my son, now just returned from studies overseas. Successful studies, I might say. Ought to be, for what I paid for them." He paused for polite laughter. "Now Byron here has become quite a poet, I'm told. He's given a number of readings in London, and has been quite well-received." There was an unmistakable note of pride in the old man's voice. Byron wondered why he should be so surprised to hear it.

"So without further ado, let me call upon my son to give us a verse or two."

Byron stood up to a polite applause, which was eclipsed by Emma's enthusiastic clapping.

"Thank you," he mumbled. "Thank you." He was clutching a tattered folder of loose paper, which contained all his writings. He hoped the natty outfit he had selected would impress his audience; the trousers were daringly cut, rather more tight-fitting than was usual. His velvet waistcoat was yellow, not the more customary dark colours. If his father disapproved, he did not show it. Perhaps he was attempting to come back some distance toward his son. Byron dared not look at Emma, who was sitting on the floor, in front. She was beaming. From the corner of his eye, he could see that she was beautifully dressed in a long, form-fitting dress, with silk inlays of the same colour. The contrast in texture made it a rich-looking garment; all the more so given the simple pearl necklace which lay on her dark throat. Her hair was swept up into a tight knot, and light curls had been pulled down to frame her face. The girl was going to drive him mad.

He cleared his throat. "These poems, the one or two that I'll be reading this evening, were all written at college. One of them, I have never read before, and I dedicate it to my mother." Again at the periphery of his vision, he could see Emma's face fall. "I'll begin, then, with one I've called *Carpe Diem*:

*Distantly, a prophet speaks, but*
*we turn the words away.*
*For love is wisdom all it's own,*
*there is no other way...*

*Winter's bony fingers raise*
*and beckon to her side.*
*We tremble in her icy gaze, but*
*love shall be our guide*

*And in the frozen, silent wood*
*beyond the snow-filled tracks,*
*love leaves no mark upon the land, tho'*
*keen as any woodsman's axe*

*So the time to seize the day,*
*is now. The clock has stilled*

*for love's misplaced the key, but*
*the sky's foreboding: each breath is chilled*

He looked up from his papers. No one said anything for a moment, and he thought he must have failed. Suddenly Emma clapped vigorously, and shouted "Bravo!" The other joined in.

"Well," said Bailey, in his booming voice. "I'm not sure I understand it, but some nice images there."

"Yes," said Byron. "The Brits are quite fascinated with Canada, and all it is about. The imagery went over quite well with them, too.

"Read on, son. Let's have another one." His father seemed relieved that the poetry was not too obscure, decorous in the Victorian manner, or ribald.

"All right. This one is special, and I have given it the title: *Convincing*. Rather a convincing title, if you like." He snickered self-consciously. Pause.

*Was there ever a word as trivialized as 'love'?*
*To declare the point, take ten steps above!*
*So the moment arrives and the expression's wanting,*
*words are devalued and doubts stay haunting;*
*that the message intended is short of its mark*
*and detail is lost so the picture is stark*

There were eight more verses, some of which were more intensely erotic than the times may have countenanced, but Byron skipped over passages that his university colleagues would have enthusiastically received. Nevertheless, he was kept on his feet for nearly an hour. This went beyond courtesy: they enjoyed his work. He knew that reading to an audience was a drug for them. There were very few pleasures that could rival it. He pitied the working classes who had no time for such indulgences, nor money for lamp oil or electric lights. He dared look directly at Emma. Her face shone. She had both hands clasped in front of her; her pose was one of total adulation. He was on a collision course with the consequences of his weakness, yet he felt powerless to do anything about it.

The next morning, he rose with his father to accompany him to the warehouse. The ailing Edwin Bell was expected by the steamship *Manitoba* sometime that morning. This was just a month over the anniversary of his first trip to Red River, on the *Anson Northup*, forty-three years ago. Edwin was now sixty-six. Byron was very fond of his father's partner, and looked forward to seeing him. He also wanted an opportunity to speak with his father about his future. These things, for the time being at least, helped keep his mind off the lovely Emma.

Winnipeg, the population of which now stood at better than forty-two thousand, was the northern anchor of the wholesale trade. It would be seven years before the term 'Gateway City' was to be used in an exuberant column in the *Winnipeg Telegram*, but already it was clear that all east-west trade of necessity needed to pass through here. Indeed, in excess of sixteen million dollars worth of business was being done by the wholesalers alone. The newly-elected federal government had established stiff tariffs which effectively diminished the north-south commerce that Byron's father had built his business upon, as had many others. The railway was now the dominant influence in the warehouse district, which was clustered north and west of the junction of the Red and Assiniboine Rivers, rather than the shipping docks. The tracks and roundhouses of the Canadian Pacific Railway lay just north of the Bloode & Bell warehouse properties, and only that year had a spur line been laid alongside an addition to the warehouse.

When Byron and David arrived, men were already at work unloading box cars of goods into the warehouse. The loading platform had been built at the same level as the rolling stock, so that time was used efficiently. Except for the navvies, who were hired by the shift boss on a casual basis, Byron knew most of the employees by name. But they greeted him indifferently. Unlike women, other men, he noticed, were not particularly drawn to him. He dismissed it as a necessary consequence of being the owner's son.

The warehouse itself was a massive structure of Tyndall limestone and heavy timber, not unlike many others of the day. A local architect, Charles Wheeler, had designed and organized the building as David had wanted. It, like the Botterill warehouse just half a block away toward the river, was a severe building, taking its beauty from the elegantly integrated relationships of arches, spandrels and mullions. Walking into the structure gave David a sense of power and wealth, as well as solidity and permanence. To think that one day it might be his, made him feel unworthy.

There was no sign of the *Manitoba*. Upon his return from the docks, Byron busied himself with some bookkeeping at the request of his father. He hated the tedium of it, but it passed the time, and it seemed to please David. When the noon whistle blew, all of the crews stopped work, seized the tin pails which contained their midday lunches, and left the building for shady spots along the river. There the breeze, cooled by the water, afforded some relief from the summer heat. David announced that he was driving home to take lunch with Mary, and asked Byron if he wished to accompany him. His son declined, saying that he preferred to wait for the steamer; the heat robbed him of appetite in any event.

The rows of columns under his pen had a hypnotic effect. Sitting stooped over at the heavy wooden desk reminded him of Oxford, and he slipped into a reverie of recollections about his time there. It had been pleasant, though his friends were few, and his interests narrow. The university had been like a cocoon, away from the real world, where all of his physical needs were taken care of. He thought fleetingly of writing to one or two of them, but the moment passed. What could he possibly tell them of Manitoba? They were urbane; this place was not, for all its pretensions. They had sophisticated tastes; this place was a pretender to high society. His friends were cultured; he knew no one here who fit that description. His thoughts jumbled, he dozed.

Jolting awake to the touch of a light hand on his shoulder, Byron mashed his knee against the inside of the desk well. Looking up, he saw Emma. There was no one else around, and the Regulator on the wall showed nearly twenty minutes after the hour.

"Well, I thought I'd find you here. What a surprise to have you all to myself, for a change." She walked in a circle, looking up at the rows of file cabinets containing the company records. "I have never really seen much of this place, only this musty old office. Father believes that the warehouse is no place for a lady. Won't you show me around?"

Her eyes dropped to where he was rubbing his knee; it was obvious he had given it a sharp blow. "Oh, have you hurt yourself? On my account?" She dropped to her knees and laid her hands on his thigh. Looking up at him, she widened her eyes. "Tell me where it hurts?"

He pulled away by rolling the chair backward on its hard rubber wheels. Her fingers felt electric. "The warehouse is really a stuffy old place. Not much to see, really, beyond a few old bags and crates."

She laughed at his discomfiture. "Oh, I'd still like to see it, and if we don't start our tour now, then father will be back, and catch us." With that, she walked to the staircase. "Come on. Let's walk up, and we can take the elevator down. I've not had a ride on it yet, and I want to save the best for last." She hurried up the stairs, and Byron, who limped exaggeratedly across the office floor, was left behind.

"Emma!" he called. "Emma, you really must wait for me." He could hear her giggling as she ran up the stairs to the top floor. There, bales of oakum, tow, hemp rope, felt paper and other highly flammable goods were stored. As in all other such warehouses, the heaviest and least incendiary items were on the lower floors. On the fourth level, there was a rich odor of wood and canvas, oils and tar. She was nowhere to be seen. He called her name again. He was conscious of his heart thumping so violently in his chest, that it was nearly painful. And he knew that it had nothing to do with the four double flights of stairs. He tip-toed along the aisles of silent goods; there was no sound beyond his labored breathing, and the occasional squeak of the wooden floors.

There was a sharp cry at his ear, and as he turned with a start, she leapt upon him, bowling him over onto a rack of folded tarpaulins.

"Emma," he protested. "You mustn't do this." But there was no insistence in his voice. The feel of her rolled against him; her face, inches away from his, was intoxicating. She kissed him. Mashing her lips to his with enthusiasm, if not experience. He was transported by the sensations her full, moist lips created, and his groin thickened. It had never been like this with the slatterns who had crept into the dorms at school. He could not imagine such an urgency was possible. He groaned into her mouth, and she drew back.

"You must teach me the ways of men and women," she said intently. "I know so very little, but the thought of it makes me shivery, and my woman's parts become quite soaked." He opened his mouth to protest again, but she put a gloved hand over his lips: "You have already seen me once as God made me. I feel your fondness for me against my leg." She was suddenly coy. "I may not know everything, but I know lots. The boys I know have such swellings, but I have never seen it. And I want to." She stood up, and began to unfasten her dress.

"Emma! This is my father's warehouse! What if someone should come?" He was ready to faint with the thrill of what she was doing. His heart hammered in his ears. She seemed a vision in the filtered light of the dusty windows. Her clothes slid from her in layers, though the heat of the season and her age kept those to a minimum. She looked down at him, almost scoffing as she spoke. "Who will come? All the workmen are away, for at least half of an hour more, and we shall hear them on the stairs in any case." As she dropped away the last of her clothes, now clad only in stockings that rose to mid-thigh, she spun around, arms over her head, hair billowing. "Now look at me. Do I please you? Am I as beautiful as the girls you escorted in England?" She wrinkled her nose at him: "Am I too thin?"

He had drawn himself up on his elbows, gasping, filling his eyes with her.

"Oh, look at you, will you? You're like a landed fish! Come on: I want to see all of you." She crouched at his feet, and began to tug his shoes off; then his trousers. Soon, he was naked from the waist down, his engorged cock flopped across his belly. She was fascinated with it. The way she was squatting before him, knees apart, he could see the dark wedge of tightly curled hair where it disappeared into a tight, pink fold. He groaned, but she took no notice. Taking his maleness gingerly between thumb and forefinger, she moved it gently from side to side. He whimpered again. "Emma, please ... " he protested weakly, but for no purpose.

"It's so hard," she whispered. "Does it hurt when it's like this?" He shook his head feverishly. Moving over him, so that her slim legs were on either side of his, she gripped it in her small fist. "It's such a beautiful thing," she said in a hoarse voice. "Just holding it like this —" she squeezed it again — "makes me feel funny inside. Really good inside. Oh, it's so beautiful, I could kiss it." She lowered her head, and her long hair trailed across his thighs and belly. He stretched, taut as a bow under her, and ejaculated in thrusting spurts onto his shirt. He sobbed with the intensity of it.

"Oh!" she cried, sitting back. "Oh my goodness! Did I do that?" She leaned forward, resting a hand on his hip, and dipped her forefinger into his seed where it had dribbled onto his stomach, and tasted it.

"It's salty! Like ... like ..." There was a sudden noise from a floor below them. She sprang to her feet, snatched up her clothes, and fled to a distant corner. Byron was stricken, and looked around wildly to see what she had done with his clothes. He dressed like a madman, tearing his small clothes as he tugged them on. He was running his fingers through his hair when two labourers rounded the corner from the stairwell. They showed surprise when they saw him standing there, his shoelaces untied.

"I, uh, was ... I was showing my cousin around the warehouse, and she seems to have gotten away ... that is, I seem to have lost her." He looked sheepish. The two men glanced at each other, then back at him. "Carry on, then, lads. Don't let me get in your way." They nodded, making for the gantry that was off one of the loading bays. As they did so, Emma reappeared, waving brightly to them as she passed:

"Oh, Byron, you should see what a lovely view there is of the river from over there." She was slightly disheveled, there was no mistaking it, but cool as a sweep inspecting a hearth.

The two men exchanged a knowing look. "Gotten away from 'im? I should say not!" Byron was sure he heard one of them snicker in a low voice, as they moved away. His cheeks flaming, he descended the stairs with Emma, who fussed with her hair, and repeatedly asked him whether it looked all right.

Back in the office, Byron was further upset to see his father had returned, obviously much earlier than he had planned. The old man was not in a mood for trifling; it was apparent that he had just been reviewing Byron's work, and had noted the lack of much progress. Frowning at Emma, he said, "Girl. Have you been in the warehouse, when I had expressly forbade it?"

Without waiting for an answer, he looked at Byron. "Have you no sense, boy? The warehouse is a dangerous place for a girl. It's dark, and there are sharp things about, and open trap doors. Oh my. Where are your senses?" He looked at one, then the other. Emma objected, saying that it was her fault; that she had insisted on a proper tour, and that Byron was very careful. David shook his head. To Byron, he said, "You look untidy. And what's that mess all over the front of your blouse?"

At a shrill, three-note blast, which echoed melodiously among the large buildings, Byron broke into a smile. "There's the *Manitoba*," he cried. "Uncle Edwin's here!" And he ran out of the building toward the river like a boy with a hoop.

# V

This must be what it is like to commit a crime, Byron thought to himself. Not even the pleasure of seeing his father's partner could dim the anxiety he felt over his encounter with his cousin. Over and over in his mind, he related the reasons why it was wrong: her age, her relationship to him, his age, his parents' trust. And it was a criminal act as well, he was sure. Yet, for all the torment he underwent, he brushed it aside as a man might clear dirty dishes from a table with a single swipe, when he thought of Emma. Alternating between temptation and fear, it was his craving for another encounter with her that succeeded; it drove him wild with worry. But he felt he could not help himself. He resolved to leave. But where? He had never really had to think of his own future, given that it had always been taken for granted that he would assume the family business. That looked increasingly unlikely, and unattractive in any event. His last thought before falling asleep was that he should avoid the girl at all costs.

He began to accompany his father each day at work, surprising the old man with his efforts. Each time he thought to broach the subject of leaving, he could not find the right words. He was not sure where he would go, or what he would do. One thing was certain: his father would not be keen to put him back on the sales circuit again. He had to prove himself.

Yet even as he put in long hours at the business, he nevertheless remained at the office over the noon break. He kept hoping, for all his efforts to will the contrary, that she would turn up again. But several months passed, and he avoided her at home, and saw her not at all at the warehouse. Though disappointed, he began to relax, let his guard down. As time passed, he thought he might be able to get a better grip on matters when she was around, now. Take control. He was, after all, the elder by several years. Then unexpectedly she turned up again at the office.

This time, she walked through the door, having rung the bell first.

"Hello, Byron," she said coolly. "I see I've caught you alone again, just as the men are going off for their dinners." As he greeted her, she walked quickly to the chair where he was sitting, and knelt at his feet, taking his hands in hers. She was wearing a brightly coloured, print cotton dress, with a high neck and an empire waist. It was fitted snugly under the bosom, but cut full below. She had drawn it up so that it was not soiled on the dusty floorboards.

"I have many times wanted to come and see you, but I was afraid that everyone was suspicious; that they all knew. I know it's silly. But I had to feel certain. Then I thought you were very cross with me for what I'd done, so I was worried ... "

"No. Not cross. It was too wonderful — but — "

"Oh! It was," she interrupted. "It *was* wonderful. It was the most wonderful thing that has ever happened to me."

Byron squeezed her hands. "But we mustn't ... "

"Nonsense," she said abruptly. "There's no harm in it. And I want more. I want to see you again; your glorious manhood. I want you to show me the things a woman must know about real love. Who else will teach me? Some ruffian in my neighbourhood? There are plenty of them that - "

"Please don't talk like that. Wherever did you learn to talk like that?"

She stood up. "Oh, stop arguing with me. I know you like it too. Let's go find a place where we can do sweet things." She tugged him by the hands, and he stood up, hesitantly, but not reluctantly. The claw in his gut was getting control of him again, flushing away whatever remnants of reserve remained. She started for the stairs, but he held her back.

"We simply cannot go up there again. I know a better place, around back, where the sacking is kept. No one will think to look there." Self consciously, he led her behind the rail cars standing on the siding to a tall shed. It smelled musty, and the only light streamed down from a dirty window set high on the east wall. The roof was corrugated tin, and pigeons clattered and fussed at its edges.

She started to remove her clothes, and he stopped her. "We must be more careful this time; there are people about. Lie down here - " he gestured to a knee-high pile of large sacks, stacked flat on a pallet. "I want to look at you." She sat, then fell backward, arms crossed over her head, covering her eyes. Her feet remained on the floor. "Do what you will," she whispered. "Oh, Byron."

He dropped to all fours between her knees. With her help, he shoved her dress and petticoats up to her waist, and took her underclothes slowly past her ankles. She was exposed, and he fell on her with a gasp. Under his nostrils, her pubic hair was damp and faintly musky. The warm wetness of her yielded under his lips, then his tongue. She drew her legs back, opening herself to him, gasping at the sensations she was experiencing. Fumbling with his buttons, he took himself out, hard as granite.

Emma cried out. "Oh, Byron. Oh Byron. That feels so ... so ... wonderful." Her cries resounded under the metal roof. "Oh ... oh ...oh ... "

Under his own hand, he felt his tension building; he lapped at her slackness like a cat. He sensed, rather than saw, the muscles of her legs bunching with the rhythm of his own rocking motion. Her hand reached out and grasped him firmly. At once, she squealed, louder than he might have wished, but now he was oblivious to all but his nearing completion.

Suddenly, and at the point of his release, the door flung open with a slam, sending the pigeons on the roof into a flutter. "I say! What in *bloody* hell is going on here?" It was Major Botterill, a bag manufacturer and friend of Byron's father. As his eyes grew accustomed to the light inside the shed, he recognized the two figures.

"Oh my God in Heaven! Sodomite!" he shouted. Byron's erection glistened and bounced obscenely as he lurched and attempted to cover himself. Emma simply kept her eyes covered. Botterill's eyes darted over her nakedness, bare from waist to stocking-tops. "Oh my God!" he gasped hoarsely. "The defilement of a child! Before God, what *disgrace* you bring on your father!" He spun on his heels and stormed away, leaving the door wide open. Now Byron was truly frightened, and he turned to Emma, who was weeping softly. He stammered something incoherent, but her voice was clear:

"You shouldn't have done that to me," she sniffled. "You never should have done such a thing to me."

Byron felt a white heat at the base of his skull, which spread to the point where he was nearly blind. He put out his hand to steady himself.

# vi

The Chief of Police of the city of Winnipeg was a tower of a man by the name of Benjamin Whitehead. With mutton chop sideburns and flowing gray mustaches that entirely covered his lips, he was an imposing man, even without a uniform. His preference was to go bareheaded, rather than sport the forage cap that completed his formal outfit, for with it, he could not pass through doorways without stooping. Chief Whitehead was recruited by the city council to clean up the downtown, exile the growing criminal element, and contain the red light districts now centered around Toronto Street, east of Colony Creek.

It was a timely call for the burly policeman, for his rough methods had attracted growing attention from the local churches in Brampton. The *Brampton Herald* had picked up the story, and had begun to ask searching questions about a man whose death in custody had never been entirely explained to anyone's satisfaction. It was time, Whitehead had decided, to leave the ungrateful citizens of this middle-sized Ontario town behind. What a coincidence that Winnipeg should come calling.

It was true that Winnipeg had difficulties which were associated with the "immigration problem". There were rough saloons along Main Street. Bootlegging and prostitution, robbery and theft were persistent nuisances which in the councillors' view, required a firm hand. And, the Mayor had winked, "a *free* hand". It was an assignment entirely to Ben Whitehead's pleasing. And he had set to work with a will. Woe betide the thief who was caught red-handed. A sound thrashing worked wonders on the would-be recidivist. The prostitute who strayed beyond the clearly-understood limits, in the hopes of snagging a better class of trade, was put aboard the next train - east or westbound - with dire warnings of what should befall her should she return.

Pleas of 'not guilty' in the courts fell, as felons and triflers alike were expected to admit to the charges, or suffer the wrath of Chief Whitehead's hand-picked staff. These minor failings of due process were largely overlooked as the citizenry of Winnipeg delightedly reclaimed their streets back after dark. Of course, crime remained, but it was contained to the docks, the red light district, and the areas near the immigration sheds. In the latter case, it was not so much viewed as a matter of locals preying upon often frightened and disoriented newcomers, it was seen as the natural outcome of an immoral, heathen sub-class, who plundered one another as an inevitable result of their barbarism. Chief Whitehead didn't bother much with the immigrant class, unless they interfered with proper folk, in which case the full weight of the law descended upon the malefactor. There were few recommendations for bonuses or commendations that came out of the newcomers. It was the merchant class and their property that wanted watching over, and he was just the man to do it. A keen political nose, had the new Chief, and it served him well.

Though he could beat a man to death with his bare fists — the rumour was that he was a prize-fighter back home in Britain, up from the Welsh collieries, who had dispatched an opponent or two in his short time in the ring — he was curiously fastidious about his hands. He was known to wash them several times a day, and he kept a pitcher and bowl in his office for that very purpose. Now, he sat at his desk, picking at his nails with a two-penny nail he usually kept tucked behind one ear. As he did so, he stared at Byron, who sat in a thin wooden chair opposite the chief's very tidy desk. There was not a single document, or so much as a lead pencil on it. The truth of it was that the chief did not fancy himself a shuffler of paper. There were others for that sort of thing.

Byron made no attempt to hide his dismay. He was ruined, as far as he could make out. The Major had gone straight to the police, and they had created quite a stir when they had arrived at the warehouse, for David had returned to the office, and Emma was hysterical, crying out only that she didn't know what had happened.

Byron had never seen his father so disturbed. He drew the officers aside, and conversed with them in low tones for several minutes. Byron watched, until his father shot him a glare past the officers which was so venomous, that Byron looked away. Moments later, he had been placed under arrest, and escorted to a light surrey with a black canvas canopy top. It was a few short minutes to the Rupert Street Station, where after a short wait, he was ushered in to see the Chief of Police himself.

There was, incongruously, Byron thought, a cuckoo clock on the wall, its long chained weights near the end of their drop. It ticked at a furious rate, in time, he thought to the pounding of his own feverish heart. The two officers who had arrested him stepped back into the corners of the room. In all, they had barely, between them, uttered more than a dozen words. The blind to the only window was drawn, so that the room was filled with a curious light that flowed through the oilcloth material. The cuckoo sounded two o'clock, with shrill, two-note sounds. More than once, Byron opened his mouth to speak, but thought the better of it; he had heard of the fierce new police chief, and he was not about to provoke him.

"Do ye have an idea of what is done to molesters of children in our slammers?" he asked suddenly. He had a curiously high voice for someone so large. He held up a thumb, with forefinger tightly curled around. "This is you going in." He opened his fingers to form a circle: "This is you coming out." Byron's eyes widened as he caught the man's meaning. He had heard that desperation in gaols made men turn on one another for comfort, that violent sodomy was common within high prison walls. And only the weakest, the lowest were victimized in this way. He began to shake, willing himself not to cry.

"Ah. Remorse. That's good." To the others he said with not a trace of irony: "Ye don't often see that in the common felon." He turned back to Byron. "Now then, we have a number of factors to consider.

"Ye fancied a piece of tender cut chicken, then, did ye. It's nothing to me,

77

understand. Old enough to bleed; old enough to butcher, is what I say. But in the process, you have," and he held up his sizable hand, raising a finger, "committed an act of gross indecency, public nudity, sex with a minor of an age where consent is irrelevant, and, of all things, incest." All four fingers were up. "There are doubtless other crimes, if I look in the Criminal Code. All told, I'd say ye be looking at ten years or more in the federal prison. Quite a price for a piece of tail, wouldn't ye agree with me?" He leaned forward, his dark eyes intense behind tiny round glasses which sat on the bridge of a thick nose, many times broken over the years. The wooden tilt chair under him squeaked in protest at the shift in weight.

Byron could not hold back his tears. They flowed freely down his cheeks, and he hung his head. Whitehead looked disgusted; rolling his eyes. "The man plays with babies, and he whimpers like one," he said to the others. Behind Byron, they nodded and smiled in the shadows. They had seen this played out many times before.

Resting his elbows on the table, Whitehead folded his fingers under his chin, after a searching look at his nails. "Well, there's some good news, Master Bloode. Ye happen to be the son of a big taxpayer here in town. That helps. Goes to mitigation, ye might say. I doubt that there'll be a formal complaint, after ye father speaks to Major Botterill, which'll see no criminal charges in the end."

Byron raised his head, disbelieving. He pulled through his nose, for the mucous was running over his lip. He looked at Whitehead, not willing to ask him to repeat it lest he had not heard him right. Whitehead saw the question coming. "Oh, but don't ye be thinking ye be getting off scot-free. Oh no. In fact, I think ye'd wished we'd sent ye through the courts."

He stood up, and took the seat cushion from the chair under him, and placed it on the desk. Byron was mystified. The chief walked over to a magnificent *Peerless* gramophone on a tall corner table, and wound it up, carefully adjusting the long brass horn, which had its own stand, so that it was oriented to the centre of the office. The machine began to play ' 'Mid the Green Fields of Virginia' as he unbuckled the thick leather belt that encircled his vast torso. The others stood up, as if on cue, and walked over to Byron. He had barely enough time to utter a protest, which sounded more like a bleat than an objection, before they seized him, tore away his trousers, and laid him across the desk, pressing his face into the seat cushion. It stank of old rubber.

The first blow across his naked buttocks was so sudden and sharp that it drove the air from his lungs. He could not utter a sound. The second blow had the same effect so that he thought that he might faint both from its effect, and the way his face was being held against the cushion. The edge of the oak desk cut sharply into his pelvis. Each successive blow took him to levels of pain he thought he might never experience in his life; it was as if his buttocks and flanks were on fire. The cylinder in the player warbled on noisily, the lyrics ludicrous in the circumstances: " ... let me hold you, let me soothe you, for you're back 'mid the green fields of Virginia".

At last, a scream tore its way past his lips. A high, rending shriek that blended with the now shrill chorus of the recorded song. He jerked and pulled at his captors, but they held him easily, and merely forced his face harder into the padding. This was well-choreographed. There had been others who had wailed to the accompaniment of unknown vocalists captured for all time on a wax cylinder. Finally, as Byron thought he would surely pass out or die, either of which would have been merciful, the tune faded, and Whitehead relented. Byron slid sobbing to the floor, as the police chief mopped his brow, and examined his hands distastefully. "See to it that he doesn't bleed on my toss rug," he ordered. "Get him cleaned up, and throw him out."

He squatted at Byron's head. The bulk of his massive legs nearly rended the seams of his blue serge trousers. He clasped his hands in front of him, resting his forearms on his thighs. He was breathing heavily, for beating a man properly was no light duty. "Now see here," he said. "See here." He slapped Byron's face sharply. "Stop, or I'll rewind my gramophone. Stop it. Accept ye punishment like a man, for the crime of child defilement be not worthy of anyone calling himself a man.

"Listen close: I don't want to see ye face in my city for a good long while. So see that rich father of yorn, and ask him to buy ye a ticket to far away. Or ye be back here for another dance, the next time me or one of me men lays eyes on ye."

Byron decided not to go home that night; he could not face them. For a time, he wandered the streets, head down, hair over his face; passersby took him for a derelict. The stains in his seat where the lacerations had started to bleed looked as if he had soiled himself, and people turned away in disgust. Uncertain what to do or where to go, and fearful that the pain and fatigue might cause him to pass out on the streets, he stole back to the storage shed where he had been discovered with Emma. It was never locked, as little of value was ever kept there, and by working his way around the back lanes, among the waste and the shadows, he was able to install himself in the out building without being seen. A good thing it was, too, for each step was a fresh torment, and he wept freely in his anguish and humiliation. Once inside the shed, he collapsed upon the very platform that only hours ago he had pleasured himself, and drew himself up into a fetal position which eased his pain. Some scrap sacking was sufficient coverlet. His body shivered and convulsed in a state of complete distress, but his only thoughts were of Emma.

Those thoughts were confused. This girl, almost half his age, had seduced him, toyed with him, then turned on him. The ordeal he had suffered at the hands of the police was nothing to that which he was now to undergo. This was going to be a permanent stain on his life, that nothing could ever remove. Emma was a child, and he should have known better; more than that, she was his first cousin. His family would be humiliated by the scandal. Perhaps the business would suffer. He thought fleetingly of ending his life, as a melodramatic gesture of despair, but as he tried to contemplate the manner of it, blackness took him.

The origin of the term, 'Huguenots' is not clear: it is ascribed by some to the Protestants of Tours, who assembled by night in a tower which was supposedly haunted by the ghost of King Hugo. Others think it is a corruption of the German *eidegenossen*, meaning 'confederates bound together by oath'. However they came to their name, the life of a seventeenth century Protestant was not an easy one in the face of vigorous and cruel persecution. When the Dutch East India Company decided that the future of their victualling station at the Cape of Good Hope at the southern tip of Africa lay in its colonization, in 1688, free passage was offered to, among others, two hundred Huguenots. So Cape Town became the nucleus for the settlement of South Africa by a fiercely independent and stubborn class of people. The British, whose rapacious appetite for conquest and commercial exploitation was to covet the same rich *veldt*, agricultural plains, found them a surly lot, nearly two centuries later, hot-headed, touchy, and not submitting easily to discipline. In time the expression gave way to 'Boers', from the Dutch, *boor*, and the German *bauer*, both meaning 'peasant farmer'.

The history of uneasy, if not outright rancorous relations between the Boers and the British dated from the seizure of the Dutch colony at the Cape in 1795. The swell of English-speaking settlers brought with it an insistence on Imperial laws, the most irritating of which was the abolition of slavery in 1833. More than five thousand Boers, accompanied by their slaves in greater number, moved north and east in great *treks* to the communities later to be called the Orange Free State, for it lay across the Orange River, and further north, the Transvaal, after the Vaal River. Further north still, was the mighty Zulu nation, and the inability of the Boers to defend themselves against it lead to their request for British help.

A rebellion against the imposition of British annexation in 1880, known as the first Boer War, lasted only four months, but the farmers of the Transvaal were able to inflict punishing damage to British troops, most notable of which was the decisive rout of the English at Majuba Hill. Discovery of gold in the Witwatersrand brought a rush of *uitlanders*, foreigners, and the Boers felt more threatened than ever. Taxed heavily, and with no voice permitted in governance, the *uitlanders* petitioned Britain for redress, and it soon became apparent that the issues could not be resolved peacefully. Great Britain and the two, small, white, Protestant republics began an inevitable slide toward war, which saw an outbreak in hostilities in October, 1899.

These events were followed closely around the various reaches of the British Empire, and nowhere more enthusiastically than in Winnipeg. Notwithstanding strong objections of the French Canadians in Quebec and St. Boniface — the strong French-speaking community across the river from Winnipeg — it was considered patriotic to support the efforts of the Imperial Crown, the motherland. But the war was going badly for the English soldiers initially, until a massive force under Lord Kitchener began a systematic destruction of the Boer armies. By 1899, it was hoped that the war would soon be over.

But thoughts of the war and national events were far away from David Bloode's mind. He had been outraged that Botterill had gone to the police: this was a private family matter, no matter how the Major tried to rationalize his actions. A telephone call to the chief of police had brought some relief, in the sense that the man had used his usual good judgment, and had released Byron without charges. He had mentioned, somewhat ominously, that Byron "had been strongly cautioned, in lieu of more formal attention". Emma had been bundled up over her strong protestations and put on the train, sulking, for St. Paul, to stay with Byron's sister. A hasty telegram to Christine vaguely spoke of a "family emergency", but that there was "no need for concern". But where was Byron? For the balance of that day, and all of the next, he was nowhere to be seen.

And it was not that efforts weren't being made to discover his whereabouts, for both David and Mary, the next day, anxiously drove about the city looking for their son. It was not until the second day after the event that the boy was found by a workman at the Bloode & Bell premises. Looking for sacking to use as packing, the labourer had been startled to find the delirious son of the owner under remnants of filthy burlap.

It took Byron the better part of a week to recuperate. Initially he was feverish from loss of fluids, then as he regained his physical health, his shame kept him from rising from his sickbed. So his mother's ministrations kept up rather longer than perhaps was justified. But he realized that he could not hide in his bed forever.

One morning in early September, as he lay with his arms folded behind his head, looking out the window, he thought that it was time to face the inevitable. Outside, those trees which he could see had started to change colour; it was odd how, come September, the leaves turned as if someone had thrown an enormous switch. He realized that he had not thought about natural things for a long time. It was a clear day; the kind of glorious sunshine that one experiences in abundance on the prairies. His room was flooded with light. The kind of place, he reflected, that one could hide away in forever.

Suddenly, the door swung open, and his father walked in. In his reverie, Byron had not heard him approach, though it seemed that the old man wanted to catch him, before Byron had an opportunity to pretend that he was asleep: his usual stratagem.

"Good morning. I see you are looking more yourself." Byron searched the words for a sign to suggest how this was going to go. Would they throw him out? Restore the condemned man to health and hang him? What had Emma told them? Had the little witch minimized her participation, and made him out the drooling beast? Under this mélange of fleeting deliberations was a powerful current of fear, which underlay the realization that he had never had to take responsibility for himself — or anything else, for that matter.

"I am feeling well, again, I must say. Though my posterior is still sore." David's anger at the beating his son had received had been boundless at the time. But he was compromised in his response to it. He knew that Chief White-head had cut a corner, so David felt constrained to pursue any sort of objection. However, as the week passed, he thought that perhaps a thrashing wasn't such a bad idea after all. Hells bells: he would have gladly thrashed his son himself. But the thought that Byron might have died from it remained a chilling one.

"Perhaps if I had taken a hand to you when you were younger, you might have learned a little about responsibility and self control. Hmm?"

Byron said nothing, but turned to look out the window. The humiliation he felt coloured his cheeks. He sniffed. There was nothing to say.

David sat on the edge of the bed, making the steel springs under it protest. "I must know. Ah ..."

Turning his head back to look at his father, he realized what was being asked.

"The truth," his father said quietly.

"I did not take her," said Byron. "We had no intercourse." He felt as if his face was aflame.

"I am grateful for that small mercy," his father replied. "There are degrees of wrong. That would have made a bad situation wicked."

Byron opened his mouth to add more, but as he drew in his breath, David cut him off with a glance. "If you are about to relate to me how your cousin was an active participant, save it for your reckoning with God. She is a *child*, for heaven's sake. Only a purblind fool could not have understood that. The relationships that exist in a family are fundamentally ones of trust. Love, dependence, belonging, care: these are nothing without trust. Most people understand that as a matter of intuition. But not you."

Folding his arms in front of him, Byron hung his head. There was nothing to say: his father was right. He had violated the sanctity of what it meant to be a family.

"Perhaps it was a mistake to send you away for an education. I fault myself, for not taking the time that I should to teach you things, rather than building my business. Perhaps, in the end, this is my doing." He tugged at his fingers wistfully. "Your mother has been very hard on me, you know."

"This was not your doing, father. It was mine. I got carried away, and I was a fool. I will speak to Mother. The truth of it is: I am glad we were discovered. Who knows what ..." He fell silent at a pained look from his father.

"Let's speak of other things. You will not be returning to the business, at least for a while."

At the shocked look on his son's face, he went on. "As you know, there is some trouble in the South African Colonies. Canada has decided to send more men. I think you should be among them. You can ride; it's been a little while since you shouldered a gun, but I think you probably still have the general idea."

It took a moment for this to sink in. War? His father was sending him to war? His instinct was to object: what did he know of a warrior's arts? South Africa? He knew nothing of the dark continent. Quite frankly, it frightened him, but he was loathe to admit that.

"South Africa? Me to go to war? I don't think ..."

"This is not a matter that I want debated. I have had enough with your mother. Her experiences with armies — the one under Sir Garnet Wolesley that came here in '70 — are ones she'd prefer to forget. Victorious soldiers are a vile, cruel lot, and their behaviour here left an indelible stain on your mother's consciousness, I'm afraid. I'm not entirely sure that she knows the same Wolesley is now Great Britain's Commander-in-Chief, which would offend her even more deeply.

"But properly-led, properly-disciplined, the military can provide the kind of discipline and structure which I think you need. I think that you've probably had it a little too easy. Moral lapses don't occur in a healthy mind. You need to balance your considerable intellectual skills with physical and spiritual dimensions, as well as self-control. You can get that in the army. If it be necessary to put yourself in harm's way, then so be it. There is harm of a far worse sort."

"Are there alternatives we can ... ?"

"There are, but you can choose them by yourself. If you wish to oppose me on this, then you must leave. Think of it as atonement. You have trespassed against your family; now you must balance the ledger. I want you away from here for a while; it is for the best. And while you have the benefit of distance — which should bring with it a perspective of its own — I want you to reflect on what you have done to all of us, and condition your mind to a state where such weaknesses will be a thing of the past."

As his son took in all that he had said, including silent reflection on the police chief's injunction to leave town for a while, David outlined what he had found out about Byron's possibilities with the Imperial armies of Great Britain.

"It seems that Canada was turned down when offers of military assistance were first made. But the Boers, to everyone's surprise, gave the Brits a rather dreadful series of setbacks, as you probably have read by now. It seems that we can help, after all. Now, I have a little influence, here and there ..."

*Book Three*

# SOUTH AFRICA

# i

The parting had not been easy; Byron's mother had been stiff and cool and his father had been reserved. The tension over David Bloode's decision for his son, and his wife's disapproval of it — together with her revulsion at what Byron had done — was palpable.

It hadn't made him feel much better when David told Byron of Mary's anxiety; how she had ministered to him through the nights that he was ill. Despite that bit of cheering news, Byron was miserable. His military training had not gone well. He had barely passed the qualifying events of marksmanship and riding. It was apparent that the sergeant-major was of the view that better men were there for the choosing, but he had been instructed that Byron should be accepted. It was the way of the monied class, the powerful, even in Canada.

Now, as the troopship *Milwaukee* lay at anchor off the South African coast, he tried for the third time to draft a letter to his father. If matters were to be put right, the time to start was now. He and his father had corresponded in a desultory way while he was at Oxford, and Byron had always treasured those letters. Perhaps the way to begin was to come at it indirectly. Set down routine things, innocuous. A letter like those of old. It might be that in the weeks ahead, the letters could become a little more revelatory, and the process of restoring family grace made a little easier.

Byron was lying on his belly in a narrow bunk. At eye level, a porthole was lifted so that the breeze could be caught. Though it was yet early morning, the day was already getting hot. He licked the end of the stubby pencil, and wrote upon the paper he had placed on the back of his paybook.

*December 16, 1899*
*2nd Troop, 'B' Squadron*
*1st Canadian Rifles*
*My Dear Papa:*
*Here we are anchored along Cape Town. It is a good sight to see the steamers anchored here. The shore is all rocky and mountains. One of the closest is Table Mountain; it rises quite a height, and is flat on top.*

*We weighed anchor at 5:00 on November 15, and dropped anchor almost four weeks to the hour. I have become quite close chums with a Cuthbert Copeland, who is quite a bright fellow from Carberry, Manitoba.*

*18th. We have moved a little closer to the wharf, now. There is a heavy wind blowing off the shore today, and we can see the sand flying at the foot of Table Mountain, which reminds me of Manitoba at seeding time. I suppose that you will be well into taking orders for next season, by the time you eventually get this.*

*I wish that we could get at the horses to clean them, now as we have lots of time. They are slung so close together, all we can do is scrape the hair off their backs with a hoe. It comes off in great clumps. Forty of them have died on the trip, which isn't bad, really when you consider how awful it was for them.*

*25th. Sunday. Christmas Day, but who would know it, but for a mug given to us by the Queen. It is quite sturdy, like the old girl herself, I suppose, and bears her picture. But most of us have no idea where to keep it safe. We're in Cape Town at last, and being shipped out by rail to Kroonstadt.*

*26th. More delays. I've opened the letter to scribble a few more lines, as this is a last call for the post. Don't worry if you don't hear from me for a while, as they have told us to let everybody back home know that mail will be spotty once we are engaged in training. There is a fine spirit among us, and we all want to have at Mr. Boer, but it will be some time yet, about a month, depending upon how quickly the horses recover. The train is to pull out within the hour, and wouldn't you be amazed to see what we're travelling in: mooo!*

*Your loving son,*
*Byron*

It was a neutral thing, empty of anything personal, but it was contact. A man off to war needed connections that tied him to more comforting things. He handed down the letter to the corporal who was making his way along the track, stuffing the letters and cards into a sack, and stowed the stubby pencil in his breast pocket. It was hot, and the sweat poured from under the high, white helmet, that bore the maple leaf. In either direction, six hundred men milled alongside the train of freight and cattle cars that were their conveyance to the remount station at Stellenbosch. The horses had been loaded for more than three hours, but there was no accounting for the delay, the last of many, and all of which had gone without explanation. It was part of the military mind-set that Byron was beginning to find irritating. Everyone was treated as an automaton; an unthinking creature who did as he was told; nothing more, and certainly not less. As an officer, although the lowest rank possible, that of ensign, he expected more.

By the time the training of the green soldiers was complete, and the horses restored to their former fitness, replacements found for those that had been destroyed during the passage, feed obtained and the multitude of other organizational and supply matters attended to, the war had started to go badly for the Boers, much to the relief of the English, who were still smarting from the early punishments that the doughty farmers of the little republics had visited upon them. In February of that year, the sieges of Ladysmith and Kimberley had been lifted, and in March, Bloemfontain had been taken. Field Marshal Frederick Roberts, Earl of Kandahar, hero of the Afghan and Indian wars, and now the supreme commander of British forces in South Africa, had proclaimed the Orange Free State to be British territory. His army was marching on Pretoria, and Kroonstadt was soon to be put under the Union Jack.

Morale was high in the Canadian contingent, and all were eager to be in on Roberts' march to Pretoria. however, 'C' battery, and a squadron of cavalry, Byron among them, were given orders to proceed back to Cape Town. Most expected that this was for prisoner-of-war duty. There had been considerable traffic in the shipping of prisoners out of the country, and green soldiers were often assigned to this. It was easy work, and Byron found the Boers cooperative enough, though he understood not a word of their grunting, hooting language. Still, it was an annoyance to be moving backward. He was caught up in the excitement to do battle, having no real idea how it would be. He could not imagine that these ragged, rather pathetic-looking creatures could put up much of a fight. Inwardly, he was somewhat relieved at that. It was easy to feel confident surrounded by an enormous army, properly turned out in full kit and caboodle.

It was with horror that they were detrained and marched up the quay to board the *Columbian*. Non-commissioned officers shouted down muttered protests, as once again, the enlisted men and junior ranks were told nothing, beyond the matter being of the "highest secrecy". Even though Byron was as uninformed as anyone else, he was regarded with suspicion for some time; as an officer, he was perceived to be on the inside of such goings on. Not to share information was viewed as lack of trust. It was only after the ship had been at sea for two weeks that a pervasive rumour held that the destination was Mafeking. The city had been under siege from the start of the war, and its Commander-in-Chief, Lord Baden Powell, was getting desperate. There was considerable public pressure for the lifting of the siege. The Canadian guns were to accompany Major-General Frederick Carington's Rhodesian Field Force, which was to strike from the north. This was so plausible, and not denied by anyone of senior rank, that the men settled down. They had other things to concern them in any event, for the passage would be most unpleasant.

The route was a circuitous one, which would take them west and north, around the Cape of Africa, to a desolate port called Beira, in Portuguese East Africa. From there, a combination of rail and forced march would bring them around to a point where they could descend upon the beleaguered town. There, it was hoped that the siege forces would be surprised by a pincer movement of allied troops converging from both directions.

The trip at sea took fifteen days. The weather was hot and rough, and to add to the misery, the master missed the landfall, so anxious was he about the sand-laden shallows. The horses, so brought to a state of good health by their time ashore, now were reduced to a state of distress. One was slung overboard, having died. But by the end of April, Byron and his mates were loaded, along with their gear and mounts, on the narrow-gauge railway that would take them inland, to Bamboo Creek, just over sixty miles from the sea.

Lying atop bales of sweet-smelling hay, he had little to do than watch the strange countryside roll by. It was more agreeable than the marshy lowlands where Beira was situated. Byron pulled out his pencil and small notebook for which he had bartered in Cape Town. Turning backward so that the fetid breeze would not interfere with his writing, he started another letter. This was dated April 25, 1900. It would arrive in Winnipeg much blacked-out by the censors.

*Dearest Papa:*

*We have had yet another sea-voyage, this time bringing us to a point where we can reach Rhodesia, thence to Mafeking. Or at least, that is the rumour, for we have never been actually told anything for certain. Yet it seems obvious. No doubt by the time you read this, the siege will have been lifted by our efforts.*

*This is a very strange place, called by some the "white man's grave", for it is said that non-Africans live no more than three years here. Last night, as it cooled (it gets rather cold here at night, you might be surprised), a "fever mist" came out of the ground. So we were very glad to be high up on the freight carriages. As you might expect, there are a lot of nigger-men about, and a frightening lot they are too. They seem to have no love for us, though it is on account of their freedom that we are here in the first place.*

*As you know, my chief function as ensign is to look after the company colours. I have them folded up in my pack, until we are on maneuvers. Then they are to be deployed. But a good many nasty-minded fellows have told me that I shall be a target for the Boer sharpshooters, for that reason. Still, being forewarned is forearmed, so do not worry. I shall be careful. I have the same rifle as all others, and a Colt .45 strapped to my waist. I look quite the bandit in my cowboy hat, which is preferable to the helmet in bright sunshine.*

*We have just had a rain of sparks from the engine, a common occurrence, so it looks as if I shall be called upon to do duty with wet sacking.*

*More later, Byron.*

While he could not bring himself to deal with it in his letters, which he kept as antiseptic as possible, the hours of idleness were time to reflect on those matters which had brought him here. He found it odd that he could barely bring an image of Emma to mind. The way that she had turned on him had been disgusting. His earlier infatuation had been displaced by an anger, then resentment. But now there was nothing. She seldom figured in his daylight musings, but she still had the power to enter his thoughts at night, stirring his sleep. The image of her in his father's warehouse, that day, had seared itself into his subconscious, though when he awakened, aroused and distressed, he could not fetch the construct of her face. It was quite puzzling, for he refused to accept that he had seen her merely as an object of gratification, a receptacle of his lust. There was something quite wrong with that, wasn't there?

He decided to engage Copeland on this topic. His friend was a handsome fellow who seemed to have all manner of intimate experiences, for he spoke of them often and in considerable detail. Other men gathered around, from all ranks, for Copeland could spin a yarn with the best of storytellers, and there were many who thought that some of the more salacious details had been made up. But he was nonplused by criticism, and there was no shortage of audience for his tales.

"Copeland," Byron began, one afternoon as the train from Bamboo Creek made for Marandellas, a further three hundred miles away. "What sort of a woman would you like to marry?"

"Marry?" snorted Copeland. "Marry? I shouldn't know. I've never considered it. I'm having far too much fun at the moment. Too many girls, too little time." He smiled, looking dreamily at the passing landscape. "No, I shouldn't want to be bogged down with a wife for a good while yet." He looked at his friend. "Why? Are you hot for someone in particular to bed every night? Did you leave her behind, then?"

In spite of himself, Byron blushed. He envied Copeland's easy way with women, to hear him tell it at least. "Well, I did leave someone behind, but it was not like that. I hardly knew her, but she was a fiery sort. Hot-blooded, you might say. You wonder, one wonders whether ... " he picked at the seeds of the bale he was lounging on, and tossed each mote over the side of the open freight car, as if it were a grenade.

"Whether what?"

"Whether that's what love is. I mean, I hardly remember her face, now."

Copeland roared with laughter. "Aye. But there's other parts you could recall in great detail, I'll wager!" Those within earshot turned to look at Copeland. Another salacious story? They were interested, but he waved them off. As a second lieutenant, he had sufficient authority to command a little privacy. He became serious. "I do believe you're blushing, man. Is it guilt you're feeling, then? You had this woman, and now you feel some sense of obligation?"

Byron cringed at the word, 'woman'. Copeland took this for another reason: "Ah, yes. Perfectly natural, especially if it was your first."

"It wasn't my first!" A protest, sounding slightly petulant. "There were others, in England." Desperately wanting to sound experienced, even blasé.

"Then perhaps it was love, I couldn't say, never having been more than temporarily in that state. The fact is, a man *in erecto* has no effectively functioning brain, in any event, wouldn't you agree?" He was grinning broadly. "Who was she?" There was no answer. "Were you her first one? That can make quite a difference."

The drift of the conversation was beginning to alarm Byron. "Yes I was," he said. "Let's leave it at that."

"Aha!" cried Copeland. "Now we're getting closer to the reason you're on this God-forsaken train. She's up the spout! Had your way with her, and run off to war; her with a bulge in her tummy. That's it."

This sounded as good a story as any; far better than the truth, he supposed. "The thing is, she condemned me, for what we .. er ... that is, what we ..."

"Oh for God's sake man, out with it. You fucked her. She's unhappy. It's all part of the standard ploy. The only way she'll let you off the hook is if you say you'll marry her. They're all the same. Can't wait to do it, then miserable afterward. You did the right thing, getting out."

"Well, I'm not so sure. This really was the easy way out, actually, once I'd gotten used to the idea that I was actually going off to kill people. Better that, than face -"he stopped short, realizing what he was about to disclose. He looked away, his eyes shiny. Shittles! Could he ever hold his head up again?

Copeland studied him for a long moment. It was apparent his friend was not going to tell all that was involved, but it was equally evident that there was considerable torment associated with it. He put his hand on Byron's sleeve.

"I worry about you, old man. You might be too soft for all this."

# ii

The men of the 2nd Troop, 'B' Squadron, 1st Canadian Mounted Rifles, were a mixed lot, drawn from across Canada, though all but three of the eight troops of the battalion were from eastern and central Canada. Troop 2 was composed of men from Virden, Brandon, Portage la Prairie and Winnipeg. Their commander was a short, energetic lieutenant by the name of Young, who had cheated on the minimum height requirements to join. He had commanded a militia troop at Virden the previous summer, and nine of the volunteers from that experience had come with him. He was resentful of Byron, and did not consider that the lean red-haired puff had earned a commission, but had obtained it by influence. And this was not to be a force where that was the case. Nevertheless, he had become resigned to the fact that nepotism was inevitable in this country, and given that the Company's colours were to be the principal responsibility of the man, there was not significant harm to come of it. In fact, the word among soldiers was that the standard-bearer was a high-turnover position in any war. But throughout, he remained abrupt with Byron, where an exchange was absolutely necessary.

Byron, for his part, felt wounded by the snubbing, but was content to associate with the non-commissioned officers, and enlisted men, though principally he sought the company of Copeland. Lately he had been having bad dreams, imagining that Copeland had been killed, and the men somehow blaming him for it. Copeland was right: the guilt was creeping into his life like a stain, colouring his view of the world. This wouldn't do at all, he told himself. But it was more than a matter of vanity and appearance; it was that he felt he did not fit. He was out of place at his father's business, and now here he was on a troop train, no more at home with pennant and gun than he would have been in a gas balloon. He wished that he had thought to bring his father's letters, and the hints they contained of his family's history. Why was the old man so damned taciturn about his past; where he and Mary had come from? It was almost as if he was ashamed, that if by ignoring it, hiding it, it did not exist.

He stared out into the jungle, now dark and closing in, like a shroud. He shivered, both from the notion, and the surprising chill that came virtually as if on a switch, once the sun disappeared. He was conscious of Copeland's laughter as he told a joke to his mates, just behind him. How comfortable the man was, with anyone, and how the others seemed to adore him. Byron felt a sudden pang of envy. Next to Copeland, he felt clumsy and irrelevant. The inverted pips on his shoulders burned into his flesh. He should have insisted upon enlisting as a private soldier. There was Copeland and twenty-odd members of the Manitoba Dragoons who seemed perfectly at home in their station, content with their lot. There was a sudden burst of guffaws again, at another story. A shower of sparks drifted by from the labouring engine, and it seemed for a moment as if the laughter had become palpable, lighting the surrounding coolness. He felt a slap at his leg, where his puttee was wrapped between boot and cuff. A voice spoke from the darkness, where a face was barely limned by the glow of a fat pipe.

"I say, Bloode, did you hear that one? Come on, it's your turn. Tell us a joke from your private school in England."

He coloured, glad of the darkness. He was hopeless at jokes; a poem, yes. But one thing was certain: were he to relate a poem, they would pitch him off the train altogether. No doubt about that. There was nothing worse than a flat joke. Unless it was to refuse to try at all. So he dug into his recollection; he remembered a story told by a friend in Oxford. It was about dons, and the peculiar hierarchies at college, but he could adapt it, he thought..

Several others took up the cry: "Well?" "Come on, then?" "Ah, never mind, reverend. Can't pull a white rabbit from a coal miner's hat!"

Byron cleared his throat. "It seems a certain corporal, who shall go unnamed, was sitting in his tent, doing up dispatches. One of the enlisted men of his troop came in and said, uhmm, 'Excuse me, corporal, I know you left instructions not to be disturbed. But the Pope is outside, and wants to see you'.

He paused, to let this particular absurdity sink in, then continued: " 'Oh, and the Regimental Sergeant-Major is here as well, and he wants to see you too. Whom do you want me to send in first?' " There were some chuckles.

"The corporal thought a bit, chewed on the end of his pencil, then said: 'Better send in the Pope. All I have to do with him is kiss his ring.' "

There was a pause, and the top of the car erupted in raucous laughter. He had done it; he had won their applause. He beamed in the inky blackness. Perhaps the way to being held in another man's esteem was in many such small steps; was love this way, won by degrees? But he was acutely aware that a single careless step could remove it. He begged off another story, telling the truth that he had no other to offer. And the chatter slid away from him. He dozed, a degree of contentedness easing his thoughts for the moment.

Too soon, he was roused from a fitful sleep to assist with the sanding. It was their turn to grit the track so that the undersized engine could make the grade. Next, at first light, it was wooding-up that was necessary, for the locomotive burned fuel at the prodigious rate of a cord and a half an hour where there was anything of a rise to the rail bed.

It was with considerable relief that the troops were permitted to disembark from the train at Marandellas, a town well inside the Rhodesian border. It was a picturesque place, carved from the jungle, and featuring most of the amenities that Victorian civilization had to offer. There were restaurants offering reasonably good fare, shops with a generous selection of goods on view, even a theater. The men could only fantasize about the comforts of the hotels they marched past, on their way to the campground where they would be setting up their ten-man, bee-hive-shaped tents. It was here that leave had been granted, as part of the necessary restoration of the force which had been continuously on the move. There lay ahead six hundred miles of rugged terrain to cross, surrounded by sullen tribesmen who had suffered at the hands of the British Army during the Matabele Wars as recently as four years earlier; beyond that, the Boers, in strength, tightening their grip on the town of Mafeking. It was here, in Marandellas, that the men were first formally told of their destination, though by then it was anti-climactic.

The settlement had seemed large as they had advanced upon it by train, but by the end of a couple of hours or so, the men had explored everything there was to see. The taverns and the 'sporting-house' were placed off limits by the provost, much to the annoyance of the troops. The 'social ladies' disported themselves about the second-floor verandah, and were nude, or nearly so. It reached the point where there were so many men milling about below, that traffic could not pass, and the local clergy had become outraged. Sin was tolerated in the shadows, here, as anywhere else. But righteous indignation was provoked by the sight of undressed women, albeit black or coffee coloured, openly taunting men with obscene words and gestures. Never mind the fact that, despite the best efforts of the missionaries to cover them up, most local natives felt the requirement of additional clothing silly and unnecessary. The establishment was closed until the force had decamped.

Once, at the edge of town, Byron saw several men seize a young native woman, and manhandle her toward the dense bush at the edge of the jungle. He could see fear in the whites of her eyes as they rolled like those of a panicked mare. Three or four of them laughed as she was bundled from view; the last one beckoned to him, to come and join in the fun. He remained rooted, torn between an urge to go for help, and horrifyingly, an even stronger urge to go and join them. It was not so much that it was the same predatory creature that had clutched him when he was with Emma, which fondled his prurience now, but the fact that he had been included, which made him feel as if he should participate. He wanted to run with the pack, tear at the heels of sheep, and once blooded, howl at the moon.

He started at a touch on his shoulder. It was Copeland who had obtained two bags of dry sherbet and a licorice straw. He handed one to Byron. "I say, couldn't you hear me? I was calling you." He looked to where Byron was staring, puzzled. "What's going on, then?"

Byron related what he had seen, omitting how his emotions had torn at him. Copeland seemed unconcerned; perhaps indifferent would have been a better term, Byron thought.

"Damned stupid of them, raping locals. We've strict orders about looting and fraternizing. What they're up to is court martial stuff." He sucked at the straw. "Mmmm. This is quite good. Let's get out of here, so we're not caught up in anything should the provost come around."

"Should we report it? I mean ..."

The other made a face at him. "Those are our comrades at arms. In a very few days, we're going to be relying on those chaps to watch over our backs. We're going to need them. What do you think?"

Byron tore open the paper pouch and inserted his licorice tube. He tried to imagine the ordeal the girl was going through, and wondered whether they would kill her to keep her quiet, or offer her trinkets. He pondered whether a negress, or a mixed-race girl at least, would feel the same about the violation as a white woman. It was with a sudden rush of queasiness that he remembered that he was of two races, though his parents didn't speak of it very much. He folded the bag and put it in his pocket.

"What's the matter? Too sweet for you? I'll take it back if you like, though the stuff makes me bloody thirsty."

"No. Thanks. It's very good. But I can't get out of my mind what's happening back there. I mean, we're supposed to be here to free these people; enforce the laws of the British Empire. You know, that sort of stuff. Not rape and kidnap and Lord knows what else. Couldn't we at least go back and tell them to cheese it? The provost is coming?"

Copeland stopped and looked at him. "What's the matter with you, Bloode, old man? Think about it: it's their risk. Their fun - their folly - however you want to look at it. Mix into it, and you'll lose on all counts. Most of the mistakes we make in life come from feeling when we ought to think, and thinking when we ought to feel." He craned his head back and tilted the remains of the sugary powder into his mouth. It made him sneeze. "Right now, I venture to say, my friend, that you're feeling rather than thinking. Forget about it. Niggers don't notice things the same way we do. She's probably enjoying herself." He started walking again, chewing up the black licorice.

He called to someone he recognized some distance off, then turned back to Byron for a moment. "Listen, you red-haired twit: you'd better toughen up before we get to the war zone. Remember, you came here to kill people, not to read them poetry."

His tone was amiable enough, but the words chilled Byron.

# iii

Just north of Mafeking was Colonel Harry Plumer's Rhodesian Regiment, a force raised by Colonel Robert Baden-Powell. When war broke out, the Boers laid siege to the city with its nearly nine thousand inhabitants. Baden-Powell refused to surrender, though serious privations were being experienced by the populace. Plumer had not many more than seven hundred men, so there was not much beyond rather impotent harrying of the eleven thousand mounted horsemen that could be done. What was needed was reinforcements and field guns. It was decided to send on an advance force from Marandella, consisting of a pair of artillery officers, two guns with a supply wagon, forty other military personnel, including infantry from the Queensland Mounted Infantry. In addition, there were local drivers who had been retained to provide mules for the guns and wagon, and other supplies. Very few of the horses were sufficiently recovered from the trip so far to proceed with them. Byron was the ensign designated to accompany the first detachment.

The assembly was instructed to proceed at all possible haste to the support of Plumer. Though the track was well defined, and local scouts were employed to ensure that the way was not lost, the convoy nevertheless travelled slowly. On either side, for the beginning of the march, was thick, impenetrable jungle. Mysterious and dark, the gloom was riven by cries and roars of strange beasts. Moreover, there was anxiety over the Matabele, who had been punished by the British earlier on, were ever-present, though only fleeting glimpses of them could be seen. At night, anxious sentries listened to the muffled thumping of drums, and sharp cries of angry men. It was difficult to rest under such conditions, even though the dust and heat of the trail enervated the men. All were anxious to make Bulawayo, which was the railhead for the Western Railroad route to Mafeking.

The night before they expected to reach the town, Byron lay in his tent next to Copeland. Eight other men slept fitfully alongside them.

"You awake?" someone said. "This is a bloody 'orrible land. Some of the fellows came across an enormous great snake, eighteen feet long it was, with a pair a skinny black legs sticking out of him. Bulge in the belly as poor old blacko was being had for dinner."

Someone else cut in: "Drop out of the trees they do, and crush you and eats you. If you're lucky, you're dead when you start to get swallowed."

"Aye," said the first. "When the lads killed it, they cut him open, and there was this fellow's head and chest half dissolved, his mouth wide open in a silent scream."

"By the bright eyes of Jesus," breathed another. "And listen to that thumping. Can you all hear it?"

"Mmm. Yes. Dammit. Those infernal drums are a colossal headache that won't go away. Annoying as hell; I suppose that's the purpose."

"Do you suppose we'll be attacked? That's the rumour all day."

Copeland's distinctive voice entered the conversation; Byron could imagine him in the dark, amused look, arms behind his head. "Nahh. If it was going to happen, it would have, already. We're less than a day away from Bulawayo. There's a detachment at least of the Protectorate Regiment out of Rhodesia stationed there. They'll be well-mounted and properly armed, so ... "

There was a voice from the far corner: "What bloody good will they do us, then? They're thirty miles away, and we could be stewing in Matabele cooking pots by the time they even hear about us. If there's an attack. Blasted field guns aren't going to be any use in close fighting, in the dark. With black men you can't see anyway."

And another: "I'll be glad when we're out on the veldt, away from this bush. It gives me the creeping what-fors, it does, to be so hemmed in."

Copeland snickered. "Well, my fine lads: since no one seems to be asleep, why don't we have a few hands of whist?"

It lifted the mood. The first man who had spoken said, "Say Copey: why don't you tell us a story? That should put us all out in a flash." There was general snickering.

"Come to think of it," said another, "Matabele spears might be welcome after one of Copeland's stories.

"All right, lads. Did I ever tell you about St. Peter and Jesus going fishing?" There were groans all round. "No. Listen. You know Peter from your scripture. A good man, a brave man, but his weakness was that he assumed things. See, if someone laughed, he figured that they were laughing at him. If they scowled, he thought that they were cross with him. He simply assumed the worst.

"So one day, he took Jesus with him in his boat, out fishing. Jesus had just got himself settled in the stern, when Peter stands up and yells to the other boats: 'Hey fellows. You want to catch fish, come with us. See how it's done properly.' Naturally, they all followed him out, to where the best spot was.

"Soon, he dropped the sail, tasted the water, took sights off the coast, and held a moistened thumb up to the wind. 'Here,' he said. 'this is where they are. Don't make a sound, 'cause you'll scare them off.' And it was true. Just beneath the water were hordes of fish, Jesus could see that.

"So Peter lets the nets out gently. All the others followed suit. 'Why aren't you casting the nets? says Jesus. 'We'll scare them,' says Peter importantly.

"Jesus taps on the side of the boat, carefully, so that no one sees him, and the fish dive for the bottom of the sea of Galilee. The nets come up empty. After a few tries, all the other fishermen get angry. They're yelling at Peter. 'You idiot!' 'What do you know?' And like that. Poor old Peter was all destroyed over his failure.

"Jesus says: 'Hmmm. This fishing business is not what it's cracked up to be, I'd say."

Someone spoke from the darkness, "There supposed to be a point to this story?"

Copeland was silent for a moment. "It's a Basque parable. It's supposed to tell us a few things. I'm surprised you don't see it."

It was about the folly of assuming things, of taking things for granted, Byron thought to himself. But he was afraid of appearing stupid — or patronizing — in front of the enlisted men. Minutes passed without anyone saying a word, though it was apparent from the measured breathing that all of them were awake, and had the story in their thoughts. For a moment the drums were forgotten, as each man wrestled with the point of the tale.

At length, Copeland spoke. "Jesus was a man, like any of us. In fact, the Bible tells us that many times. It follows that he had a sense of humour. He was playing a joke on Peter, but Peter didn't get it. He just assumed that Jesus was single-minded about everything, and had no time for humour. So of course, that possibility didn't even occur to him, even when Jesus made a wise-acre type remark."

Copeland rolled on his side, and closed his eyes. "You see boys, our judgment on things can be no better than our information. Assumptions can take us way off. We got sentries out. There's a battle plan. There's a bit of high ground we're on. We got local advice that's been right on, so far. We're close to Bulawaya. Hell, boys, there won't be no attack tonight. Get some sleep."

For a long time, Byron stayed awake; the drums no longer intruded into his consciousness. Copeland was a blacksmith's son from Brandon. He had finished school, and was casting about for something to do with his life, when Young's militia out of Virden, headed for South Africa, seemed an exciting opportunity. It was true that he read voraciously, having nearly consumed the entire contents of the Carnegie Library in Brandon. He was the sort of man who read his instruction pamphlet for his Lee-Enfield, cover to cover. Did this explain why he was so wise? Byron had four years at Oxford, yet he felt like a bumbling fool next to Copeland. The private soldier had more natural leadership qualities than most of the strutting martinets whose sleeves and shoulders bore the ornaments of rank. He knew that Copeland had refused promotion, offering that others were more worthy. But it was plainly not the case. The man was self-contained, comfortable with himself.

It was as dark as he had ever known. There were no fires outside, lest they illuminate the camp unduly. All that broke the stillness outside was the insistent throbbing, and the regular calls of the sentries, one to the other. The earlier unease he had felt returned like an unwelcome visitor; all the more discomfiting given that Copeland and the others were asleep, the sometimes raucous sounds of weary men sleeping filling the tent. He had never thought much about his own mortality, no more than he had given much consideration of what purpose would underlie his life. The idea that he and his comrades could be set upon at any moment, and have their lives taken away in horrifying circumstances seemed very real. Even likely. At once his imagination took hold, and he conjured all sorts of painful means of destruction. He could see his own corpse; now it was dismembered. He could see the triumphant dance of crazed savages gyrating among the disgusting remains of his fallen mates. The terror was so real, that he was ready to sit up and seize his pistol. Only the strongest exercise of will prevented him from leaping from his bed, and displaying his fright to the others. In truth, it was only the fear of looking the fool that was the greater of the two.

Outside, the sentries called to one another in a sequenced code, and the sergeant reported in: "All's well."

The next afternoon, they arrived without incident in Bulawaya.

Spirits were high among the men as they arrived in the vibrant town of nearly five thousand residents. This was a progressive settlement, with electric streetlights, motor cars, and ice. The British South Africa Company took on the responsibility of sponsoring a proper welcome for the 'heroes for the relief of Mafeking', and the soldiers were treated to chilled ale, sausages, fresh French bread in the peculiar thin baguettes, and pudding. When the train was loaded at the station, and ready to leave on the 9th of May, a large throng turned out to cheer the sixty men on for the last four hundred miles of their journey.

As the train puttered south, signs of combat became apparent. There was a sniper alert. While Byron initially had been delighted to have been assigned to a cattle car, as opposed to the open coal cars, he now envied their steel sides. The slatted vehicles of the type in which he rode offered little protection against the enemy marksmen with their Mausers. The remaining bales of hay and boxes of supplies had been stacked against the sides, and the troops lay sweating in the dusty aisle, listening for the strike of a bullet. These came frequently enough so that no one could relax his vigilance. Already the spotter, whose function it was to scour the rails ahead for blockages or other forms of sabotage, had been shot in the hand; at that he was lucky, for he was holding field glasses to his eyes at the time. Only five miles an hour faster, and he would have been killed instantly.

The meeting with Plumer's force at Sefetili on the 14th of May, 1900, was jubilant. Byron felt that these experienced, battle-seasoned men would be able to share their knowledge of the Boers, and how they fought. With such men as mentors, he thought, and the field guns they had fetched these many thousands of miles, the British now had a formidable means by which the relief of Mafeking could be accomplished. They were now not more than thirty miles from the beleaguered city. But as it developed, it was not to be a walk in the park that many of them thought it might be.

# iv

In the face of the massive army that was arrayed against them, the Boers improved upon their hit-and-run tactics. That it was hopeless didn't seem to have occurred to men who were fighting not only for family and hearth, but freedom and a way of life their ancestors had spilled blood to maintain. Guerrilla warfare escalated. Railway lines were cut, sometimes as frequently as a half dozen times a month. Sorties were attempted against Cape Colony, where both British and Afrikaner citizens were numerous. English soldiers were fired upon under cover of white flags of surrender. Reprisal shootings of civilians began, and the severe grip of martial law began to flex on the entire theatre, on Boer and non-Boer alike. Soon, military courts were sentencing captured rebels to death.

As Byron's troop train puttered southwest on the Western Railway, he and his comrades were unaware of the efforts of the Boers to invade the southern provinces, where the English forces were thought to have complete dominance. There were frequent stops, because the rails had been torn up, or a barricade of ties had been wired to the rails themselves. At such intervals, it was necessary for a troop to deploy, and scout the area, then guard the work party while they set about restoring the tracks. The actual repairs seldom took long, as it was apparent that men travelling on horseback did not possess the necessary tools to do permanent damage. The small parts had been carried off a short way, but there were sufficient replacements on board, so this did not pose much of a problem.

There had been two month's recuperation for men and horses, as well as drill in firearms, close combat, and riding in formation. The horses responded well to proper feed and exercise, and were restive at being confined again. On the occasions when it was his turn to turn his mount out and patrol the veldt — Cossack post, it was called by the men — Byron was struck at the vastness and the stark beauty of the land. It looked very much like the Northwest Territories, out beyond Brandon, save for the anthills, which seemed to be everywhere. These little mounds ranged from twelve to fourteen inches. The rolling countryside seemed empty and forlorn, for the winter of the Southern Hemisphere was well upon them.

On a patrol near the village of Pitsani, not far from Mafeking, Byron had become nearly hypnotized by the dull brown, featureless landscape, and was lost in reverie. At first he did not comprehend what his partner, a ruddy-faced sergeant from Winnipeg named Bob Bricker was saying. The man was about twenty feet off and slightly to the rear; Byron sensed rather than heard the dread in the man's voice. He swung his head in the direction of his companion, whose arm was extended toward the brow of a low rise, perhaps a quarter mile off. The ground had been steadily gaining as they travelled, and the highest point was their destination. From it, they would have had a commanding view of the entire countryside. Though they were at least fifteen miles out of camp, they were unconcerned, for there had been no reports of significant Boer activity since their arrival. It was felt by the leadership that all of the enemy's efforts would be directed toward the tightening of the stranglehold on Mafeking, before relief could arrive. Indeed the high command was satisfied that the enemy would act in an entirely predictable way, though in fact there was no reason whatsoever to believe that the wily Boer would do so. Of such errors are empires lost.

A tightly-bunched squad of men was hurtling down the slope in their direction. Boer commandos. As yet, no shot had been fired, for the distance was too great. It could suggest that it was intended to take them alive. They had only to wait for five minutes or so, and both men could have been picked from their saddles like tin cans on a fence.

"Bloody hell!" the sergeant shouted as he wheeled his mount. "Where in hell did they come from?" Asking the obvious, but revealing his anger at the careless briefing the lieutenant from the British contingent had given them that morning. "Let's be out of it!"

The sudden excitement gave Byron some difficulty with the horse he was on. It tended to be a bit skittish since their arrival, but well-found horses were in short supply, and he was trying to work with the animal. He lost frustrating seconds of time fighting the animal into a circle, and by the time he put the spurs to the animal's flanks, his sergeant was well off, lashing his own beast with his forage cap.

It was a gentle grade descending, which gave the horses the advantage. But the enemy had the same advantage. Byron dared not look back, to see whether they were gaining on them, but bent low over the withers. The sweat from the great neck muscles of his mount flew back into his face, and he urged it on with high cries that telegraphed his fear to the creature. Ahead, he could see the other rider snatch glances back; after each look, he redoubled his efforts with the hat. It was plain enough that the Boer raiding party was closing the distance between them. He gasped as the horse gathered for a leap suddenly, crossing a shallow ditch that he had not seen. Concentrate, dammit! Another jump like that, and you'll be unseated. He admonished himself, trying to calm his emotions. His heart raced, and his vision blurred with the ambient breeze their swift movement across the veldt created. The tears drained across his cheeks. He could not shake the lurking anxiety that a thousand pound animal could not run so fast over uneven ground like this without stumbling, and he focused his thoughts into fervent prayer that this should not happen.

Up ahead, Bricker seemed to be gaining ground, even though the grassland swelled upwards again in a slow roll. He was now several hundred yards off, and Byron dug in his spurs, certain that he was drawing blood. On the great beast thundered, his hooves beating a staccato drumbeat over the parched sod, his nostrils flared wide, showing the lining of his nasal passages bright red with the effort. Behind him, dull popping noises signaled that the Boers had commenced shooting at them, perhaps trying to bring down the horses, for the shots seemed low, striking the ground only yards ahead.

With a cry that was carried down to Byron, the sergeant and his animal went down in a flurry of arms and legs. The horse stayed to earth, but miraculously the little sergeant came up running, his arms outstretched, and calling to Byron, who now rapidly closed upon him. As yet, Byron had not looked around to see where the enemy was. The man called his name, the voice edged with panic. Byron was now almost upon him, but had not slowed his horse; rather the animal had started to swerve to avoid the running man, whose arms were waving wildly.

"Take me sir," he cried. "Swing me up behind you! Come sir!"

Byron swept on by.

"Don't leave me to these barbarians! Bloode! For the love of Christ, don't leave me!" His exhortations abruptly turned to cries of condemnation: "God-DAMN you to hell for this! Come back, you craven bastard!" His cries faded as the space between them increased. Byron was sure in his misery that the pursuers would stop to secure their captive, or dispose of him if the sergeant was foolish enough to make a stand with his pistol.

But Byron shut himself to the sounds of the man's voice and to the searing vision of the man's eyes. He sunk lower into the beast's flailing mane and became one with the animal. On he fled, and the tears stung his eyes, though he crushed them shut with a force of will he had never experienced.

# V

Captain Marthewicke-Jones of the Queen's 9th Fusiliers looked sneeringly disdainful, but that was his usual expression. He avoided Byron's eyes as if it was a painful matter to consider the direct gaze of a colonial soldier. Particularly in these circumstances. He laid aside the double-sided sheet of paper, and with a tight mouth and narrowed eyes, he appeared to stare at the canvas wall of his tent.

"I'm not a bit happy about this report, Bloode. Not a bit." He spoke to Byron, but addressed his comments to his own lieutenant, omitting the usual strict courtesy that required rank be prefaced to an officer's name. All of the field operations in that sector were being managed by Marthewicke-Jones, and since his arrival at the line for the relief of Mafeking. there had not been a single man lost.

"Let me see if I understand you: you were surprised by the Boer. You and Sergeant Bricker fled. But you have no idea of what befell your man? I mean, how is that possible? No idea? Were you so intent on saving your own neck that it was every man for himself? To hell with discipline and looking out for each other? To hell with an officer's obligation to ensure the enlisted ranks are secure before his own retirement from the field? What?"

The blood rose at the nape of Byron's neck. He fought the urge to say something intemperate. The man addressed him as if he were an enlisted rank.

"We had no intelligence that suggested the presence of the enemy so close," he said slowly, fighting the emotion in his voice, which was an alloy of anger and fear. He looked intently at the lieutenant who had briefed them this morning. With a faint smile, that man seemed to be more concerned with what he appeared to have stuck under his thumbnail, than with the tableau playing out before him.

"Are you suggesting, sir, that abandoning a man in the field is somehow related to the morning's briefing? Are you not aware that this war is being fought on horseback? Riding skills are supposed to be the reason you bloody colonials were brought into our fight in the first place. What?"

"Let me be as plain as I can, sir," said Byron. "We were both riding hard, keeping our heads low over the withers for the shots in pursuit were intense. I could hear them whizzing all about me, and I wanted to present as small a target as possible. At one point, Sergeant Bricker was abreast of me, but in the confusion, I cannot be sure of what happened to him. A ball may have taken him, or his mount: I heard nothing. " He was conscious of his face flushing as he approached the lie, spanned it, and continued.

"I considered going about when I realized the chase was no longer on, but I was vastly outnumbered. Perhaps as many as a dozen," he gestured to the report, "as I have written there."

Emboldened at the captain's silence, he added, "Better it seemed to me then, as now, that you have the information as to the strength of the enemy, and his whereabouts, as opposed to two men captured, or possibly dead."

"Dismissed," said Marthewicke-Jones abruptly. "I shall report this to the major; you may hear again from me on this subject."

As Byron walked away, Marthewicke-Jones looked again to his lieutenant, with the expression of a man who has taken something spoiled into his mouth, but cannot bring himself to spit it out.

"Bloody hell, what drives such men?" he muttered. "Something smells to high heaven about that story. One doesn't expect gallantry from these colonial fellows, but to have no idea where your man is, or what happened to him? I smell the pungent breath of a coward, my friend. I think I shall have to keep my eye on that boy. See that he's seconded as standard-bearer to us. It's a good fit, given that, what's-his-name ... "

"Gifford," said the other man lazily.

"Yes, Gifford. Gifford has damaged his leg and shall be out of the saddle for a time. Get him on with us, and we shall soon see whether we have taken the proper measure of him."

# vi

In fact, a dozen men from Byron's regiment were taken by Marthewicke-Jones, to make up for the effects of dysentery, which had lately swept the ranks of the 9th Fusiliers. The guns which Byron and his colleagues had escorted to the outskirts of Mafeking, four breech loading 12 pounders, three 2.5 muzzle-loaders, and one breech-loading Maxim, were now being dispersed among the forces which were assembling for the relief of the city, and no objection was raised to a reassignment of the troops. Not that there could have been in any event. Once in the field, Canadian troops were entirely subordinate to the British.

Within forty-eight hours, Plumer's northern column had met the Canadian contingent at Jan Massibi. After a day of rest, two columns of men and armament marched on Mafeking, now not more than twenty miles away, in the valley of the Molopo River. After about half the distance had been covered, a halt was called, and the entire force stood down, with the exception of the outriders.

It was a relief for Byron to get off horseback. Holding the standard of the 9th Fusiliers was tiresome, for it was no mere pennant. A heavily embroidered flag, it was, with a thick golden fringe about three of its edges. The cooks had swung into action even before their wagons had rolled to a stop, and great cauldrons of soup were being set upon fires, bread was being cleaved into dipping chunks, and tea billies were being set next to the soup. Byron's stomach grumbled, a little more urgently now, as he dug his mess kit from his saddle bag. The cold porridge they had taken at breakfast seemed an eternity away. He took his place in line, according to rank, at the rear of the other officers. He noted with satisfaction that their ration included white bread, not that coarse brown local stuff that was the lot of the enlisted man.

There was a distant shot. Then another. A pop-popping sound that belied its lethal message. Men scrambled to the decks of wagons for a better look. A cry: "The Boer! It's the Boer!"

With a sudden muttering cacophony, troops swarmed in all directions to their arms and horses. Gun carriages were detached and swung to face the incoming riders, whose shouts could be heard but not understood over the veldt. Close on to the last of the scouts, two men from the British South African Police, fell from the saddle at once, and a groan went up from the assembling men. Officers' calls went up, repeated by the barking non-commissioned officers. Byron took to the saddle, standard in hand, suddenly wishing that he was left-handed, so that he could, if necessary, deploy pistol or sabre. He had no greater weapon in his right hand than the brass pike that capped the hickory staff of the Fusiliers' colours.

With a cry from the sergeant-major, whose neck veins stood out like cording, Byron's column moved out at a trot. He was directly behind Marthewicke-Jones, who twisted momentarily to look at Byron. His eyes glittered under the tip of his helmet, and his thin moustache was stretched tautly over a thin lip.

"Stay with me, Bloode. Do not let the 9th down, or I personally shall serve up your guts to the vultures." He snapped back to the fore, and as a second group of Boer soldiers appeared at the top of the ridge, he gave the command to give chase at a gallop. The sergeant-major's bellowed shouts were lost in the thundering of hooves.

If it was intended to give chase, Byron thought, then they were at a disadvantage. All of the enemy were on the south side of the Mopolo River, and there was not an immediately obvious place to ford, without risking considerable exposure to Boer shot. And if they should have heavy guns beyond the ridge, why ... he nearly fell from his mount as an artillery shell exploded not fifty yards from where he was. The shrapnel breathed by him in an evil whispering. Behind him, shrill cries sounded of men who were struck or who had their horses cut from under them. The stench of cordite hung in the air. There was for him a sense of unreality about what was happening, like a macabre dance in which the partners were constructed of sound and rage.

Marthewicke-Jones swerved in the approved manner of barrage avoidance, but the column began to break up in confusion. Byron followed close to his commanding officer. Next to him, Copeland had caught up, calling his name. Byron looked over to him, but what Copeland was saying through a smiling set of clenched teeth was lost in the return fire of the Canadian guns. The Boers seemed to be somewhat less than a mile off, with three major positions along the high ground to the south of the river. Their shot was falling randomly at first, with no seeming effect on the gun positions of the British forces, but by degrees, the explosions crept closer, so that it was soon apparent that a direct hit could not be far off as the cannoneers found their marks. The guns had to be moved, at least to elevations roughly proximate to that of the enemy. Two squadrons were recalled for that task.

As the remaining men reached the river, it seemed to Byron that the Boer were falling back, rather than rushing to close with them in battle. It soon became apparent why. The rapid-fire Vickers-Maxim 37 mm automatic guns began to open up on them. These were known as 'pom-poms', from the sound they made. British-made, these weapons fired a belt of ten one pound shells at a rate of one every one or two seconds. Though designed for use in the British navy, the Boer Transvaal government had thought they might be quite useful in land combat. The guns utilized a smokeless powder, and in consequence was hard to detect. These shells fell among the British troops with dreadful effect, especially upon the horses. Then in the confusion, the smoke and the incessant din, Byron felt a great slap at his right calf. He was sure his leg was broken, so great was the force, though curiously in the excitement, he felt no pain. Then the staff in his hand was struck, severing the wood just below the flag.

He looked over to Copeland, who seemed to have both hands full with the task of controlling his horse; the eyes of the beast rolled wildly as his nostrils flared, showing pink. His own animal was going down, then, sinking slowly as if caught in a bog. Red-flecked foam showed at his nostrils as the gelding tried to lift his head. A lung injury. It would be over in seconds. As if in a dream, the horse fell to the left, twisting its great head up in a last effort to remain upright. Soundlessly, the beast died, falling heavily onto Byron's uninjured leg. The impact shook the offside limb from its stirrup, and Byron felt a jolt of pain pass along the entire length of his body. There was a burst of brilliance, then darkness.

# vii

Though Mahon and Plumer did not realize it at the time, they finally routed the enemy from what was to be called the Battle of Sanie Station, so named for the smattering of white brick dwellings near the banks of the Molopo River, so that the way to Mafeking had been cleared. Scouts soon brought the news back to the exhausted force, and the decision was taken to ride in to the beleaguered town. Their jubilant welcome was not witnessed by Byron, who lay in the bed of an ammunition wagon until he could be transferred to a field hospital. The shrapnel that had glanced off his thigh had badly bruised the flesh and snapped the bone. He had been lucky, for his leg could have been mangled, as were so many others.

The surgeon who set the fracture did so perfunctorily, saying only, "Stay off it a week, and four or five weeks from now you'll be back on a horse." The same night, Marthewicke-Jones made an inspection of the hospital, followed by an adjutant with a clipboard. He consulted with the doctor in low tones at the foot of each bed, then either passed on or tapped the metal frame of the collapsible cot with his swagger stick. No comment meant a trip home from the looks of those poor bastards who were passed over. A tap meant a brief stay in bed, then back to active service. Byron thought that this was a chance to return home with honours. It was not to be. Marthewicke-Jones looked at him coldly, then conversed with the doctor, jerking a thumb at the bed-ridden soldier. Byron flushed, feeling like a malingerer. But there was no doubt: his leg was broken. Crutches for this boy for the next month at least, probably more, the doctor reported. Shrugging disdainfully, the officer rapped the bed frame and passed on.

Two days later, his fresh orders came. As soon as able, he was to report to the detainee camp at Potchefstroon for guard duty. Potchefstroon was a grimy little town, some of the others told him, about a week's march to the southeast, just north of the Vaal River. It was only a half day by rail from Johannesburg, but for military men, it might as well be on the other side of the earth. Guard duty! What an ignominious end to a tour of service in the South African War. But deep within, Byron felt a sense of relief. Marthewicke-Jones returned three days later, and handed him sealed orders.

"You are to present these to Colonel Sleppard upon your arrival. He will open these, and set out your command." He turned to walk away, hesitated, then addressed Byron further:

"We found poor Bricker," he began. It was impossible not to notice Byron flinch. "Bullet in the back of the neck." He paused. Byron was silent, unable to look the officer in the face.

"Amazing thing is, he was alive when they picked him up. Alive, but paralyzed, of course. He has not spoken yet, but when he does, I shall be at his side, and shall have great interest in his account of your skirmish." He looked at Byron for a long moment.

"Nothing to say?" he sneered. "No relief that your subordinate, your comrade-at-arms is found alive, if grievously wounded? Ah. I thought not." And he spun on his heel, marching stiffly out of the ward. Byron groaned inwardly. Was there to be no end to his torment?

Copeland came to visit, but was appalled by the depression in which he found Byron Bloode. No story, no joke, no kidding about seemed to matter to him, and Copeland gave up, frustrated. It seemed an over-reaction to a broken leg that was on the mend without fever or any of the other complications that this infernal country produced. He came only once again, then said his farewell to Byron.

Some days later, Byron heard Copeland was "missing in active duty" as the euphemism went, and some blamed it on his bloody-minded insistence upon smoking a pipe even at night, which was an irresistible target for the Boer snipers. It was speculative, for he had not been found, and his troopmates' sense of loss turned to anger, as it often does, and they blamed him for his own destruction.

# viii

Concentration camps were not invented by the British. Don Valeriana Weyler y Nicolau, Spanish military leader in Cuba in 1896, had rounded up all the inhabitants of the western provinces of the island, in what he termed a system of *reconcentrado*. Forced into walled and fortified encampments, men, women and children died of starvation, disease and brutality in the thousands. Essentially non-combatants all, their imprisonment was thought to deny insurrectionists their support, and to wage a dreadful form of psychological warfare.

Kitchener, now in charge of the overall war effort of the allied invasion force, had been mulling over the idea of bringing in all Boer civilians to a form of humane detention, so as to deprive the guerrillas of their succour. Safely locked away, farmers' crops, homes and outbuildings could be put to the torch; no roaming fighter would find food or shelter anywhere in the countryside. Though it would be another year before Lord Kitchener put out his memorandum formally approving internment as an instrument of martial policy - under which more Boer children were to die than all combatants of both sides put together - the camp to which Byron was assigned was well into its operation.

The camp at Potchefstroon had not yet the foul reputation it was later to claim as the worst in the British system of civilian confinements, but there were signs that infamy was not far off. Situated in a low lying corner of the veldt that closed on the scrabble of shacks that was Potchefstroon, the reason that the camp had been established here was that the small farming community was now on the spur line of the Central Railway, and it served as a convenient collecting point for the Transvaal and the Northern Orange Free State.

Originally, wall tents had been pitched upon wooden platforms to house refugees caught between warring sides. Then two clapboard barracks had been built, though of the poorest quality. The roofs leaked, the walls admitted drafts and mosquitoes, and there were no private accommodations for men and women. Finally tents were put up anywhere that was the least bit level on the ground within the confines of the ragged barbed wire enclosure. Soon the enclosure would be enlarged, then again, as upwards of seven thousand souls were forced inside. The death rate would exceed thirty-five a month. The latrines were soon overwhelmed, and it became necessary to haul away waste to a ravine, a quarter-mile distant, where a fortified tower housed those unfortunate enough to draw that particular guard detail. There was no escape from the stench, for the structure - and the camp - were constructed down from the prevailing breezes. There was simply nowhere else to dispose of so much human waste.

Byron was appalled as he hobbled on his crutches from the troop transport to the command centre. The man in charge, Major Cornell Noseworthy, appraised his new lieutenant with a cool eye, tugging gently at his tight, upturned moustaches.

"Really, dear chap. Just *once* I should like to have a man with all of his functioning parts. This practice of sending me damaged goods is quite tiresome. Really." He snatched up the brown envelope that Byron handed him. Eyeing the man, he added, "Quite a swarthy chap for a red-headed bloke, what?"

Byron said nothing, but shifted on his crutches. They bit under the arms, and his good leg was aching with the sustained weight of his body. Noseworthy noticed, but did not bid him to sit. He frowned as he read what was written.

"Well, I can see that I shall need to keep a careful eye on you, Mr. Bloode. Nasty bit of business at Pitsani? Man down in the field, and left for dead? You won't be taking home the Queen's Scarf at this rate, I'm afraid."

Byron reddened. "May I see that, sir?"

"Quite out of order, dear friend. I have here all I need to know about you."

"About my command ... ?" Byron started.

"Your command?" Noseworthy sneered. "Your command? A bloody colonial in your condition, with your checkered experience?" He snorted delicately, as if he had smelled unwashed poverty at church. "I have a troop of *hensoppers* who will do anything for an extra ration of potatoes and flour, who keep order in the camp. And three enlisted men; one a corporal. You shall be their commanding officer. Snell, the *sergeant* who had that chore is off with galloping dysentery."

It was humiliating. A sergeant's duty was well below his commission. And *hensoppers*. He had been in South Africa long enough to know that term referred to those who surrendered, those who tried to make deals with the enemy, or who betrayed their countrymen. They were hated by the majority of the others in the camp, the *bittereinders*, those who would resist to the bitter end. A protest formed on his lips, when another officer strode in, a major, giving him the briefest glance, taking in the maple leaf shoulder patch that marked the Canadian contingent. He sniffed, and addressed Noseworthy, but turned to look at Byron: "The replacement for Snell?"

"Yes sir, Major Crumley. Just in. I've just announced his command."

Byron snapped to attention, saluting stiffly, then lost his balance on the crutches and fell to the rough plank flooring. He was sure that his face was the colour of beets, which made him forget the shooting pains in his freshly-healed leg. He scrambled and groveled on the rough plank flooring. The two men chuckled behind gloved hands, Noseworthy breaking into whooping laughter as Byron sprawled upon the floor. They walked outside, still laughing and shaking their heads. Bricker, thought Byron. The ghost of that man, with his outstretched, imploring hands, would haunt him forever. Cowardice bore a cost, and Byron could only wonder what price he would have to pay.

# ix

There was a dreary routine to the camps. There was not enough food, clothing or blankets for the detainees, and all of the prisoners' time was expended in the repair of clothing, the tending of gardens, minding the sick, the haulage of waste and the other mundane tasks of staying alive. Byron had little to do with the camp monitors whose responsibility it was to keep the others subjected to the rules. Only one would admit to having some understanding of English, and it was through him that Byron issued perfunctory, unenthusiastic instructions. He spent as little time as possible inside the camp boundaries, for the air was fetid with the closeness of confined humanity, and the misery was everywhere as palpable as the malevolence with which he was regarded by nearly everyone as he hobbled by on his crutches.

One morning, he passed by a man reading to a group of children. He was speaking in the guttural tongue of the Afrikaner Dutch, and the children listened raptly. As Byron slowed, he flipped the page of his worn volume, and began again, this time in accented English. Byron could not place the inflection. The man had a wondrous voice with the timbre and cadence of a natural story-teller; as he read, he seemed to know the verse by heart, and rarely glanced at the page, rather looking directly at Byron:

*a little girl, lovely and black of brow,*
*is lugging liquor from the cellar now;*
*as I watch her struggle with her tavern-tasks,*
*I weaken - my pitying spirit asks:*
*who will consume this brew that claims her care?*
*Why are her little feet so cold and bare?*

*Most mighty God, you are omnipotent;*
*that you are just, this sight gives dark dissent*

He closed the tattered cover, and lifted his head to the children, saying something that scattered them. Byron watched them go, ragged, thin goblins with wide staring eyes and old faces. The poetic metaphor was not lost on him, but the fact that such a medium would be employed drew him intensely to the man who now struggled to get up. It was apparent beneath his ragged trousers that his left leg was a prosthesis, no more than a whittled sapling protruded from one cuff, and he required a cane to stand.

He had thick hair, well streaked with gray, and large, flowing moustaches to match. He had not shaved in some time, and in consequence had a thick growth of stubble that covered most of his face. Underneath bushy eyebrows, bright blue eyes shone with warmth and intelligence that belied his tatterdemalion appearance.

"You speak the Queen's English well, then," Byron began.

There was a flicker of a smile. "Aye, sir. The Boer tongue, Ruthenian, Polish, French, of course, German, a touch of the Congolese dialect, and Zulu better than King Shaka himself."

"Very impressive."

"Nothing more than necessity required at the time," the man replied modestly.

Byron was overcome with a sudden wish to know the man. He extended his hand, and hopped closer. "Byron Bloode, lieutenant of the Canadian contingent." He did not notice the other members of the guard detail take interest in the gesture. Had he looked, he would have seen expressions of surprise, suspicion, and disgust. But he did not.

"Vladimir Dudych, free man, at thy service." His grip was firm, and Byron sensed a sinewy virility under the rags he wore. He appeared to hesitate for a moment, then grinned. "Free man might not be the proper term is these circumstances, but I announce myself to thee thus, regardless of present conditions."

"You were reading a piece of verse just now ... I did not recognize it."

"No surprise there. Not many born outside the Ukraine would recognize Taras Shevchenko. The patron of all free men of the Ukraine."

"You are Ruthenian, then?" Byron was aware that the settlement of Manitoba's Interlake district and the northern parklands were beginning to be settled by sturdy immigrants from the Ukraine. Strange, insular folk who kept to themselves, and were not well-regarded by the established communities. He had never met one till now, and he was intrigued.

"How is that you come to be here, in this ... this camp. Surely this is not your fight?"

The other man sighed, leaning heavily on his cane. "Sometimes, the flight from evil takes one to worse evil. All my life ... " He appeared to be contemplating painful recollections, for he had a distant look. "Evil. Humanity's most enduring legacy is the terrible wrongs we do to one another, in the name of the highest principle. And for what?"

Byron shifted his weight on his crutches. His leg was improving by the day, but it could still not take his weight, and Byron favoured it, to be sure it healed properly. Somewhere in the distance a child screamed, a pale, forlorn sound, more a giving up than a protest. It seemed to underscore the truth of the profoundly bleak statement far better than intuition or experience. He attempted to draw the conversation back to his question: "So how then, does a man from the Ukraine find himself in the South African controversy?"

A mirthless chuckle. "Not by a straight line, let me assure thee, Canada."

Byron was intrigued by the use of the English intimate tense. Unlike the French, or the Italians, the English use of the intimate 'thee' and 'thy' had fallen into disuse in all except the elderly. Even there, it was considered quaint, and quite passé. A loss, he thought. Another of the ways in which we extend the distance between us. It was probably a consequence of the admix of languages with which he was fluent, often one word serving for another, and pronunciations interposing from one dialect to another.

"Born to indentured parents in Ruthenia, orphaned at six years, conscripted in the King of Poland's Army at eleven. Private guard for a German prince at sixteen, a paid soldier for King Leopold in the Congo - " Here he broke off, the lines along his jaw tightening. "And finally, the Transvaal, working as a security man for a well-to-do Boer family whose kraal was under constant pressure from the Zulu. Now here."

"There must be a lot left out in that ... " Byron was hailed from the front gates. It was a regular officer of the same rank, Hanifan. An aloof fellow much like the others, he was frowning. As Byron turned away from Dudych, his eyes fell upon a handsome young woman, whose intense blue eyes gazed at him with an expression he could not discern. Usually, there was no mistaking the hatred the Boer harboured for the invaders, but this was something different. Engaging, but cool. She was nearly as tall as he, poorly dressed as were all the detainees, but proud, even haughty. In her hand she clutched a thick bouquet of *varkblomme*, pig flowers dug up for their roots, a sign of extreme poverty. She made no effort to hide them as she saw his glance.

He tugged at the bill of his dun-coloured helmet, about to say, "*Mooi meissie*," pretty girl, but thinking perhaps "*meurou*," honourable mistress, would be more appropriate. Uncertainty over his terms resulted in a mumbled "Ma'am". She nodded curtly and passed on. He stared after her.

"*Uitlander!*" Foreigner. Dudych snickered as he limped off: "It's *verdomde*." It's forbidden. "Be careful."

# X

The siege of Mafeking had been lifted in May of 1900. Britain went mad, and a faddish term was coined, 'to maffick', meaning to indulge in riotous celebration. Ladysmith had been liberated just two months before. The prolonged battle for that unimposing tin-roofed town had left more British and colonial troops as casualties than the entire force of Boer farmers who opposed them. The first British officer to ride among the hard-pressed town was Captain Gough of the Rifle Brigade, who upon encountering the commander of the beleaguered forces, General George White, was asked, simply, "How are you, Hubert?" Such restraint was demanded by the upper class Britisher. Openly expressed emotion and abandonment of protocol just wouldn't do.

These events and associated niceties held little meaning for Byron. He was miserable. The only other colonial troops were Australians, who though gregarious and flamboyant, kept to themselves. His superiors seemed to regard him with suspicion, notwithstanding he had found a way to disclose that he had been at Oxford for a number of years. He knew himself to be introverted, and preferred the company of intellectuals and scholars to those who chose to pursue a life in the military. But friendships seem to depend upon someone else extending a hand: he just could not find it within himself to understand what was necessary for friendship to occur on his terms. In all his associations, he reflected, he was the passive partner — and this included not only his family, but his ill-fated relationship with Emma.

On his next pass through the camp, he made a deliberate attempt to search out Dudych. The man intrigued him. No scholar, but a self-taught, well-experienced man, who didn't seem to fit the pattern of the Boer prisoner. He hailed a corporal of the 12th Rifles, who wore a patch over one damaged eye, and asked him about the Ruthenian.

"Oh, aye sir, I know the man you seek. Watch him with care, sir, for he's an agent. Sentenced to death, he is, by firing squad. Next week, I should think it is." He scratched his head under his helmet. "One less scroggy to worry about."

Byron was stunned. The man was an old cripple. What could he have possibly done to deserve the firing squad? There he was, seated on an upturned wagon bed, from which the wheels had been removed. As usual, he was surrounded by children who listened to him raptly, silently, some with their eyes closed. Dudych saw him approaching but kept reading from the tattered volume as before. He spoke in the Afrikaner Dutch in a lilting voice that seemed to smooth out the naturally choppy inflection of the language. As Byron paused and waited, the older man turned the page and began to read in English:

*A cloud is floating, following the sun;*
*It spreads its scarlet coat-flaps in the sky*
*and calls upon the sun to settle down*
*on the blue sea, and there be covered up*

*As, with red quilts, a mother might her child*
*One's eyes rejoice to see it ... one brief hour.*
*One's heart relaxes and communes with God.*
*And then the fogbank, like an enemy,*
*covers the sea and all the rosy cloud -*
*The thick gray mist spreads darkness in its wake,*
*and in that darkness it enshrouds one's soul*
*So that one cannot know where one should go.*
*One awaits dawn as children await their mother ...*

Some of the children understood, but most became restive and fidgeted at the familiar but hated language. He dismissed them, and turned to Byron.

"So, my gaoler, you have come again?"

"I am intrigued by the verse — which you seem to select for my benefit. Is it always so gloomy?"

"Not at all, Canada," replied the other. "Indeed, it is rather uplifting and hopeful writing. Shevchenko's life has much in common with we who suffer now. You British abuse us now as did the Poles fifty years ago. That is why the children listen so closely. Poetry is the soul's looking-glass. It enables us to see what is there all along."

Byron's heart surged. This was the kind of discussion that he had enjoyed at Oxford. The purpose of poetry had been a constant source of debate. "Shevchenko: he — that is written in English?" He gestured to the volume Dudych held.

"It is in the Cyrillic script. But here, see, I have written the English in pencil on the opposite side." He pointed with a stubby, dirty finger to heavy, square letters etched in dark lead pencil.

Byron stared at the text of another rhyme on the same page, and asked, "Would it be possible to borrow it for a little while?"

"No." The answer was abrupt. "Not possible."

"I would take good care - "

"It is not a matter of your trustworthiness. I have only a little time left. This book is all that I have."

Byron was reminded of what he had just been told. "What happened?" he said simply. "How is it that you ... " He sank with some relief onto an empty barrel. His leg was healing well, but it was still weak, and he yet required the crutches he had been issued a month earlier.

"How does a man end up like this. Good question. One I think about a lot. Part of it is this country. Fierce, beautiful, but unforgiving. And I think it brings out the worst in a man.

"I was getting too old for the life of a paid soldier. Leopold - the King of Belgium? Was offering pay in gold sovereigns for policing-work. Well, 'forest guards' is what we were called, supposed to supervise the Congolese militia. When I got to Leopoldville - well, Bolobo, really, well up the Congo River, I took ill and was bedridden for a time. Infection in this leg," he tapped it lightly with his cane, "so I was out of things for almost two months."

He leaned back against the axle, wrapping his tattered coat more snugly around him, for it was overcast and cool. "But it was obvious to me that rubber was king. This maniac Leopold and his dreams to play with the big boys and have an empire, wanted the costs of his army - people like me; you never saw such a hodge-podge of hired men in uniform - he wanted the costs recovered as well as wealth returned to Belgium.

"When I was well enough for duty, my corporal was issued our kit, including seventy-five cartridges. Imagine my shock when we were instructed that upon return to camp we were to account for each one, and for each one missing, we were to bring back a right hand."

Byron stared at him. This was some sort of macabre joke. He opened his mouth to say as much. The other man held up a hand. "It was far worse. If the villagers who were taxed in rubber, failed to meet the amount set for them, they could lose ears, hands or feet in consequence. Oh yes. The floggings and mutilations and killings. Not soldier's work, but it was ... well, it was ... " Words failed him, and there was a wetness around the man's eyes. Perhaps it was the cool breeze. "We warmed to it, let me say. We were like gods, with the power of life and death, and no fear of consequence. So a firing squad holds no terrors for me. I deserve what fate has in store; I am ready." He flipped open the book he was holding, squinted, and began to read:

*Why do I feel so heavy? Why so weary?*
*Why does my soul in wailing grief lament?*
*Like a starved child? Ah, heart oppressed and dreary,*
*What do you wish? What is your discontent?*
*Are you for food, or drink, or sleep aspirant?*
*Sleep then my soul! Forever sleep apart,*
*Shattered, uncovered ... let the senseless tyrant*
*Rage ever on ... close, close your eyes, my heart.*

Byron noticed with a start, that the woman he had seen earlier had quietly seated herself on the other end of the wagon, and was listening to the reading. As Byron looked at her, she eyed him coolly, and deliberately returned her attention back to Dudych, who had finished the verse, but remained staring at the opened page. Byron spoke:

"I feel your sadness for the things you have done and witnessed. But that was in the Congo. Why are you being punished here for things that took place there, and so long ago?"

"I came to the Transvaal because I heard that the Boer farmers would pay for help against the Zulu. This country has much in common with my beloved Ukraine: the open spaces, the glorious sunsets, the proud independence of these people." Here he smiled at the young woman. "Stella, this is Lieutenant Bloode. From Canada." He turned to Byron, saying, "I give you Stella van der Koop."

As Byron touched the brim of his helmet, she nodded, and said in a thickly accented voice: "Papa Dudych is helping me improve my understanding of the

English language to me." She spoke in the rigidly formal tones of one who speaks in a newly attained fluency in another language.

"From your speech, those lessons go well," smiled Byron, taking in all of the details of her lovely face. This was not lost on Dudych, who chuckled, a raspy, dry sound.

"In our land, the Ukraine, a woman who has heavy, dark brows, is considered to be the most beautiful of women. The most graced. Would you not agree, Canada, that Stella van der Koop is so?"

The woman blushed. Byron was captivated by her. This conversation had an air of unreality about it, given the setting. He tore his attention away from the woman.

"You still have not explained how ... " He did not want to say it.

"I found work with a *Kommissie*, exploring the country and making it safe for settlers. Then I settled as a *bywoner*, a guard on a large farm called *Bakenlaagte*, in charge of a small troop of *Kaffirs*. Our job was to keep the marauding blacks from killing our cattle, stealing produce, or worse. I hoped one day to have my own kraal, but there was never enough money. But I ate well, had a warm place to sleep, and for the first time in my life, I was content with my *woonplek*, place where I lived. Then came this war, capture, and ... I was put on trial for spying for the enemy, and given my history with the Belgian forces, it was a foregone conclusion. Now they propose to shoot me on Tuesday."

Byron frowned. "Can't anything be done? An appeal?"

The woman laughed scornfully. "Appeal? There is no appeal from the decision of the Tommies. Look around you. Daily, new families of women and children arrive. Soon this miserable place will be ... " She struggled for the right word.

Dudych offered, "Overwhelmed?"

She nodded vigorously. "*Ja,* overwhelmed. And then we will all begin to die, as even now the children suffer and die from the measles. They have no appeal." Tears started from her eyes, and she rubbed at them angrily for the show of emotion.

At that moment, a pair of private soldiers walked by, and their sneering comments could not be missed by any of them.

"Well look at this fine little picnic. I thought there were rules against intercourse with them black-hearted Boers."

"I'd fancy a little intercourse with that nice bit o' snug, mind." Snickers.

Byron stood up angrily. He was about to call them to attention, when the woman put her hand on his forearm. The shout died on his lips. He looked at her, sinking back to his seat.

"It is of no use," she said. "It will only be worse for us. When our parties of women — those who still have the strength — go out foraging for roots and fuel, there is constant harassment from those sent to guard over us. If you anger them, it will be the worse for us." Her left hand still lay on his forearm; he glanced at it, and saw that it bore a single slender ring of gold. She caught the look.

"*Ja.* A widow. Married not four months before I lost my man. Father and two brothers all with the Kommando, and not heard from in over a year."

"I'm sorry," said Byron. "But our men harass the women?"

She looked at him as if he were stupid. She withdrew her arm. "You suggest to me you are not aware that women give themselves for bread and meat?"

Byron was stunned. This was the army of Britain, whose officers were committed to gallantry and chivalry of the first rank. Yet with shame he remembered the treatment of the black woman he had seen dragged off into the underbrush, and Copeland's remarks that were indifferent, if not selfish.

Dudych spoke softly. "It is said in this land, and we be the living proof of it, Canada, that an Englishman carries his honour in his pocket, and is no slave to his word."

It was too much for Byron. He stood up again, and without speaking, walked away. Dudych looked at her, and spoke in Afrikaans: "It pains me, but I think he may be of some use."

She nodded, lips pursed thoughtfully. "*Ja.* A decent man, maybe, but weak."

# xi

Efforts Byron made to make complaints about what he had heard, and his formal request to have an investigation were rebuffed. Indeed, Major Crumley had summoned him to his quarters, where, visibly angry, he had torn the report into small pieces in front of him.

"Are you aware of the serious impact upon the reputation of Her Majesty's men-at-arms, to say nothing of morale, that this ... this *drivel*, these most unwarranted and scandalous accusations could have? This is an outrage."

Anger — any extremes of emotion always had the effect of unsettling Byron. He had distant memories of his mother and father quarreling when he was a child, and somehow, the terrible anxiety that it produced then remained with him always. So it was now. Flustered by the officer's reaction, he tried to explain, but was shouted down.

"How dare you impeach the credit of the men under my command? On the word of a filthy Boer bitch, who has plenty of good reasons to stir up the enemy, no less. My God, sir. Have you taken leave of your senses? Get out of my sight!" He turned to his paperwork, angrily shuffling documents, muttering about "Bloody colonials," and other references that Byron could not hear.

As he left, there was no avoiding the sneering glances of his fellow officers. The major's voice quite obviously and intentionally would have carried beyond the flimsy door of his office, and the story would be well-embroidered and passed through the ranks before mess that night. He was humiliated. And he had not even broached the subject of Dudych's court martial and sentence. He now realized that it would be futile.

The Tuesday morning that Dudych was executed, Byron could not bring himself to get out of his bed, having not slept all night. He protested reveille, arguing that he was ill, and turned to the tent canvas, wrapped in his blankets against the damp. It was a bleak day, and a light drizzle was falling. The firing squad was to be assembled near the cremation grounds, where dead animals and those who had died in the camp were taken for disposal. There was a very great fear of disease, and any death, human or otherwise, resulted in disposition in this way. Though the grounds were to the southeast, so that the village and the camp were upwards of the prevailing winds, now and then the wind veered, so that the stench borne by the oily smoke enveloped the huts and tents which were well below the townsite. A mile away, the collective report of the nine rifles in the squad was clearly audible. He flinched. The image of the lame Ukrainian flung back in the chair to which he was bound tormented him until he fell asleep. He was awakened by an enlisted man who handed him an object.

"What is it," he asked, rubbing his eyes. "Mail?"

"No sir," the soldier replied indifferently. "It's a book. It belonged to that spy they shot this morning, and he gave it to the Captain saying it was to be given to you. So here it is." He spun on his heel, and ducked through the tent flaps into the rain, which still pattered on the canvas.

Byron looked at the worn leather volume, quite thick, with loose pages and tattered edges bound within by a faded piece of ribbon. Touched by this unexpected gesture, he gently untied the fastening, and opened it. Because of the way it was wrapped within the volume, it fell open to a particular page. His eyes moved from the Cyrillic script to the penciled words beside it.

*The poplar and the willow-tree*
*the tempest bends indeed.*
*It breaks the oak and down the field,*
*it rolls the tumble-weed.*
*And such is fate: this one she breaks,*
*This other merely bends,*
*And you she rolls, and does not know*
*where all your travel ends.*

Byron studied the hard, square letters through moistened eyes. They were more fresh than some of those that had been written on the same page, and others. It was an intimate farewell from a man he barely knew. It said everything about Byron that he had feared for a long time: that he stood for nothing, that no principle for him was carved in oak, nor would he make deliberate choices about anything important in his life. Indulgence and fear drove him. He was here in this war he neither understood or wanted to be involved in by a confluence of events that were shameful to reflect upon.

He dried his eyes with the corner of a blanket, and rolled from the creaking collapsible cot. Dressing, he determined to seek out Stella van der Koop. There was someone whose company he was anxious to have. He threw the tent flaps aside and started to leave, then returned for the Shevchenko. As he picked it up, he wondered at the emotions simmering within him, and for a fleeting moment, he thought of Emma.

# xii

Reading to Stella gave him enormous pleasure. She made him repeat words she did not understand, and explain them to her. She would say them over and over again, rolling them on her thickly accented tongue. She read to him the same verse, though she had much difficulty with the words, and to get at what she was looking at, he would lean over her, sometimes accidentally touching her hand as he pointed out the syllables, thrilling at the nearness of her.

On one occasion, she pushed him gently, saying that she must stink like a goat, as there were few opportunities to bathe. He laughed, saying: "Surely you must have heard of Napoleon's preferences?"

"Which were?"

"When he was returning home from battle, he would send a message ahead. It would read:

*'Je rentre; tu ne lave pas'.*"

"Which means?"

"I am coming home; don't bathe."

She whooped with a sudden laugh, clapping both hands to her mouth. Then blushed, her face darkening even under her tanned skin. Pensively, she said, "I have not laughed since I have come to this place; I thought I would not again." And then coyly: "Are *all* men like Napoleon?"

Two days later, Byron was assigned to command a detail assigned to watch the women as they foraged for roots. Stella was among them. As the group dispersed across the rolling veldt, looking for the ubiquitous *varkblomme*, and wild maize from which the staple mealie was ground, Byron watched Stella. Without giving any indication that she was aware of his gaze, she broke away from the three women she was with, and sauntered to the crest of a low *kopje*, hill. The enlisted men with Byron squatted on the grass, rifles across their laps. This was easy duty. A woman could not run far enough to escape, and even if she did run, there was nowhere to flee, for the countryside for miles about had been scourged. Gradually, the group of thirty women dispersed, all bowed, looking intently at the ground. At the blast of the corporal's whistle, they were expected to return.

Byron followed Stella, his heart thumping as if he were running in a dead heat. He turned to look at his men, but the three of them were engaged in idle chatter, sitting cross legged now, passing a water flask back and forth. He could hear their uproarious splatter of laughter at some joke, and a whinnying response from another, but the words were lost in the distance. He walked backwards over the knoll, and still there was no apparent interest from them, so he turned toward the woman he had been following. She was waiting, a short distance away, a dark figure on a field of dry, brittle grass that rose above her knees. Suddenly, she slumped to the ground. Even at this short distance, she was completely covered from view. Alarmed, Byron ran toward the place where she had been moments before. There she was, lying on her back in the heath, smiling at him. She was chewing a long stem of grass in a way that he took to be wanton. His heart seemed as if it would take flight; his mouth was dry, and his limbs trembled. She laughed.

"Sit down next to me, before you fall down. No. Lie next to me, or we shall be discovered."

Breathlessly, he lay near her, reaching for her. She held him back, though gently.

"Now you tell me how you came to *ons land* with these invaders. I want to know everything."

He relaxed and let his head fall back on the dry sward. He related the story of the past several months, skirting around his involvement with Emma, and carried through to the present day. She listened attentively, and questioned him on his departure. She was perceptive. Slipping a work-worn hand into his, she whispered, "You're not telling me everything. There's something ... something that is missing. Someone, perhaps?"

As she saw him redden, she laughed. "Oh, that is it. You have left a ... what is the word? A woman ... hmmm, no. There is a special word ... "

Byron spluttered. "No, no. I miss my dear family, that is all."

She artfully changed the subject, but she gave him a cheeky smirk that suggested she did not believe him, that there was indeed more. "Tell me again of your *trek* from Beira. It must have been terrible hard for you."

He related again how Plumer's guns came from 'C' Battery, and their mounted escort was from Carrington's Rhodesian Field Force. He rambled idly about their meeting with Mahon's southern column at Jan Massibi. Stella seemed interested and squeezed his hand as she snuggled closer to him. He was acutely aware of her body next to him as she asked him questions about the invasionary force. "I had no idea so many men had come to fight us. We are but a poor handful of farmers. And you have the large guns, also?"

"Oh yes," said Byron. "Four of our own Canadian breech-loaders, twelve-pounders, three two-point-five muzzle loaders, and one breech loading twelve-pounder Maxim. Quite a formidable little force, really."

"It worries me, for my people, that you are so strong." Her face was nearly touching his; he could feel her warm breath on his throat. He was engorged with excitement, and he thought fervently for other neutral things to talk to her about. He talked to her of the gun emplacements they had helped dig at Ramathlabama, and of the battle where his leg had been broken at Sanie Station.

Almost imperceptibly, she had moved against him, until she was nearly over him. Now his excitement was evident, for he could feel her thigh against him. He broke off: "This must be so boring for you. I'm sorry, I've rattled on like an old soldier." She raised her head over his, lips parted, eyes half-closed, and was about to speak, when in the distance a shrill, piercing blast of the corporal's whistle sounded. Byron leapt to his feet, brushing the shreds of dried grass from his tunic.

"Help me," he gasped, his ardor fading with the threat of discovery.

She laughed as she brushed his back. "That was very foolish. You should have looked about before jumping like a *springbok*. You have much to learn if you want to fight like a *kommando*."

Byron was not listening. "You go on ahead. Straight back. I'll work my way around." With an anxious look around, and seeing nothing, he ran below the crest of the hill, putting as much distance between him and the woman as possible. His heart was racing now, as much with the panic borne of narrow escape as with the effort of running in the high grass with sabre, revolver and small pack. But already he was thinking ahead to the next encounter with this intoxicating woman, and the possibilities. Oh, the possibilities.

# xiii

Reveille's trumpet call sounded two days later. Barely had its reverberations died away, than Byron was roused by a shaking at his shoulder. "Byron! Byron Bloode, it's me, Copeland!"

Byron rolled to his side, rubbing his eyes. "Copey? But you were ... you are ... "

"Dead?" the other man laughed. "Not bloody likely. A few days wandering the veldt, hiding from brother Boer, but nothing more serious than a lamed horse. Stepped in some sort of hole, if you please. Precious little glamour in that, I'm afraid.

Byron was delighted. "Tell me you've been assigned here. It's absolutely awful. Couldn't be worse - "

"'Fraid not, Byron old son. Off to Pretoria soon. Marched all night we did, thank goodness we're to ride the rest of the way by rail, once the carriages arrive. Say, how's the leg? Looks like you're moving it all right. Cast is gone."

"Still a bit tender, but healing by the day. I'd like to get back to active duty; I can't stand much more of this prison duty. I say: how long do you have?"

"Not much, I'm afraid. They're hoping to be assembling the wagons any day now. But I will come back and visit, if they'll let me get away. Listen, I thought you should know: poor Bricker came out of his coma for a few minutes, then croaked."

Byron's heart lurched, and fear thickened his tongue. "Did he ... did he ... "

Copeland looked at him and cocked his head slightly. "Oh, I know the chat. They all think you left him out there to die. The Brits have this funny code that as one's superior officer, you have this obligation to die as well. Of such stuff are heroes made. It's actually preferable to die in the struggle so that your grieving family can have a medal to hang on the corner of your portrait. For God and country, and all that." He studied the worried look on Byron's face.

"Look Byron, old fellow. I don't know what went on out there. This lot has struck terror into me all right; who am I to judge? But your old friend Marthewicke-Jones was very keen to hear what he had to say. I gather whatever he did say was not very much, and equivocal. He didn't last long. What I wanted to tell you was: watch out. Marthewicke-Jones has it in for you, everyone knows that. Just keep your nose clean."

Byron felt ready to weep. It was true, a man could never outrun the vile things done in self-interest. "Copey ... " he began, reaching for the man's arm.

Copeland made no secret of his unwillingness to hear what Byron may have been ready to say. "I'd rather not know just now. And a piece of advice for you: don't tell a soul what took place, because even if you've done nothing wrong, things can be twisted around. Believe me. Listen, I must go, but I promise to come back and visit soon. Get well and rejoin the Canucks. That's where you belong."

With a light slap on the shoulder, he ducked under the tent flaps, and was gone.

It seemed as a dream to Byron. He felt terribly alone. Even the morbid thought that Bricker had gone to his grave with his dreadful secret afforded no relief. He was a coward, and as unfit for military service as the *hensoppers* were regarded by their countrymen.

Later that day, he roamed the camp looking for Stella. She greeted him stiffly, and shrank from his furtive touch. Puzzled, he beckoned her to the rear of the barracks, where a lean-to and a pair of tents afforded slight privacy. He seized her, urgently, saying: "I must talk to you. I ... " He was conscious of her body, the warmth of her. "I need ... "

She hissed at him. "You fool! They watch us. We must not ... "

He seemed oblivious, clinging to her, burying his face in her hair. "You don't understand. I must talk to you. I don't care who sees us in this wretched camp, I only care about you."

She was resisting him now with a strength that surprised him. "Stella," he said. "What *is* this? What's gotten into you?"

Firm hands seized his shoulders and pulled him back. "Not you, matey, not this time."

Startled, he swung his head to see Crumley scowling at him. A pair of enlisted men he had never seen before had him by the shoulders. Their grip painfully crushed the flesh under his epaulets, and he opened his mouth to protest, but he was cut off by a snarl from Crumley.

"You are under martial arrest for high treason. You will surrender your side-arm and come with me." He slapped the swagger stick under his arm, spun on his heel and marched away to the gates. The enlisted men dragged Byron along after the officer, for their prisoner's legs seemed about to fail him.

# xiv

Robert Hicks, the officer attached to the Judge Advocate's office assigned to defend Byron was a mouse of a man. His thin moustaches and small wire-framed glasses gave him a timorous appearance which alarmed Byron, particularly since the role of prosecutor was assumed by a nasty-looking sort by the name of Crench. Both men were of equal rank, major, but one seemed far the superior litigant. The panel was chaired by an aged colonel, Winthrup Dangerfield who was a veteran of the Relief of Khartoum, the Zulu wars, and other exploits. With him on the panel was Major Crumley and a Captain Charles, the latter an overweight man who sweated profusely regardless of the weather.

The particulars of the offence were in the nature of 'fraternizing with the enemy', and the disclosure of "information causing, or likely to cause harm to Her Majesty's interests". The British military believed in swift justice, and a court-martial hearing was convened within two weeks. During that time, Byron was held in close custody, with a guard at the door of his makeshift cell at all hours. Contact with anyone except the apologetic Hicks was forbidden. Only letters to immediate family were permitted, and Byron availed himself of the opportunity to compose a letter to his father.

This was no easy task. How does one, wondered Byron in an agony of despair, announce to one's family that he is on trial for treason, and the penalty if convicted is death by firing squad? His hands shook at the thought of it, and he could discover no easy way to come at that in the note, so he decided for the moment at least, to leave that fact out. He wrote:

*Dearest Father:*

*It is with considerable regret that I put pen to paper this morning. My last letter spoke of the broken leg, and how lucky I was in this dreadful war, that my injury was one that would cause no permanent harm. Indeed, the leg has healed quite nicely, and the crutches have been discarded. My current duties during my convalescence have me assigned to a prison camp, which hardly has been what I expected. But I have done my duty, as you demanded of me.*

*After several false starts, and much gnawing at the end of the pencil he had been provided, he continued:*

*I struck up an association with one of my charges, an old Ruthenian mercenary who had quite the story to tell of his life. Quite a fascinating man, really. He served under the King of Poland, the Kaiser, Leopold II, but wrongly interned, I think, but no one here seems to believe that a miscarriage of justice has occurred at all. The belief is that I told him things that I shouldn't have. How they can suggest that is quite preposterous, since he is dead now. It is possible that someone overheard us, and got quite the wrong interpretation of it, for all we really discussed was poetry. I hope to sort it all out soon.*

*Anyway, they've organized a sort of court martial. I think the whole thing's trumped up, possibly orchestrated by the commanding officer here, who seems to have taken a dislike to me from the very first day. But I have an advocate assigned to me, and he assures me this is all probably a mistake of the most colossal kind, and I shall be vindicated in the fullness of time.*

*I'm sending this note along to you just in case this makes the news back home, and I don't want you to be worried.*

*Good-bye, and say hello to Mama. Tell her not to fret about anything; I shall be fine.*

*Your son*

He read and re-read what he had written before passing it, unsealed, to be reviewed by the military censor.

The two weeks initially seemed to drag on interminably. He saw little of Hicks, who persisted in a rather worrisome indifference to the case. Perhaps it was a matter of the man's personal style, thought Byron, and tried to relax. In spite of his anxiety, he was always glad to see the man, for no other visitor came to see him. He knew that Stella would not be permitted; that would have been quite preposterous, really, for she too was a prisoner in her own right. On one occasion, four days before the trial, Hicks seemed more preoccupied than usual. He settled wearily into a ladder-back chair, and spread his file over the tiny table between them. He called for the chamber-pot to be emptied, as he found the odour quite repelling. Byron hardly took notice of it at all, so accustomed had he become to its noxious presence, and was impatient for news of further developments.

Hicks peered at him over his little round glasses. "They seem to be quite serious about you, my boy. I have been trying to negotiate an arrangement for a set penalty, but my learned friend is having none of it. Rather firm about the whole thing."

Byron felt fear take hold in his guts. "But what can the case possibly be against me? Some snippet of conversation had with an old man, now dead. I mean ... "

"Oh, they say they have witnesses to your, ah, indiscretions. My colleague Crench has spent some time with a Marthewicke-Jones, who has some serious allegations of cowardice, which they propose to offer in evidence. I'll need to hear your version of it, but I rather seriously doubt that they'll get away with it. Not much probative value, but highly prejudicial."

Byron's heart sank further than he might have thought possible. He swayed in his chair, so despondent was he at this piece of news. "That old story again.

They believe what they want to believe, that's all. And nothing will ever change their minds."

The next day Byron did not rise with the wake-up call, for he had nothing to get up for. His morning meal was bread and water, served in tin containers by his custodians, and they were indifferent when - or if - he ate at all. There was a furious pounding at the door, and the face at the small window opening was Copeland.

"Copey!" Byron shouted with joy. "Dear Copey! See what they have done to me! How glad I am to see you!" It was really true: the value of friendship often goes unmeasured until the day it proves itself.

"Byron, you silly bugger. The whole troop's agog with the news. Treason! We think it's quite impossible. Listen: they won't let me come in, so we have to converse through this little window; ol' 'jug handles' here'll be listening to everything we say, so don't give me the battle plans for the attack on Kloopdorp." He snickered at the guard, who maintained a professionally stony face.

"Honestly, Copeland. I have no idea what it's all about. I think my troubles have to do with Marthewicke-Jones, who's hated me from the very start."

"I think you're right, there. He's very suspicious of you after the patrol with Sergeant Bricker. In fact he came to see me, you should know."

"What did he want?" asked Byron anxiously.

"He asked me whether you had given me any details on what happened on that patrol. He seemed to suggest that I knew more about it than I was letting on, and that it could be quite unpleasant for me. I couldn't very well say anything about what I didn't know, so I was as firm as one can be with a superior officer."

Byron let out his breath in a low whistle. "He's like a dog with a bone."

"So it would seem. Then this ruffian Crench shows up, a couple of days later. His slant was to try and put contradictions to me, making out that though you had no idea what happened to Bricker, your story to me was that it was all a blur, and that it was impossible to sort out things, just that Bricker was suddenly no longer there. I said that was hardly a significant change in your story - and he got quite shirty with me, I must say."

"I'm feeling very much put upon. It's as if they want to make an example of me, and regardless how weak their case, they'll bull it through. No matter what." Byron was conscious that his voice was wheedling, revelatory of his despair.

"Well, Byron, old man," said Copeland as the guard touched his shoulder, "Buck up. If they call me to testify, I shall tell them what I know of you, and apart from being a traitor, you're not a bad bloke."

He looked at Byron's stricken face, and quickly added, "A joke, Byron, a joke. Keep your spirits up, man."

# XV

It was a pleasant day in February of 1901. The boundless South African sky was in the full glory of summer, and under the eaves of the mess which was to serve as the court room, white and black crested *hoopoes* twittered and called their double-noted warble. Byron stared at the birds flitting back and forth past the unglazed windows, wondering whether one them might venture inside. Not likely, he thought: who would voluntarily give up one's freedom? He turned to Hicks, who sat scribbling beside him, and was struck again at how ineffectual the man looked across from the ursine Crench, barrel-chested and intense. He shivered at the prospect of being questioned by the man.

The first witness was Marthewicke-Jones, as they expected. He spoke of "dereliction of duty", and referred at length to the British officer's code of conduct, in particular the obligation to defend fallen men. While he spoke, he glared with loathing at Byron, who shrank from the naked contempt in the man's eyes. He concluded by saying, "In all my service, I have never come across what can only be explained as the vilest cowardice."

Hicks creaked to his feet, saying altogether too mildly for Byron's liking, "I say there, really, I must object. This witness is coming to a conclusion which is quite insupportable. And even if it was, that would be for your Lordships to decide. Besides which, it's all quite irrelevant, unless what Mr. Crench is trying to do is sully the reputation of the accused, before he gets on with the main thrust of his case. Prejudice your Lordships, if he might." He sank to his chair, bones protesting.

The chair of the tribunal, Colonel Dangerfield, rolled his eyes. "Captain Marthewicke-Jones is one of our finest officers, and a man of exceptional courage. I know the man personally, having served with him in the Zulu War under General Buller. Not only is his opinion admissible, I should think it ought to be *invited*. Need I say that you are out of order?"

Hicks scratched at his pad.

There was a parade of witnesses who attested to the inordinate amount of time Byron spent in the company of the executed spy and the woman, van der Koop. To each of these, Hicks merely asked whether there was any apparent attempt to hide or behave in a surreptitious way; the answer was uniformly negative: the accused made no attempt to conceal his association. These were important points to make, Byron was sure, but they just did not seem to be made with any of the histrionics that he associated with the manner of a barrister. He wanted each element of his case to be driven home emphatically, and it was difficult to sit still while the old man plodded on in his methodical way.

The following day, when court was called to order, the orderly rose and called the next witness: "Mrs. Stella van der Koop!"

Byron sat back in his chair, aghast. A prosecution witness! How was this possible? What could they hope to extract from her?

A few moment later, she took her place behind a small table, and was sworn in by the orderly. Seconds later, she was offered a chair, but she declined. Byron willed her to look at him, but she did not. Her eyes kept averted from his. He put this down to her reluctance to be there at all; surely they must have intimidated her into this.

Slowly, under careful questioning from Crench, she recited the facts surrounding their meeting. Then to Byron's horror, she related what had happened when they were out looking for roots on the veldt. In a clear voice, she provided details of the information Byron had given her about the Canadian expedition from Beiria, and their strength.

A hot blaze of shock blinded Byron. Dizzy, he lowered his head to his hands. His breathing was laboured and heavy, as if suddenly stricken. Hicks looked at him and whispered in an avuncular manner: "Pull yourself together man. Sit up."

Crench passed a book to her and bade her read the pages which were marked, and she did so.

"This pocket diary — it is in Afrikaans?"

"It is."

"And does it contain all of the information you have just related to this court-martial?"

"It does; you know it to be so."

Crench recovered the small volume. "And the name on the inside cover, Pieter Greijling? Who is he?"

"My ... brother." Visible tears welled in her eyes.

"Your brother," smiled Crench, indifferent to the woman's distress. Turning to the panel, he announced, "May it please your lordships, I should like to have this diary received in evidence. I shall establish that it was taken from the body of a marauding Boer commando shot by our troops January 21, whose name matches the very name on this book." With a sneering glance at Hicks, he said, "You may take the witness."

Hicks got slowly to his feet, still making notes. Byron swiveled his head to look at the panel. Dangerfield looked stonily ahead, and was inscrutable. Crumley looked as he always did around Byron: impatient and out of sorts. Charles sweated and seemed to doze, though his eyes flickered over the woman, in a way that a man might peep through a keyhole. There was no discernibly favourable portent here, and Byron turned back to Stella in an agony of worry and feelings of betrayal.

"So," said Hicks. "How came your brother by this information?"

"He heard it with his own ears."

"And how so? Were you not alone with Lieutenant Bloode?"

"My dear brother lay not more than five paces away. He was sure to have heard it all."

"Ah," exclaimed Hicks. "So this was all pre-arranged, was it, the snaring — trapping — of Mr. Bloode?"

"*Ja*," she said simply. "It was."

Byron was stupefied. The intensity of affection that he had felt, and the way in which she had reciprocated; the way she had touched him, so intimately, had been a ruse to get him to natter on about things which he considered so inconsequential. It was past betrayal. This itself was a crime.

"Were you promised anything for your testimony, your freedom, perhaps?"

Over Crench's objections and strong reservations from Dangerfield, she was allowed to answer.

"Yes."

"And it was ... ?"

"I would be permitted to know the location of my brother's grave, and he would not be burned in the cremation grounds." Her shoulder shuddered with barely repressed weeping.

Hicks pressed her. "Yet you tell us you lay with this man in the presence of your own beloved brother, put your hands upon his body, to coax information from him? I'm afraid I don't understand. You are a married woman, are you not? Where is your sense of decency?"

She flared, more tears starting. "You don't understand? Let me make all of you understand!" Her voice began to rise. Byron did not recognize her now, as she threw off the mantle of docility. "This man is — *stormjagers* — to me." She used a word that meant a dish cooked so poorly that it made one violently ill; though few understood the expression, fewer still mistook her meaning.

"I would have given my body to him if it be necessary to help my beloved brothers rid *ons land* of him and his kind." She looked for the first time at Byron, glared at him, and spat. "We have fought the Xhosas and the Zulu and the Matabele. But we have never confronted an enemy with less honour, less decency. You cannot defeat our men, so you punish their women and their children. You disgust me as surely as you must disgust all civilized people!" She sagged, as if the speech had taken her last reserves. Hicks sat down, shaking his head.

Byron took the witness rail the following day. His mind remained reeling from the extent to which he had been fooled. Hicks' strategy now was to emphasize youth and foolishness in mitigation. But he had not promised much hope. The case seemed overwhelming, what with the incriminating statements reduced to writing in a dead Boer's pocket, twelve miles away.

In answer to Hicks' deliberate questions Byron detailed all that had transpired since his arrival in South Africa. He skirted around the incident with Bricker, sweating so profusely that he felt as if his guilt was stamped upon his forehead. Then Crench rose to question him, assuring the panel that he had "... but a few questions of the accused."

"You do not deny that you abandoned Sergeant Bricker, then?"

"I did not use the word 'abandoned' Major; I simply said - "

"It is all the same. You left him for dead. And in any event, you cannot give a proper account." Before Byron could answer, he went on. "In fact, you provided a version of events to Corporal Copeland that was in contradiction to the story told to Captain Marthewicke-Jones, did you not?"

Byron seethed at the unjust nature of the question. "I don't know how you could ask such a question. Only days ago, Copeland told me that he had assured you there was no contradiction."

"Since you have stained my honour, Mr. Bloode, let me explain the nature of my conversation with Corporal Copeland. When I spoke - "

Byron could not contain himself. All the rage generated from the previous day boiled over. "If you wish to testify, sir, then take the oath and subject yourself to cross-examination, as I have!"

Dangerfield reprimanded Byron. "Be responsive, witness. Be responsive and not argumentative. It shall not help your cause."

Crench turned to the panel, saying simply, "I believe, my lords, that I have effectively revealed the true nature of this man, this man without honour or regard for propriety and decent conduct. No further questions."

Upon completion of submissions, the panel retired for twenty minutes before they returned with a verdict. They were unanimous: guilty. After hearing submissions on the issue of penalty, they retired for more than an hour. Byron could not speak without his teeth chattering. He tugged at Hick's spotless sleeve.

"They have been after me all along," he rattled.

Hicks looked at him, expressionless. "You are a stupid man, Mr. Bloode. You look, but you do not see; you listen, but you do not hear. Your stupidity and your fear are your best hope for mercy. Though I think Charles is persuaded, I think the others are not. It will not go well for you. Your vanity and your insularity have let you down. Somewhere inside you must find the strength to think and act with courage and determination, traits which thus far you seem not to possess."

Stung into silence by this rebuke, Byron fought back tears, and sat motionless in his chair.

Finally, the three men returned. Charles looked diminished, and stole into his chair like an uninvited guest. Dangerfield faced the brace of men who now stood to attention, awaiting his pronouncement. He picked up a sheet of paper, upon which he had scribbled some perfunctory notes.

"The charge upon which Lieutenant Byron Bloode has been found guilty is the most serious one possible in Her Majesty's Army. If allowed to go unpunished, and severely so, it would send a signal that we lack resolve, that we lack moral fibre, that we countenance betrayal of our brave lads in the field."

With a sidelong glance at Charles, he continued, "We are unanimous. The prisoner shall be taken a fortnight hence to a place of convenience, and there and then after having had the opportunity to speak his last, and make peace with his Maker, he shall be suffered to die by firing-squad. May God have mercy on your soul ... We are adjourned."

As these words penetrated the fog of Byron's thoughts, he sank to his chair. He had known it all along, as he galloped past poor Bricker pleading for succor, that he would be condemned. And now it was coming true. In this sudden realization of finality, of reckoning, the doubt lifted, and he straightened, rising to his feet again. In the hour when hope becomes impossible, there is still prayer. Prayer for reconciliation, for peace. If he had not lived thus far well, then he would face death with dignity and resolve. But oh, to see his father but once again.

"Papa," he said softly, "Oh papa."

# Book Four

MANITOBA

# i

West, out past the tiny village of Headingley now, the land had yielded to orderly, well laid-out fields. Twenty miles to the west of Winnipeg, settlement thinned out considerably, as did the traffic. The roadway followed the north side of the river, and as much as a half hour might go by without someone passing. As they did so, however, their response to a man straining between the shafts of a cart was without exception one of surprise. Jan could hear them comment to each other, or exclaim out loud over his horseless wagon, pointing. He paid them no attention.

Shortly, he came upon a small group of men on horseback. One had dismounted and was urinating in the ditch. This was a subject of considerable mirthful commentary by the others. Then they saw Jan. In small movements, they moved their mounts so as to block the road. Some got out of their saddles, grinning at the spectacle. The man in the ditch returned to the roadway, buttoning his trousers, sneering.

"Well, what in hell have we got here?"

It was clear they were not going to allow him to pass, so Jan came to a stop. What right did they have to impede a man's passage? He had a long way to travel, and he was barely half a day into the trip. He dropped the shafts and unslung his harness. He stripped off his blouse, for it was soaked with sweat, and flung it over the wagon. He turned again to face his human obstacles.

What manner of man was it that took the time to torment another? Even if there had been two or three, Jan could have driven them off, perhaps. But five, with one watching from horseback further off? Jan squinted in the bright sunlight at the man sitting his horse apart from the others, but he could not make out his features. His friends had formed a semi-circle around Jan and his vehicle. The one in front, Pisser, seemed their leader. He was laughing. Laughter as free from mirth as a snarl.

"You fuckin' *bohunk*! Come ta take up good Canadian soil fer *nothin'*. That is, when yer ain't workin' fer wages less than a man can decently live on."

He pushed Jan with the heel of his palm. Jan knew that the other could sense the coiled threat that lay within his well-muscled chest, but he stepped back with the push all the same. There was a time to fight, and a time to back down. Only a fool would confuse the two. He lowered his head, hoping that an attitude of submission would appease them. It was galling. He had a club tucked away on the wagon bed, but he could not drive off all these men with a length of wood. Besides, they might use an attack as an excuse to shoot him.

Emboldened by Jan's apparent obeisance, the others chuckled, and walked over to the cart, shaking their heads in exaggerated disbelief.

"Nothin' but a beast a burden!"

"Think on it; pulling a cart like a god-damned ox!"

Jan heard them, and remained silent, his expression impassive as they seized the edge of the wagon and toppled it over. With its tall wheels, it went over easily, with a crash as the stove tumbled out, and wagon and contents slid down the shallow ditch. Parcels, tools, and sections of stovepipe came to rest in brackish water.

There was a chorus of laughter as some of them started to walk down to pick among the scatter, but the man on horseback called to them.

"Enough. Let's be gone from here. We have the best part of the day to reach the quarries. Fun's over. Let's be on our way."

Without much objection, the others agreed, even the one who seemed the most aggressive.

"Well, I already pissed, so there's no sense in going down there again. What could a baloney-eater like this have of value anyways?"

They swung into their saddles, chortling and calling out to one another.

"Did ya see how she went down, all feathers flyin'? Hee hee!"

Then they were gone.

Jan looked at the wreckage, dismayed. Squatting beside the overturned cart, he was relieved that nothing seemed to be broken. But everything needed to be unpacked, and he would need his rope and blocks to right the cart. There was nothing for it but to begin, and with a loud sigh, he wrestled the cast iron 'Mont Blanc' onto its griffin-claw feet, away from the cart. He was grateful that the brittle metal had not cracked.

As he straightened over the stove, he became aware of a presence. A horse coughed, and Jan jumped up. It was one of the men who had accosted him, the one who had sat some distance off from the others. Jan stepped back a pace or two, watching for the others with narrowed eyes.

Without a word, the stranger dismounted, and his horse wandered off to the side of the roadway, pulling at the long tufts of timothy. Walking down to the overturned cart, he bent his knees and put his back to it. Holding his fingers under the rail, he looked at Jan.

"Well?" he said quietly. "I can't do this alone."

Jan looked at him uncomprehending. After all, this was one of those that had just bullied him. The man stared straight ahead, still crouched against the cart. And then:

"Today or tomorrow?"

With a suspicious look around, Jan slowly took up a position on the other side of the wheel. The other counted.

"One, two, three... heave!"

They raised the cart a few feet, and held it.

"Jesus, this thing you've built is a little overdone, don't you think? One, two, and *again!* "

Breath whistling from both men, the cart righted with a lurch. The two wrestled it back to the roadway. The stranger studied the harness cut for a man, and shook his head, faintly amused. Slipping off his jacket, he capered down to the stove.

Jan followed him, and seized the opposite side of the stove. With a count and a grunt, the implement was hefted. Jan looked the man in the eye, whose face was now less than three feet from his own. He had clear blue eyes, and a thick thatch of black hair starting from under his hat, a peaked, round-brimmed felt hat that many plains people wore. A bony nose topped a massive mustache that drooped over each corner of his mouth. The other stared back at him, the weight of the stove showing in his eyes.

"I know," he said, "let's stand here until we sink up to our knees in this ditch." But there was no malice in his voice. "Sideways, now," he gestured with his head, "let's go. Now!"

With more grunting, the stove was carried up and positioned over the axle, for balance. After the rest of the bales and parcels were returned, the stranger went to his horse and took down a sack strung from a ring near the pommel. He took out a packet of grease paper, and a canteen. Returning to squat against one of the tall wheels, he offered something to Jan, who did not move.

"Go ahead. It's salt pork, and damned good salt pork if I do say so myself." Jan took the morsel, and chewed slowly. So far, he had not said a single word.

"Well, in all, there's no real harm done," said the stranger. "Just delayed you on your way a bit." He took off his hat and mopped his brow with his sleeve.

"They's angry, is all. I'm not sayin' that excuses anyone for anything. But they see you Galicians comin' along, takin' over, getting good land for nothin'. Workin' for undercuttin' wages, keepin' to yourselves, not bein' like the rest of us." He sighed. "So they's angry; maybe a little afraid, is all."

He stood up, put his jacket on, shaking the sleeves to get his shirt cuffs down. "We're hopin' to get on at the quarries at Stonewall. But we been told that a whole trainload of Galicians was swarmin' up there to get the jobs. Everybody knows they'll work for next to nothing, so it's a little worrisome. Yeah, well, we'll see when we get there, I guess."

He stepped over to Jan, extending his hand. "Well, ya just about talked my ear off, so I'll be on my way."

Jan did not take his hand. He still held the salt pork in his own. The other withdrew his offer quickly, and jogged over to his straying animal. He mounted and left without so much as a glance back. Jan watched till he disappeared over a rise.

It was a small thing, but it would always bother Jan that he refused the man's hand. Even though the fellow had done him no wrong, and had helped put right what his companions had wrought, Jan's suspicions and his persistent belief in the fundamentally evil nature of all men, could not be overcome. It was when a man was at his weakest that they struck. So never turn your back; give no quarter. Tightening his lips, he leaned to his traces, and with a rattle, the cart moved forward.

# ii

The prairies were the floor of the world. Similar and yet dissimilar to his native steppes which unrolled like a verdant carpet at the foot of the Carpathian Mountains. There, a promise of mountain-fed stream or forest screen was never far away. Here, inestimable flatness was broken only by muddy, sluggish streams that meandered so unpredictably, a man might have to cross them a dozen times in a week just to move in a straight line. Here one might see ragged copses of willow and poplar, or scrub oak. It seemed a patient land, enduring the efforts of man to comb the snarls and tangles of natural lines into the angular dimensions that comfort him: fence and furrow, house and stable, road and gate. These had pushed the unkempt face of nature back, though to a lesser extent as he made his way northwest. He knew well enough too, that this land occasionally shrugged its broad shoulders, wreaking havoc with those who would be masters of the soil.

Grasshoppers had come, as recently as 1875. In such numbers did the plague arrive as to consume everything before it. In the Whitemud settlements, even the potatoes were lost. Not a green blade remained after their passing, and the stench of the rotting heaps of locusts made breathing nearly impossible. Droughts came intermittently, desiccating the countryside so that crops withered, and animals perished for want of drink. The soil was as packed and unyielding as stone, reduced under the intensity of an unrelenting sun to dust as fine as flour. No well-joined sill or felt-damped threshold could keep it out. And every now and then, those torpid rivers threw off their natural traces and spurred by winter run-off, became feral torrents that carried all before them. Vast stretches of flatland, cultivated or otherwise, lay under a silent, smothering flood. Jan had heard enough on the trip out, and at the sheds, to know that this was no easy land to tame.

A man could be embraced and rewarded, or resisted and destroyed by the land. Settlement was on its terms, with necessary compromise and alternatives. Like the oil pits of Boryslava, he needed to listen to the land, feel her, experience her. The land yielded lessons to those who would seek to understand. The teachings of his home would be useful, but this was a new place, and he could not afford to be arrogant.

Arrogant. It was odd how a thought could take his mind in an entirely different direction. Perhaps random thinking was a function of simple repetitive work. Not like labour at the winches, which had more in common with torture, so completely did it expunge all thought but one: the quitting bell. Others took him as arrogant, a man who aspired beyond his peasant's station. But it was nothing of the kind. His reluctance to trust, his experience with predetermined attitudes toward him and others from his homeland, made him distant, self-protective. He feared and distrusted authority, which he believed to be persistently applied with harshness to people such as he.

There was little point in becoming engaged with people who almost uniformly seemed to take a certain view of him, his intellect, his rank. His reserve was taken for impudence, for arrogance, quite out of place. He was a strong-back, a creature of burden who was permitted with his kind to enter the country to fill an empty land. Theirs was to hew the wood, draw water, and produce the yield which would justify the railways and warehouses that were in turn the badges of prosperity for the proprietors and brokers, wholesalers and financiers who held the ties to the national purse.

Yet he was arrogant, if confidence in self, and belief in will were any guide. He knew he would succeed. He would meet this land, now *his* land, not as conqueror, but as beneficiary. And he was supremely confident that he would coax from her that which he needed to survive.

Jan shifted in his harness; it chafed at the left shoulder where he tended to take the greatest weight. For a moment he felt chagrined, for he had allowed himself to indulge in prideful thoughts. He knew that God could look into his thoughts, even anticipate them. Shevchenko muttered at his ear:

*But you, my precious Lord, will seal*
*the lips that foul would be*
*and that high-sounding tongue that says:*
*we are not vanity!*

"Ay! Ay!" Jan cried aloud, wondering. What kind of being is God? Is He a warm, generous, tolerant God? Or harsh, unforgiving, and without mirth? Could he stand a joke? Or afford a man a little margin? What, Jan wondered, would they talk about if He were actually walking alongside. To hear some of the priests tell it, He'd want to know about recent sins, attonements and the like. What good works had been wrought in His name. And little else. How did a man relate to a God like that, except on his knees. *Where is that Lord who would forbid Our souls to think and teach?* Taras again. Perhaps a distant, fearsome and forbidding God was a necessary thing, to keep the comprehension of the *idea* of God just beyond the grasp of mortal men.

But try as he might, Jan could not summon such a version of the God that *popá* Kudryk had imbued him with. This was not what he had understood scripture to portray either, not this. Though most of His agents on earth were eager to preserve their own authority through a stern God, Jan was not having any of it. No, God was a companion, someone to call upon, someone to share the worries of the day with, help draw the load. *Cast thy burden upon the Lord, and He shall sustain thee.* So went the instruction.

"Christ help me," he muttered through clenched teeth as he struggled up the incline of a creek bed. No disrespect here: merely an unvarnished plea to inspire the inner man for a last reserve of strength to get the job done. How many times had he been rebuked for uttering the Lord's name in this way? Yet who more than a peasant needed such a plea so often? Such explanations fell on deaf ears, and it escalated the debate to pretend a personal relationship with the Almighty. Clerics would only shake their heads. Stubborn, prideful man.

But out here, in the vastness of a land he would soon call his own, once he had seized his soil with his bare hands, a man needed a God who would live with him, struggle with him, argue with him, and close with him in the hard choices that confronted him.

So he settled that a man could have precisely the kind of God he wished. For did not the idea of God live in the heart and mind? And could not a man do any more than the limits he set for himself? Were these not related thoughts? *Popá* Kudryk had told him once that the care of the soul was a personal responsibility. Not to be handed over to the village priest weekly for a scrubbing, like a soiled undergarment. But a matter for daily attention. These were difficult issues for Jan, and he would complete circles in his thinking, becoming confused then convinced by turn. Perhaps there was a touch of madness in a man striding along and conversing with someone who was not physically present. But then, what of that? What need had he of the opinions of men?

"So, Christ. You have me drawing like a beast. A test, this, for past or future misdeeds? Vanity perhaps? Am I too proud in Your eyes? Or was the taking of a life, even in such circumstances, a matter for reckoning?"

Was it possible, Jan considered, that this business of sins and atonement meant that the Lord was nothing more than a bookkeeper, whose cosmic grasp of all good works and misdeeds needed an accounting at the final reconciliation? He could hardly fathom such an Overseer whose concerns lay with such trivial detail. God was a Man of ideas, surely, not some distant counterman piling and adding villainies and homages like grubby coins in a userer's shop. No. Intent. That's what God considered, and that lay in the heart.

Looking about, he shouted, "Do you see into my soul Christ; do you know me?" He laughed. "I am your servant, me, though you have set some terrible tasks before me! When will you ease my burden?"

He listened with his heart, and heard nothing. Though there were no assurances, there was nothing to dismay him either, and he began to whistle. The thin notes danced across the plain like smoke. Whistling was good for the soul, like singing. A fearful man can neither whistle nor hold a tune. The sound that is borne of fright is that of surrender, a forlorn thing. You will send me a sign when you're good and ready, he thought.

The cart bounced and jostled behind him, tugging at the shoulder straps, the shafts twisting in his hands. It seemed at times to be a living thing. Slowing, the shafts pushed against him, the momentum of the moment urging him on. Sometimes a start was a test, for the thing became churlish, reluctant, demanding. The weight against his shoulders, neck and arms was a constant presence. The shafts embraced him, and threatened to topple him on an embankment should he move without care. The harness that secured him to the whiffle-tree was a snare from which there was no escape. And the steel tires of the narrow wheels, muffled by the packed soil of the trail, hissed in a rhythmic breathing of a avenging angel following closely on.

Jan's contemplations were interrupted by the appearance of two figures ahead on the trail. Both labour and thought tended to keep his head down, though he looked up now and then to the horizon. But there was no science to it, and often his deliberations kept him staring at his feet for most of an hour. As he approached, he could see off to the left in the trees by the creek, a farmstead. They were fewer and farther between, now. It was English, he could see that. The house faced the roadway, at right angles to it. The barn and outbuildings were set back of the house, almost as if cut to a pattern. All along the road toward Portage la Prairie and beyond, the pattern was the same; even the whitewash and red ochre paints seemed to have been stirred in the same bucket. The French along the plain at St. Xavier tended to be more casual about the layout of their farmsteads, organizing them with an eye to efficiency. And in his homeland, the house always faced south, so that the *khatchyna*, west room, which contained the kitchen and living place would have the benefit of the late day's light, while the sleeping room opposite would catch the first rays of the new day. There was the matter of luck and positive influences as well.

As he drew closer, one of the figures, a woman, scuttled back to the house, emerging a few minutes later with what appeared to be a rifle. Jan was unsettled by this, for when he had first seen them, they appeared to be in the middle of the road, whacking the surface with shovels. A strange thing, this. The man, about fifty or more, Jan guessed, leaned on his shovel and waited. He raised his hand to his red-faced wife, who looked to be about the same age, and she skidded to a stop where the yard accessed the trail.

"Watch yourself, Casper," she called, clutching what was now clearly an ancient shotgun of very large bore, maybe a ten-guage. Its forestock was held on with a generous wrapping of wire. Probably hand-loaded black powder shells filled with unpleasant things like nail heads, fence wire cuttings, stripped nuts or gravel, Jan thought. He kept a wary watch on her from the corner of his eye. Since the man ahead was in the middle of the road, Jan came to a stop several paces away. He set the shafts down, and mopped his face with his *khustra*, headscarf, which itself was soaked with sweat.

"Watch yourself, Casper," the old woman called again. "He looks dangerous. Probably one of them ones that raided us last night."

The man waved her off once more. "No thief ever broke sweat like this fellow." He looked directly at Jan. "Good day to you son. You look like you could use a drink of water."

Jan nodded. "Yes. I am grateful."

"Ha!" the woman cried, picking up on the accent. "I suspected as much! He's one of them foreigners, with no respect for British decency and good order. Look at him! Naked as a -"

"Give it up, woman," her husband said firmly. "Here's an honest man, or I'm no judge."

His wife looked as if she might say something more than faintly critical of this last statement, but appeared to think the better of it. She was a lioness contained, just barely, by the cage of her husband's authority. Instead she turned, still holding the gun at the ready, grumbling something about being slain in their beds one night.

He turned back to Jan, a smile creasing his sun burned face. He wore no hat, which was unusual in a day when every man, whether he worked indoors or not, wore some form of headgear. It was as much to mark good sense as it was to signal station. He offered his hand.

"Casper Clement," he said. "That, you've probably guessed, is my wife Beatrice. Pay her no mind, for we've been robbed overnight, and she's in a foul mood about it. Pull your rig in here, and we'll fix you up with a drink."

"Thank you," replied Jan. The man's grip was firm, honest. "Jan. Jan Dalmynyshyn."

The other looked back at the cart. "I was going to ask you what happened to your horse, but I can see you're set up to operate without one. Doesn't seem like a practical way to travel, if you don't mind me saying."

Jan lifted the shafts with a sigh. "It is a question of money. I have agreement with you: this is no practical way to travel, not today."

As they entered the farmyard, Clement looked up at the sky, squinting. The top of his head was bald like a monk's, burned and peeling. "Yep," he said. "Must be nearly ninety already. Hot as Hades. If we don't get some rain soon, the crops'll fail. The wet's been threatening to come, but each night, just a bluster. Maybe tomorrow."

Jan walked over to the well, but Clement called out: "No, no, over here! The rain barrel on the north side of the house. There's still a bit left. Well water's no good out here. Seems west of the Red River, the water's salty. Oh, the odd sweet well occurs, but God only knows where it might be. You find a good one, and fifty paces away it's unfit." He plunged a dipper into the cool barrel in the shade, offering it to Jan, who knelt out of the sun to take it.

"We've tried. We've had well diggers, water-finders, witches and even government experts out here, but no luck." And as an afterthought he added, "And may the Good Lord save us from 'government experts'. Half of them got their jobs because of some uncle who works for a Minister somewhere in the government. Then they come out to see me, at my expense, to tell me what I'm doing wrong! You know?"

Jan swallowed loudly, nodding his agreement and understanding. He had lived in three places: the Ukraine, America, and now here. The systems were different, but each had its competing tyrannies, and the effect on the poor man or the man without influence, was the same. He rose, returned the empty ladle and walked over to the stock trough, brimming with dark water.

Clement called out. "That's not fit to drink, I told you..."

Jan shook his head. "With your leave — I need to wash myself -"

"Hell's bells, man. Dive in if you want to."

Jan stood at the narrow end of the wooden reservoir grasped it with both arms, bent at the waist and immersed his entire upper body in the coolness. He stayed beneath the surface for several moments, then arose with a splutter of exhaled breath and scattered droplets. Clement was laughing.

"I've never seen anyone enjoy a bath so much. Made me feel almost clean just watching."

Jan wrung out his *khustra*, and mopped his body with it. "I'll be on my way, with thanks," he said.

Just then, Emma Clement stuck her head around the corner: "If you're coming for soup, it better be now. I'm not running some fancy road house with bill of fare, open all hours."

"Well, I think that includes you, Jan, I suppose. You go on ahead. I want to rinse off a little myself."

Jan stared at him, then back at the house, uncertain. His had been a mixed welcome.

"Oh, go on in," said Clement as he turned away. "She has a rough way about her, to be sure, but she wouldn't have asked if she wasn't prepared to set a place for you."

Jan walked slowly to the open door. It was dark beyond, for the curtains were drawn against the sun. It smelled of cooking food, and the aroma made Jan's stomach rumble. It was all the bolstering he needed. He stopped at the threshold and knocked at the jamb. There was no answer. Hesitantly, he stepped into the gloom, pausing to let his eyes adjust. He was startled by a voice, low and resentful.

"Who the hell are you?"

He turned quickly in the direction of the voice; it was low, off to one corner of the room. He could make out the outlines of a man, seated. He looked to be about thirty or so, but as his eyes allowed for the dark, he could see that the fellow had an old, bitter look to his face. Moreover, he had a faded military tunic drawn over his shoulders; the brass buttons gleamed dully in the shaded room. With a start, Jan realized that the man was missing his right leg. Before he could answer, both man and wife appeared at once at the door.

"Ah. So you've met Nathaniel. Our son. Come sit at table," said Clement in his broad, welcoming voice, gesturing to Jan.

There were two places set opposite; two large bowls full of thick soup, two spoons, with a plate of sliced bread between them. Jan was a little uncertain, for there were four occupants. But the seated man did not move, and Emma took a seat in a rocker near the stove, placing a skein of wool on her lap. Jan could not help but see that the shotgun was standing against a sideboard, within arm's reach. The hammer was still cocked.

"Excuse my boy, here; Nat, we call him," said Clement with his mouth full. "He takes after his momma a little bit when it comes to hospitality. Sit. Sit."

Behind him, his wife clucked loudly, then after a moment said only, "He's eating, isn't he?"

It was true. Jan was devouring what was placed before him without further hesitation or formality. That he was hungry was obvious. But he felt caught between warring members of the same tribe. No answer, no conversational approach seemed to afford safe avenue, so he ate. The stew was wonderful. In addition to shavings of what he took to be venison, there were carrots and potatoes, dumplings and greens. The bread was thick and fresh, and drew up the soup like a wick. He deliberately chewed and rolled the morsels around in his mouth, forcing them to yield every shred of flavour before swallowing. "Mmmm," he said between mouthfuls, "it is very, very good."

"Why is there no place for me at table?" Nathaniel Clement suddenly demanded. "Am I not part of this household?"

His father looked at him in exasperation. "You had your soup in your chair, already, where you always eat. Come sit. Come then."

His son did not budge. Jan looked from one to the other, then bent to his spoon again. He was wary, keeping an eye on both of them, as if there might be trouble. Clement looked at Jan, his face was neutral, though Jan sensed a certain resignation.

"He's not been the same since the war - "

There was a commotion as Nathaniel got up awkwardly. Standing uncertainly, he said with petulance in his voice, "I suppose you're going to talk about me now, like you always do, as if I'm not here. Well, I'm *not* here!" He stumped out of the room with a crutch held under his good arm. He seemed furious.

Clement sighed and laid down his spoon. "His brother died of an ear infection when he was three. He seemed to get over that. Was the smartest boy for miles around. Read like a parson; do sums like a banker. Everyone, us included, figured he'd do well.

"Won a scholarship in '85 from the Daughters of the Empire, to go down east and study law. Could hardly afford to let him go, what with working the farm and everything. Lord knows it wasn't what it is today. But it was a great opportunity for him; maybe he wouldn't end up working the land. Maybe there'd be something better. A career at the Bar, maybe a judge one day. But what did he do? What did he do with this opportunity? Ohh!" He laid his hand alongside his face.

He shook his head, weary, then took up his spoon again. Pointing it at Jan he said, "Joined the army. Joined the ... army!" He was obviously not a man given to pungent expletives, but he was clearly searching for one now.

Jan moved a mouthful of dumpling over to one side. He was not ready to release it just yet.

"So he goes to war, then? There is fighting?"

"Well, it wasn't really a war, though them that went through it called it that. Got everyone to a fever pitch, it did. But it didn't amount to much in the end."

"Where was it?" asked Jan. "And what was fighting over?"

The older man sighed, leaning his elbows on the table. "It seems like wars don't need to be over much. Is any war worth a ruined son?" He gestured with his head in the direction of the doorway.

"Up in the territories, on the South Saskatchewan, there were farmers, mostly French-speaking half-bloods; probably most related to them just east of here.

Anyway, with the coming of the railway, and the buffalo gone, they started to get worried about what was going to happen to them. Then when surveyors showed up and started to carve the land without a mind to their homesteads, the worrying was on in earnest. They sent for Louis Riel to speak for them, who'd been involved in similar troubles back in '70 here in Manitoba, who was teaching or preaching or something in Montana. He had no better luck getting the government to listen then, than he did in '70. Why, I don't know, except that down east they blamed him for everything that went wrong out here."

Jan pursed his lips. In his time at the sheds, he had heard of this man. His name arose during the discussions about ownership of land, and whether it could be taken away. While everyone agreed that it was unlikely, Riel stood as illustration of the fact that the government could, under the guise of the public welfare or some other high-sounding principle, take away what had been freely given, or hard earned. It was no secret that the courts were well stocked with former politicians and the toadies that served them; they could hardly be expected to side with the little man against government and its ally, big business. Anyone who could read an English newspaper understood that the stench of scandal perpetually emanated from the grant of contracts, the awarding of positions, and the exchange of money and influence.

Clement got up to fetch a large kettle of tea which was simmering on a small parlour stove. This was a sign of modest wealth, for it enabled the larger kitchen stove to remain unused, a blessing in scorching weather. Holding it with a piece of doubled toweling, he continued.

"Of course, Riel couldn't lay claim to all the stupidity that was going on back then. I was barely twenty, and many of my neighbours grabbed their weapons and marched against Riel under a Major Boulton - a fine piece of work, that fellow - " he said grimly, as he poured the black liquid into a tin cup. "It's a wonder that only one was killed in the end."

Beatrice looked up from squinting at her work. "I remember that if it warn't for your father, you'd have gone off too."

"Oh, hush Bea, that's beside the point. Time makes you see a little more clearly, now doesn't it?"

Jan knitted his brows. "But the war..."

"Oh yes. Well, this is just background, see. So here they are, 1870 happening all over again. Same reasons, same folly. Government does nothing. I suppose they were too busy making each other wealthy. Josephine! So after Riel sets up another sort of government of his own, like he did at Fort Garry, they decide to send in an armed force of police cavalry, to nip the whole affair in the bud. Not send in assurances that no one'd be put off their land, oh no; just send in the troops.

"Well, what do you know, at Duck Lake, this rag-tag group of farmers and plainsmen runs them off! And doesn't the eastern press go half wild about it! Show of force! Example needed! To Arms! It was almost laughable if it warn't so pitiful."

Jan was fascinated by the account, particularly the old man's perspective on it. Casper seemed to see the injustice of the thing. Jan said as much, swallowing the dumpling at last, reluctantly:

"This is an unjust thing to do, then..."

"Good Lord in Heaven, yes. A force of more than four thousand was raised under General Middleton. And then who shows up on our doorstep after less than six months at school, but our Nat, dressed in red twill and Glengarry cap. I could have wept — and I have since, God knows. But there he was, his chest all puffed out, ready to have it away with the rebels. He was only with us the night, as his Company was in the vanguard, and Middleton was eager to get on with the business of scrawling glory in other men's blood. But not a wink o' sleep did the three of us get.

"I asked him, 'son', I says, 'would you feel the same if it was our farm that was threatened, and it was me facing off against the government?' 'That's different,' he says to me. 'Not the same at all. It was the same government that had given us our place; why would they take it away?' It was no use. He wouldn't be told. Besides, there was nothing for it. He'd signed up, and that was that. The next time we saw him, he was missing a leg."

Behind him, his wife sniffled a little. Clement himself had moist eyes. He cleared his throat loudly, and spooned the hot soup, lifting it, but setting it down almost immediately.

"Took two balls in thigh and arm almost at once, during the ambush on Middleton's forces at Fish Creek. First man down. From what I hear, the army surgeon couldn't wait to get his saw into him. But that saw ... that saw cut much deeper than bone. Something else is gone, and I suppose it might have been that evening where I planted doubts about the cause that did the real damage. Can a normal man fight if the cause be not just?"

Jan cleared his throat, and Clement looked up, seeming startled. "Well, haven't I been the bore," he said quickly. Jan started to protest, but Clement waved him off. "Haven't even asked your destination. Where you off to?" he said this as he was rising; it was clear the visit was about to conclude. Jan had the sense that perhaps the farmer felt that he had shared a little too much of himself.

"I have been promised a homestead, south of Ukraina." He mopped the remains of his soup with a thick crust.

"And you're walking the whole distance barefoot drawing your rig! Whew." Clement led him to the door. "Good that you stopped with us, son. Hope I didn't prattle on too much about our troubles." Once again, he waved off Jan's attempts to protest, or express thanks. His wife was still sniffling, so he said to Jan, "I'll be right along. Why don't you top off your water jug from the barrel back there?" And he turned back into the house.

Blinking in the bright sunlight, he filled his container and returned to his cart. He stood between the shafts, adjusting his *khustra*, unwilling after such hospitality to leave without a farewell, he was hailed by Nathaniel Clement.

" So you're on your way. Good. If the old man had any more time, he'd have spilled his guts to the point where he'd be even more unbearable than usual." His voice had a hard edge to it; his eyes glittered as he looked Jan over.

"What kind of man pulls a wagon like a beast?" he asked evenly. Jan had it in mind not to answer, but the answer came from Clements, who had reappeared at the door.

"A man who makes his own way no matter what the obstacle, that much is plain. Come," he called to Jan. "I'll walk you to the road."

As Jan felt the familiar tug of the harness at his body, he felt ready. He expressed his thanks again, simply. As they came to the trail, he saw a dark patch of freshly turned earth where he had first seen the two standing. Curious, he asked what it was.

Clement rubbed his smooth chin. "It's where we buried our dog."

Jan was puzzled, but thought it impolite to ask further; Clement continued nonetheless.

"Last night, we had two chickens taken, a row of carrots, and our dog Cameron was killed. Both his back legs were taken, so I suppose it was Indians that did it. They'll eat dog, you see; it's a delicacy, though it hardly commends itself to me. He wasn't the brightest beast we ever had, but I'll miss him. I buried him up here on the road, because his spirit will continue to watch the yard. If the Indians saw that, they'd keep clear for sure."

Jan shook his head at this; this was too much to understand. With a final handshake, he set off at a brisk pace. Clement called after him, something about stopping in again, but his voice was caught up by a late-stirring afternoon breeze. Jan did not look back; he had more information about this place, its history, and the responses of people to it. He needed to think about each part, and store it away. Later, tucked under his cart, Jan slept fitfully. He dreamed of Farmer Clement's' legless son and legless dog pursuing him along an endless highway.

## iii

For a time, the days ran one into the other; hot, clear, and with barely a breeze in the afternoon. Fewer travellers passed by now, though their reactions continued to be surprised. Still, there were queer sights out here in the settlements, what with tinkers and travelling sales agents, tramps, laid off Chinese coolies, and immigrants of all description. A man shouldn't be too surprised, and it remained a custom to touch the brim of one's hat as a stranger was met. Or nod. Only these damned men in sheepskin coats didn't acknowledge a body on the trail. Of course, with most of them, both hands were taken with the burden of the moment, and this was particularly true for Jan. So he kept his head down. From snatches of comments he could tell that he was not one of those highly regarded:

"Did ya see that? Didn't even look at us!"

"Huh. Whaddya expect? Ain't got no manners, these baloney-eaters!"

Jan was entering the broad flatlands south and west of Lake Manitoba. Covering the western corner of the province, the prairie occupied a variety of land forms; bluffs, glacial lake beds, ridges and swales, and rolling till plains. But its impression of uniformity was created by the dominance of major grasses: big bluestem and Indian grass, with some side-oats grama and cordgrass, as soil moisture levels fluctuated. However, by far the most intrusive vegetation was the appearance of orderly rectangles of new domestic crops: wheat, oats, barley, flax and corn seeded in rows as straight as the hand of man could effect. Such plenty, Jan thought. How could one man manage to sew, tend and reap such abundance? His pulse quickened at the thought of such possibilities for himself. To own land was one thing; he was very close to that. But to become rich? To have more than enough?

To steady himself against such giddy thoughts, he looked for variety among the plants at the thickly grown edge of the trail. He had been startled to see the pale white anemone, the same flower in his native land which was said to possess magical properties. He took that as a good omen. Here was a clump of Siberian Yarrow with its startlingly white flower and serrated leaves. Moonwort, sedges and purple thistles, chickweed and ubiquitous buttercups: all were plants he was familiar with, and there was a certain comfort in a new land whose soil was obviously as accommodating as that which he had left. He was on a glory road, a solitary pilgrimage in a fertile land, and his heart swelled.

*In bloom the land*
*Around them lay as they did bend*
*Their steps toward Bethlehem ...*
*'Twas midday, and the blue*
*Of sky was bright and seemed to bode*
*A mellow day*

The cerulean prairie sky by day teemed with birdlife. He could not have known that, less than a century before, the skies often became darkened with the passage of great flocks of winged creatures. The trumpeter swan, passenger pigeon and whooping crane were long gone from the heart of the continent, though once they flew in such numbers as to defy belief. Plovers, curlews, willets and the raucous marbled godwits still clamoured over the prairie grasses, however, and Jan lost track of his attempts to count the different birdcalls.

At sunset, swaddled under his cart from the humming mosquitoes, Jan could hear the ticking call of the yellow rail, the rusty gate screech of the red-winged blackbird, and the distinctive treble note of the sharp-tailed sparrow. If he were near a marsh, which he tried to avoid because the mosquitoes seemed even more rapacious close to water, the hootings and bleatings of countless water birds remained with him until sleep took him. Prairie chickens, so stupid they could be killed with a stick, provided many evening meals.

One morning in early July, he came to the edge of a gully through which the Whitemud River ran. He reckoned by the hand drawn copy of the map he had made in Winnipeg, that it was not more than a few miles to Tanner's Crossing, just south of the Riding Mountain. Stopping for a moment, he saw a wagon with a white canvas fly, large and expensive he thought, on the other side of the shallow rivulet. Without giving it much heed, except that it seemed to be standing directly in the middle of the roadway, he spun his own vehicle around, so that he could descend the bank using his weight on his heels as a brake. For this he needed to put his boots back on. They seemed tight and uncomfortable, even though he had deliberately purchased two sizes larger, so that they could accommodate extra lining for the winter.

Straightening and looking again, he saw that the wagon had not moved, though two men stood at its rear, hands on hips. A woman was there as well, sitting off to one side on a rock, legs drawn up, and resting her chin on her knees. Assuring himself that their presence was benign, he began the descent. Once into it, he regretted not taking out the rope he used for steeper declines; the cart strained at him, threatening him with a brisk plunge to the bottom. But his back strained against the traces, and his arms pulled at the shafts, bulging the biceps and forearms as he skidded down the slope.

He was sweating heavily with the effort. His boots dug channels in the packed dirt; he leaned back almost level with the trail. The cart began to pick up speed, bumping and shaking, the contents rattling about. Then in a moment, it was over, and the cart came to a splashing rest in the creekbed. His buttocks were sore; he was glad he had sewn a large square of sailcloth on the seat of his trousers. Looking up, he was not surprised to see the three staring at him in some wonder. There had been a warning shout from one of them; he supposed that it must have appeared as if he were going to crash into the wagon just a few feet ahead. In addition to the older man, there was a woman who looked about the same age, and a younger man with a thin, unfriendly face. There were enough similarities to suggest this was a family.

"We thought you were gonna lose it, for a moment there," said the elder man with a grin. "Good thing you didn't, or we'd a had more trouble than we got at present."

"Damn near did us in," said the younger, with obvious exaggeration.

Jan stood up and whacked his rear with his hands. "You have trouble?" He could see now that the rear wheel had collapsed.

"Yes, I'm afraid so," said the other, staring ruefully at the wheel. "We're planning to take one of the team into Tanner's Crossing for a replacement." The team of matched Belgians had not been unhitched, and they stamped their great plumed feet in annoyance.

Jan walked over to the side of the wagon. "It can be fixed, this?"

"Shoot! I doubt it. Look at it." He pointed to the two spokes that lay in a split felloe. "Wheelwright that put this together oughtta be taken out, shot and pissed on!"

From inside the wagon came a feminine voice: "Father, your language!"

Jan looked up as a woman's hand drew aside the rear curtain, and a face as lovely as a cloud looked out. Mary, Mother of God! It was the most beautiful face he had ever seen: strong, intelligent, and luminous, framed by soft, dark hair. Beguiling eyes looked down on him, transfixing him. He was acutely aware of her appraisal of him; the flickering glances over his bare chest, the faintest of smiles licking at the corners of her mouth.

Then she smiled openly. "Oh. Forgive my father. His language choice is not always the best, but he's quite put out about the wheel. We all are."

The younger man, apparently her brother, sneered. "I don't think you need to worry about language choice in front of this fine fellow. From the sound of it, I wouldn't think -"

"Don't be a boor, Henry," she cut him off.

The elder man stepped forward. "The name's Cartwright. Now isn't that appropriate? Henry. This here's my wife Gladys," the old woman nodded silently, "and these quarrelsome two are my daughter Ervina, and Henry Junior. We're making for Gilbert Plains, where our home is, and we were hoping to make Tanner's Crossing before dark. Now this."

With effort, Jan tore his gaze away from the dulcet Ervina, and looked at the wheel again. "It could be fixed," he said, nodding. "I could try..."

The boy spoke quickly; there was a hard edge to his voice. "He's just a Galician tramp, father; should he be allow -"

His father interrupted. "Well now boy, don't be ungracious." Turning to Jan he spoke apologetically: "Don't pay him any heed, he can be downright rude sometimes. If you'd care to have a try, we'd be grateful ..." He trailed off, glaring at his son.

Jan walked back to his cart for his tool box, conscious that Ervina was watching him. Pointing to a deadfall, he directed. "I need that trunk cut, long as can be. For levering. Someone hold the team. We must pile rocks under axle."

"You heard him," called Cartwright. "Mother, Ervina, watch the horses, make sure they don't move. Henry, take an ax to that deadfall. I'll help you with the rocks; what you say your name was?"

Jan extended his hand. "Jan Dalmynyshyn." The other's hand was firm, but not callused. This was not a man used to hard work.

The wagon was levered up and the wheel quickly taken off once the kingpin was struck. Jan lay it on its side. The hub was crimped where the felloe had failed. Straightening it with an axe would be easy enough, but a section of the wheel needed to be replaced. He took the axe and walked off to a thicket of white oak along the creek bed. Looking this way and that, he selected several grown curves from boughs he thought might match. Returning to the wagon with his armload of branches, he chose the one which most approximated the radius of the wheel. With his woodworking tools, he fashioned a piece to match the one he had cut out of the wheel. Fitting it in several tries to the loose spokes, he at length drove the fitting into place with the axe. With slats from the wagon bed, and small rope soaked in the creek, he locked the spokes into place by fashioning splints. Hefting the big wheel while the others pried up the wagon, Jan knocked the pin back in place.

"You must watch as you go," he said. "It will work some, perhaps, but if you go slowly, it should last for today."

Cartwright was all smiles. "Can't thank you enough, my boy. This is a Godsend. Thank you indeed."

The team strained at the load, and the wagon moved up the slope. Jan walked along for a few paces; he was pleased to see that the repair was holding. It wouldn't last long, but long enough, he thought, to get somewhere where a replacement could be obtained. At a touch on his arm, he looked up. It was Ervina.

"We are truly grateful," she said. "If you are in the Gilbert Plains area, you must stop in. The Cartwrights. Everyone knows where we are. Thank you so much."

Jan shivered under her touch, unable to do more than nod. This close, he could see her eyes were an unusual olive brown, under dark brows. They were eyes, he was sure, that would come back to torment him in his sleep.

*Ah, those eyes so brown and sparkling,*
*And those brows so dark!*
*It is they my heart awaken,*
*Make it pound, and - hark!*
*Laugh in glee and pour out verses*
*Sing and whisper of*
*Starry nights and cherry orchards,*
*And a dear maid's love and my sweet Ukraine!*

"Come on, girl," called Cartwright. And in moments, they were gone, vanished over the rim of the gully.

Jan now considered his own position. He was several hours behind, and the sun was starting to slant in the afternoon sky. The struggle up the incline would be difficult, he thought, and would probably require his turning blocks and rope. He wondered why there had been no offer to help him. The three men could have shouldered his small vehicle up the slope in no time, but they had left without any hint of willingness to reciprocate. It seemed almost as if his labour was taken for granted, worth nothing. He felt a small twist of resentment. Perhaps in future he would not be taken in so. He wondered about the girl, as he rinsed and wrung out his *khustra*. She was a beauty, that. He stood motionless for a long moment, holding the image of her. Well, there was nothing for it but to begin the task, and with a sigh, he took out the heavy coils of rope.

# iv

In 1848, nine-year-old John Tanner watched with his family for three days as the huge Northern herd made one of their regular twice-yearly crossing of the Little Saskatchewan River, at a ford that would shortly become named after him. So many buffalo that a boy might have thought that the world to the west of the crossing was nothing but buffalo. Singly, then in groups, grunting, dew claws rattling, a deep shuddering telegraphed their coming like a rendering of the earth. Great shaggy heads lowered, they snuffled and snorted and bawled their way across the river in an unending flow of living flesh that tore the earth and roiled the river bed, foul with the excrescence of beasts beyond number. This being the autumn, the Cree lodges on the south side were being struck in readiness for a move to the wintering place in the north hills; the *Odanah*, meeting place, it was called.

This was a place well known to the Tanners. In 1796, John Falcon Tanner had traveled the area by canoe with Saulteaux traders working for the North West Company. Seven years before, he had been kidnapped by Shawnee on the Kentucky side of the Ohio River, downstream from Cincinnati, at a place still called 'Tanner's Creek'. Soon after, he was sold for twenty gallons of whiskey to the Saulteaux, and became known as *Shawshawabenase*.

None of this, of course, was apparent to Jan. The history of a place is revealed only inferentially, and then only upon deliberate inquiry; a man might pass through without any understanding of why a town existed, or why a people had come together. A man in search of a future might pay no mind to the past; what was done was done, though a fool might hold onto a grudge. But a man wishing to secure a future had better heed what had gone before. If the purpose of wisdom is vision, then its life is experience. Jan had yet to make that leap.

What presented to his eyes was a scrabble of shacks on the riverbank bordering the busy commercial main street. False-fronted shops, fieldstone office buildings, an ice house, butcher shop, implement dealer, and in a thicket of wheeled vehicles, a feed and livery operation with a hand-made sign that proclaimed 'The Commercial Livery Stable, A. McKenzie, Prop.'. There, near the wide door, was the Cartwright wagon resting on a jack, the damaged wheel already off. Only the boy was in sight, and it seemed to Jan that he gave him a guilty glance, though it was one that was quickly masked by something else; disdain perhaps.

Jan carefully looked about, but there was no sign of the woman. He wondered at the disappointment, why it should be so keen. The gulf that separated them was as vast as the plain over which he travelled, yet there lay within him the mote of a possibility that she had found him pleasing.

Soon enough, he became aware of the attentions of others. Small boys flung horse turds at him, jeering.

"Bohunk, Bohunk!" they cried. "Horsey-man! Horsey-man!"

Bystanders laughed and did nothing to stop the petty torment. A few even tossed a jibe or two themselves. It seemed certain that the waves of eastern European immigration were still a novelty in Tanner's Crossing. Though there were settlements of such newcomers to the north and west, this community was pretty much of a sameness from what Jan could see. The Indians had been long banished to the farthest corner of the valley; there was a Chinese laundry, and that was it. All other faces were white, all attire was singular, and expressions seemingly united in their exclusion.

Jan resisted the temptation to speed up. The ground sloped toward the river, and the cart seemed to be urging him on. Off to the left side, Jan could see an Oriental watching him, scuttling across the verandah in front of what appeared to be his business establishment, the 'Go-Along Laundry and Bath House'. The fellow called out to Jan.

"Big man! Big man! By here!" He beckoned with one arm as he pulled open a high gate between his building and the bank next door. Jan briefly considered the baying pack of children, and turned in. The gate closed behind him, and he came to rest in a well-stocked woodyard, fenced completely around by a palisade of rough milled timber. He turned from his shafts and faced his host.

The Chinaman was dressed in a three-quarter denim smock, well-vented at the sides, and worn over his black pantaloons. His thinning hair was twisted into a single tight braid that hung to his shoulders. His features were permanently coiled into a grin, though it may have been a lifetime of strategic obsequies that conditioned him in this appearance. Grinning, he approached Jan.

"I am Lieu Gao Lung." With a gesture to his two-storey building, and a broader grin, he continued, "So, 'Go-Along' Laundry. Not so clever, hey-san? You like our Tanner's children?" More smiles.

He pointed to a tower-like structure at the rear of the building. It was open, with two landings upon each of which an ingenious hopper had been built to supply wood to the boilers for the laundry and baths. A zig-zag of stairs reached from ground to upper level.

"I need two cords carried up there, each place. " He held up two fingers. "I pay you two dollars (he pronounced it *dallah)* you have two meal, bed and bath. You big, strong, you take no time, hey-san?"

Jan needed no careful review of his situation to see that this was an unexpected but welcome respite, both from the urchins in the street, and from the routine of his travel. And a bath! How much he craved the idea of something more than a wallow in a muddy stream. Without a word, he gathered up an armload of stovewood, dry, split birch, aromatic in his nostrils, and started for the staircase. The older man stopped him, and pointed to a hod leaning against the wall.

"Use that. So. You take no time." Grinning still, he disappeared into the back door, with just the faintest shaking of his head.

An honest cord of wood measures eight by four by four feet. It took Jan the better part of the afternoon to carry all four cords to the hoppers. As he shouldered the loaded hod, his biceps and thigh muscles stood out with the strain. He was as lean and fit as steady hard work can mould a man, but what kept him going was the thought of a warm soak. By the time he had loaded the stovelengths as directed, his back and knees ached in a burning concert of pain, all of which seemed focused at a point at the base of his skull. The bath. Oh, for a hot drowsing.

The bath was drawn for him by what Jan took to be one of the owner's silent sons. Soon he had stripped off his sweat-drenched trousers and was luxuriating in the soapy heat of a galvanized tub of steaming water. He lay back and closed his eyes. He had not taken a real bath since Pennsylvania, not one like this. What a luxury it was. People laughed and pointed at him on the road. "Stinking peasant," they said. But why would a man choose to be foul if he had an alternative? At home the reek of hard work was what set apart an honest man from a felon. But here, people were quick to judge, to condemn.

He slid down into the water, and rolled a wash rag under his neck against the bite of the narrow rim of the tub. Head back, he lay dreamily with his eyes closed, listening to the rumble of distant street noise, and the thump and slop of the laundry operation below. The warmth enveloped his body. He allowed its embrace to take him, to reach deep within the root of him. He felt himself stir, and he started, guiltily. Glancing about, he could see that he was alone. If necessary, thin curtains which looked like badly-worn bedsheets on tightly stretched cord, could have been drawn between his bath and the five other metal bathtubs. He settled back, sighing, closing his eyes.

Unbidden, though in truth the thought was never out of easy reach, Ervina's face drifted into his mind. He examined and re-examined her image as if he held her head in his hands. Turning her this way and that, tenderly as a lover, he recalled her hair, her brows, her lips parted over white teeth. The eyes, olive-gray, dancing to some inner joy - or was it mischief? - reflected a gaze that was direct and warm. The scoop of her collarbone, and the gentle turn of slender shoulders; she was so close he could feel her warmth against him, smell the tracings of soap on her skin, white where the sun had not browned her. Suddenly, he was tumescent, his thighs slowly contracting and lifting his groin in gentle surges. The dirty, soapy water slopped at the edge of the tub, spilling gently onto the wooden planked floor. He clutched at himself as he imagined her private places, the sheer intimacy of conjoinment.

Screwing his eyes tightly to keep her evanescent features in view, he struggled with himself, hands moving faster yet, oblivious to the slop and splash of his bathwater. At the moment of his release, he arched his back, crying out softly, "Ervina, Ervina!" as if to keep her but for a moment longer. Moaning barely audibly in this way, he settled back into the cooling water, still holding himself, his urgency fading as rapidly as his fantasy.

The was a faint rattle of crockery. Jan opened his eyes. There was the Chinaman sitting on a high stool at the foot of the bath. He was pouring a second cup of tea from a dainty pot bound in wicker. Jan sat up, blushing furiously. The Chinaman looked at him, grinning.

"You enjoy your bath, I see. So." Nodding. Then continuing:

"We charge next man half price for bath, if he use same water." He took a sip from a tiny cup without a handle, "but in this case, I don't think so. Hey-san?"

Jan opened his mouth to speak, but no sound came out. He was swept between outrage and shame, unable to decide how to respond. He stared at the placid little man sipping his tea, nodding pleasantly. His emotions subsided. Would he have felt so quick to forgive if it had been a white man who had intruded upon his private moments? He wasn't sure, but this fellow seemed benign. Jan shrugged.

"A moment of weakness, I did not know anyone was about. I -"

Gao Lung waved him off. " You enjoy bath. It is enough. I bring tea. You dress, we talk later. So." He slid off the stool with a whisper of cloth, handed Jan a cup of warm green water, and drew the stool with the teapot on it to the edge of the tub. Only the faint creak of the stairs told of his exit. Jan wondered at the depth of his urgency that the Chinaman should have entered unnoticed, brought a stool, drank tea and watched him thrash about in his bath like some prurient, panting boy at the turn of manhood. It would take a while to get over this one, he thought as he leaned back with his tea.

# V

Jan was lost in thought. The going was smoother now that he had passed out of the valley of the Little Saskatchewan, by way of the Odanah Pass. Thank the Blessed Virgin that an old man by the name of Nestor Cramps kept a team at the far end of Tanner's Crossing to help wayfarers with the passage through the hills.

He had stayed on at the Chinaman's to stack wood for five days, so the extra money had enabled some luxuries, like fresh bread, smoked meat, and the lease of Cramps' tandem team, though only one of his Percherons was used. Pulled his trap as if it weren't there, Jan thought. Both he and the sour old man sat one behind the other on the big horse's back, legs dangling like schoolboys. Cramps kept up a steady stream of invective, requiring nor seeking response.

"Worked for thet Chinee feller Go-along, did ya? He as weird as he looks? Don't know why folks don't clean their own clothes. I heard the Chinee eats babies. Delicacy. Heard it on good authority. 'Course, even a sniff a thet savagery an' we'd burn the sonofabitch out. Mark me."

Jan shook his head behind Cramps, listening to his venomous prattle. He was thinking that he had been well treated by the Chinaman.

Following his bath, he had put on a robe which had been left for him. It was ridiculously small over his enormous frame, but the silk cloth felt sensuous against his skin. The Chinaman had taken his blouse and trousers to be washed; indeed, there they were on a span of clotheslines near the woodpiles.

At the bottom of the stairs, the Chinaman's two boys — Jan guessed about twelve or thirteen, sat on the floor, staring at a square of wood which was marked off in smaller squares, seventeen each way. On the playing surface, for it was evidently some sort of game, sat pebbles, light and dark. From time to time, each boy would break his concentration and pick up a new pebble with index and middle finger, slapping it down in a new intersection with a crack. After watching the play for a time, Jan could make no sense of it. There seemed to be no object, no prize or goal. The moves were not apparent or obvious. He had watched, fascinated, until he became aware of Gao Lung next to him. The old man moved like a housecat.

"Your clothes dry soon; it is warm and dry tonight," he said softly. "You find this game interesting?"

Jan rubbed his jaw. "Its purpose eludes me. What is the prize?"

"Ah." replied the other. "Must your opponent be beaten? Must you always seize something that he has? Perhaps a game with honour should have only as its object a reckoning between players, hey-san?"

Jan was puzzled. "What is the point of playing if there is no winner, no prize?"

"This very old game, perhaps four thousand year. The great Emperor Shun make this game to strengthen weak mind of young son. One hundred eighty white stones; one hundred eighty one black, for weaker player." The younger boy playing black looked up sharply, then slapped his next move loudly, saying something in Mandarin that Jan could not comprehend. The old man nodded approvingly, commenting in the same language. He turned to Jan.

"He gives warning that the other about to lose place. It is honourable. Purpose of game is to seize territory, by surrounding space, or opponent's stones. When much space taken, not necessary to, hmm" here he paused, looking for the right word. He slapped his hand lightly. " Ah. *Diminish* opponent. Is enough to say, 'I think there is nothing more to be done.' Hey-san?"

Jan looked back at the board. Fascinating idea, this, to align oneself with one's opponent to succeed. A new way to look at opportunity. He could see now that there were groupings in several places; several struggles were going on simultaneously at different parts of the board. Pebbles were being placed suddenly with rapid cracks. Each player needed to keep track of parallel campaigns. Jan watched until dusk, as the younger boy, spurred by his father's reference to the lesser player taking the black stones, went on to secure territory, in some cases surrounding his brother's pieces, until the elder conceded, it being obvious that the frontiers of the opposing groups were in contact. Gao Lung pointed out nuances of play, the small courtesies, strategies. It was at once complex and simple. Jan was entranced, and was eager to know more.

He was thinking about the game as he trudged along, having left Cramps pawing at the coins Jan had placed in his palm. It was an engaging idea that opponents could combine strategies to assist one another. He was tempted to dismiss it as having no practical application in the world he knew and understood, when he was abruptly hailed from some distance behind: "Halloo there! Where you going?"

He did not slow his pace, but turned his head suspiciously to consider the approaching newcomer. He was a short man, slender, with a neat but threadbare appearance. His clothes were those of a faded businessman, dusty, with scuffed boots. Not a single item belonged out on the trail. About thirty years old, Jan placed him, There was a quick, intelligent look about him, but the eyes seemed to dart from side to side, giving him the appearance of a man afraid of being overheard. He chewed tobacco and spat frequently, but only to punctuate sentences, or as Jan was to discover, for dramatic effect.

"Wait up," the stranger called. "Jesus. Where you going? I been near runnin' the last hour so. Don't you ever look back?" He drew abreast of Jan and took off his battered hat, mopping his brow as he did so. He was leading a heavily loaded mule, a big one, with large floppy ears. An American, Jan thought. They seemed to have a fondness for mules; big strong beasts they were. Intelligent. Jan had seen many of them in Pennsylvania, especially at work in the mines. But Canadians didn't seem to fancy them, unless you counted the railway companies. Yes, an American, this. Who else but an American would go to such an effort to have company on the trail?

"Jan Dalmynyshyn," he said, conscious of his accent. He kept moving.

"John? Good ta meetcha John. The name's Whyteas. Whyteas C. Snow. The C don't stand fer nothin', but my ma thought it sounded classy. My friends call me Whytey. Whytey Snow. Ain't thet hilarious? Medical Doctor, phrenologist, and purveyor of fine patent medicines and medical devices. Thought we might walk along apiece. Actually, no. I was hopin' to sit on your tailgate for a spell, but I seen you ain't got no draft animal. What happened to it?"

The man seemed harmless enough. He wore a pistol of some kind, but it was holstered high on his belt and had a flap covering the butt. There did not appear to be a rifle slung on his animal. There were no covetous glances at Jan's belongings, when he thought that Jan might not be looking.

"No horse." His expression was neutral. "Maybe one day."

"Son of a gun," said Snow quietly. "No horse. I ain't ever seen no man pull his own cart before. Seems like she goes along real nice though. You come all the way up from Winnipeg?"

It seemed unnecessarily intrusive, but Jan nodded his head. "It's not being so bad. No rain. But hot. Very hot."

"Youse can count your lucky jiggers that there ain't been no rain. Turn this miserable trail into a quagmire inside of an hour. You'd be in a fine pickle then. Whew. You gonna take a break soon? You look like you need one."

It was true. Though Jan had stripped to the waist, his body was soaked with sweat, and the *khustra* knotted around his head needed wringing out. But as Stefan had advised him, a man didn't just get tired and look for a place to flop down. There were natural breaks to a journey, and you just kept on until they showed themselves. They were approaching the ford of a small creek, and where the bank was shaded by a tangle of poplars seemed to be a good place to rest. Lowering the shafts, Jan unslung his harness. Snow hobbled his mule, which immediately started to tear at the tufted grasses as if this were its last meal. Jan walked down to the stream, untying his head scarf. Behind him, Snow began to whistle noisily as he clattered with his pots and snapped dead sticks for a fire.

The cold water was restorative. Jan mopped himself with his scarf, then tied it around his scalp. Straightening, he could see that Snow had a fire going, and a coffee pot set at its edge. He was chewing on something, and he offered a piece of it to Jan.

"Smoked sausage. Go on. Best you'll ever eat. Picked some up from Mennonites down south a here. Go on." Jan took the morsel, examined it warily, then popped it in his mouth. It was good, and he snatched suddenly as Snow flipped him another piece. Jan walked back to his cart and began to check it, looking for loose pieces, tightening knots. Snow called over to him. "Sit down man. Give it a rest. Coffee's almost ready. Ain't had my coffee today, and I just ain't any good without it."

Jan shook his head. "No time. Got to get moving."

Snow seemed incredulous: "You call that a break? I been following you all mornin', and your pace didn't hanker for a minute! You gonna kill yerself! Come and set a spell; it's my coffee, and yer plenty welcome to it."

Jan thought for a moment. Who was this man, and why was he being so friendly? Gestures of friendship made Jan suspicious; all of his instincts were alert for betrayal. This was how he perceived the human condition: always seek the advantage. The surest way to disengage a man's natural defences was to offer friendship. Still, he could not deny the feeling he had of isolation. And here was a man who was clearly better off than he, and offering to share what he did have, so far, with nothing asked in return. He shrugged, and returned to the fire, squatting down beside Snow.

"Good," the other said, tossing Jan a tin cup.

The liquid was lukewarm, and tasted stale. He had developed a taste for coffee in Pennsylvania; coming north, tea seemed to be the preferred drink, though coffee was catching on. He made a face. Snow caught the grimace.

"OK. OK. I'm the first to admit that it's not the world's best coffee. But it ain't bad for yesterday's leftovers, don't ya think?"

Jan did not reply, but asked, "What is a phren ... phrenologist? What does this do?"

Snow laughed and spat mightily into the fire. "I'm glad you asked, my friend. What it means is that I can tell a lot about you just from examining the shape of your head. Each bump and hollow tells me something different. It's been around for a thousand years - phrenology, that is, not your head - but only recently has it developed to a science."

Reaching up to his scalp, Jan felt the irregularities dubiously. "From this you tell ... what?" he asked, his expression showing his disbelief.

"Well now, a number of things. I'd have to do a full examination, a course, but even from here I can see things that tell me a lot about you." The look on Jan's face was unchanged.

"You've got - everyone's got - forty-two different organs what makes up the brain. It's true. Each one's got a mental power that is greater or lesser in different men. I could show youse a chart; it's all been worked out more'n a hundred years ago.

"You've got yer affective powers, comprised of yer propensities and yer sentiments. Then you've got yer intellectual powers, both perceptive and reflective." He smiled unctuously. "I know this's complicated stuff, being highly technical an' all, but here, let me give you an example:

"Right here - " he gestured to the top of his forehead with two fingers. "You've got prominent, well-defined contours that indicate to me just by lookin', straight off, that you think a lot 'bout things. Always ponderin' the why of it. An' them ridges behind yer ears; well now, I couldn't say without checkin', but I'd guess you're a pretty ornery kinda fellow, if someone was ta get between you an' what yer want.

"Anyway - " he looked into his mug, "It's all scientific, and takes plenty a trainin'. But I'd need ta do it properly. Could give ya half off my regular fee."

Jan wasn't listening at this point. How could anyone know so much about a man, not having spent more than a couple of hours with him? It was as if Snow had peered through a window on his soul. If he was a cheat, he was a damn good one. He shook his head, and dug at the embers with a twig. A strange man, this.

When the sun's rays slanted low over the southwestern sky, and the first mosquitoes started to make themselves felt, the two men halted for the night. Jan felt exhausted, though this day's toil had been no different than the previous. It was Snow, he decided. The man talked unceasingly, barely pausing to take breath. It was becoming apparent why he had chased Jan; for him, connection with other human beings was nourishment. Jan needed large periods of time in which to think, to reflect. He wanted to practise his English, calling out to the vacant prairie, without fear of being taken for a madman. He needed to recite his beloved Shevchenko in his mother tongue, without attracting attention from those who would not understand. He felt self-conscious speaking English to this man, for he felt it was only a matter of time before his thick accent drew some adverse comment. Wearily, he pulled at a twist of dried bully-beef, as he built a small fire. Later, having draped his cheesecloth around the wagon bed, he crawled in.

"I'll be jiggered," said Snow, pushing his hat back. "That keeps the bugs out?" He looked at his own bedroll doubtfully as he took a quick pull at the small bottle he kept in his coat.

Jan nodded. "You can try."

"Whew," breathed the other man, tucking away his drink without offering.

"I'd just as soon not sleep another night with a blanket around my head. Them beasties is fierce. Suck a man's blood dry, they would." Without further comment, he scuttled on hands and knees in beside Jan, dragging his sleeping robes. Jan lay on his back, as he preferred, but the other man lay on his belly, resting his chin on the back of his hands, staring at the dying embers of the fire. His breath was noticibly sharp with the reek of liquor.

He lifted the screen to spit out his wad into the fire. "Jesus! Lookit them hordes a flies!" Swatting and cursing, he tucked the edge of the cloth under; Jan sighed and rolled over, falling asleep even as the other man continued to natter.

The next morning, they were away in the false light, before the sun had spread its roseate fingers across the eastern sky. Snow had started to grumble, but when it become clear that Jan would leave regardless of complaint, he left off. For a time, uncharacteristically, Snow walked along in silence. Perhaps he was sulking, but his expression seemed nonplused. By and by he turned to Jan.

"Where you going? What's at the end of the road for you, anyway? Youse in such a dad-blame hurry. Fer what? Too late for crops. Three months to winter, anyway ..." He looked at Jan expectantly. "Not that it matters to me, a course. I can wait fer my coffee. Jazus: Where you going, anyway, such a hurry."

Jan pondered this question. He was loath to share anything of himself with anyone. This stranger was nothing to him. Yet it seemed to be the way of things in North America, particularly out west. Everyone wanted to know your business. Where you were going, and where you were living. How much money you had, and who were your kin. It was not that there was malice in it; since most everyone was dirt poor, it seemed more a matter of misery loving company. It was a bit like the Old Country; well, back in Kameneta-Podolak.

He sighed, conscious that Snow was looking at him. Something inside him was giving way. Small, like straws being washed from a mud dam, but tangible nonetheless.

"Land," he said. "I go to have my own land. I have not seen it yet, and the winter is coming. This is why I must not waste time. It is possible to rain ..."

Snow pursed his lips. "Land, eh. Well, from what I hear, you'll need to go north a Dauphin; maybe even over to the Carrot River valley in the Saskatchewan. All the good land's been grabbed up by the speculators and the bluebloods ages ago, 'less'n you've registered."

Jan felt a thin stab of panic, which he suppressed by leaning into his harness and quickening his pace slightly. Snow noticed this, keeping up.

"Hey, I'm sure there's lots -"

He was cut off. "I am told that there is plenty of homesteads. I have the name of the Dominion agent. Others have told me there is much land with plenty of wood."

"Of course! I forgot. You Galicians don't want open land. Beats me all to hell why you wouldn't want land you could sink a plow into straight off, but there you go. Sure, there's plenty a land if youse not averse to clearin' it. Plenty fer the askin'."

These last words came out hurriedly, as if he was afraid that he had offended Jan. This was a new feeling for Jan, whose recollection for more than two years was that few showed him even the barest tracings of respect, and no one deferred to him. He felt always on his guard, and there was no obvious reason why that should change. Snow was chattering again.

"Never wanted no land of my own. No siree. Too much of a ... well, holds you down too much, I'd say." He jabbed the air with a skinny finger for emphasis. "God knows there's easier ways to turn a dollar."

Jan cocked a suspicious eye at his new companion, but it was hard to take him seriously. "It does not look as if you are a man of privilege. What are your bundles holding?"

Snow took off his hat and gestured grandly as he trudged along. "I have here the newest patent medicines and devices of medical therapy available. Some fine cure-alls. I'll be offering them for sale as we hit the larger centers. They won't last long." He looked up at Jan speculatively. "There's nothing wrong with you, is there? "

There was a half smile on Jan's face. Snow saw it and chuckled. "I didn't think so. You look healthy as a ... well, healthy as a horse." The irony seized both men at the same time and they both began to laugh. Snow had a high whickering laugh, which made the joke seem even merrier, and they both stopped to regain their composure.

His smile fading, Snow looked away. "Let's get going. I got my own reasons." He moved briskly on, and for a time he was silent. This suited Jan well enough, and neither men spoke until, nearing a copse of scrub oak, they saw a figure sitting on a length of deadfall, his horse standing not far off. He had seen them, that much was certain, and Snow stopped suddenly, his face working.

"Sonofabitch!" he muttered, with an emotion Jan could not identify. "I'm done fer."

# vi

Sergeant Rishton Jones stripped off his gauntlets and tucked them under his bedroll. It was too hot for gloves. He took off the broad-brimmed Stetson hat that nearly all the Mounted Police members had adopted in place of the silly pillbox hat that was still official dress. Cowboy hats, the brass sneered. Quite out of order. But what did they know about months in the saddle? He had stitched a handkerchief inside the rear liner, so that it hung down to protect his neck from the heat and the flies. With a finger, he wiped the sweat from the inner band, and settled his thin haunches on a length of deadfall. A trim man, there were premature flecks of gray in his longish hair and heavy mustache. He had not shaved in several days, and he wore his dusty red uniform jacket open.

The flannel undershirt was grubby from the trail, as indeed was his entire kit, from cap to high leather boots.

The weather promised little relief; the sun beat down on him like a forge, but he paid it little mind. In the British navy, he'd had his fill of cold and wet. One night a storm so fierce that his own ship nearly foundered brought a terrible sound to the men on deck . Later he would discover that a shipment of prize cats being taken to New York by the steam packet *Alice,* had been put overboard by a superstitious crew, in the hope that this would save them. Jones had never forgotten the hideous wailing of hundreds of drowning cats, and he always associated rain storms with that morose event.

The insects hummed in the tall grass as he squinted off in the distance. Two men. He could make out two men; or was it a single man leading a cart? He replaced his hat and took a bell-shaped meerschaum pipe from the upper breast pocket of his serge tunic, tamped it full with a practiced ritual, and crossed one leg over the other. Hunched forward, he puffed comfortably, waiting for the little procession to cross his path.

Lost in his musings, Jones suddenly raised his head. The little party had stopped, still a way off. One man leading a mule. The other ... the other pulling a cart behind him. Odd. But why had they stopped? This attracted his professional suspicions, but he did not move. His revolver was in its holster tied to the saddle. He hated wearing the thing, and always took it off once away from barracks. The carbine was scabbarded on the offside of the horse now grazing not ten feet away. His eyes drew back to the two men, and narrowed.

The man with the cart stepped forward, and after a moment, the other followed, hurrying a little to catch up. The first man was big, well-muscled, and stripped to the waist. His body shone with sweat. The other seemed dressed like a dandy, or one of those eastern swanks out for a little taste of the frontier, but the outfit had seen better days. His instincts telegraphed calming signals, and he saw no reason to take precautionary steps.

Quickly they came on, and it became apparent that the big man would haul past the seated policeman without so much as a word. The man with the mule seemed uncertain of what was required, looking from his implacable companion to the policeman and back. As they came abreast, the sergeant stood up.

"Now hold on, boys; steady on a moment." The gravel in his voice did not disguise a British accent, faded now. It seemed to lend his modest command a certain courtesy. The two men stopped, looking at him. The shorter, older man began to wheedle: "Aw, what we done, officer?"

"Seems passing strange that you boys would come upon a man on the trail, and not pay him so much as a 'how-do-you-do'. You wouldn't be on the run, or anything like that, would you?" There was no sternness in his face.

There was nervous laughter from one; stony silence from the other. Jones had seen it before in other newcomers; that resentment, that suspicion of police officials. Funny how assumptions and beliefs maintain themselves, as long as they serve the function which brought them into existence. He remembered the first time he had encountered a uniform up close. Ten years of age, he had been running along the wharf at Thames Pool. At the time he was a 'fetch boy', a messenger for the Thomas Cook Travel Company, when he crashed headlong into a Cornet of the 11th Hussars. A newly commissioned ranker, he was done up full dress in pipeclayed belting and gleaming high boots. Jones remembered looking up at a magnificently whiskered face and bulging eyes topped by a splendid forage cap. Here was the pride of England off to the Crimea. The soldier laughed him off, though the boy's head had driven mightily into his crotch. The laugh in retrospect seemed more of a gasp.

"God bless you sir," cried Jones, doffing his cloth cap. "Hurrah for England!"

The officer had tottered off, fluttering his hand dismissively at the lad. How the scarlet trimmed warrior had seemed the embodiment of a proud country. He could see that in the way passersby nodded, or touched the brim of their hats. But these people ... his thoughts came back to the men before him.

These people. This man in particular, the Galician. Official costumes sent powerful signals, as it was intended. Red serge had been chosen for the Mounted Police because it was felt the Indians would respect the Queen's soldiers. He recalled stories about the original patrol out of Macleod in '75, where poorly outfitted members picked up the blue greatcoats discarded by deserting American pony soldiers. That patrol narrowly avoided death at the hands of marauding bands of Sioux, who took them for the hated 'horse soldiers'. And if it hadn't been for the interventions of Jerry Potts, the legendary half breed scout, they would have been butchered, so great was the rage inspired by the military dress of the United States 7th Cavalry. What had this immigrant suffered at the hands of uniformed men, that he should be so suspicious, so resentful?

Jones spoke to the American. "Jones, Rishton Jones. Sergeant of North West Mounted Police." He offered his hand.

The other took it, gingerly, nervously. It was wet to the touch. Why was the man's hands sweating? Jones was prepared to wager a month's pay this one was on the lam for something.

"Whyteas. Whyteas C. Snow. The C don't stand fer nothin'; it's just that my ma thought it'd give me a bit a class. Heh heh. Everyone calls me Whytey."

"Whytey," said Jones, nodding his head and looking over at the loaded animal. "What're you packin', Whytey?"

There was a curious tension between the three men. No menace, but a tension.

"Medicines an' medical supplies. Patent devices an' the like. Have a look if yer want. All first class stuff." He warmed to his presentation. "Hemorrhoids? Hernia? The blinks? Need some starch in your wedding tackle? I can fix yer good."

"I bet you could, Whytey," said Jones, seemingly losing interest for the moment. He turned to Jan who stood in his traces with the faintest shadow of a scowl. Putting out his hand, he said, "Jones. Sergeant of Mounted ... well, I guess that is not exactly right. My horse here has thrown a shoe, which kind of leaves me unmounted. I suppose you and I have something in common straight away."

For a very long moment it looked as if Jan would not take his hand. There was nothing threatening in the officer's eyes. If anything, they were neutral. His gaze was direct. By this time in his life Jan had developed something of a beast's instinct for survival. Trust no one. Expose yourself as little as possible to others, and keep the guard up. But now and then, all that was unnecessary in the circumstances, though he still preferred to err on the side of caution. But the memory of the stranger who had returned to help him after the thugs he was with had toppled his cart, still bothered him. He could still see the outstretched hand.

"Jan Dalmynyshyn." He gripped the other man's palm. Jones could feel the strength in the callused hand.

"You boys planning to stop in the next piece or so? I'd be pleased to sit down with you a moment or two." He took out a massive pocket watch, flipping it open. The brass cover, worn smooth by frequent handling, glinted like sunlight released. " 'Bout time for the midday feed, I'd say. You interested?"

Snow chortled, relief evident in his expression. "Why shore! Never too early fer a snack, I always say. I was thinkin' of how nice a cup a coffee'd go down just now. Why don't we ease on over to that willow thicket yonder, an' settle in?"

The three men sauntered over to the spot where Snow had pointed, not more than a stone's throw from the trail. The tension was still there to be sure, but not so palpable. They had not taken the measure of the newcomer yet, nor he of they. But all three had private mysteries they guarded carefully. It is a canon of manhood that he who acts without sufficient thought is certain to fall into danger eventually. So regarding each other tentatively, carefully, each according to his nature, they sat down to break bread together. Behind them, a breeze ruffled the willows for a moment, like a sigh.

Putting his pipe back between his teeth, Jones puffed thoughtfully, squinting his eyes as the smoke plume masked his face for a moment. He pushed the broad brim of his hat back with his thumb. It made him look more benign; jauntier, maybe. The others looked at him, waiting for him to begin. He was the authority. His dirty uniform a constant reminder of the power of government to command obedience. Jones took his pipe and tamped it with a stone the size of his thumbnail.

"Either one of you gentlemen got a sharp knife? I'd like to cut up my tobacco into some decent sized plugs, and the blade I have can't hold an edge for love or money."

Without thinking, Jan dug out the knife he had taken from the two would-be thieves, and offered it to him by its end. The skull gleamed in the sunlight. Jan cursed himself inwardly. It was stupid to have shown anyone something he had stolen, especially a policeman. He felt himself getting warm, as he watched Jones' sudden interest.

"Say. Isn't this a fine snickersnee!" The sergeant turned it over in his hands for a moment. Then bent to cutting the dark brown plug. He continued, speaking out of the side of his mouth, clenching the pipe firmly between his teeth, saying, "Whew. Sharp as a stropped razor!"

Jones lit his pipe and puffed calmly, his eyes flickering back and forth from the American to Jan.

"Anyway. I'm looking for some Indians. I don't suppose you chaps have seen any?" Without waiting for an answer, he went on. "No, I don't suppose you have. If they don't want you to see them, then you don't see them." He looked at them, his face an interrogatory.

It was Snow that answered. "We ain't seen nothin'. What'd they do, anyways? Didn't murderize no one, I hope." He looked around with the faintest hint of a shudder. "They can be real savage, I've heard."

"Now where'd you hear such a thing, Whytey?" said Jones amiably. "We haven't had many massacres in recent years. There hasn't been a scalp lifted in these parts for, what? A month?" He eyed Jan, with the barest flicker of a wink.

"My ol' man tol' me," said Snow peevishly, ignoring Jones' feeble attempt at humour. "He come to Red River just after the Sioux troubles in '62. Whew. The stories o' torture 'n horror, of what th' Sioux did to decent folk. Burnin' alive, 'n such. Broiled over their own stoves. Scalpin' an' chopping off a man's nuts.

"Then when the Indians 'n breeds took over at Red River in '70, they shot down a man in cold blood, just for disagreein' with them. Th' ol' man seen it with his own eyes. He was there. Then they buried th' poor sonofabitch alive. Once a savage, always a savage, is what I say. They don't think like ordinary people. Shit and damnation. That's all we need; bunch a murderin' thievin' scalpin' Indians sneakin' around." It was a speech delivered without his usual enthusiasm, and he fell silent, darting glances here and there.

Jones shook his head. "Who said anything about murder? I simply said I was looking for some Indians -"

Jan remembered the Clement's dog. "What is it said that these people do?" he asked the policeman.

"Well, to tell you the complete truth, they've been doing a little stealing here and there. Nothing too serious. Not to get too excited about, but they are a nuisance. And since taking property without colour of right is an offence under the federal criminal code, that's where I come in." He looked dreamily off in the distance.

"Yes sir. Thieves, thugs, swindlers and bully-boys. That's my regular diet. This is why it's a welcome relief to rest a short spell with regular chaps like yourselves." He looked hard at Snow, who seemed uncomfortable under his gaze. Jan had the uneasy feeling that this policeman was never off duty. Even his disarming manner seemed calculated to advance interrogation.

There was no harm in offering the information. "People I stop with south-east of Tanner's have things missing; dog killed."

Jones nodded. "Dead dog's sure sign. I've been following them for a while. Counted up eight dogs so far. Probably be a dozen afore we're done." He handed back the knife to Jan, after another long look at it.

Snow looked puzzled. "If yer followin' them, and yer know they're killin' folks' animals, then why don't yer run them in?"

Clasping his fingers behind his head, Jones puffed contentedly at his pipe, tilting his head back. "Now that's a good question." He paused, taking his pipe out to spit a mote from his lips. "Yes sir. A good question.

"These renegades are off the File Hills Agency up the Qu'Appelle. Not far to the west of the border. Now, there's four reserves at File Hills, see; Starblanket, *Okanese*, Little Black Bear, and one to the south of all of them, *Peepeekeesis*. Not one of them but *Peepeekeesis* has more than a pot to piss in.

"Now the agent at File Hills is an interesting chap. Bill Graham. His father was head of Indian Affairs here in Manitoba; guess how young Billie got his job? Anyway, Bill's favorite word is 'de-indianize'. He thinks that the salvation of the aborigines lies in civilizing them - making white men out of them." There was a tone to his voice, Jan noticed, that suggested considerable skepticism.

Snow caught it too. "Well what's wrong with that? Helluva lot better than sneakin' around stealin' an' eatin' dogs and God knows what else. Besides, everyone knows theys all gonna die off, anyways. Nearly all gone in the Dakotas."

Jones stretched his leg out, rolling his foot inward so that the spur on his tall boot was out of the way. The yellow stripe on his breeches was almost obscured by trail dirt He batted at it absently with the back of his hand, and the dust rose in small puffs. "No doubt about that. Thinking is that there won't be a red man left inside of ten years, only his breed cousins. Between disease and drink, hard to see how that'll turn around much, and the way we treat them, we're not helping. Which brings me back to Graham.

"You see, *Peepeekeesis* is his pet de-Indianizing project. He starves the other reserves to build up *Peepeekeesis*. Moves some out - the ones that cling to the old ways - and allows in the Christians and farmers, and the industrial school graduates. They get all his attention."

He dug at the bowl of his pipe with a dirty fingernail. "But just in case you fellows get the idea that somehow *Peepeekeesis* was a bed of roses, let me put you straight. Back in '85, the top man for Indian Affairs was a fellow by the name of Reid. Hayter Reid I think it was. Was an agent out of Battleford at one time. His thought was that you could civilize primitives who were working with stone tools a short time ago, all at once. So he issued instructions that no modern farm machinery was to be purchased for their wards — they had to make their own. So working with sharpened sticks, and the like, was the only way that Indians would appreciate the modern reaper and such. Heh heh!" He laughed without mirth.

Jan thought of the tools of his homeland; the hard implements he had wielded in his youth. Not a one save the wooden plough of his neighbours was drawn other than by a man or a woman's back. And here money was available for native people to have what was needed to become self sufficient in this land, and were not permitted. It seemed madness. Did a man need to put his hand in a fire to know it was hot? Could a man not learn from other men?

Jones continued, weaving the thread of his tale like a master storyteller. "So Graham thought that this was good sense. When one of his deputies, fellow by the name of Schmidt had a surprise inspection from one of the new inspectors — Hamilton this man's name was — it was found that the machinery that was invoiced to the federal government for the reserve was sitting on Schmidt's farm, well-used. When Hamilton complained to Graham, he was fired for his trouble. Get the picture? Nope. Things aren't good on any of these reserves, especially Starblanket, which is where our friends are from."

"Do you pursue the man called Graham?" asked Jan.

Jones laughed his dry cackle. "There's no criminal complaint. Who would complain? Not Hamilton, if he ever wanted to work in this country again. The red man? He's got bigger things to complain about, and no one's listening anyway. Nope, there's doing right, and there's doing the right things. I learned a long time ago that one can't always correct wrongs head on. And there's some things bigger than a man's ability to change them. Believe me on this."

Clearing his throat and spitting, Snow broke in. "You still haven't answered me: you know who they are; you know they's thievin'; why don't yers run them in?"

"Well," Jones answered, "I suppose you might say, I am. You see, I have no complaint from any of the farmers that've been troubled. Nothing more than a dog or two, and a row of carrots here and there. Sure, it's an annoyance; some of them are plenty pissed up about it, but they chalk it on the side of the cost of doing business in this country. When this lot jumped the reserve, we were requested to bring them back, because they didn't have permission to leave. No pass, see.

"But there's a problem. The pass system was imposed by the agents on their own, as punishment for the rebellion in '85. But there's no actual law to that effect, see, though these agents think that they are a law unto themselves. So while I have no actual authority to bring them in, I did take an oath to keep the Queen's peace. So I let the rabbit run to see what he do. Good advice, boys. Wished I'd learned it early on."

He tapped the side of his pipe against a stone, watching the still warm ash tumble out. "They're heading back. Like everybody does sooner or later. The tracks we make cross and criss-cross themselves and others. Big circular route, to be sure, but heading back. My guess is that they seen the land transformed. Settlements and farms, railroads and telegraph lines. No game. And everywhere disapproving, unwelcoming people. Nothing for them but resentment, thick as auntie's jam. And they sure as hell know I'm following them."

Jan pondered these last words. Disapproving, resenting people. He could understand that. More than the labour, the hunger, more than anything else, that was the thing that made his own pilgrimage so difficult. How much more must it be so for the people who were first of this land, and now outnumbered, and who were on the verge of disappearing. *Os de liudy, nasha slava, Ukrainy*, he thought to himself, in the poet's words. The glory of Ukraine lies in its people. Not so here, it seemed. Or at least, not all people.

He stood up, shaking sentiment from him like trail dust. The day was passing on, and he wanted to get some distance behind him before the mosquitoes came out at sundown. The other two stood up as well.

Jones tucked his pipe away. "I suppose it'll be all right if I walk along for a stretch?" This seemed to be a statement more than a question, borne of years of exercising authority over others. Jan could almost see the turmoil in Snow. No, he did not want the policeman along. But he did want the protection the red coat offered. Without further comment, the three men, cart, mule and limping horse formed a caravan, and headed off to the shaggy bluffs that marked the western edge of the Riding Mountain.

# vii

The campfire had burned low. Now that wood was more plentiful, a bigger fire could be set, for the nights were getting chill, even though the prairie sun was scorching by day. There were now three men draped under the wagon bed, for Jones had stayed with them for two days. He was planning to have his horse re shod in Dauphin, or 'Dogtown' as most still called it. This day, he had even stripped off his red jacket, and had pulled Jan's vehicle for a while. He was fit, but at the end of a ten mile walk, he gladly surrendered the cart's shafts.

"Don't know how you do it, man. But you have my admiration."

That night, as they lay near the fire, contemplating the sun's glorious extinguishment across the western horizon, Jones raised his jaw in the direction of Snow's pack.

"What manner of oddments be you peddling, Whytey?"

Snow stood up, stretching and farting, stamping his feet as he walked over to his gear. He passed back a quart-sized brown bottle marked *Corning's Mixture - The Remedial Elixir to Kings and Popes*. And below that, mysteriously, 'patent pending'. Jan sniffed it suspiciously; it was redolent of wood and tar. Its taste, however, was like the vodka peddled to the oil workers, though perhaps thicker, more bitter. He threw back a heavy draft, and passed it to Jones, who sipped at it tentatively. Jan immediately felt a loosening of his neck and shoulder muscles, and a slight euphoric rise. He reached for the bottle again. Jones' face worked as he swallowed; he exhaled through his teeth as he exclaimed: "Well now, doesn't that tingle your pisser?"

"Gentlemen, may I have your undivided attention," Snow announced with a flourish, taking out a wooden box with two miniature drawers built into the front. Holding up a metal ring lined with a series of tiny spikes inside a protective spring, he gestured with the open palm of his other hand. He was transformed in speech and bearing.

"From Dr. Foote's Sanitary Bureau, 'The Timely Warning Device'. Prevents nocturnal emissions by waking the wearer. Weighs but two drams and saves pounds of drugs and worry. It has been allowed a patent by the U.S. Government, as it is most useful in the early stages of Spermatorrhoea - that dreaded loss of vital substances which results in nervous weakness, spinal trouble, insanity and paralysis. It causes no discomfort to the relaxed organ, and does not excite it as do other articles intended for a similar purpose. Price: two dollars. No further nocturnal emissions and resultant weaknesses, or money cheerfully refunded."

He rummaged further, both Jan and Jones remaining silent, even awestruck. A man would as soon put a number four wolf trap on his private parts, their expressions declaimed.

"Aha!" Snow held aloft a large green bottle with a large label upon which was written, *The Sorrell Company, Hot Springs, Arkansas.* He tapped it with a short, thin cane he'd dug from his pack. "Antidote for poisoned blood. There is nothing in life more discouraging than realizing you have impure blood. It leads to dismal thoughts, and frequently to suicide. You feel shut off, alone; afraid of contaminating your friends. Nothing but misery. But the marvelous hot springs treatment drives all impurities from the blood, freeing you from even the most violent forms of this malady. Only fifty cents per bottle, and you'll save that much on the free recipes for emetics alone!"

He was into it now, standing and calling upon his audience, eloquent and persuasive. "Step up, my fine friends. What ails you? Have the doctors given up? Have you no relief from disease and irregular bodily function? Do you suffer from that which is only whispered about? Glandular reluctance?"

The other two had taken several long pulls at the brown bottle, and were starting to snicker; their reserve was failing.

"Do you have: nervous prostration? lung troubles? gout or locomotor ataxia? writer's cramp? giddiness, dyspepsia, female weakness, prolapsus, dropsy or varicose veins?" With a flourish of his cane, he shouted suddenly: "Then consider *Professor Wilson's Magneto Conservative Garments!*"

Jan was awed: dyspepsia? prolapsus? dropsy? Diseases he had never heard of.

With a rattling din, Snow unpacked several shiny pieces of galvanized tin suitments, riddled with hundreds rows of tiny holes. Small leather straps were mounted at intervals.

"Behold the nerve cap. Seven dollars! And you'll never suffer headaches or toothaches again!" He place the helmet on his head. "The nerve and lung invigorator. Twelve dollars." He grunted as he struggled to secure the straps for the large chest piece behind him.

"Jesus, Snow," chuckled Jones. "You look like a knight in armor. Where's your lance? Say, is that suit bullet-proof, or is that how those holes got made in the first place? Your last customers, maybe..." He broke off and began to cackle in earnest.

Jan grinned and swigged at the bottle before handing it back to Jones. Snow looked ridiculous.

"Now don't laugh my friends. I'm having trouble here because my waistcoat's a tad too thick. The garment is to be worn next to the skin..."

"Next to the *skin*?" roared Jones. Jan could not help himself. The thought of all that pierced metal against bare flesh, as a form of disease prevention, seemed as ludicrous as it looked. He joined in his companion's laughter; as it took them, they roared, falling backwards. Jan drummed his heels. Snow was unmoved, and continued, oblivious.

"I have here bottles of *Brewster's Medicated Electricity*, a perfect, functioning, electric battery in every bottle. A safe and positive cure for headache, catarrh, neuralgia and smite. It will hold its strength for two years, provided it is well corked. For only a single dollar for each bottle, you'll not have another sick day in your life, if taken daily as a preventative." He took a generous sip, and the tin hat fell off at the same time as the breastplate slipped from his shoulder, to hooting and applause from the two men.

"Electricity. Yes, indeed. The wonder cure of the coming century, available now in various appliances. Consider the *Mioxrl Electric* body battery: nature's vitalizer to build up and strengthen the sexual organs and liver. Forget those dangerous copper belts charged with acid. This continuous current device addresses neuralgia, lumbago, restless nights, incipient paralysis, falling of the womb, lack of vital force, decay and seminal weakness." He addressed Jones boldly, staring sternly at the teary eyed man:

"Will you be fitted sir? Let me give your vital organs new life, and banish shaky nerves and night sweats forever."

Jones was red-faced with laughter. "Stick *that* thing under my woolies? A continuous electric current? I'll bet it shall give me vitality. Hee hee! Snow! Do people actually buy this stuff?""

Snow's capacity to entertain and promote was boundless. His stage presence was considerable; his elocution remarkable. He was animated by his products, many of which seemed aimed at the darkest anxieties of a credulous society overwhelmingly preoccupied with sexual vitality and the elimination functions. He regaled them with devices, pills, potions, condoms, and suppositories that they took for oversize candles, until they faded under the influence of *Corning's Mixture*. It was a sorry trio who awoke to the steep rays of the late morning sun.

Not one of the three had much to say for the next two days. It was as if the release had left each man stripped and unguarded, and time was required to reestablish boundaries between them. Even Snow had fallen uncharacteristically silent. They were a day out of Dog Town, or Dauphin as civic pride now insisted. The policeman had not given any cause for alarm, though all his conversation could be taken as gentle probing. They had seen no sign of the Indians Jones had been following, but "they were there, never fear, if you want the complete truth," he had said, and given that they were on foot and probably hungry in the bargain, not far off either. This too, had made their indulgence in intoxicants the other night seem doubly foolish.

When they could see the smudge in the distance that was Dog Town, they elected to stop for the night in the lee of a copse near a small creek. As the sun began its decline beyond the prairie horizon, Jones began his evening ritual of rubbing down his horse with handfuls of black mud, to protect it from the flies. Jan was rolling out the muslin to drape the wagon, when it became apparent that the three men were not alone.

"Bloody Saints in merciful Heaven!" gasped Snow. "Hist, Sergeant!"

Looking around, Jones saw that at the edge of their campsite, where the willows were the most dense, there stood eight dark faced men, one nearly a head taller than the others. Jones turned back to his mount, scooping handfuls of soil inside the legs where the hair was the thinnest. Snow gaped in disbelief. He looked back at the motley band of Indians, seeing that their dress, though European in cut, was badly worn. Each one wore a hat which looked as if it had been run over by cattle. Their appearance would almost have been comical, were it not for the air of desperation about them. To Snow's considerable anxiety, one of them advanced a few steps and raised an ancient musket from under the dirty blanket he had draped over his shoulders.

"Food." he said simply, his voice hoarse.

Jan stood up, and reached for the flour bag on the wagon bed. The man with the gun spun around and pointed it at him, shaking his head. Jan dropped his arms. Back to the policeman, who by now had turned to face them, he spoke again, "*Micim.*" Food. He shook; whether from rage or from hunger, Jan did not know.

Jones had his hands on his hips. He was unarmed, as usual, and his dusty red serge jacket was slung over a willow bush. His flannel underwear was grubby, with great dark crescents of dried sweat under his arms. He had not shaved in two days, though his kit was already laid out for the morning, as he did not want to get to the post in Dauphin "looking like a vagabond", as he had put it. Nevertheless, for all his tatterdemalion appearance, Jones still exuded authority. He eyed the newcomers confidently; his voice was clear, almost conversational.

"You're a little early for a supper, but I think we can throw an extra can of water in the soup, eh boys?" He looked over to Jan and Snow, who watched wordlessly.

The man with the gun had a thin, nasty face. His eyes narrowed, and he advanced upon Jones with quick, short steps. He looked up at Jones, who seemed to tower in front of him, and spat.

"*Kakepa 'tisiw!*" he said, looking at his comrades over his shoulder. He is a fool.

With a sudden motion he struck the side of Jones' head with the gun barrel. The slap sounded sharply in the evening air. Jones' hat fell to the ground.

The policeman put his hand to his temple, which was bleeding. The other man backed off and repeated, "Food." And looking at Jan and Snow, he said, "Get food now." Now the gun was held at the hip, the barrel sloping upward, pointing at Jones.

The two men scrambled to the wagon, as Jones looked at his hand, stained with his own blood.

"Look here, don't go filling your boots," he said stepping forward. "You're welcome to what we have, but there's no need for this. We mean you no harm."

"You follow us. You take us to your prison where our *nistesak*, our brothers, die."

Jones shook his head. "That's not the plan. But put the gun away. Give it to me." He said this in a gentle tone, and stepped forward, reaching for the musket pointing at him. With a soft boom, the muzzle belched flame that set the front of Jones' shirt afire, and pitched him on his back with great force. He lay near the legs of his nervous horse, unmoving. The stench of black powder hung in the air. The Indian looked at the prostrate body in seeming disbelief, dropping the weapon. As one, they all turned and disappeared into the dusk.

How much time had passed? A hundred heartbeats? Twenty? Jan could not believe the suddenness of the violence. He had seen desperate men before, yet there was innate to the thoughts of rational men the insistent denial of evil. This cannot be happening. The worst will not come to pass. He breathed deeply, willing the shock to leave his brain, his body. He was vaguely aware of Snow's sniveling behind him.

"Jesus, Jesus, o Lord sweet Jesus. Look what they done."

Jan knelt beside Jones. The man was still alive, but there was considerable blood spreading across the front of his shirt. Opening the sticky buttons, the wound looked ugly, and seemed to be where the heart lay; Jan wondered why he was not dead.

"Snow. You are doctor. You can help." Snow did not move, merely twisted his hat in his hands. He looked as if all the fears of a wretched childhood had caught up with him at once. Jan thought he might tumble to the ground.

"Get the medicine. Help me. He should not die."

"Why'd he hafta go fer th' gun? Tell me that. It's his own fault. Stupid man. Just like a lawman ta do sumpin' stupid like that."

Jan left the unconscious man and approached Snow. Without pausing, he hit the peddler with the back of his hand. Snow went down like a fallen balk of timber. He yowled like a man mortally stricken, and well he might have been had Jan caught his temple rather than the top of his skull.

"I do not ask again," said Jan grimly, turning back to Jones. "Get what is needed."

Snow fairly bawled. "I can't do it!"

Jan turned to face him again, his fists clenched. Snow cringed, backing away into a seated position, holding his head with one hand, and putting the other up as if to ward off Jan.

"I would if I could, but I'm not a doctor. Not a real one, anyways. I'm a helper to an animal doctor. I only read about doctorin'..."

Jan looked with a puzzled frown at the pack of medical supplies that Snow had only moments before taken off his mule. Snow saw his glance.

"It's not my stuff; well it is. I came by it - I bought it - I mean, it *is* mine." He fell desperately over his lies like a man in a pack of wild dogs.

Jan looked at him with disgust. "Come. Help. Whatever you can do. Bring a cloth." He knelt again over the fallen man. Snow came snuffling up beside him, with a piece of blanketing. Jan stuffed it over the wound and rebuttoned the shirt now soggy with blood. Resting back on his knees, he looked at the unconscious policeman helplessly. Snow lowered his head like a dog at a fallen pot roast.

"Turn 'im over. Then we'll see if th' bullet came out, or if it's still in there. It's better if it came out, long as nothin' vital was nicked." Together they eased him onto his side. Snow produced a small folding knife, and slit the mountie's shirt between the shoulder blades. There beside the spine was an enormous bruise, with a pronounced swelling at the centre.

"Jesus Sweeney!" exclaimed Snow. "There's the bullet. Maybe his backbone is broke, an' if it is, he'll not take another step even if'n he doesn't die from somethin' else. Man's better off dead, anyways, if'n he's to spend the rest of his days in a litter, bein' spoon fed an' pissin' in a bottle."

Another voice suddenly intruded. "*Pasikow ná?*" And then in English: "Is he getting up?"

They both looked up, startled. It was one of the Indians, the tall one. Jan looked quickly about; it had not occurred to him that they might return, and he cursed himself inwardly for his carelessness. Yet no other sign suggested they were about to be set upon by the others. Indeed the spent musket still lay where it had been dropped. Nothing suggested a renewed attack. But neither man moved. As the dark figure approached the fire, a battered hat was removed with both hands. Hair as fuliginous as a raven's wing fell around the face of the newcomer. With one hand, it was swept back as the stranger knelt over Jones, and both men were agape when they realized that the warrior who had lent menace to the earlier encounter was a woman.

# viii

A woman. When her parents realized that their daughter would not only be tall, but taller than the men in the village at Starblanket, they were distraught. Consultations with the medicine people yielded some hope, but only in the sense that Kinipi, She Moves Quickly, was imbued with special powers. Their verdict was that she live alone, apart from men, from the time of her first blood. Her powers should be allowed to concentrate by the expedient of contemplation and study. The other medicine women of the village would have much to teach her, but she would exceed them all, it was felt.

As time passed, this state of affairs did not sit well with Kinipi. She envied the young men who were free to move about, often breaking the strictures of the Agent's rules, leaving the reservation to hunt, and secretly participating in the old ways of worship expressly forbidden by those put in charge by the government. No one was sure when she started dressing in the clothing of men, but soon her tall figure, more than half a head above the others, could be seen whenever the young men assembled for storytelling or adventure. This was not thought improper or indecent, for she was considered powerful, and worthy of respect. Her male clothing set her apart. Though she did not speak often, deference was paid to her least utterance.

This was obvious in her language. In ordinary conversation, but particularly in relating stories and legends, the speaker used the qualifier *maci*, apparently. Its purpose is to convey the idea that the narrator believes what he is saying, but has no first hand knowledge of the facts. There was a tradition of healthy skepticism among the Cree Nation which was reflected in their everyday expression. In consequence, there were many words for 'maybe' in their vocabulary. But not so with the medicine people. Kinipi was emphatic and direct in her speech, which reflected a confidence borne of special gifts.

It was in the missionary school that Kinipi had her special difficulties. Speaking the Cree tongue was forbidden, and children were chastised with a willow rod across the back for breaking the rules. The rod was applied across the bare buttocks in the case of boys; over the bare back where girls were punished. The priest was a thin, sullen and unhappy man, feeling he was destined for better things than this vile backwater. All of the Bishop's attention was directed to *Peepeekeesis*, several miles to the south. He, Father Estevan Creeder, had nothing but the heathen dross; those who would not be moulded to the civilized ways of Christian living. So he flailed away with his willow rod, hoping to accomplish by wrath what learning and the Church's direction were slow in the getting. But as he prayed at night, feverish as he thought of tender, budding breasts shivering with the blows he laid across slender backs, he wondered if his soul was slipping beyond redemption.

Kinipi was stubborn. The complexities of English grammar seemed to her to be unworthy of the effort, for it was a barren language.

Creeder raised his rod, which doubled as a pointer, and intoned: "The inkwell is *here;* we place it *there.* Understand? Repeat."

Kinipi shuffled at her desk, which was almost too small for her gangly frame. She raised her hand, as demanded, but did not wait to be recognized. "In our language, we have *óta*, here, and *neta*, there, but within reach and sight; and *nete,* over there, out of reach and out of sight."

Creeder's thin lips tightened. The other children waited for the explosion, but Creeder, anxious that the case be made for the superiority of the Queen's

English, launched into a discussion of the idiomatic expression, losing them entirely. There were few touchstones in the curriculum that the reluctant pupils comprehended with any enthusiasm, nor were the lessons relevant to their condition, but they all wore expressions of practiced attention, while their minds wandered to other things.

"Can you no understand that it is literacy; *literacy*," he shouted, "that will enable you to move from a primitive stone-tool culture, to the modern day. You are of an illiterate, backward and confused peoples, whose only hope — and I mean, *only* hope, is to learn to read and write proficiently. Skills your parents, and their parents never had." He had a congestive disorder, in consequence of which his nose ran, and spit flew from his lips as he held forth on subjects near to his heart. His given name among his motley students was *mitakikom-paniw*, snot-flyer. Like all impatient men, he had a vision of where he wanted to be, but not the means by which to get there, or to help others develop the necessary strategies. The cultural gulf yawned between them, but Creeder was oblivious.

Later, the students would talk quietly among themselves, in their own language. There was a sense of anxiety about the sharp criticisms Creeder regularly made about them, and their people.

Kinipi looked around and up, over their heads, conscious of their respect. "Yet it does not harm us to learn reading and writing of the English word, for it is the way of those who now number far more than we. Whatever lies in store for our people, it will certainly involve the *wápiskisiw*, they who are white. But never forget: we are *Anishinaabe*, the People. And we always will be."

When the scheme was shared with some of the bolder young men to leave the reserve to go on a great hunt, it surprised no one that Kinipi would be going along.

Nowhere was there a propitious sign; the young woman could see that the land on all sides was barricaded with the fences and furrows of the homesteader. On the first day, they were shot at by a farmer dressing a white-tailed deer in the distance. Their small group was driven off the road by two wagons which purposefully drew abreast so that no room was afforded to the travelers. They were shouted at, cursed, or viewed suspiciously, though pains were taken to conceal the only firearm they had in their possession, an ancient musket. On the second day, they decided to travel by night. It was on the third day that their meager supply of food ran out. Thereafter, they were reduced to stealing vegetables from the edge of a garden, and seizing inquisitive dogs when their curiosity exceeded their protective instincts. It was not long before the resentments kindled by hardship were turned upon Kinipi.

Initially, the change in mood brought jeers and petty sarcasms aimed at no one in particular. Then it became a matter of blaming; the next stage in the breakdown of the group. This trip had begun with such hope. The degree of conquest of the land could not have reasonably been foreseen by young people who had lived all of their short lives confined to a small tract of rough land devoid of both game and much crop bearing soil. It then became held that the power of Kinipi to ensure the favor of *kisemanitow,* the god of all things, was diminished. One of them, *Pehew,* he-waits-for-him, called 'Peter' by the missionary teacher, declared himself leader, seized the gun, and spoke recklessly of what he intended. By now, they were all aware of the mounted policeman who followed them, but curiously did not try to catch up with them. Peter's anger, borne of fear, was fueled by the despair of the others. Kinipi pleaded with them in vain. The respect she had enjoyed until now had no force in the face of the hunger, failure, and disgrace that now seemed to be looming inevitably before them.

Peter was the first to lose heart. It was Peter who was to shoot Sergeant Jones. It was Peter who was to condemn Kinipi as the source of their ill fortune; but it was all of them who drove her away.

As she related this to the two silent men, Jan built up the fire so that it blazed. They had shrouded the wounded policeman from the mosquitoes, but the fire helped drive the pests away. The woman turned Jones on his side. A feeble moan emanated from his lips.

"There is no blood. The ball has not come out - " She gasped.

"What is it?" asked Jan kneeling at her side.

"Here. Feel this." She gestured near the top of the spine. "It can be felt. It can be removed."

Jan nodded. "We see that before, but this man," he pointed to Snow, "thinks that his back is broke from the shot. Better to let him die, perhaps."

Kinipi turned on him with a scowl. "Better to let one of your people die? Bring me a sharp knife. I will tend to him."

Jan mistook her intent. He did not move, refusing to participate in a killing. She looked at him for a moment, uncomprehending. Then she shook her head, speaking to no one. "*Kakepátisiw.* He is a fool. Get me a knife, if I am to remove this bullet."

The sergeant was suffering from a spinal cord contusion, which for the moment left him deeply in shock, and completely paralyzed. The slug had entered through the lower chest, traveled upward next to the heart, broken the collarbone, and grazed the spine. The shock wave created by its passage rendered the man unconscious, and the pressure on his spine by the lodged bullet would keep him there. Kinipi understood that whatever damage had been done inside the man's body, it was good to let the wound drain for a time, but the ball itself must come out; she had seen the poison wrought by even a deeply imbedded splinter. It could kill.

As she bent to the task, Snow suddenly seemed to come alive. "Here," he insisted, "pour some o' this over him, and the knife before yer start." He offered a bottle of Corning's Mixture. "Do it; it's as good a disinfectant as there is. Least, around here, anyways." He leaned over the woman to watch, as Jan held the fallen man on his side.

The bullet was surprisingly easy to extract. It was very close to the surface.

The cut was rinsed out with more of the patent medicine, and bandaged with a piece of his own bedding. During the entire operation, Jones had not made another sound, and as they watched him toward dawn, Jan thought that he would probably die. Dozing and watching, it was only when the eastern sky had lightened considerably that they noticed that Snow had loaded his mule and stolen away. But the policeman was not dead yet, so Jan reluctantly agreed to remain for another day. What other choice did he have? Besides, the woman interested him, and he felt drawn to her. He decided that it was as much for her that he remained with Jones, as any sense that somehow this mishap could be tied to him, when the body was found.

They were some distance off the main trail, and they considered whether it would be wise to seek help. Kinipi had no confidence that she would be treated fairly by the authorities; Jan had the same misgivings about his own involvement. He had thrown the old musket into the creek. That could be construed as the act of a guilty man, should Kinipi betray that fact. They elected to remain where they were and attend to the wounded man.

Jan watched as Kinipi fussed over the man. He could not comprehend it. He was her enemy, and was herding her and her countrymen back to a place where they would languish. It made no sense. If the man were to die, he could be rolled into the water, where he might not be discovered for months, if ever. Yet he could not entirely disregard Jones' expressions of friendship toward him. The man had even pulled his wagon along for a time. True, it could have been to insinuate himself into Jan's confidence, to get him to lower his guard. He cursed his alienated and divided life. In this land, trusted by no one, he trusted no one. All that mattered was the quest for his own land; this pilgrimage to an unknown sanctity guided by a polestar imagined, not seen. But he was increasingly troubled by stray thoughts that suggested this was not enough by itself.

A man had a tangible and enduring relationship with the land, true enough. An affiliation with God was necessary for reflection on the spiritual wellsprings of a man's life, but it was the interconnection with other human beings that provided the embracing form for a real existence. And it was this emptiness in his own life that Jan examined that long day. Was this the source of his worry? He studied Kinipi as she chewed a mouthful of cattail roots to make a poultice for Jones. Her black eyes glittered intently as she studied her patient. She brushed away a stray wisp of her hair as she lowered her head, absorbed in her task. He was attracted to her. It was not just her physical beauty that made him stir; it was her strength and sense of purpose. It was at least as strong as his own.

That night, after the policeman had been dragged under the wagon and blanketed, Jan squeezed in beside Kinipi. There were small courtesies and elaborate gestures as he tried to avoid touching her. Kinipi kept her eyes averted, saying nothing.

For a time, he lay on his back silently, as she. The awkwardness of the close quarters inhibited both of them, and though they were exhausted by their long vigil, each was wide awake and restive. The nearness of one to the other was exhilarating, and the slightest touch of her hip or foot as either of them stretched, or adjusted to the uneven ground, sent a thrill through Jan. Though it was cool, he was sweating.

For Kinipi, the upbringing of a Cree woman prized modesty and restraint above else. Even courtship between two who had obtained the necessary approvals for marriage were still subject to the stern supervision of the old women in the village. Though they might be allowed to snuggle together under a blanket, should their relative positions hint at larger improprieties, they would be subjected to the cries and light blows of willow whips of the chaperones. Yet she was glad that this man had offered her his shelter, even though she had reservations about him. Physically, he was big and strong, yet his hands hinted at an inner gentleness. He stood almost a head taller than she, and she was glad for this. It made her feel like the other young women, and she wondered at such a need, and how it comforted. She turned her body slyly to look at him, imagining his strong profile in the dim light. At the same time, he turned his head to face her. For an uncertain number of heartbeats, they considered one another.

She moved her head toward his shoulder. He brought his arm up and gathered her in. She drew close to him, the heat from her body palpable the length of his. Her hair smelled faintly of woodsmoke, exotic and mysterious. He felt a claw clench its talons in his belly, and a hotness fill his groin. He pulled her hair aside gently, and touched his lips to her temple. She murmured something unintelligible, and burrowed closer; so they stayed for a few moments longer.

The urgency he felt could not be denied. Roughly, he unbuttoned her trousers, and thrust his hand into the warmth between her legs. He groaned.

"*Anwástin.* Be calm," she said, surprising herself, for she had no such experience with men. "Let me help."

She lifted her hips and slid off the worn garment. Jan hurriedly pushed his own breeches down to his knees. The feeling of his flesh against her softness was intoxicating. She cried out at his initial thrusting, which brought him to completion almost immediately. Panting, he lay within her, taking his weight on his elbows. Allowing the delicious tension to rebuild.

She looked up at him and smiled. His head was almost touching the underside of the wagon. She touched his face and said softly, "*Kihtwám?*"

"What does that mean?" he asked huskily as he felt himself stir in her body.

"Again. More," she said.

# ix

Jan shivered inwardly in anticipation as he sat behind the Dominion land agent, his legs dangling off the bed of the buckboard. He had declined to sit with the agent on the only seat, given that the man was fat by any standard, and his commodious rear end took up most of the bench.

"I gotta show ya the property, and you've got the right of refusal, a course. An' ya gotta sign for it, afta examinin' the survey pegs, ones on the road allowance, anyways. May as well go together, but I sure ain't walkin' while you pulls that thing. Take my buckboard. It's govermint issue, so it ain't much, but it'll get us there if'n my old Belgian don't die on the way. Heh heh." There was no interest in the man, nor warmth. He surveyed Jan as if he were taking a sack of rubbish to the tip.

Jan had left his belongings with Kinipi, whom he felt would guard them with her life. "I am yours, now," she had said simply. And he was glad. He had felt reborn in this new relationship with another human being. *Mikinákos,* she had taken to calling him. Turtle. For he carried everything he owned upon his vehicle and slept under it at night.

There had been surprisingly little fuss overall when they had arrived with Jones. Kinipi had fashioned a drag from two poplar saplings, lashed together at the apex and put behind the saddle pommel. The wounded policeman traveled roughly, but there were no alternatives. There were expressions of outrage and consternation as Jones was brought into the detachment compound, and Jan related in his most contrived, halting English, the events that had befallen the Sergeant. He did not mention Snow. He left them with impression that Kinipi had traveled with him since his arrival in Manitoba, but told them sufficient detail to make it sound credible. Very few questions were directed at the woman; she was Indian, and, well, a woman. When she answered softly in Cree, eyes downcast, rolled eyes were turned back to Jan, who confirmed "she not speak much good English."

As the cart rumbled down the road allowance — little more than a trail much poorer than the one they had traveled previously — the agent chattered dispassionately, without looking for response. He seemed to be talking to himself, and every now and then he would hawk wetly, and spit to one side. As he turned off what Jan considered to be the main trail, onto what appeared to be worn wagon ruts in the grass, the agent began to call out the names of settlers who had gone before, and who had taken properties close to the principal roadway.

"Mycho Yankowitch, come in '96. Wife Maryka. Two children born here; eight in all; one other run off the same year. Cleared acreage: three, almost. André Grumachuk, come in '96 too. Wife dead same year; six children. Cleared acreage: two and a bit. He'll not last. Boris Urbanoski, wife Gilda. Yaselda? Fourteen children, that one. One dead last month. Cleared acreage: four and a half, since he was here in the Spring of '95. Pays ta breed strong sons. There's ol' Nastyshyn. Hermit since his wife got bedridden. He'll lose his place, sure, if'n he don't work it. That's the conditions, see."

And so it went, the fat agent nattering. Names and statistics. Small commentaries related to disease, misfortune, or the extent to which will foundered before nature. There were few happy narratives.

Jan heard the words distantly; he looked neither to left nor to right, though images of sod and poplar shacks, clearings torn from scrubland, and ghost-like figures flickered at the periphery of his vision. No comparisons would be undertaken, no false starts, no judgments passed. The agent commented that they were now not more than a mile from "Your land". The words surged through him. He was within minutes of taking possession of his own land. His own land. The words resonated in his thoughts with a more powerful rhythm than ever before, yet on the same strings of disbelief. He fought the urge to speak it aloud, for he thought he perceived a trace of disdain in the fat man's voice. But the agent was at worst an indifferent man, neutral on all matters save that of his own advancement. His job, his conversation, his life turned on statistics and facts.

"I record facts, is all, and send 'em on. Government wants to know. It's free land, sure, but there's clearance expectations and such. Gotta be homesteaded properly." He droned on, oblivious to the fact that Jan had not spoken a single word in response.

At last the vehicle bumped to a stop; the mangy old Belgian drew off to the side of the trail to graze, the bit crunching in an enormous mouth. The frogs croaked incessantly, and the flies buzzed in the hot sun of late August. Far off a woodpecker beat a tattoo. The agent studied a tattered map, pencil in one hand.

"This is it," he said, jumping down with a surprising agility. "Come on."

Jan sat motionless, the exhilaration leaving him breathless. The soft, punky smell of the woodlands around him filled his lungs. There was a fertile intensity about this place. The emotions welled up in him, tangled and impenetrable as a windfall. The still air, the yielding earth beneath his dangling feet, and the water in which life teemed seemed a happy, perpetuating existence, in which he would soon participate.

"Awright, let's see," said the agent, pushing up the brim of his narrow hat with the blunt end of his pencil. "Your land runs from this stake here, to the next. Let's see, about eight hundred an' eighty paces, then north again the same. A quarter section." He turned to look at Jan who had slipped off the buckboard, and was walking slowly to the stake which was first pointed out. On either side of it, to the passing eye, the land was indistinguishable. It was covered with poplar and willow, though here and there were clumps of scrubby oak and solitary spruce. In the distance, above the lesser growth, was a stand of tamarack. Here and there, natural clearings occurred, and the land rolled gently to a broad creek which meandered in a northerly direction.

"Th' creek's roughly the eastern boundary, so it's not quite a full quarter. But every other year what the water takes away, she'll give back the next, so — "

He stopped, as Jan fell to his knees, tears streaming silently down his cheeks.

Bending to the earth, Jan slowly clawed away the tangle of tall grass and surface decay, to the thick black soil beneath. Scooping up a handful of loam, he sniffed its musty bouquet deep within his nostrils, tasted the bitter richness of it, and crumbled it slowly between his fingers. Clasping his hands, he made the sign of the cross, and gave silent thanks.

The agent had seen many such displays since his uncle, the Assistant to the Deputy Minister of Supply and Services, had obtained the position for him. The job wasn't much, but there was to be a better appointment soon, he'd been promised. Patronage was a fine Canadian tradition, predating the confederation of the provinces. There was no reason not to expect something a little more to his liking any day now, he was thinking. Yet here he was, fourteen months later, assigning and escorting peasants to overgrown lots that were entirely unworkable as far as he could see. He looked at Jan with an expression somewhere between pity and contempt, and felt nothing. He scratched his buttock and pulled out his watch. It was time to get going; he was impatient with this peasant's grovelling in the sod. He shook his head: this one has no wife, no brats to help with the clearing, and from the cut of him, as bare-assed poor as the rest of them sheep-coats. How soon would those prayers of thanksgiving turn to curses of reproach? Well. We'll see.

But Jan, swaying ever so gently on his knees, saw not the tangled virgin bushland, but fields of rye and oats, and orderly rows of lush vegetables. He saw a gabled, whitewashed cottage facing east, with a sleeping loft above the kitchen, and an outbuilding for the stock. And in the distance, he saw the onion shaped spire of the True Faith. He saw the future as certainly as he saw the soil before him, and he had seen it since the beginning of his consciousness as a man. He saw it all, in truth, too clearly.

# Book Five

# KLONDYKE

# i

The squaring of a tree trunk to timber with an adze is no easy task. Quite apart from the physical strength required to move the blade through the wood and bark, there is coordination of hand and eye in several dimensions: horizontal, vertical, as well as linear. Moreover, the trunk itself diminishes in diametre as the work progresses from base to crown, and that must be taken into account in the consideration of the final product. Man and tool move together, and the apparent ease of the skilled labourer belies the concentration of effort that is necessary to produce a useable balk. That quality the Cree called *atoskata*, which loosely means, 'to work at it', but also includes more general notions of patience and persistence. It is the premier virtue of the hunter and the leader, and in Cree culture, what is a necessary precondition for maturity.

One bright morning in August, 1900, Jan was squaring logs near his Manitoba homestead, a single stroke to each beat of his heart. Thus paced, a man could work all day. He had been at task since the first blush of the coming day. The sweet pungency of spruce sap teased his nostrils, and he was surrounded by a spreading tapestry of wood chips, white against the trodden ground. It was warm, and he had stripped to the waist; the muscles of his back and arms rippled with each swing of his implement. Having cleansed herself as she did at the beginning of each day, Kinipi stood naked in the window of their two-roomed dwelling, watching him, the sounds of his work nearly muffled. The sight of his body filled her with a welter of carefully contained emotions: longing and pride, possessiveness and affection. Beyond those, there simmered a strong, more palpable reaction. A peculiar melting sensation, that began in her stomach and flowed through her thighs to her feet. Her heart beat faster, and the back of her mouth was dry. She wanted him. And in the manner of her people, she felt no shame or reluctance to make demands of him. She smiled to herself.

Placing a hand over the taut skin of her stomach, she rubbed it gently. She was late arising this morning, and though the sun was well up, she had not yet dressed. Such loitering was but another sure indication of mysterious changes afoot. Another week to be sure, but she was nearly certain that a child was growing within her. She willed him to look at her, but she knew that this was a competition she could not win. Her husband was a man whose will could be narrowly concentrated upon the task at hand. The window behind which she was standing was a case in point: it was a finely-crafted affair, consisting of four good-sized panes. The glazing had cost Jan a full week's wages felling timber, but he was determined. He had taken care with the framing and mullions. No one in Kamadeta-Potselak had real glass, other than the priest and the church. Not only would he have a proper window, but it would be a large one, and be mounted so that it caught the rising sun. It was a badge of triumph: one of many such small steps toward the realization of his dreams.

As she watched, there was a movement in the distance that caught her eye. A flash of red. Perhaps a cardinal. As she turned back to silent communion with her husband, there it was again, through the thick poplar leaves fretting under the desultory morning breeze. And again. This time she could see that it was a man on horseback. Then the red coat. Now she could see that this was a policeman, and he had turned in toward them. Her lust yielded to anxiety. What did he want? She had never had an encounter with a policeman that did not turn out to be unpleasant; there was nothing in her intuitions that suggested that this would be any different. It was apparent that Jan had not noticed him yet, for nothing had changed in the rhythms of his work.

The rider had a thick moustache that drooped at the corners of his mouth, and a bell-shaped pipe, a *barunka*, Jan called them, dangled from his lips. From the motion of his jaw, she could see that he worked at the stem of the pipe, even though it seemed obvious the thing had gone out. The broad-brimmed Stetson was pulled low against the morning sun, for he had been riding in an easterly direction until he had turned off at their property.

Over the past year that they had taken up residence on his land allotment, he had managed to clear a quarter acre, and erect the shell of a cottage in which the woman now stood. Potatoes, corn, beans and onions had been planted, and the crop promised to be lush. His work over the winter at cutting ties in the Turtle Mountains for the Lake Manitoba Railway & Canal Company, had brought sufficient income to live and to purchase planking for the house construction. Other locals had to make do with poplar log huts, which some had improved upon by coating them with clay. A few had whitewashed the exterior, though it was a costly extravagance, but it was becoming more common. Soon, thought Jan, he would whitewash his own place, and finish building a proper hearth. This was a home which, when completed, would keep out the foulest weather, and all but the most persistent vermin. It was heavy and persistent labour, but it was work for himself and the woman who now shared his life.

This coming winter, the rail would reach Sifton, north of Dauphin. If the fortunes of the Company held. There were persistent rumours that the Lake Manitoba Railway & Canal Company was out of cash, and those men whose arrangements permitted them to leave their homes for extended times, like Jan, counted on the extra cash that the tie and fuel cutting work brought. Jan needed more glazing, nails, and milled planks to finish his place properly. Then there was a barn to build, then fences to surround the land he would clear. In his mind's eye, he would call into being the vision which had brought him to this spot. It would happen, even now as the beam he was creating took shape beneath the measured blows of his adze.

He was happy. Kinipi was a decent woman, whose only disadvantage in his judgement was her silence. He knew that other men eschewed shrill, voluble wives, but he took comfort in the sound of a woman's voice, whether it called for errant children or sang over the wash. Though he had withdrawn from the company of most men, and rarely offered a comment which might be considered revelatory, this was not, he felt, a condition in a woman which he would have freely chosen. He was learning the odd word and phrase of the Plains Cree people, and Kinipi for her part, could now make basic requests in the Ukrainian language. But their conversations were short and to the essence of the thing required. It was frustrating, for he felt that the decorous qualities of speech were in many respects as important as its utility. But this was a small annoyance in the scheme of his present life. He was slowly getting accustomed to the sound of his own voice, which seemed to have the effect of a drug on her. As he taught her the basic intonations of his mother language, he would read to her from his beloved Shevchenko, at night, abed, by the light of a single candle set in an empty tin.

*A cloud is floating, following the sun;*
*It spreads its scarlet coat-flaps in the sky*
*And calls upon the sun to settle down*
*On the blue sea and there be covered up*
*As, with crimson quilts, a mother might her child.*

She warmed him at night, responding to the passion with which he fuelled his readings, and the images he translated for her, with her hands upon his body, fervently matching his ardor on those evenings when they were not so expended in the field to take pleasure in one another. She cooked and swept, and stood beside him with axe or pry bar meeting him blow for blow for most of the day. But as of late, she had tired quickly, and the thought had occurred to him that she might be ill.

In all, she was a fine companion, and he was grateful to God for having placed her in his way. He had suggested to her that upon completion of the church at Ukraina, which he thought might be in the Fall, from what other settlers had said, they should be properly married. It seemed to be a matter of indifference to her, for she was of the view that her vow had been taken the first night they had lain together, under the cart.

The only shadow that had fallen upon these tranquil arrangements had occurred one late winter morning that he had been to town, to purchase a new file, a barrel of ten-penny nails, as well as some seed potatoes. Coming out of McLintock's Dry Goods Trading Company, on the other side of the street, holding her skirts high above the insistent, creeping mud, was Ervina Cartwright. He had almost forgotten her in the preoccupations of building a new life, but the warmth of their initial encounter, and how it had left him for some time after, came back like the blast from an open boiler grate.

The curve of her lower leg, just above a muddy, buttoned boot, was enticingly exposed by the careless way she held her garments. As she picked her way along what passed for a sidewalk, she must have felt his gaze upon her, for she stopped, suddenly, and turned toward him. Their eyes met.

He looked at her directly, but had been so shaken that he was unable to arrange his features into a smile. He stood rooted like a post. Later, he would wonder what it must have been like for her, to have this grim-faced man staring at her, wordlessly. Her expression had wrinkled into a puzzled frown, then she had turned quickly away, and was gone. All the way back to his property, as he trudged between the shafts of his cart, he examined and re-examined the shards of this chance encounter, wondering at the luck and wealth of a man so fortunate as to possess a woman such as that.

Hard work soon diminished such thoughts, but the lovely Ervina would steal into his imaginings. He remembered *popá* Kudryk's stern injunction to guard against man's inherent nature, which was to push the most insistently and to crave for that which is the most unattainable. Besides, he had cautioned himself, he already had the company of a good woman.

He became conscious of a horse behind him. He could smell it. As he turned, he could see Kinipi in the window, her brown body bathed in the early sunlight. The nipples on her slim breasts stood out like copper coins. Even at forty paces, he could see, or perhaps sense, the anxiety that made her features taut, and kept her, unashamed, in plain view. He looked up, shielding his eyes with a flat hand over his brow, for the stranger had come around so that the sun was behind him.

In an instant, Jan knew it was Sergeant Jones, the man he had cared for after the shooting. He did not need to glance at his woman to know that she would have recognized him as well. The events of that night were still too recent to have faded. He seemed well enough now. His uniform looked new, in contrast to the shabby outfit he had been wearing when last they had seen him. But it was unbuttoned, as before, and the revolver was in its holster, wrapped around the military-style pommel. Jones swung down from the saddle, stretching his legs this way and that as he pushed his mount away. The mare was drop-reined, so she wouldn't stray far. He pushed the brim of his circular hat back, and extended his hand. His face was relaxed. This unexpected visit was not trouble, Jan thought, at least not right away.

"Good morning, Jan Dalmynyshyn. It's been a while." Then a smile: "Called or not, like the gods, the police always come sooner or later."

Jan reached for him. Tentative. "You did not die, then." Then sheepishly: "Perhaps that is obvious."

Jones smiled. "No. I had some luck, and some help, I suppose." He squatted, and looked around. Jan heard his bones crack and pop. "This your place, is it?" Knowing that it was. "You've done some fine work here in a short time. Makes many of your neighbours look poor."

Jan nodded.

"And she?"

"It is my wife."

The policeman pursed his lips, moving his head up and down slowly. "Anyone else here?"

Jan didn't like the sound of that. But there seemed only the casual idleness in his voice that he had remembered from before. "She is the only one."

Jones looked up at the sky, which only moments before had been radiant. Clouds were starting to form, and the wind was up a little. The sweat cooling on Jan's body was cool, and his flesh puckered. "Hope it don't get up a rain on us, now, but I think it will, more than likely. Any chance of a little tea?"

As they walked to a rough bench near the house, where Jan did his woodworking in mild weather, Jones noticed that the woman had vanished. "You know," he said, putting his hand on Jan's muscular forearm, "I never did thank you for what you done. You could of left me to die; wasn't your affair. You did right by me. Only reason I'm around these days is because you didn't leave me to rot."

Jan shrugged. "It was nothing." He called to Kinipi to boil water.

Jones sat on the bench, and took out his pipe, picking at it. "Well, I owe you my life, and I'm grateful." Jan nodded, and called again; this time, there was an answering word from inside. In Ukrainian. Jones looked surprised, but said nothing.

Later, as they sat sipping strong black tea without sugar, Jones took in the sweep of the place. "You got a lot of hard going before this place is a going concern," he said amiably. "But you done well so far. Yes indeed: you done well." He nodded toward the clearing. Jan had the sense that he was building to something, but taking a very long way around. Maybe the man was just trying to put him at ease.

"Thank you."

"Never had a family member, far as I can remember, that ever worked the land. Making things grow is not in our blood, the Jones clan. Closest was my granddad. He was a poisoner." He looked at Jan with an expectant grin, but Jan was unsure where the conversation was going.

"'Tickles Tom', is what they called him. Old Tickles. He poached fish on the side, when he weren't down the coal mines, as a hewer. Now see, there's a special art to poaching salmon. You can throw poison in, and up they float, all funny coloured, and bright pink in the gills. Or there's lots of ways. But Tom, if he had done well for a night, would find that part of the brook where the water was deep, and the old trout would just sit there, with enough of a flick to the tail now and then to keep steady.

"So he slides his hand in slow, just under the belly, so. He had his fingers upended in a claw, held close to the ground. Up near the gills, he'd stroke the fish's belly, easy. No rush. Darned if that ol' fish wouldn't come right up to the surface, by and by. Almost as if it was paralyzed. Then: a finger in each gill, and you got him. I only seen it once, mind you, when I was a wee boy. But it was like magic. The things you can do if you've got patience, and you don't listen to them that says it can't be done. But you got to know your fish. It's not enough to just watch it, then do it successfully. You got to study them, get to understand their nature."

See the rabbit run; watch what he do. The words came back to Jan from their encounter on the trail. While Jan pondered the significance of what was being said, the tone in Jones' voice evened. It was more serious. "I know you and your woman been wondering why I'm here." He paused, as if unsure as to where to go next. "Well, the truth of it is, I been in a bit of a dilemma for a while now.

"You see, I know you was the one that probably did in those two bandits back in Winnipeg last year. You should have never taken that fancy knife off one of them. May as well have painted a sign on your backside. But from what I can figure, they probably came on to do you some mischief; they were well known for that sort of thing. From the records, and that; it's not too hard to figure out what they was up to.

"So after I recovered from the wounding I got, thanks to you, I filed the report of my patrol. Damned if those Indians - all but the one who shot me - eventually went back to the miserable place they left. No choice. Really. Then the reader's office picked up on these two unsolved homicides, and my notes, and there's going to be a follow-up. It's been giving me a lot of trouble, all this. So I asked for the file, you know: to finish up. Here I am."

As he listened, Jan felt a chill, and it was not just the weather, which was deteriorating quickly. All he had worked for was about to slip away. The sergeant saw the faltering expression, and lowered his head. He gripped the nearly empty tin cup with both hands.

"I did my duty. That's what I'm paid for. But ... well, bein' right is sometimes not enough. The thing is, I'm pretty sure what you did was self-defence. But there's a ... there's a real feeling of animosity - ill-will - against your people right now, and you see it especially in the courts. I don't think you'd stand much of a chance, frankly, if I took you back to answer the charges."

"Take me back?" said Jan slowly. "You take me back?"

Jones reached into his breast pocket and pulled out a much-folded paper. "This here's a warrant for your arrest, on two charges of murder. It's a legal order, that gives me the right to arrest you; take you back to Winnipeg."

The look of alarm was evident. Kinipi came out and stood behind Jan, her hand on his shoulder. The strain evident, for she had been listening beyond the open door.

"Now, this here paper gives me the *right* to arrest you; it doesn't say I *have* to, first time I see you. Police discretion, see. I'm not taking you back, at least not today."

"When?" Then more suspiciously: "Why do you play with me?"

The policeman looked at him directly. "Don't be a fool, Jan Dalmynyshyn. What I'm giving you is a chance. I'm coming back tomorrow, with help. You better be gone."

Kinipi gasped. Jan looked about, at his beloved holding. "Where shall I go?

I cannot leave what I have started here." Small tears like birdshot rolled down Kinipi's cheeks. Jones looked wretched. He upended his cup, spilling the leavings on the ground.

"I don't know. That's not my problem." After a moment of silence, during which the woman's breathing could be heard underscoring the tension of the moment, he added, "Look. I think this thing will go away in a while. I shouldn't be saying this, but the right thing to do isn't always going to be the letter of the law. The file needs to be closed, and as far as I'm concerned, I'll do my best to see that through once I come back tomorrow, and you're gone."

Kinipi said to Jan in an anxious voice: "You can hide for a few days, then come back."

Jones shook his head. "Uh uh. Not going to do it. There's too many who'd know, and we'd be back. You're going to have to disappear for a while. A good while. Sorry, but that's how it is."

Jan looked over his shoulder at the woman, then back at the policeman. "But where would I go? There is … " He broke off, disconsolate. This couldn't be happening; what he had striven for could not be snatched away from him. Almighty Jesus in Heaven!

Clearing his throat, the policeman stood up. "That's up to you. They found gold up in the Klondyke last year; you must have heard about it. There's thousands, tens of thousands that are on their way there, by all accounts. Might be as good a way as any to lose yourself, and who knows? You might even strike it rich."

He strolled back to his mare, and swung up into the saddle. He walked the animal over to where the two of them were, and looked down at them for a moment. "There's no doubt in my mind who's the angel, and who played the devil in this affair," he said. "But me knowin' that, and the way it'd likely play out in court for a man like you, are likely two different things, these days. Sad thing to say about our justice system, but take it from me: it doesn't always work for the ordinary man - especially … well, let's say, a fella from abroad.

"Look at it this way: a year or two looking for gold, as opposed to maybe ten or fifteen years in the jug. Doesn't seem to me to be much of a thing to ponder." He pulled up the mare's head, and turned her for the road. She was jumpy, and eager to be off, back to the stable. He reined her in.

"Sorry it has to be like this. It isn't fair, but I think I've done what I can to even it out. I owed you, but it's more than that. So long, Jan Dalmynyshyn. Good luck to you." He looked up at the frowning sky. "Looks like a cat-screamer of a storm coming on, folks." And with a brief glance at the woman, he was away.

For a very long time, Jan sat where he was, and Kinipi remained standing behind him.

# ii

Jan's life had been a series of departures: from the wooded verge of his beloved Ukraine, from the oil wells at Boryslava, and from the coal pits of Pennsylvania. Now his own property, with the beginnings of a fine house and gardens. It was as painful as the tearing of his own flesh. Kinipi had been silent; frustratingly so. Her eyes wet. Shall I come? she asked him without speaking. He marvelled at the affinity of human beings who could communicate with a glance or a shrug. He had shaken his head.

"The property is gone if we leave it. You must stay and work the land, as you can. This is our home, and I will come back and claim it. You must stay."

Her shoulders shook with the weight of it: should she tell him of the child? She had decided against it, for he had enough grief as it was. There would be enough of that to carry without being fearful of other things. It had alarmed her to see tears in his eyes, for he was such a strong man that such expressions seemed out of keeping. In her culture, a man bore his woe without flinching. Yet she knew that there was a point beyond which a man could not go without inner destruction. Her man seemed close to that now.

He had departed before the first light, with small goods and food rolled into a blanket, and slung by a length of rope over his shoulder. He wore his *khustra* under a broad-brimmed hat. His boots were draped by their laces around his neck. Old habits died hard. Looking back, he could see that Kinipi had followed him out to the road, head bowed and arms folded in front of her. She was weeping, he knew that, and a lump tightened in his throat.

*she stood beside the beaten path*
*like some pale poplar swaying;*
*as thick as drops of dew at dawn,*
*tears down her cheek went straying;*
*through floods of grief she could not see*
*the world that 'round her slept*

He had stopped at the home of his newest neighbours, and had told them of his desire to go to the Klondyke to search for gold. Ahapii Boberski shook his head upon being told.

"All the gold a man could ever want is black, and underneath your feet," he had said in Ukrainian.

Jan's cheeks flamed with this truth being expressed. He asked nothing from men, but respect. He felt that his stature had been diminished by this venture, but he supposed that this was nothing to what would happen once the police came and began questioning everyone. Murder, he thought. Suspicion of murder. What would his neighbours think of him then? Would he ever be able to retake his place with pride among them? Too late for such thoughts, he mused. Time enough for that worry when the moment comes.

He had been reluctant to ask Ahapii to look in from time to time on Kinipi. He had enough of his own worries, what with four children and a sickly wife. Their accommodation was a poor hovel, and the children were pale and filthy. Jan had brought two rolls of tar paper over the previous autumn, so that the forlorn roofing could be made waterproof at least over the sleeping platforms. Boberski was a proud man, and had insisted that this was a loan of short term duration, and that Jan would be repaid in full. Jan had insisted that there were no ledger pages between friends and neighbours, and had been certain that one day soon, the opportunity would be there to return the kindness. Sure enough, there he had been, knocking at the rough planks that passed for a door. Jan shook his head: how could a man who worked the land with such enthusiasm as his neighbour, have no idea how woodworking tools were used? Perhaps, he considered, the man had very few tools at all. Suddenly he had regretted not doing more.

When he heard of Jan's plan to walk to the rail at Brandon, he had a suggestion.

"There's a threshing gang in town, looking for experienced men. I know you have the experience with the steam engines. You might find work as well as free passage, for they are working west. The machine came in on the railway two days ago. I saw it myself, wheezing and smoking. A grand machinery, it was. One day, such a beast will stand on my soil." His enthusiasm was as apparent as it was pathetic, Jan thought. Wizened, filthy and impoverished as a vagrant, it seemed unlikely that the fates would change their minds about Ahapii Boberski. A shame. For he had one of the most generous hearts God had managed to fit into a small though hardy frame.

The threshing gang seemed to be a promising idea, unless their work was to be confined to this area. He had taken the thirty-six dollars he had saved from his efforts over the winter, divided it with Kinipi, and the additional work could augment his modest purse. He might even be able to send some home. He would look into it. He might go to the goldfields; he might not, but it was good to have a destination that bore promise; at least, until something better happened along. Threshing might be the thing.

The crops were ripening, now, in mid-August. It had been an ideal year for growing, and the rich soil of the prairie parklands, much of it in these parts yielding its first crop ever, had delivered of a richness that suggested assurances for the future. The sight of such lushness honed the edge to Jan's sadness, as he walked along. It was true that a particular unhappiness brought its own cerecloth, beneath which there was no joy in anything else. Hope he had, though in short supply. But joy: much seemed to lie in what might have been, rather than what was. And just as he was near to closing his hand around the substance of his dreams, it evaporated.

He had heard of the threshing gangs: these were the means by which farmers could get their crop off quickly, for a proportion of the yield. No need to invest in equipment or labour, even if such unimaginable sums were available.

But few men were tempted to go with the gangs, for the work on their own holdings was all-consuming.

Poor Boberski could not leave his wife, for she was sickly. Jan had seen her when he had helped with the roof, and had thought at the time that death had a firm grip on her. She coughed and hawked and spat thick gobs of phlegm into a metal container. It was all she could do to haul herself from her bed to empty herself, which she did with a lot of moaning and calling on the Almighty for help. Jan remembered looking at his neighbour in silent embarrassment, as the sounds of the struggle raged. Ahapii shrugged. He took his lot with remarkable aplomb, as was characteristic of these stoic people, his countrymen. But his circumstances prevented much in the way of supplemental earnings, and the living was very hard.

Up ahead, he could see the scrabble of shacks and barns that surrounded the more prosperous buildings hard on the railway terminal. There was a loco-motive there now, sending black plumes of coal-fired smoke straight into the air. There was prosperity in those man-made storm clouds, he thought. You could tell that from the way the settlement was growing. It was still early, but there already was considerable traffic on the way into town, most of it the well-to-do farmers in their wheeled vehicles. No one stopped to offer him a ride. Those who had settled before were clannish and indifferent to the non-English newcomers, and many barely disguised their contempt. Others, like him, were on foot, but were so burdened with produce or other wares that there was little opportunity for chatter. So he walked on.

Entering the town, he wondered where the gang recruitment was taking place. Or perhaps they had left; Ahapii was a little vague on detail, as usual. Some of the more prosperous establishments had built wooden sidewalks in front, so as to keep their customers out of the mud. When it was dry, as now, the roadways were hard as paving. But when it rained, the streets transformed into a glutinous dark paste that clung to hem and heel like mucilage. Pondering which way to turn, he stepped onto the platform in one direction, while look-ing the other way. He collided with a passerby, giving him a start. His victim, a woman, gasped audibly, for he had stepped on her foot.

"I am at fault –" he began earnestly, backing off and nearly falling. He was further stunned to realize it was Ervina Cartwright. "I am at fault ..." he began again, feeling stupid and clumsy. His face was red, and he fought the urge to flee which had inexplicably come over him. She was doubled over, favouring her foot.

"Help me over there," she commanded, gesturing with her head toward a bench in front of McLintock's. She raised her elbow.

He took it, feeling the warmth of her flesh through the thin sleeve. He lifted her, and thought that perhaps she was a *russalki*, wraith, perhaps an angel, for she weighed nothing.

"Ouch," she said lightly, "you'll pull my arm out. You don't know how strong you are." She sat down suddenly as he released her; dropping her arm as if it had burned her. She looked at him with a grimace. "I shudder to think what damage you would have done if those –" she gestured to his boots around his neck - "had been on your feet."

Now his face was carmine.

"I say –" she peered at him closely. "Now I know you. You're the kind fellow that helped papa on the trail, with the broken wheel. I heard that you had settled around here somewhere. Why haven't you come to see us?"

Jan was dumbfounded. That she would remember him, a mote? That she would have an interest in his whereabouts: a peasant farmer? That she should sit here with him, chattering. A *bohunk*? It was beyond belief.

She had lifted the heel of her boot to the edge of the bench, and was working the toe. Her face was askew with the effort. "It hurts. I don't know how you did it, but my toe feels like you broke it. Well, are you going to say anything at all, or just sit there like a sack of potatoes?"

"The fault is mine –" he began again, lamely.

She laughed. "I think we've established blame. Now what about compensation?"

He looked at her, dumbfounded. "Compensation?"

"Compensation?" She mocked him gently. "Yes. There's nothing for it but you must rub my foot to get the circulation back. Especially the middle toe, which feels positively mutilated."

"Rub your foot?" he muttered.

"Yes. Get down, and take off my shoe. I have good stockings, so be careful. You have big, rough hands, and I don't want a run or a tear. Come on." She pointed her toe outward.

He furtively looked both ways along the street, but there was no one nearby, much to his relief. This seemed like such a private thing. Ponderously, he got to his knees in front of her, shooting a glance at her face to see whether she was toying with him; whether she would, once he was down, put the toe of her boot to his head. But all he saw was a wonderously beautiful woman smiling, a little mischievously he thought, down at him. His fingers felt like carrots as he fumbled with the tiny button of her boots. Her foot under her hands felt like a small animal, a hare, perhaps, as he caressed it awkwardly.

"Not there. There." She commanded, pulling the hem of her dress further up than he had ever seen a proper woman behave. For a few moments he squeezed and rubbed her foot, feeling the small bones, and the five miniature protuberances under her sock. It began to arouse him. He became conscious of his heartbeat: was this animal within beyond his control?

"So why have you not come to see us?" she repeated dreamily, her head back, eyes closed. "After I told you to. We did not repay you for your kindness to us that day. I have always felt badly about that. We were rude. It's sort of a family trait. So why, then? I heard you live with a very pretty Indian woman. Is that true?"

She pattered on with the voice of birds. He was entranced. That she had remembered him was a shock which forced into the background the more urgent of his problems at the moment, not the least of which was the warrant for his arrest. But come the army of Herod, he was not going to let go of that delicious foot before it was absolutely necessary.

"I have no excuse. I thought that perhaps you said such a thing out of kindness. That's how you appear to me, to be a person of great kindness." He bowed his head, focused on his work, glancing now and then at the curve of her lower leg. This was becoming intensely erotic; he could feel it. He wondered whether she could.

She laughed with pleasure at the compliment. "Of *course* I meant it. Of *course* I did. I may talk altogether too much, but I do mean what I say. All right then, that feels much better. You can stop." Jan gave up the foot as one might hand back a prize fairly won. He was conscious of his lowered breathing, and his state of excitement. He wondered if she had noticed, which was why she had asked him to stop. Looking away, he could see others approaching, and decided that they were the cause. Maybe she had realized what this looked like. He sagged a little, and looked at her as he raised himself to the bench again. Her face was intensely alive; her eyes danced. She gave away nothing of her inner thoughts, but his attraction to her must be obvious, he decided. His blushing had not let up.

"It is better now?"

"Oh, good heavens, yes." She swung her head forward, opening her eyes. It seemed to him that she had coloured a little, for she drew her foot away, perhaps too quickly. "You have, er ... healing powers in those strong hands. Where were you going when you stampeded over me, anyway?" She put on her boot quickly, and stood up, brushing down her skirts.

"I was looking for the threshing gang. I was told –"

"Oh, then why didn't you ask me?" she said gaily, the moment of faint awkwardness gone. "I've just come from there. My brother - you remember that boorish lout, don't you - is negotiating with them to come out to our place. But there's some kind of problem, it's all sort of terribly boring, so I walked over here. Come on, I'll take you there." She raised up, stretching on her toes, fists behind her. "Umm. I'm still a little sleepy. The walk will do me good."

Walking beside her, Jan felt like a prince. The sound of her voice was as musical as his *balylyka*, on a good day. He scarce heard the words, but allowed the music of them to flow through his being, like congratulations, or a blessing. He half closed his eyes, and forgot all else but the spell of the numinous creature he was with. When she looked at him, the intensity of her olive-gray eyes was such that he would look away, as if her gaze might penetrate his thoughts.

"Over there. Can you see it?" She pointed.

The steam tractor was sending off plenty of smoke; already a small crowd had been drawn to it, which explained why so few people were about on the streets. On the edge of the settlement, past the dirt-filled raised platform where stock and heavy items were unloaded from the trains, was a Cockshutt painted red and black, with white striping, on massive, six-foot wheels that were ribbed with triangular steel lugs. The power take-off had a long, tan-coloured belt attached to a saw blade, itself about four feet in diameter, and several men were feeding logs through it.

This in itself was a marvel to watch, for more wood than a team of twenty men could dispatch was being reduced to stove-lengths in minutes. As he watched, Jan realized he was seeing the future, when such instruments would replace the efforts of men. Would life be easier with these devices, or would it be much worse, as men's labour became unnecessary? It was a fleeting thought, for there were other things to distract him. There were no policemen about, though he kept a furtive eye for them. And Ervina was about to take her leave.

"Well, I do hope you will come out to see us. Oh. There's Henry, my dear brother." The way she said it, expressed little genuine affection. The man approached them, scowling.

"Where have you been? Father's gone off to look for you. We're ready to leave." Beyond the briefest of glances, he took no notice of Jan.

She seemed inured to his rudeness. "I say, Henry, do you remember Jan, the man who fixed our wheel on our trip out? He's ..."

He took her by the arm. "For heaven's sake, Ervina. Will you take no care at all where you wander off to, and who you end up with?" With a glance back at Jan: "These people are quite rough, and can be unpredictable."

She jerked her elbow out of his hand, annoyed. "Let go of me, you lout. Why must you be so ignorant. He's to see the threshing people. About a job, I think?" She looked questioningly at Jan. "Maybe he can help do the harvest at our place." This was clearly intended to annoy her brother, who turned and stalked back to the activity. She watched him go, shaking her head.

"He really can be a pig, sometimes. He's not all bad, but now and then he's really, oh ... abrasive." She settled upon an adjective that was obviously but one of many she was considering. "I'd better go and fetch father, or he'll be cross with me too." She closed with him, touched his arm, and said softly: "I hope to see you again. Goodbye."

The warmth of her lingered like a dissipating spell. Then he turned to the small throng of milling, shouting people, and sought out the foreman. He was easy enough to pick out, as all persons in authority are. He stood apart, hands on hips, brooding under a broad-brimmed hat, of the sort that Sergeant Jones had worn. Jan approached him, and upon reaching the man, he doffed his hat. The other appraised him coolly, without reciprocating the gesture.

"I am looking for work."

"Are you. What can you do? I've no shortage of lifters and helpers."

Jan explained that he had experience in the coal fields of Pennsylvania, with steam engines used to pump water and lift the cages. He could operate, maintain and repair. The man looked dubious, as he scanned Jan's much repaired, tattered clothing. "How's a steam engine work," he asked with the faintest trace of a sneer. "Got any idea?"

Jan coloured under the question, for it was more in the nature of a taunt than an examination of his understanding of modern machinery. But he wanted the job.

"I know the standard Corliss engine, which was used in the mines. The steam created by the boiler expands into the cylinder, pushing it one way, then as the steam comes into other side, it pushes it back. Piston rod pushes through stuffing box, fastened to cross-head, connecting-rod, and so to flywheel. Simple." He offered a small smile.

Any hint of a sneer was gone. "You got papers?"

Jan shook his head.

"Well, the statute of '94 requires that I only hire them that has proper qualifications, as engineer. Besides, I got one. Candell Kerr." He jerked his thumb to the man on the deck of the tractor. He chose not to elaborate that Kerr was a man partial to heavy drink, and threats notwithstanding, always seemed to be able to lay his hands on a bottle, no matter where they were. Maxwell Roberts was anxious to demonstrate to the syndicate that had entrusted him with a four thousand dollar piece of equipment, that he was a competent manager. And that he would get his bonus for performance. His operating costs ran to three thousand dollars for the season; gross earnings might reach five thousand. All that was in jeopardy if his engineer failed him.

Now here was a man who would not draw the pay of a certified engineer, but who seemed to understand machinery. He looked him over. A good-sized, handsome man, with an alert, intelligent face. Not the usual shuffling *bohunk* that spoke barely a word of English. He put out his hand, and Jan took it.

"Roberts is my name. I don't usually run my team with a separator tender. The grease work and maintenance gets done by men on rotation from the tank and bundling crews. But I'll take you on approval for a week, and if you do prove out right, then I'll take you on, at er ... let's say, fif - forty-nine dollars a month." He still held Jan's hand, as if now suddenly afraid that he would disappear. He was ready to go another six dollars, if necessary.

Jan nodded, and took away his hand. "Done. But another two dollars if I prove out."

# iii

A separator tender must keep the threshing separator running smoothly, and constantly checks the machine, oiling and greasing the bearings, and adjusting the belts. The machinery had to be level, and the cylinders, sieves and concaves needed to be adjusted according to the weed content, the moisture level of the straw, or the particular crop. Jan knew nothing of this, but he was confident of his understanding of machinery, and he felt that by observing the men who were doing the job now, he could quickly get an understanding of what was necessary.

This was how he spent the rest of the day. The rig was scheduled to move out the following morning, and his thoughts wandered from images of Ervina's foot, to Sergeant Jones, and many an anxious glance scoured the edge of town for some sign of the police, or the bright cotton shawl of Ervina.

The engineer, Kerr, seemed congenial enough, though Jan quickly determined that it was the bottle that made him so. Nevertheless, the man knew his equipment, and he moved between tractor and separator, calling out instructions, and cautioning the spike pitchers who stood at either end of the feeder, not to get too close to the whirling tines on the band-cutter, yet keep the insatiable maw well supplied with grain. He would listen with a cocked ear to the machine, worried that it was becoming choked, or running too fast for want of a proper supply of grain. He was relieved that Jan would take over at the separator, for it was warm going already, and the sun barely up. "Don't know how long I'd a lasted, boy. There's plenty demand for us properly trained people, without working an outfit that's cutting corners."

The fireman was an ugly fellow by the name of Wibbins. Jan had never seen such a well-muscled human being. Short, thickset, and stripped to the waist, Wibbins was drenched with sweat. The boiler was fired with straw, and it was consumed nearly as soon as it was forked into the narrow door. In consequence, Wibbins pitched the straw with a steady rhythm, while a helper behind him forked bundles to the deck. Wibbins was in constant motion. His long hair was tied behind his head with a length of leather lacing, and his ponytail flew like a greasy pennant. Jan noticed that the man's eyes took in everything around him; the change of workers, newcomers, Kerr's comings and goings. It was as if he fed the blazing throat of his master by instinct.

Gradually, Jan realized that the swarm of shouting, labouring men had a particular pattern, from the bundlemen who drove from stook to stook, loading the sheaves for the separator, to the engineer and his crew. Walking about, peering at this aspect of the operation, and that, was Roberts, who from time to time would grab a pitchfork, and help load the separator, urging the others on. Or he might call for a jack, because the thumping machine had settled in the dark soil, and the belt was starting to run arhythmically. It was the same as the huge steam pumps that drew out water and pushed fresh air to the shafts of the coal mines in which he had toiled back in Pennsylvania. They needed constant attention, but properly minded, they were rarely shut down.

By watching then helping - without pay - Jan learned the subtleties of the steam engine. In fact, it seemed to him that the principal secret was lubrication, and lots of it. All the same, any machine has its mysteries, and the great steam engines seemed the closest thing to living beings he had ever seen. So it was now: the panting of the boiler, the deep exhalations of the stack belching the pale grey smoke of the burning straw into the clear prairie sky. The tractor pulled them along effortlessly, several wagons and cabooses in a row, each filled with men and equipment. And oh what a grand thing it was to survey the passing countryside from the bed of a vehicle, rather than having to proceed on foot, alongside, as he did with the tie wagons which hauled for the railway company. It seemed to him that one whose lot it was to travel on foot was forever condemned to a lower order of men, with whom he now had little affinity. He was a landowner, a man of some consequence, not to be trifled with. He leaned back, and Ervina stole into his thoughts.

As they moved from farm to farm, each having been approached by Roberts' agents well in advance so that a ready supply of work was assured, the only obstacles were the slow prairie rivers that wound their serpentine path in such convoluted coils that they were often obliged to cross the same stream several times. It was necessary, where there was not a well-established ford, to construct a bridge - or reinforce the existing one - in such a manner that would sustain the enormous weight of the machinery. Roberts had seen more than one steam tractor collapse the bridge upon which it had tried to pass. So he insisted on caution and over-building as the marks of each exercise. But Jan was indifferent. Hard work was a balm to a troubled mind. As far as he was concerned, he needed to be away for as much as a year, perhaps longer, and as long as he was earning money, he was as content as he might be expected to be under the circumstances. The vision of his farm was a keepsake as certain as the tiny pouch of soil from his beloved Ukraine, that even now was tucked with his belongings in the bunkhouse - or caboose, as it was called - rolling behind them.

The back end of the bunkhouse was tiered on either side with three levels of sleeping ledges, no mattress or pillow. The cost of a blanket was a day's wages: exorbitant, but no choice offered. The lower bunks were preferable to the uppers, for the heat from the cookstove and the summer sun combined to make the air fetid. Doors could not be opened at night for the hordes of mosquitoes would have made sleep impossible. As the newcomer, Jan was relegated to the uppermost bunk, though he was later advised by Wibbins that he was free to dislodge Cliff Waymack, the half-breed who fed fuel to the fireman.

Jan had been accepted into the ranks in the same way that a group of prisoners opens to accommodate a new arrival: without ceremony or observable enthusiasm.

Besides Waymack and Wibbins, there were two reclusive but hardworking Chinese brothers who worked as labourers. An American soldier, Cantlie, whose career had been cut short by a defective rifle that had scarred and twisted the right side of his face terribly, four sullen *Métis* who kept much to themselves and spoke French to each other in low tones, made up the balance of the crew in this corner of the sleeping arrangements. The cook, who seemed to have but a single name, Franco, was the oldest man of the crew. He moved gently, in accordance with his frail appearance, and had a peculiar habit of speaking in a whisper, almost a croak. At cards, he would cackle nearly silently to himself, for no apparent reason. The mainstay of his culinary efforts was porridge, though the evening meal was a stew; a thick soup, really, made the thicker by the addition of more porridge, or such game as might be secured from time to time by Roberts, who always had a rifle at the ready.

It occurred to Jan that all these men had at least one thing in common: they were all dispossessed, and all of them worked as hard as any he had known in the oil pits of Boryslava, or the coal mines of Pennsylvania. He had seen it before: that frenzied quality found only in men whose jobs were maintained solely at pleasure of their masters. Men for whom fair treatment and generosity were accidents of fate rather than expected traits of character in those who profited by their labour.

Of the citizens who now made up his tiny world, if Kerr and Roberts were the distant monarchs, Wibbins was Prime Minister. Not a man overly given to good humour, he was accustomed to having his own way, and would order the others about like a petty lord. It gave him a small delight to ask a man to fetch him a dipper of water, even though that man might be settled in to his blanket, bone weary from the day's efforts in the field. But no one wanted to take him on. Even Roberts tolerated his petty bullying, feeling that there was an inevitable hierarchy that developed among men of the working class, and he was in no position to alter what God had wrought.

He was conscious of Wibbins eyeing him, tugging on his jaw, sniffing loudly. That Jan seemed to know his way around machinery appeared to irritate the fireman. His was a world of flame and heat and sweat and constant motion. His life was ruled by two unblinking brass-bound thick glass eyes of thermometer and pressure guage. He saw himself as slave to technology; Jan seemed master, who could coax the machinery from a hiccuping arrhythmia to the deep breathing that ensured smooth transferral of power from piston to blades. That either task was as essential as the other did not matter for Wibbins. He was one of many such men for whom perceived advantage in another gnawed him like a rat's tooth.

While Wibbins was undisputed ruler of the labourers, horse-handlers, and other low-skilled men, it was not obvious to Jan why this should be so. He had physical strength, true, but at least in those early days with the crew Jan saw no physical bullying or threat to use force. Nor, thought Jan, would Roberts have tolerated anything which might threaten the stability of his crew. In cards he was petulant and preening by turns. There was nothing obvious that would drive one to conclude that this man was a natural leader. It would not be until much later that Jan would realize the smoky but persistent truth of it: Wibbins took himself to be better than the others because of race, and no other reason. It would be later still that Jan would come to understand that Wibbins did not simply assume that: it was yielded to him by the others.

It rained rarely that summer, but on those rare wet days, all but the Chinese participated in card games. Roberts would not allow gambling for money, but the game was spiced by playing for short lengths of peeled willow branch, called 'stickies'. All began with the same number, and yielded or took them as the worn cards permitted. Each man showed his personality in his playing. Wibbins, dropped each card with the heel of his palm loudly thumping the stained plank table. The American soldier uttered a string of curses with each card, whether he was favoured or otherwise. The Métis were quiet, but asserted their cards firmly, perhaps even defiantly, keeping their eyes on the other players' cards. In this arena at least, they yielded no ground to Wibbins or any of the others.

Waymack had only one eye. The damaged socket had been filled with a plug of white glass, and it gave the man's gaze a hideous quality. Perfect for card games, Jan thought, but utterly inconsistent with the way in which he allowed himself to be pushed around by Wibbins. When Waymack held a hand that was superior to that of the fireman, he could not suppress his glee, and the triumphant smile he valiantly tried to hold back as he gently laid the cards upon the table, switched and danced at the corners of his mouth like a man who has only just understood the joke. Wibbins, at least in this small dimension of life's complexities, understood the luck of the draw, and would greet his own bad fortune with exaggerated accusations of fraud and deceit, though it was intended as a general amusement of the others. And so it was, except for Franco, who never showed mirth when it was appropriate.

For his part, Jan enjoyed the games, to which he was admitted as equal. In Pennsylvania it was not this way: he was expected to play with the other immigrants: the Poles, the Ukrainians, the Russians. They were a mindless way to pass the evening hours or rainy days when no work could be done - though these were few that summer. No one cheated. This among other things were part of the murky niceties that were necessary for working men to survive in such a tiny universe. He copied the other men in their use of the English language, and so in generous measure learned to embroider his speech with the profanity and vulgar irreverences of the Canadian west.

The talk that summer increasingly was of gold. In the Klondyke, far to the north, came the storied whispers of riches beyond a man's imagining. Gold, and lots of it for the picking. Gold in the streams and the hills; gold lying on the forest floor as a man might see pine cones, and imbedded in the ancient chilled sod like stars in a frozen firmament. On one occasion, taking their mid-day meal near a prairie school south of Rapid City, Wibbins walked over to the thin schoolmaster who was dozing in the shade, enjoying the summer respite. The fireman walked back with a faded red atlas, and with the others hunkered around him, he laid out the two pages that illustrated the Dominion of Canada. Roberts and Kerr sauntered over; Jan thought he could see worry - or something - flitting across their faces. Wibbins could read, though he rarely did, and he assumed the pose of lecturer.

"Now here's where we is right now," he dug at the page with his dirty middle finger. "Just west and south of Rapid City. Our next job's in the Northwest Territories." He gestured vaguely at the enormous expanse of page coloured yellow. "We finishes in Medicine Hat, here. Right boss?" he glanced at Roberts, who nodded.

"If the weather holds."

"And this is the gold fields up here." He outlined with a dirty finger a wedge the apex of which abutted the Arctic Ocean and drew alongside the green shape marked 'Alaska'. He whistled. "See here, it says 'Klondyke'. This is the gold fields, they say." He gestured over his shoulder with his thumb. "Thet fella there told me he'd be long gone for the gold, but he's got wood legs, so's he's only good fer teachin' an' little else."

Jan jerked his head up sharply and squinted at the reclined figure, but his hat was over his face. From the look of him, he could have been Casper Clement's son. He thought about going over to the man, for his father had been generous when Jan had need, but he hesitated: the boy had been bitter and hostile then; likely not much had changed. With a trace of regret, he turned back to the open book, and Wibbins was holding forth.

" ... so what I been hearin' is that there's two ways to get there. Out to the sea, then up by steamer to here ... " he bent further and squinted. "Skaguay. Yeah, that's it, Skaguay. Then ya gotta walk over these mountains up ta here. Hah. Gotta be a thousand mile walk if it's a yard.

"Or you can go up this way, through Edmonton, overland. An' that's gotta be even *further*, 'cept they's no mountains to walk over. Probably take ya a month ta get there."

Kerr snorted. "A month! How about six months through the worst terrain you ever saw." He shook his head and walked away. But the others were mesmerized. Even the two Chinese boys had crept close, taking in all that was being said. Jan noticed that they rarely seemed to miss anything while yet maintaining their distance. He turned again to Wibbins, who seemed in a reverie. The American soldier Cantlie was agitated.

"My ol' man's partner went to the gold in the badlands in '76. Course, I was just a kid then. But he came back richer than ... than J.P. Morgan, ya know. Had all this gold. Let me touch it, he did. Emptied a poke on the kitchen table, an' out tumbled all these nuggets. Christ on a whiffle tree: I'll never forget that sound as them shiny little fuckers hit the table. One day, I says to myself. One day I says. I was gonna make that sound fer myself." He looked off to the northwest horizon as if in a trance. Almost under his breath, he muttered, "I'm owed. Christ knows I'm owed."

Roberts had heard enough. "Time's up, boys. Let's get back to reality here. Wibbins: that book needs to get back to the schoolhouse." He took it from the man as the fireman struggled to his feet, and handed it to Jan. "Jan, run this back there, would you? I want a word with Mr. Wibbins here." He was annoyed, and he put an arm around the man's shoulder in a way that did not suggest affection, and as he walked off, Jan heard sharp language.

Reaching the dozing schoolmaster, the man stirred at Jan's approach, and lifted the brim of his hat. "Everyone pissin' their pants to run off to the goldfields?"

There was no mistaking that voice. It was Nathaniel Clement. Two wooden crutches lay on the ground beside him.

"I return your book." Jan held it out, but the other didn't move.

"Put it on the stoop."

Jan did as bidden. He turned to go, and the other spoke. "Don't I know you from somewhere? We met before somewhere? Be hard to forget a big bastard like you."

Jan turned to him and said evenly, "Yes. Your father took me in and gave me food. Was very kind. I had been on the road many days, and I was hungry. You were unhappy ... "

Clement sat up, dragging himself back to rest against the building. There was no hint of recognition, for he was as self-absorbed now as then. "What do you know of unhappiness you big ... What do you know? How'd you like to get around with no leg? Don't you think I'd like to be off to find gold with everybody else?"

Jan could see that nothing had changed with the man - not much more than a boy, really. What kind of a teacher he made, Jan could only be dubious. Suddenly *popá* Kudryk came into his mind, and he remembered the patience, gentleness, and the encouragements of him. So unlike this bitter man.

"Maybe there is no gold," he began.

"Pash!" Clement scowled. "I get the papers from Brandon. Not right away, of course. But the stories are clear enough. They're taking *tons* of gold outta there. Tons of it, don't you know? And it's just sitting there for the picking, like blueberries, only bigger and there's more of it." He laughed, short, mirthless. "Isn't a fellow around here who's left, just about. It'll be hard to get the crops in, right enough. But who cares. There'll be gold to spend this winter, so let the wheat rot where it is." It occurred to Jan that not a single seed of generosity flowered in this man.

There was no further point to remaining, particularly as work had restarted, and Kerr was standing off in the distance, hands on hips, looking at Jan. The very image of impatience, him.

"If you don't go off for gold when you're able, you're a fool. I remember you now. The man who pulled a cart like a horse. Perhaps you are a fool." He settled back, tugging his hat over his eyes. "Why did God give me my brain and this stump, and a man like that has ... "

Jan did not hear the rest. As he walked away, he thought of two things: the power of the lure of easy riches, and the utter emptiness of encounters with some men. Both occupied his thoughts for a time, till the sheer weight of heavy labour forced all thinking from him. But that night, as he heard the fitful stirrings of the others, he could not sleep, for gleaming images held fast in the frozen muck had seized his fancy.

# iv

George Washington Carmack shaded his eyes, considering the stranger standing in front of him.

"Bob Henderson," said the other, with no hand put out. "Found a little trace of yeller along Gold Bottom Creek, an' I'll trade it fer some o' that salmon yer puttin' up."

It was hot that Yukon July of 1896, and Carmack was disinclined to get up. "Set yerself down, Bob." He called to his partners, Skookum Jim and Tagish Charlie, who were sweating at the fish-drying racks. "Hey boys, take a rest. Fetch up the tea-pail, here. Got a little business come our way." He turned back to the stranger. The man was looking at the two Indians with no attempt to hide his disdain. "Hard ta say what stinks more: the fish or them." He laughed dryly, attempting to draw Carmack into the joke. Carmack ignored him. An American, he had seen Indians diminished to the point of non-entities, but in truth, he preferred their company. None of the venalities of whites, that he could see, as long as there was no liquor about.

"We was thinking about doing a little prospecting ourselves, once we got the fish up proper," said Carmack. "Why doesn't we team up an' look fer claims, that way cover more ground. Jim here says it's gonna be an early freeze-up, so time's ... "

"Waal," Henderson cut him off. "I don't know. I mean, well, maybe I'm a little untrustin' fer a blue-noser, but ... "

He scratched his forehead, pushing his hat back. The lice eggs glistened in his thick hair. "Yer welcome, a course, ta help me look. But 'fraid I have no use fer the likes a them. Turn yer back a second, an' everythin' that's not tied down is gone. No thanks."

Carmack was indifferent to the other's hate. It was a common thing. "Well then, I think we'll just go our own way." Henderson nodded, as if they had been discussing tea with or without sugar.

"A course, I got the promisin' part a Gold Bottom already staked out ... "

Carmack shrugged. The following month, in the loose bedrock of the Klondyke River, the three men found the golden horde that touched off the fabulous rush of '98: " ... thick between the flaky slabs, like cheese sandwiches," said Carmack later. History has not recorded whether Henderson reflected on the cost of his prejudice.

It was mid August when Cantlie ran off to expatiate his aggregate demons. Foregoing the two weeks back pay he was owed, he disappeared one night, just outside Moose Jaw. The others saw it coming. The man had become increasingly obsessed with the idea of vast riches, and could speak of little else. At the card table, he was alternatively remote and indifferent to the game, and feverish in his need to chew on the latest morsel of information, which he would work and re-work until there was no telling what the truth was. Both Roberts and Kerr tried to intervene in these discussions, reminding their men of the folly of chasing off after a dream, and the distances involved, the hardship, and the plain fact that thousands - even tens of thousands - had preceded them. But this was variously ascribed to selfish interests on their part, and the fact that both men had a share in the profits of their enterprise.

"They's already got money," Cantlie had grumbled. "Dunno why they'd wanna talk a man outta gettin' some for himself."

It looked as if Wibbins might be next. One night, as he shuffled the cards seemingly endlessly, he looked out at the remainder of the sun's dying blush on the western horizon. Up against the cheesecloth screen, the mosquitoes kept up an electric whine, and in a nearby pothole, frogs chirruped a steady chorus on rusty springs. Wibbins was not his usual self. He seemed wistful.

"Wonder where Cantlie's got to now?" he said, almost to himself. Waymack's good eye glittered in the lamplight, but he said nothing. One of the Métis, a lean, well-built fellow named Georges Forest swept his head about.

"He's gone. Deal the cards."

Wibbins turned on him with a snarl. "What's the matter: sore 'cause you ain't the guts to do what he done? Spend all yer life picking straw, is that it?"

Forest looked at Wibbins with an unrelenting hatred in his eyes. "*Foure toi!*" Fuck you. Two of his friends at the table had the same look, and a third on a nearby bunk raised his head at the sharp exchange. From the back of the trailer came Roberts' voice; a growl:

"Steady on, boys." It was a command, not a suggestion.

Wibbins knew his place, but he returned the deadly look with his own brand of intensity. "I bet he's nearly there. He's been gone, what, near two weeks? Time enough to make the coast and grab one a them ships north. Why ... "

Jan got up from the table and made his way to the corner bunk. He glanced at the Chinese brothers who were uncharacteristically quiet; it was their practice to converse in their native tongue in barely audible tones. They watched him intently, and it occurred to him that they were about to say something, but they stayed silent. But there was something there, to be sure.

The next day showed grey and blustery, and it promised rain. Roberts rode off to secure a replacement for Cantlie; he was hoping for luck in Qu'Appelle, else he would have to go on into Pile o' Bones, or Regina as it was now being stylishly referred. He was off with an assurance that he would meet up with them in a week, and laid out for Kerr a schedule which, as they all knew, depended on weather. The low sky would pass soon, he told them. "Hell, this is the prairies. You don't like the weather: wait an hour."

The cortege had just established camp at the sprawling farm of a British landowner, who was fretting about the readiness of his crop. It looked luxurious to Jan, but this was a new way of considering things. The yields were so bountiful, averaging twenty-eight bushels to the acre - thirty was not unusual - that a man might be forgiven for attempting to coax a little more from each acre. That was the other thing that was odd: in Ukraine, a man could be assured that his neighbour's fields would mature at the same time, to the hour, as his own. But here, there might be a difference of days, even weeks. Kerr was in no mood to have his crew sit and wait. They would be off to the next spread, and try to get back if they could. The farmer relented: "Take her then. I've no hands anyway. All gone off for the gold." There it was again. There were constant reminders that the rainbow's end was a tangible thing.

Roberts returned much sooner than expected. With him was a short, well-proportioned man who walked with purpose and confidence. Over his shoulder was slung a large rolled canvas pack and a pair of shining leather boots. Jan noticed his bare feet straight away: *nasha lude!* a countryman! Who else would save his leather?

"Fellows: meet Yurgyn Os - say, Yurgyn, how'd you say that name again?"

"Ostastachuk." The last syllable was pronounced 'chook'; the accent was thick and the cadence slow.

"Jan," called Roberts. "Look what I found ya. Someone from your native soil! Strong as an ox, too, by whistling Peter." He swung his foot over the saddle, and took a set of bulging saddlebags off, and handed them to Franco, who cackled at some unknown joke.

Jan stepped forward, a wide grin on his face, holding his hand out. A good turn of events, this. "Jan Dalmynyshyn, from Kameneta-Holodyk. Welcome to our brigade of chaff-chasers!" His mother tongue sounded musical in his ears.

The other man held out his hand, and took Jan's in a crushing grip. "Yurgyn. I am glad to be having this job to working." He spoke in heavily accented English.

Jan replied in Ukrainian. "The work is hard and the pay not so good, but I think we shall have steady work until the cold."

Again the newcomer replied in English, even though he searched for words like a man turning over shells at a carnival. "They are not knowing hard work in this country. Where the country I live, I am knowing the hard work. I am at the coal mines by the Medicine Hat." He pointed at Franco, who was sitting on the threshold of the bunkhouse-kitchen, head reared back in silent laughter. "What is that ... ?"

"Oh, don't give him any heed. He is ... " he tapped his head.

Wibbins intruded. "Show some decent manners, Dalmynyshyn. Yurgyn here is doing his best in the Queen's English, an' you're going on like a *bohunk* in heat."

Ostastachuk had a faint smile, ignoring the slur, and spoke in Ukrainian. "I live here now. The old tongue is dead. To succeed here, I must speak the language well, and that means all the time." Then in English: "Yes. We must speaking good."

This gave Wibbins cause for laughter, and he guffawed loudly; Franco abruptly ceased his own amusement as if on cue, and Kerr ordered the lot of them to get to work.

"Reception's over. Yurgyn, throw your stuff on Cantlie's bunk; Jan, you show him where, and tell him he's entitled to no more lice than anyone else." This set Wibbins to snickering again; Franco's face was stony.

Inside the close, cramped quarters which had a sharp pungency to it not readily identifiable as the product of man or beast, Ostastachuk opened his bag and with the piety of a novitiate took out a worn violin wrapped in a soft, embroidered cloth. He handled it reverently, placing it with care on an inside corner of the straw-stuffed mattress. Jan was intrigued. "Some things from the Old Country are not so dead."

"Oh no. The songs and the poems of my forebears will live forever in my heart," said the other, this time in Ukrainian. "I may be a peasant who cannot read or write - yet - but what little I have learned will never be taken from me." He was defiant.

"But your language - our language ... ?"

The newcomer turned to face him, and reverted to English. "Hey you, man. I say I live here now. No one understand me but others like you, and you peasant also. I have land, wife some day; some day when have money. Lots." He held up his wiggling fingers in the Ukrainian way of showing plenty. "Lots of money."

It was a comfort to have Yurgyn alongside in the fields, even if his labourer's work took him far away from the machinery at times. They had much in common, including frightful stories to tell of their emigration to the new world. Yurgyn related how he had been sold a ticket by the recruiters who had come to his village, and upon reaching the coast, officials had laughed at him. He had been sold a brochure - in English - which had brightly coloured scenes of the prairies on it, and a large image of an enormous three-funneled steamer, which he had no difficulty accepting was the vessel which would take him to wealth and prosperity. Forced to work as a longshoreman, he starved himself and slept on the streets so that he could re-accumulate the cost of passage. The trip itself was hellish, for his quarters were below the waterline, and suffocating from the press of human beings. The stench was nearly unbearable, for the slop pails were constantly overflowing or spilling. Of the two hundred and eighty persons thus confined, four died of uncertain causes, and four of clearly identifiable diseases. They were buried at sea during the few times the weather permitted an outing along the lower boat deck, away from the better paying passengers. He had found work in the western coal mines, but work there was bitterly hard, with death or maiming nearly a daily occurrence. Explosions, seepage, frightened mules and runaway mucking cars; the possibilities for ruinous events were endless and constant. He had to get out. Anything was better.

Jan in turn related his stories from the Pennsylvania coal mines, and the same filth and dust and constant danger of explosion and cave-in that he had left behind. True, the wages were better than he had ever imagined, but the cost of all commodities was high. And he had the pervasive thought that he might not ever live long enough to see the land for which he had set off in the first place.

Yurgyn's addition to the group changed its dynamic. Wibbins seemed to take his arrival as some sort of personal affront. It was bad enough that there were two Chinee, a couple of half-breeds, and now the sheepskin brothers. He didn't like it, and made no effort to disguise his suspicion, especially when each reverted to their mother tongue. The least able to mount a defence against his petty bullying were the Chinese, who ironically gave him little cause for his attentions, given that they kept to themselves. Always careful to keep his sarcasms out of the earshot of Roberts, Wibbins kept up his criticisms and bitter commentary against most of the others, until one night, after Roberts had ridden off to Qu'Appelle to fetch supplies, he turned from the card table to glare at the Orientals. Their nervous, muted chattering fell silent, and they shifted uneasily under his gaze.

Yurgyn noticed this, and with a sidelong glance at Jan, he said, "You leave them alone. They do nothing to you." He looked down at his cards.

Now Yurgyn was a big man, taller than Jan by a palm's width, and fuller in the belly. For all Wibbins' strength, he was not about to pick a fight with anyone close to his size, that much was clear. But Yurgyn's words had the opposite effect of what was intended. Wibbins got up and went over to the two Chinese, who now huddled together, avoiding eye contact. He looked back at the other players.

"See. They's too good fer us. Never played a hand o' cards wif us. Pisses me off it does, no end, them thinking themselves our betters." He turned to them. "Come on then. Play some cards wif us."

There was shaking of heads. Wibbins reached under the bunk tier and caught one of them by the shirt. He pulled hard, and the cloth ripped loudly in the close space. Whimpering. Jan and Yurgyn exchanged looks, eyebrows raised. This was none of their concern, but the tension in the caboose was thick.

"What th' ... ?" There was another tearing sound, and another. The cries escalated now, this time from both of them. All men now looked over to the corner where Wibbins' thick torso obscured from view what he was doing. Suddenly he spun around, his face a mask of glee.

"Lookee what we got here, chums. We got ourselves a woman!"

There was a sound of consternation. What on earth was Wibbins talking about. Held by the scruff of the shirt, the figure in his massive hand squirmed, trying to cover a thin chest with both arms.

"A woman, boys," he chuckled again. "A Chinee woman, to be sure, but a woman all the same. Look: she got little titties to prove it!" He pried away her hands, exposing her nakedness. She cried forlornly to her companion.

"Now if this isn't a fine how d'ya do. Work like a man along us, live like a man, and her peekin' at us all along." He paused for effect. Clearly, the others were taken by surprise at this fortuitous discovery, and seemed uncertain how to react. There was more than a little prurient interest, for most had not even seen a woman for months.

"Well. We needs to be certain of this. There's only one way I know of to check for certain these things ..." He started to fumble at her breeches, and she began to squeal, writhing in his grip. Her loose pigtail came undone, and fell across her face, as she struggled to keep her clothing. Wibbins had an awkward time of it, trying to loosen her clothing with his left hand, finally giving up and tearing the cloth from her body. He flipped her under his arm as if she were a child, and held her exposed buttocks to the lamp. He was about to say something, having laid a dirty hand upon her, when with a scream, he stumbled and dropped her. Her companion had struck Wibbins on the back of the head with the piss-bucket with such force, it sounded like the meal bell.

For a long moment, the fireman stood there, then suddenly collapsed. The woman scrambled to cover herself, sobbing. No one moved. Then Yurgyn reached over and put his thumb on Wibbins' throat. "Not dead," he said simply, as if it were not out of the ordinary. "But close. He sleeps for a time; long, I think."

"We have trouble now," said Forest. "Or at least, *they* do." He pointed to the Chinese couple who were clinging to each other. "Better head out of here quick."

The man spoke in a thin voice without looking up. "We do nothing wrong. That man shame my wife; do bad things. I need to stop him. We do nothing wrong. Work hard. Mind business."

Forest sneered. "You don't get it. You Chinee. You *always* in the wrong no matter what. Born with a wooden ladle, you all are. No matter what we say. You near killed a man, just for looking at your naked wife. Last time I thought about it, wasn't a capital offence; besides, we'd all be done if that was the case."

"But where ... where do we go?" Not asked of anyone in particular.

Forest harrumphed again. "*Merde!* Anywhere but here, is what I'm thinking. Go on. Better bugger off straight away, or you'll end up with all of us in it."

Jan watched the grim realization sink into the couple's inner consciousness. Sergeant Jones' admonition about the uncertainties of the law's application came to mind, and he found himself agreeing silently with what Forest had just said. There was not going to be justice for himself, nor for these frightened people. He stood there, like a piece of rag caught on barbed wire, motionless, not belonging, contributing nothing. Wordlessly, they all watched the two gather their meager belongings and depart. Unsaid was their forfeiture of more than four weeks back pay. Silent tears streaked the woman's cheeks, as she gave a last look around, implicitly pleading for understanding. But no comforting word came from the group, beyond Forest's final urging: "*Allez!* Get on the hell out of here!"

It was another instance of failing to act that would haunt Jan's dreams for a very long time. An enormous mystery which attends on the dividing line of wanting to do and actually doing. Doubts and fears sheer by the belly of resolve, like sharp-toothed fish in murky water. But he would have another good reason to remember the unlearned lesson of these two wretched people, much later in his life.

# V

"You boys ever sat a horse?" The man called Fratnoe was dubious. One man costumed as a bumpkin, boots around his neck, and the other all dressed up like a spare bedroom. Jesus. Maybe he could get Ritter to ride herd and have the cook do double service; get these hands to ship in the supply wagon. "Ever drive a wagon?"

Jan was uncertain about the morality of lying to get a job. Not ordinarily a problem, this, if he could learn enough in a short time to prove up, as they said out here. But a minute or two on a horse, that is, assuming he could actually get on one, would reveal to the world both ineptitude and dishonesty. Better to keep quiet on specific responses, and rely on strenuous assertions of willingness to work. A meager plan.

Horace Fratnoe rolled his eyes. This project was getting off the rails before it'd begun. Almost two months earlier, Norman Lee up in the Cariboo had set off for the Klondyke with two hundred head of cattle. It was a drive that would take man and beast across some of the most forbidding territory on the continent. But last word had it that things were going well. Fratnoe had been inspired. He'd heard that beef was going for nearly two dollars a pound or more in Dawson City; hell, even a single steak in a restaurant was fetching as much as five dollars. He had more experience than Lee, had a better, tougher grade of cattle than Lee's pure bred Herefords, and figured that he could make better than the twelve or fifteen miles a day that Lee was said to be doing. A little cross with himself that he hadn't thought of the idea first. Blast and tarnation: there was some serious money to be made. He'd even designed a wagon that could be broken down and reassembled if need be.

But the matter of putting a decent crew together was a tougher prospect than he'd imagined. Only three of his regular boys stayed on - and one with a bum leg, at that. Everyone else had run off to the gold fields, caught up in the frenzy that was the gold rush, that summer of '98. Now with time running out, he was still short two hands, and decided reluctantly that these two immigrants would have to do. Sure weren't dressed for the part, what with the thick boots and long coats. Tall handsome one looked intelligent, could maybe learn what he needed; the other looked ... well, strong, is all. He'd have to lose that flowered shirt, for sure. Could always put them off along the way if better prospects showed up.

"Well, okay," he drawled, extending his hand to Jan, then Ostastachuk. "Understand me: if'n you boys don't prove up in a week, I'll have to get someone else. Ya know what I'm tryin' to tell ya? But we gotta get started. Dollar twenty a day, and a bonus if we deliver eighty per cent of our stock."

Jan was delighted, if a bit daunted that he may have to spend some time in the saddle. These animals looked unpleasant. He watched as one twisted its head, trying to bite the rider who was sawing at the reins, trying to get cooperation.

"You boys ride in the wagon for now, till I see what I got. Maybe we take a few days ta shake down the crew."

Jan and Yurgyn exchanged looks. Ostastachuk's face showed relief. At the prospect of work? Or at not having to mount one of these nasty nags? They scrambled to the wagon, which was fitted over with a tarpaulin on a frame of hoops, threw their blanket rolls in, and leapt aboard as the vehicle rattled off.

"See?" said Ostastachuk "It makes good sense to wearing your best clothes. You could see the man knows I am someone of consequence."

Jan was not so sure.

The first part of the journey, Fratnoe expected, would be easy, given that the Cariboo Wagon Road, completed in the days of the brief Cariboo gold rush, would take them as far as Fort George, though it got rougher after Quesnel. This route was known as the Ashcroft Trail, from the little town on the Fraser River. There were plenty of goldseekers who had used this route, and while passable, it was rough. They would follow the route that Lee had taken, heading north along creek and river beds, till they hit the slash cut by the Collin Overland Telegraph Company, back in '66 and '67. Should be plenty of overgrowth by now, but hopefully Lee's herd would have taken care of much of it. When the transatlantic cable was put down in '67, the venture was abandoned at a place still called Telegraph Creek. After that, it'd be a push to get to the Teslin River, but here again, Lee and God knows how many gold-crazed stampeders would be clearing the way. After that, easy sailing to Dawson. Off like a bride's nightie, then. A touch more than fifteen hundred miles; he'd need to make at least twenty miles a day to beat the weather, he reckoned. Should be able to do that with time to spare.

Jan and Yurgyn settled quickly into the routine of a cattle drive. Up before sunrise, they collected fuel and set the cook fires. Hot porridge, sweet tea and biscuits to get the men moving, then while the two hundred and eighty animals were rounded up, tents and other gear put away, and the wagon away before the herd, so that the mid-day meal could be prepared in advance. The evening meal was at a site chosen by Fratnoe, based on what he thought he could get from the herd. It was a fine balance: no point in getting there with skinny beasts worth nothing to no one. But it often obtained that the day's last meal was consumed after dark, with weary cowboys stumbling into their bedrolls before the last crumb was licked from a greasy thumb.

Ostastachuk was a chatterbox. He would prattle on without pause about everything he saw, working his adopted language like a convalescent trying to walk. Often, he would call out to the cook, known only as 'Sheddy', asking the correct English word for this or that. Sheddy was patient, to a point, tossing away ironies such as: "Yurgyn, ya say some things ya never thought of."

It was a chance for Jan to reflect. He had been away from home now nearly three months. He had not much to show for it. When the Chinese couple fled the work gang, both Jan and Yurgyn had decided to leave. The others spoke incessantly of the gold seekers headed north, and it seemed an attractive alternative to one or all of them being detained by the police. Both of them had an abiding fear and loathing of officials, particularly those in uniform. No good could have come of it, that was certain. Jones had said as much, and he was one of them.

His thoughts drifted back to his homestead. He thought of Kinipi, bent over, working the rows of vegetables they had planted. She did not know about such things, but she learned quickly, and worked hard. The image of her metamorphosed into the features of another woman. Ervina. He closed his eyes tightly against the image, seeking initially to hold it, then flush it from his mind. How could this fixation take root so quickly? He realized that it had seeded the moment he had laid eyes on her the previous year, with her family stranded at the bottom of a creek bed. Try as he might, it was impossible to banish her. There was a fine overlay of guilt to it as well. What of fidelity and his promise - at least implied - to the woman who even now was working toward making his dream a reality? *Popá* Kudryk placed fidelity above all other qualities. Without it, he would argue, the human being is no more than an animal, running from one impulse to another.

"And who has control over what we say? And what we think?" Jan could hear his voice now. "If it is not ourselves? The sins of lust and greed and avarice - these are nothing more than forms of laziness. Be firm, faithful. To your God, to your family, your friends and countrymen, and to yourselves."

Brave words. Noble. But how to flush out the vermin that persisted in gnawing at the very root of decency? He dug out Shevchenko from the parcel that held his few belongings. Burying himself in the poet's rhymes always worked. Committing to memory verses he enjoyed was always a task to be counted upon to empty the brain of all else. He opened the ragged pages randomly, and his eyes fell on a passage that he believed he had not seen before. Or at least, had not taken notice:

> *Do I deceive myself again*
> *With words so gentle and so vain?*
> *I do! But self deception's ways*
> *Are better than a foeman's praise*
> *To trust as truth, and then, down-trod,*
> *Make impotent complaints to God!*

# vi

Fratnoe was right. It was easy in the beginning. The road to Quesnel was well set up, and beyond to Fort George was better than expected. After the fifth day, they crossed the trail left by Lee, and it was apparent that the two hundred animals and three wagons of that drive would clear a considerable portion of the way. For two weeks, the procession of man, beast and implement continued in an easy routine under fair skies. Then, in the first week of August, a frontal system moved in from the Gulf of Alaska, bringing unusually cold weather and steady rain. The trail they had been following, already churned up by the hundreds of hooves that had preceded them, dissolved into glutinous, sticky mud. It covered everything. It was impossible to dry clothes; bed rolls were sodden.

It was heavy going for the cattle. Progress dropped to five or six miles a day. This worried Fratnoe, but the beasts would not be pushed beyond a certain point. They would simply lie down in the ooze, too tired even to forage. That was another problem that Fratnoe had not considered: Lee's herd had grazed out much of the available fodder, so the animals needed to range out further afield to find food. It was impossible to manage this development with the available mounted men he had, so he approached the two labourers in the wagon.

"Good news an' bad news, boys," he said with a mirthless grin. "Promotions to cowboy for both of you, but it means you'll need to leave the comfort of your present means of travel. No choice, really. Without more riders managing these cows, may as well try an' open an oyster with a laundry ticket."

It was true that the canvas cover on the wagon admitted almost as much rain as presently fell outside, the *slohta* that endured without respite. But there was a measure of comfort in comparison to the poor souls who huddled under rain slickers on horseback. Yurgyn opened his mouth to protest, but closed it, sensing both its futility and Fratnoe's mood.

Next morning under a steady drizzle, Fratnoe helped them saddle up a couple of the second string mares. "Sorry boys, this won't be no donkey ride at the seaside, but like I say, I need more outriders than I got right now. They're just rangin' too far out, and we're gonna lose a few if we're not careful. Ya know what I'm tryin' to tell ya?"

From the looks of the creatures cut from the string, they were none too pleased to be having a heavy, wet saddle cinched down just now. These animals were conditioned to expect that at mid-day. "There ain't nothing that likes his routine more than a cow-horse," said Fratnoe, as he took off his hat and swiped at the beast as it tried to nip him with yellow teeth. "Only two things about ridin': number one is, you're the boss. Number two: th' horse thinks he's the boss. Okay. Who's first?"

Yurgyn stepped forward, pulling his hat down against the drizzle. He had cut a hole in a square of canvas and waxed it for protection against the rain; it gave him a rakish look from a distance. Clumsily, he addressed the horse, climbing into the saddle as a man might scale a stone wall. It was restive beneath him, ears back, eyes rolling a little. He floundered for the reins. Seizing them from Fratnoe, he sat up straight. The animal did not move. Yurgyn flapped his legs as he had seen the cowboys do. Nothing. He clucked, then looked at his boss. A sheepish grin started on his face when suddenly the horse bolted. It passed under a deadfall propped in another tree which was, unfortunately for Yurgyn, at chest height.

He shrieked as the blow lifted him from the saddle and threw him "ass over tea-kettle" as one of the hands would later describe it, into the mud.

"That boy's a natural rider," murmured one of the cowboys, drawing on his pipe.

Jan approached his animal with anxiety evenly divided between what lay ahead, and how it might be received by the others. But how bad could it be? Cossack blood flowed in his veins; he was descended from a long line of mounted warriors that at one time had been the scourge of the steppes. That he had never been on the back of a horse seemed a technical matter only. Jamming his boot into the wooden stirrup and seizing horn and cantle with either hand, he hauled himself up as he might climb into a wagon. Under his considerable weight, the horse staggered and grunted. At the extreme angle he held himself, the saddle slipped a little. In a panic, he clenched his legs closely to the leathers, but to no avail. The saddle inexorably began to slide, until Jan was hanging nearly upside down. The chorus of laughter from the others was uproarious, all yellow teeth and hawking snorts. Fratnoe stepped over to help him slide off.

"Interestin' ridin' style, boy. Where you say you're from again?" He couldn't help himself, and with his gloved hands still under Jan's armpits, he fell back in his oilskins and whooped with laughter. Jan could not help himself, and began to snicker. All at once the release was there, and they all laughed for a time, tears streaming and snot running.

Wiping his eyes and nose with the back of his glove, Fratnoe said, "It's a question of balance, boy." He snickered again. "You could tighten the cinch-strap till yer horse couldn't breathe, but she's still gonna slip if you're off balance. Ya know what I'm tryin' to tell ya?"

Gathering himself, Jan asked in a shaky voice, "Why did you not say this before I started?"

"Some things you gotta find out for yerself, boy. Too much advice is like a doorbell on a coffin. All the tellin' in the world ain't gonna explain what you just experienced. Hee hee hee. Even if'n I did tell ya, you'd be all worried about it. So now ya know?"

"Are there other such lessons that wait for me?"

"Hell, boy," Fratnoe was now recovered, and was replacing the saddle. "There's thousands of 'em. That's what life's all about." He took the reins and handed them to Jan, repeating the manner of addressing the horse and the control of it: things he had said to Yurgyn, but Jan had failed to take in, though he had been watching. A complicated business, this.

It would be many days before they were comfortable with the animals, though it would be necessary to apply petroleum jelly to their buttocks for several days more, before the rhythm of horseback travel encoded itself as a matter of instinct. This was far better than the wagon. It was a fine thing to be astride the back of a nimble beast, well above the ground so a man could see great distances, and travel at speed in any direction he chose. In Kolomyka-Polodek, it was an unknown abundance to own such an animal, yet here there were more than twenty such animals. When he returned home, he would own a fine horse, and never again have to wear his boots around his neck when he travelled.

From time to time, he thought of Kinipi. Would she remember her commitment to him, or falter after a time, her truer nature reverting to her natural instincts and running off back to her people. A worrisome business, this: trust. As he held Kinipi in his thoughts, another paler image superimposed itself upon her, though the details were dimmer now, the fabric of those fleeting recollections having worn thin like a much-used beggar's coat. He resolved to put those meager memories away, and keep his backward-thrusting thoughts focused on his land and the woman to whom he had entrusted its care. While every step carried him further to safety, he believed, each stride took him further away from that upon which he had settled his life's ends. It was a complexity which he had no present way of resolving, save to carry on, drawn as he was by men and beasts to which he had fastened his immediate destiny.

The country through which they now passed was increasingly rugged. The trail which was easy enough to see, no longer was easy to follow. Although they kept to river valleys where they could, it was necessary to switch back where a gorge intervened, then squeeze the herd through narrow ridges, encouraged and disappointed by turns as the next length of their passage presented itself to them. Jan could see that had it not been for the unseen hands of the Collins Overland Telegraph Company, moving the herd would have been impossible. Here and there, rotting telegraph poles leaned at crazy angles; at their base was a tangle of copper wire and glass insulators from the fallen cross-arms. The wire was scrounged for an infinite variety of things, from repairing kit to adorning hats.

The season was unseasonably wet, interspersed with scorching temperatures. The animals suffered from the flies and mosquitoes, which only relented as they reached the higher country. Up here, the clouds sometimes obscured the path, or hung back, fretful, against ragged stands of fir. The sun swung a short arc over them before descending behind the mountain ridges to the west. The slopes above them were ablaze with purple penstamons and blue lupens and mountain asters. There were patches of bright buttercups and starch-collared daisies. Further up, there were flaming stands of Indian paintbrush stark against the mosses and low bush heathers and junipers. It was a beautiful place, Jan considered, and about as far away from his home in the Ukraine as he could imagine. Even the *Biskid*, the mountains of the western Ukraine, paled before these forbidding yet majestic peaks. It came on him that a man - even a fugitive fleeing the shapeless dread of a reckoning - who was otherwise content and usefully engaged, could find beauty and solace in the natural things around him.

And that it was very much the other way too, for when matters of the world pressed too close, as they had in the pits of Boryslava, there was no joy to be had anywhere a man looked.

Occasionally, the trail went in a direction that Fratnoe considered illogical. He would stand in his stirrups and look this was and that, speaking to no one in particular.

"Why in blazes does it go that way? More lost time! Why not across this way? Damon: take a ride down there and see where it comes out. Looks mighty plain to me that's the better lie. Gonna lose us the better part of another day goin' around this way. Climb down, boys," he said, dismounting. "Let them forage for a while. Sheddy, you think you can get some hot tea set up fer us in a hurry?"

As the fire dwindled under the suspended, well-blackened pail, there was a roaring commotion from the direction in which the rider had disappeared. As they all stood to look, Damon came running from the ridge, hat flying and slicker trailing out behind him. Close in and gaining was the biggest bear any of them had ever seen. It was so close they could see the saliva foaming from its black lips, and great tongue lolling from its fanged maw.

"Great Scott!" shouted Fratnoe. "Get me the goddamned rifle!" The scabbard under his saddle flap was empty, for he viewed the additional weight as unnecessary for the beast to endure. Now he regretted it. Yurgyn, who was standing on the wagon tail-gate, turned frantically to fetch the weapon, and sprawled into the bed of the vehicle, and they could hear him thumping and floundering, uttering sharp expletives in Ukrainian.

As the bear became aware of the other men and the stink of the fire, it pulled up short, skidding in the dirt. Rising on its hind legs, its poor eyes squinting, the creature must have stood ten feet. There was a collective moan of awe and fear from the men.

"Where *is* that goddamned gun?" asked Fratnoe through clenched teeth. "Nobody move."

The bear dropped to the ground and lumbered off, its hind end rolling like a clown in baggy pants. Damon dropped to the ground, sobbing. As they ran to him, they could see he had soiled himself. "H-Horse threw me, ran off," he said jerkily. "Was nearly done for. She had two cubs. Stayed to have a look. Shoulda known better."

"Never mind that," said Fratnoe. "Can we get through there?"

Damon looked at him as if he had quite taken leave of his senses. "With *that* monster in there? Have you gone mad?"

Ostastachuk came running up with the rifle, and handed it to Fratnoe, tossing it away as if it were a live snake. The other man took it in disgust.

"Johnny on the spot," he said disgustedly.

They turned away from him, and the men started again, for there was a stranger at the fire, squatting, poking at the embers to get some life from them. He rose as they crowded about, curious, a little indignant.

"Who the hell are you, boy?" asked Fratnoe in a cool voice.

The newcomer was swarthy, short, with thick black hair gathered at the nape in a greasy thong. Tiny white feathers had been worked into it. He had dark, intelligent eyes, and though he wore clothes much the same as they did, he wore plain moosehide moccasins. He wore a belt knife, and his pony, some distance off, carried a rifle, scabbarded in a moosehide sheath.

"I am Joe Smith. My Indian name is *Yontletii*. I am a *Tlingit*, a member of the Crow clan of my people. I have come to offer my services as a guide."

Fratnoe chuckled. Jan knew what he was thinking. Who should need a guide when the path they followed was so obvious an idiot could follow it. It did not need to be said, and Fratnoe simply gestured in its direction, his expression quizzical.

Smith said nothing, looking down, patient.

"Hell boy. Take a look at that right-of-way. Don't hardly need much guiding to get along, I don't think."

Smith looked in the direction of Fratnoe's open palm, nodding. "True. If following this path is all that is needed to reach where you go, you have no need of me." He met the other's eyes. "But where is the sweet water? Where are the hidden pastures? Where are the false starts beyond the end of the telegraph cut? What of the medicines you need to protect the four-leggeds?"

Fratnoe dropped his hand. "Hmmm," he said. "Don't know about that last bit. But I hadn't thought about the other. Hmmm." He rubbed his stubbled chin in his hand, and Smith sank to his knees, stirring the coals again. The others stood and watched like an audience at a play.

"What'll you cost me?" said Fratnoe suddenly. "I ain't got a lot to spare."

"Two of your cattle now, which I will take away. And if your losses are no greater than you expect, then two more upon arrival. And I will eat with you, and bring meat when I can do it."

"How do you know what I'm figurin' fer losses?"

"I do not know. But you will tell me when we arrive at the goldfields."

Jan was impressed with this simple statement, as was Fratnoe, whose squinted eyes widened ever so slightly. Honesty was not presumed in the way an aboriginal man took it for granted. A grant of trust was an act of courageous thing, and as far as Jan could see, the sum of his adult life demonstrated that it was a rare thing indeed. Fratnoe took Smith's hand with one callused palm, and took off his hat with the other. Jan took it all in: he had seen this gesture of respect many times before, but never had it struck him that such courtesies were more than affectations. In this small tableau, it meant something. You could feel it. Fratnoe was a man of his word. Men responded to it; trust was something you could almost touch, or smell.

Three days further north, and Joe Smith had proved his worth. Before the drive settled for the day, he had brought an elk down ten minutes from the camp. With a four inch knife, he reduced the beast to its edible constituent parts, leaving only the hide, antlers and gut pile behind for the magpies. That night, they feasted on a delicious stew seasoned with snakeweed roots, a favourite of bears, and when dry-roasted over coals have a rich nutty taste. He served them up fine slices of tongue, churned in brine for two days on horseback. His sense of the land enabled him to know where mountain meadows were, often not more than a few minutes off the main trail, but passed unknowingly by the Lee party.

"Damn it, boy," laughed Fratnoe. "I'm gonna make it three cows. Much more of this, an' men an' beasts will be too fat to float down to Dawson City. Fat as rats in a shit-house." Pleased was all over his face.

Later that week, the herd came to a pass so narrow that each animal was compelled to proceed in single file. The wagon had to be dismantled and carried over. For a hundred yards, the path was bounded by a steep wall on one side, and to the left, a precipitous drop nearly three hundred feet. It took all day and well past sunset. Below, broken slabs of granite studded the cliff like rotten fangs. That Lee's group or others had suffered some sort of mishap was apparent, as they could see the remains of a horse crushed among the rubble. There was something else there too, but whether man or beast could not be ascertained. Jan shuddered as he led his mount across. It was getting worse, this. But Fratnoe seemed to take it all in his stride: to look at the man, one might have thought he was out on a day ride. It was the same with the bear. The man seemed never flapped, no matter the circumstances. Jan was curious about this, for his father had taught him that fear can work for as it can work against a person.

Later, as he rode alongside Fratnoe, he asked, "You show no fear." He looked at the older man expectantly. He thought he saw a faint smile.

"Hell boy. Fear's its own antidote. After a while what scares the hell outta a man becomes just another irritation." They rode on in silence for a few minutes, a pair of trees forcing one to precede the other. Then as they drew abreast, he continued: "Gettin' old. Guess you might say I seen the elephant."

Jan was puzzled. Many of Fratnoe's peculiar expressions escaped him. He looked at his boss. "Elephant?"

He laughed. "Keep forgettin' that you're a foreigner. Funny how that is, when ya spend a lotta time with someone; get ta know him, sorta thing. 'Seen the elephant' is an old saying. Comes from the circus. When you seen the elephant, you know that's all there is, an' you might as well go home. Everything after that's … well, there ain't no more surprises.

"My ol' man was a skipper on a guano clipper. That's bird shit they mines from the South Pacific to use in fertilizer - spent ten years with him that's where I got the money to buy my place - the storms I been through. Seen a man taking a swim during a calm got eaten alive by a shark. Whew. Once we got drove up on a beach, and the ship destroyed from under us. How we all made it out is nothin' short of a miracle. You had to be there: all covered in stinkin' shit and nearly drowned. Whew. That order o' fright'll scare a freight train onto a dirt road.

"Point is: when you come through that, there's not much use in frettin' about what might happen. Fear is all about what you *think* is gonna happen, and hell, if a man ain't got control of that, well, ya know what I'm tryin' to tell ya?"

Jan nodded. He did. He was beginning to understand that one of life's important teachings was that there were always lessons to be learned. Every day, if one but looked for them.

# vii

By mid August the procession had passed through Hazleton, a scattering of shacks and tumble-down Indian longhouses, and crossed the Skeena River beyond, with only seven animals lost. But now the trail moved closer to the rain forests of the west coast where lush vegetation choked the dark forests on either side. Tall firs confined the sun to an even tighter arc, and a misty light rain fell almost constantly. It was a considerable task to get a fire going, for even the crumbly parts of the spruce and pine, close to the trunk and below the branches, had been scavenged by those who had preceded them.

There had been plenty of indication that others had come this way, for the Lee herd had thoroughly chewed up the terrain, leaving it a sticky black bog under the ceaseless drizzle. But now it became more obvious that goldseekers had travelled this road, as discarded heavier items, often of considerable value, became increasingly evident. Saddles, spades, books, weapons of all kinds, unopened crates, a toboggan and even a parlour stove were some of the things that attracted attention. At places of difficulty, where the climb was steep, or the ground marshy, there were often great heaps of materials, cast aside by those whose pace was slowed by the heavy going. Fratnoe soon tired of ordering his men to stop scrounging among the detritus of the stampede.

"Why'd ya think it was thrown away in the first place, ya damned fools. Next man as sidetracks to sniff among someone else's leavings better turn around an' head home. Ya know what I'm tryin' to tell ya?"

It was a hollow threat, for he needed every man on his crew to help with the herd now. A cow could get stuck in a bog, and it might take a couple of horses and two or three men to remove it. The herd needed to carry on. An animal which could not be extracted after an hour or two of trying was doomed. The beast was killed, or at least stunned, and the flesh would be carved from it to the level of the ooze which held it. Backstrap and shoulder, hastily taken with a hand-axe. Carcasses of various beasts punctuated the way now, ominous signs of the hardships others had suffered. And Joe Smith was gone more frequently now, often more than a day or two. Yurgyn muttered to Jan his suspicions:

"I do not like it. This. Where is that man who guides us? Living in comfort while the rot in my crotch grows well? I do not like it."

Jan understood his frustration. The rain never let up; the cattle had not enough to eat. There was only one hot meal a day - and that porridge and raisins - and the indications were that it would get worse before it got better. Someone had nailed up a packing crate lid, with the words, "Go back. Death lies this way," scrawled across it. It spooked the men, who were already harbouring their own morbid thoughts. It occurred to Jan that had there been somewhere to go, there may have been a number of desertions. But there was nothing for it but to press on. Progress was slow.

More and more goldseekers passed them. 'Pilgrims', Fratnoe called them. It seemed to Jan that it was a term of contempt, like 'peasant', but he could not be sure. He eyed them surreptitiously as they moved past the stooping cattle. Dirty, forlorn men who barely acknowledged the others as they trudged by, tugging at skeletal nags in their too-heavily laden pack trains. Forage for them was as difficult as for Fratnoe's herd. Smith had much greater difficulty now in finding feed. He warned the cowboys to keep the animals away from larkspur, which he said was poisonous. Sure enough, where the bluish plant was plentiful, the ground was littered with both horses and cattle, bloated and torn by scavengers. To Jan it seemed that the stink of death was everywhere.

At length they arrived at Telegraph Creek, the point at which the Western Union people heard that the transatlantic cable had been successfully laid, rendering their project instantly obsolete. The place was nothing more than a squatting of tents and hurriedly put-together lean-to shelters, populated by the stampeders who had run out of steam or grub or cash. Most others had carried on. There was a tavern owned by an American trader from Wrangel, who also owned the only competition for the ubiquitous Hudson's Bay Company post. Notwithstanding the free market, prices were extraordinarily high, and though a steamer had off-loaded four tons of oats, at eighty cents the pound they were too dear for Fratnoe. He had hoped to trade cattle for feed, but the Lee herd had been through only two weeks or so prior, and both establishments had enough live beef for the winter. The tavern was a place for desperate men, and he was worried that he might lose a few of his hands to drink and whores. He was determined to push through to Teslin, and gave the orders. Even so, three men deserted to what appeared to be a very desirable alternative after more than six weeks of steady driving.

The country north of Telegraph Creek is as determined an obstacle to the passage of men and tame beasts as there exists on this earth. The terrain was a steady rise at best, and at worst it was a serpentine tangle of thickets crushed flat now by the constant procession of men and animals moving with the listless determination of refugees. It claimed its toll not just in the possessions of those who were unable to carry goods one step further, but the spirits of those who had set out in the full blaze of hope. Thurgood Cobble was such a man.

A musician of middling competence from the dance halls of San Francisco, he had been caught up in the euphoric frenzies that continued for the rest of that week and beyond without respite when news of the strike in the Klondyke arrived. He with thousands - perhaps tens of thousands for all he knew - resolved to go to the Klondyke to seek his own fortune. Not hard-scrabble labour as he supposed that digging for gold might be, for he was under no illusions about that. Any gold lying about for the taking he reckoned would be long snatched up by the time he arrived. No, he would take his piano, and two of the whores named Breste and Boadice who worked with him as showgirls, and sporting ladies when the lights were lowered, and pan his gold from them that had done the dirtiest part of the work. Such tactics had served the trio well thus far, but with the depression on, and the law breathing down his soiled collar, it was time to be seeking ampler opportunities elsewhere. The Klondyke beckoned.

When the first ox in his team gave out, the other was barely able to draw the load. Of course, had he been anything in the way of experienced with any sort of droving beasts, he might have seen the signs coming. He had simply starved them to the point of exhaustion, then whipped them from there to collapse. Nothing had gone right from the start. The mud was oppressive, and the fact that cattle had been driven through some time just before had ruined what he thought might otherwise have been a fine trail.

They were without proper clothes, and his dandy but cheaply-made boots had dissolved in the constant muck. Boadice, the older one, had run off in the night after a week of whimpering. Though she took not so much as a halfpenny with her, Cobble knew she had more than adequate means of securing her way, for she was possessed of that which men covet on a level with gold. He cursed her for the loss of projected revenue, and beat her sister for good measure.

When the load on the wagon shifted over a boulder in the trail, it slewed the vehicle about with such force, that the piano broke with its moorings, and was flung with an ill-chorded, resonating crash onto the cliff face. Ruined beyond repair, but still he persisted.

When he passed the blurred line which marks the divide between despair and madness, no one could say. When Breste broke her leg as the result of a stumble in the mud, he displayed uncharacteristic calm, if not concern. His apparent equilibrium spooked her, and she called to him to carry on; others would be along to help in no time. Wordlessly he took up the whip and cut at the remaining beast. Though the wretched creature managed a step or two it could not build momentum in the slickness. Up close, one might have seen the tiny workings in Cobble's face that betrayed the failing inner man: eyes small and wetted, jaw line tight with a kinking knot at the angle, and short breaths, shallow, like a spavined horse under load.

He picked up his delicate rifle, an ornate thing bound up in brass with silver inlays that was in keeping with his predilection for excess. Small bored, it took three shots, one through the eye at a close range, to do in the beast. He walked over to Breste and as calmly shot the shrieking woman. He left her, good leg jerking under a satin dress befouled with the inescapable mud, and started for home. "End of the line," he muttered. "End of the line."

The next man he took barely had time to register his surprise, stooped in a harness secured to a sort of sled which had small and largely useless wheels under its runners. Cobble shot him where he had paused, straightening, about to greet a stranger who seemed to be going the wrong way.

The sight of Fratnoe's cattle was what seemed to push him beyond the reach of ordinary men forever. He shot indiscriminately into the herd, wounding animals with the light rifle so that the lead cattle turned back on the others in the narrow pass, and a trampling panic occurred which caused more harm than the initial shots. Into this melee waded Cobble, still silent if purposeful, using his now expended rifle as a club. One of the tormented animals, eyes rolling and hooked horns swinging, turned unseeing upon him, and Cobble was quickly brought down under their hooves. Jan could not see the man who had foolishly charged the face of the herd, and he heard no cry, but it seemed certain that the weight of the herd was upon him.

Owing to the steepness of the divide through which they were passing, and the turmoil of the dozen or so animals at the head of the drive, the herd fetched up at a standstill, animals bawling, men shouting, and horses snorting and fretful. Before long, at the rear of the drive, other travellers had caught up and were adding their urgent shouts to be let by.

Jan, who had seen Cobble go by and had noted the determined set of the man, was caught by surprise: no one had been seen wandering in a southerly direction since they had set out. He urged his mount toward the point where he had seen the man go down, wondering what would make a man mad enough to confront a solid wall of moving cattle. Four cows were down, none dead, but the groaning squawls were a deafening row, such that he could not hear the other men who were crying out. Beasts thrashed on the ground, showing a rim of eye-white in their terror, as the others milled about, unable to go back and unwilling to move forward.

Fratnoe would know what to do, but he was uncharacteristically nowhere to be seen. Jan was not about to take chances with hoof and horn; he had not yet acquired a comfort with them. Cattle needed a show of confidence as much as a horse. They were stupid creatures, true, but unpredictable in situations like this. It fell to one of the other cowboys who had made his way to the fallen animals, beating off the others with his hat, and dispatching the stricken beasts with a blow from the blunt end of an axe. This seemed to have a calming effect on the herd, and the carcasses were dragged to the lip of a drop, and rolled over, landing a hundred feet below with a wet sound as they burst open.

There was a cry. Yurgyn had been discovered, and he was quite dead. There was a tiny hole above one eyebrow where one of Cobble's erratic shots had entered his brain. He had been stepped on by frightened cows, so that he was broken, and some spillage of his innards had occurred at the groin. Dead. It seemed unfathomable that chance should end a man's life this way, when he had done nothing to contribute to the event save happen to have his head within that minute span of place where a madman had loosed his anger. The drovers were in a terrible state, and one of them went over to the badly crushed corpse of Thurgood Cobble, and began kicking it mightily, though Jan could see he had plenty of work ahead of him if he were to leave a mark that would make a difference.

Fratnoe came up, and snatched off his hat, making the sign of the cross. "How can such a thing come to be?" he asked "Had to've been a fluke thing." Jan nodded, wondering at the sheer chance of it. Poor Yurgyn: escaped the misery of the coal mines to happen across the flight of a madman's bullet.

*... Pray, brethren, pray!*
*and pray they did, as there they knelt,*
*In simple faith serenely felt*

# viii

Once Yurgyn had been buried, and the note of his passing carved into the blaze of a tree at the head of his site, *Yurgyn Ostastachuk, about 30, killed by a madman, r.i.p.* it was elected that they continue, there being no other options of attraction. The balance of the trip to Teslin Lake was bleak, for though the sun showed thinly, and the near frost kept the flies off, Yurgyn's death hung over them like an evil portent. A wagon road had already been built from Telegraph Creek to the head of Teslin Lake, for this was the 'all-Canadian route to the goldfields'. A railroad was planned, with steamer connections for Dawson City, though word had already come that the Senate would in all probability kill the Bill. Still, the trail now was crowded with all manner of travellers and vehicles. Wagons, traps, sledges and barrows plodded steadily northwards, like irregular filings in the grip of a powerful magnet.

At Teslin City, there was a glut of fresh meat, for Lee had passed through, and the corrals where the animals were to be held and slaughtered were demanding cash rather than kind. Up at the sawmill, where Fratnoe had arranged for two large scows to be built to convey the meat to Dawson, there was also a surfeit of beef, and a consequent reluctance to take more of it in payment for the vessels. Everywhere, it seemed to Jan, the singular meanness of men was on exhibition, and the operative rules of conduct revolved around profit, as much as could be got from the next man.

The good news, for that is how it came to be perceived by Fratnoe, at Teslin City was that Lee's fleet of vessels, heavily laden with the sides and quarters of his stock, had become wrecked, scattering frozen pieces of beef along the shore where human scavengers were racing to get at them ahead of the vermin. This proved to be a considerable lift for the men, and Jan felt a pang of guilt that another man's misfortune should make for leavened spirits in this way. But there was no denying that the market would be the stronger in their favour, and his share the greater. He felt the insidious pull of greed, and thought he understood that it indeed had the power to make him over into something else.

By now, it was cold, and each morning, a thin skin of ice rimmed the lakeshore. Fratnoe was anxious that they might not make Dawson, which was still more than two weeks away, even if there were no complications. Finally, after much hectoring of the mill-owner, two scows were slid into the water, and sunk, so that they could seize up. Built of rough timber, still redolent of sweet spruce gum, Jan could not imagine such vessels would float. They more resembled packing crates with upturned ends than a boat.

"Normally," the builder had said, "they'd need a week under water, so's the oakum could swell proper, and the timbers snug up against the frames."

But there was no time for niceties of construction and finish, and the sides of beef were loaded aboard and the crews pushed off.

The winds were favourable and steady from the south, even though the weather now was at winter's doorstep. A small stove was set up on each craft, so that tea and small foods could be prepared without calling a halt and going ashore. A narrow square sail set at the bow kept them moving northerly, and there was little to do except steer and bail the constant leakages.

For Jan, at last, it was a time to relax and think. Stretched out athwart, he alternated between dozing and smoking. The country now moving past him on the eastern shore was rugged and tangled, as inhospitable as a slammed door. Rock and sand and yellow clay runneled by green, clear water; these were the building elements of a God whose ingenuity must have been developed from these sparse beginnings. It was an old land, long accustomed to the distant chant and thin fires of the rugged aboriginal peoples who eked out a living from such grim terrain. Ragged trees clung tentatively to thin ground cover, and grey skies continually promised snow. Each morning now, the stern of their craft needed breaking free from a skin of ice, until they could fetch into the current or broader reaches of Marsh Lake, and the vastness of Lake Labarge beyond the White Horse Rapids.

Though it was late, there were still many vessels of all manner and description afloat and passing in the same direction. Rafts and yawls, canoes and rowboats, often loaded so that the gunwales barely had freeboard. Men, women and dogs sitting atop bales and boxes, all fervently staring northwards, with an occasional furtive glance at a lowering sky. The shores were littered with the jettisoned and the lost, the wrecked and the forgotten. It was a cruel land, Jan decided, exacting a terrible price for the privilege of entry.

He wondered why the yellow metal held no pull for him. He was not alone, for most of the drovers could only think of getting paid out so they could return home. And Joe Smith never spoke of the gold madness but with contempt in his voice. Jan had always believed as he had been taught, that purpose was a matter of being rooted in the soil, the fecund and embracing land, which would sustain him and his family. He had hoped that having conceived of purpose, he could pursue that end in a direct pathway. But it seemed that events and his own fears were disintegrating elements that were constantly interfering with his efforts to move in a straight line.

When he felt safe to return, he felt certain that nothing could deter him from his course again. Keep to himself, allow no diversions from the improvements to his property which were necessary to take title. Had Kinipi stayed true, he wondered? It was a powerful worry, for he knew her little enough, and of her race, nothing. He looked over to Joe Smith, who lounged in the bulge of the hull, giving away his discomfort only in the small way that he clutched the after thwart. The man hated being on the water. It was a paradox, for he seemed untroubled by most other things. None, that Jan could see, save this.

"What is it that makes trouble for you, Joe?"

The other man looked at him for a long moment. There was little small conversation among the men in the boats, for all of them coveted their thoughts of returning, nursing their homesickness with the intensity of revenge. It occurred to Jan that he had no idea where Joe was from. *Tlingit* meant nothing.

"I had a dream during my time when I became a man. It came to me that the spirits of the water were angry with me, for wrongs of another time. My ancestors. It was revealed to me that I shall be taken to the water, forever to live among them, there," he pointed to the faded reeds sloughing with the current, and the eddies that swirled behind the sweepers and rockfall tangles at the river's edge. "It is said that certain of us can hear their voices, when nightfall comes, by the river." He looked as melancholy as anyone Jan had ever seen.

"Perhaps you have not interpreted the signs in a rightful way," he ventured. "Perhaps there is another meaning ... "

Joe Smith looked at him with the first truly open expression that Jan could remember. Amazement, perhaps, or was it incredulity? "So you think I am a fool."

"No," said Jan quickly. "Just that, well, there is no certainty to these things, for they are of another world."

"Huh," chuffed Smith, clenching his pipe stem. "Matters of another world are as certain as those in this. They are but separate halves of the whole thing. Ask a teacher why he does not use wood from the side of the tree that the moon shines upon, and he will require you to discover the two answers for yourself: there is one response of this world, of practical things, and there is another one having to do with the spirits. Ignore one at great risk from the other." His face resumed its sad aspect, and he seemed to think fretfully for a time.

"I know about your god from the Anglican missionary. He seems to me to be a weak god, letting himself be tortured and killed by ordinary men. But it seems a fitting god for a race of ... thieves."

He suddenly looked embarrassed, though Jan could not be certain. There was silence again, broken only by the steady lapping of the water, for the current bore them along swiftly. The man in the stern leaned into the sweep oar with a firm hand, using the deflected water to advantage in the great bends of the river. A moose plunged from the shallows and reared up the bank, scattering droplets of water like a magic cloak.

"Forgive me," Smith said. "I forget my manners."

"No, it is me who must be forgiven. You speak the truth," replied Jan. "No thought in a careful man arrives full-formed and without effort. Yet this is where the gods - yours or mine - fail me, for I begin to think that everything happens according to a ... destiny. Some great plan."

"This is a very serious conversation," said Fratnoe, who was sitting in the stern with an arm over the sweep oar. "An' all we're talking about here is chance."

Jan turned to face him. It was dusk, and the man's face was shrouded in shadow. It was impossible to see his expression. Jan spoke softly: "Yurgyn cheated death in the foul mines of this country. He lived in a pest-hole built over a cesspool. He sweat in the deep coal pits and froze when he bring to the surface. He know one day he die from all this. So he leave and he die anyway."

"There's an ol' story. Seems that a citizen of a prosperous town dreamed he was going to be visited in his home by death; upon waking he rode furiously all day to a great city. He hammered frantically on the gates, demanding to be let in, and the doors was swung open by none other than Death himself. 'I'm very surprised to see you,' said Death. 'I did have an appointment in town with you today, but a more urgent matter brought me to this city.' You know what I'm tryin' ta tell ya here?"

Joe Smith nodded. "There are many such stories among my people. There is the story of the spider and the crow ... "

Their voices faded as Jan let his gaze drift over the water behind them. A troubling matter, this. Was everything that happened to a man inevitable? Or was it all chance? Should he have stayed home and seen matters through? Was this flight futile?

A flock of late-starting swans, bleating an annoyance at the constant interruptions of men and vessels, swept past him, irresistibly drawn by their own imperatives. Beyond to the south, a greater number of their kind flung their faltering wedge against the dying sky.

# ix

Sometimes it is the fate of a man's imagination that it becomes trapped in what it creates. At the end of the trail, thousands, tens of thousands of men were standing around, idling, watching, arguing and moving as if in a state of hypnosis. Having given their all in a torturous quest to reach the gold fields, there appeared to be a void in their lives that seemed to have been exacerbated by the realization that gold was not laying about for the picking. But, Jan reasoned, only a fool would have believed such a thing in the first place. Was it true that the try was all? It was a troublesome thought.

Dawson City in the early winter of 1898 was the largest settlement west of Winnipeg and north of San Francisco. Thirty thousand souls — perhaps more, for no one knows for certain — had gathered at the confluence of the Yukon and the Klondyke Rivers, on a narrow spit of land that abutted the bluffs close behind. Without benefit of paint or plan, shacks were being thrown up at the rate of fifty a day, and an equal number of high-walled tents beside. As the creeks froze up, and the ground took on its atavistic hardness, the claims emptied and the hirsute shabby men who peopled them drifted into town. To Jan's eyes, the scene at the river's edge, though partly obscured by swirling snowflakes, rivaled the clamour at the docksides in Bremen.

The last steamers for St. Michael at the mouth of the Yukon River were about to depart; their oily black smoke belched into the whiteness. Snow flakes as large as pigeon's eggs were falling in a stifling blanket onto the shabby town and into the black water. Jan shivered. He and the others stood around after Fratnoe had paid them out, conscious of being watched by a predatory lot of layabouts, down-and-outers, and whores. They had gathered to see off the lucky ones, those whose pokes permitted 'getting out', for the winter was long and bitter. "Piss freezes 'fore it hits the ground," they had heard someone say at the foot of the gangplank.

Jan asked Joe Smith what he would do now. He had money; he could sail out. But Joe had shaken his head, one trip by water was enough. A man needed to know when the gods had been generous, and he who demanded more of them was sure to come to grief, this seemed to be obvious. He was curious why Jan was not leaving, but expressed it in a way that required no answer. It was a matter of good manners, and Jan wished that all people he had met should feel so constrained by this elemental decency. For his part, he would travel upstream on foot, then across the river at freeze-up, to the place where this great influx of strangers had displaced his relatives. He would be welcome there. And so would Jan. It was the way of the *Trondek Gwitchin* people, his relations.

Before Jan could answer, he was hailed by a thin young man with skin the complexion and colour of sliced veal. He wore his hair in a long skinny braid which hung nearly to his waist. He had wispy moustaches and a feather of a goatee which curled under his chin. His clothes were ragged, but he had not entirely abandoned ornament, for stuck into his stocking cap was a long eagle feather. Behind him, Jan could see men chuckling at him, for here came another *cheechako,* greenhorn, off the river, ready to be duped. His face hardened. "What is it?"

"You're a bloody big man. Would you like to earn your keep working my claim?" The last word was pronounced 'climb' with a flat, nasal accent. There was no avoiding the sniggering around them, and the young stranger shot them an angry glare.

"What is it that you offer?"

"Room and board, and a share of the takings. I have a claim ... "

There was a collective hoot of laughter. "Tell him what you've taken out so far, Kiwi," called someone.

"Bloody dags," he muttered. His pale face reddened under the mockery, but he faced Jan squarely. "It's bloody hard work, and I need a man who is used to it, and can do what's necessary. From the look of you, there should be no problem with that. The food's poor, cabin's colder'n most, and there's not a lick of gold as yet. It's all I have to put on the bloody table at the moment." He stared at Jan for a moment, who seemed to be struggling with his instincts. He turned to leave; the look on his face seemed to reflect a lifetime of disappointment. Jan sensed he was inured to rejection. He responded to the impulse: "I will come."

Bidding farewell to Joe Smith, he picked up his single bag, and walked away with the skinny stranger, whose name was Jon Parker. He was, he explained as they walked along, Australian, "not a bloody Kiwi, which is a New Zealander." Jan was silent, for he knew nothing of either place. Parker had been in San Francisco when news of the strike came to the world's attention.

"I was there, mate, when that bloody old tub *Excelsior* pulled in, July of '97, wallowed down to the gunwales with gold. Never seen anything like it, not ever. You couldn't get a ticket on that ship back north for blood nor money. Not that I had the money." They walked on in silence, the gently descending snow muffling their footfalls.

Parker shot him a glance. "You don't bloody say much, mate. Where you from?"

Jan shrugged. "Galicia." It was his turn to glance at the other, watching for his reaction. There was none.

"Galica, hey?" said Parker after a time. "No bloody gold mining going on over there, I shouldn't think. You done any work with a pick and shovel at all?"

Jan smiled in spite of himself. He was reluctant to be open with anyone, but such a guileless question called for an answer. "I do work in the oil pits of Boryslava. I am good with the pick and shovel."

"I'll bet you are, mate," replied Parker admiringly. "What are you, six and a half feet? Eighteen stone? Bloody hell, mate, I'll bet you can swing a pick, alright."

Parker's claim was well beyond the well-established workings that ran off the Klondyke River, and along its smaller tributaries; Bonanza Creek being the most productive. As the ground kept rising, there were fewer and fewer indications that anyone was doing any excavations, though the skinny trees had been cropped as far as the eye could determine. Still they proceeded, and it occurred to Jan that there might be a reason for the japery back at the docks. He remained silent. A mystery, this. But the man seemed harmless.

"I know what you're thinking, mate," said Parker. "I'm one of them bloody loonies what's let the loneliness and the insects and the stink and the God knows what get to him. That's what they all think. My only problem ... is, ahh, I'm not a well man. Can't keep any weight on, thin as a bloody flagpole, I am. Can't do the work like I used to."

Jan nodded. Failing health was serious. And in this part of the world, more serious still.

"It's not that I don't know my business. I do. I spent seven years at the Mount Morgan Mine in Australia. I learned the demon metal well. See, there's two ways of gettin' it: there's vein mines and placer. Placer is where deposits of gold is formed by the action of rivers and floods upon the veins of gold that you'd see in quartz deposits. This placer gold is rolled and tumbled about so that the particles are rounded and smoother.

"Because it's heavier, it gradually finds its way down to the lowest levels in the gravel and such, right down to the bedrock."

Jan turned to him. "So how does this help you find it?"

"Well mate, I spent a lot of time when I got down here just lounging around the assay office, watchin' the miners coming in so excited you'd think they was going to drop one in their bloody drawers. 'Cause everyone who could squeeze in did, so it wasn't as if I was doin' something wrong or anything. Bloody hell, they'd hold up the bigger nuggets and pass 'em around. So here's what I was looking for - " his voice dropped conspiratorially, though there was no one in sight. " - the rougher the edges, the better. It is good evidence that they have not been transported far from the original source. That's what I'm looking for. You have to state your claim and reference numbers, and I been concentrating my search well up from them. 'Course, they all think I'm bloody crazy. Lot of people know the theory what I know, but the gold is so thick down at the streams, no one believes there's much left at the higher elevations. And the few places that's been tried have yielded nothing." He paused, then added. "Of course, my claim's yielded nothing so far either ... "

They trudged on for a while, stopping to pick up branches that had fallen from loads others had been bringing in. "Soon there will not be a tree left in the Yukon," said Jan.

"Oh, never bloody worry about that. Lots of trees in this part of the world: just none around here anymore. Look, there's my digs. Claim number five-bloody-eighty."

Just ahead, in the lee of a gravel cliff, was a miserable shack not more than four by six paces, with a steeply pitched roof. The entire structure was wrapped in tar-paper and nailed down with unpeeled saplings. Beyond, torn and ravaged folds of earth were being bandaged by the fresh snow. Boxes, crates, tubing and rusting implements lay about, each with their ghostly feathering. In two places, a steam rose from the ground like the breath of mother earth. The scene was fantastic.

"What is that?" Jan asked, pointing at the vapour emanating from the ground.

"Oh, that's the steam I pump underground to thaw the frost, so it can be worked. Like bloody iron otherwise. And all year round at that, mind you."

The furnishments inside the tiny cabin were as rough as Jan had expected. A sapling-sprung bed, table made from a packing crate, oil-barrel stove, and a single stool comprised the lot.

"Haven't thought out where you'll sleep, but we'll get on."

The meal that evening was porridge and raisins. In honour of Jan's recruitment, Parker opened a can of condensed milk. It was hot, delicious, and Jan began to think that his exile would not be so bad. Besides, there was the possibility of finding gold. Slim, perhaps, from what he could see. But more and more he was thinking that providence played more in the turning of a man's life than hard work and industry.

> one man in boundless luxury
> from land to land is ferried;
> and one inherits but the dirt
> in which his bones are buried ...
> there is good fortune in this world
> but who has known its taste?

The technique that Parker initially used to melt the frozen muck was inefficient, requiring more wood than he could haul by himself. Others were doing the same thing, but much lower down, near the rich creek beds. As he was able to acquire the necessary pipes and fittings, he had rigged a steam plant which demanded far less fuel, and was more effective in the bargain. To hope for gold, it was necessary to get to the bedrock and follow it for a time. The tunnels did not need bracing, for where the thaw failed to reach, it was as firm as the bedrock he followed. With Jan working the face of their digging, the work proceeded apace, and the auriferous earth was piled carefully for sluicing in the spring.

Their work attracted attention, for following freeze-up, gold seekers continued to arrive by the hundreds: on foot, by dog-sled, and on the newly-cut pack trail from White Horse they staggered in, wretched from hunger and cold, but anxious to get at the acquisition of fortune. Soon, claims sprouted not far from where Jan and Parker were at work. This troubled Parker a little, and he muttered about it. They had a good lead on excavation, but there would be increased pressure on the fuel supply, and there was little money to hire someone to fetch it, as some of the others did.

Then two weeks after Jan had arrived, a man named Oliver Millet began work on the hill high above the Bonanza Creek valley. Again the sourdoughs laughed at him as they had at Parker. But Millet suspected what Parker thought all along: that there was a primordial channel of a long-dead creek bed that harboured treasure. Working alone, he sunk three shafts in the old way; burning and digging, until he found an ancient stream bed of quartz. It was later to be named the fabulous White Channel. It contained gold, rough, coarse nuggets, hundreds of dollars to the pan. Millet had scurvy from want of decent food, and the strain of feverish, constant labours in the pit. Like Parker, he was diminishing his body for the pursuit of wealth.

Before spring, the secret was out, and men went mad staking the hills, so that there was no relief from the activities which went on at all hours. By April, the days had become increasingly longer, until by May there was constant daylight. The pall of smoke from the fires in the pits was unavoidable, for it hung over the valleys in a perpetual fog.

Jan and his companion took out some gold, but nowhere near the quantity that their neighbours were extracting. It was sufficient, however, to replenish supplies and extend their steam-pipes, a technology which others were now employing. The surrounding landscape was as barren as the face of the moon, for there was not a tree within walking distance of the City of Dawson.

Jan had built a bunk over Parker's bedframe, and had fashioned chairs from firewood they had purchased. He had nailed up cardboard packing against the walls to conserve the warmth the stove afforded. Parker clucked his tongue at all this, for he believed that such creature comforts detracted from the main task. All of his energies were required to be saved for that expenditure, for his strength seemed not to improve with the passing months.

The fact that gold had been found in significant amounts so close to where they were working annoyed Jan. But it seemed to have no effect whatsoever on Parker. He continued to work at the same pace, and was persistently optimistic about their chances of making their own rich find. "That bloody ancient creek bed runs somewhere hereabouts," he had said, ever confident. "We've just got to work that much the harder. See, this is why I needed you to come on." He looked over at the frenzied activity now not more than a hundred yards away. "No bloody worries getting help now I'd say."

Jan looked pained.

"Oh no, mate, I'm not the ungrateful sort. You came on long before anyone even suspected there might be gold up here. Oh no. You stay as long as you bloody like."

They descended the ladder into the twelve-foot hole which had been sunk like a well, the third of such excavations. The brightness of the spring day flooded the interior of the frozen pit. Half way down, Parker stopped, and Jan nearly stepped on his hands.

"What is the matter?"

Parker was silent. Peering down, Jan could see that the other man's lips were pursed, and he appeared to be thinking.

"You know," said Parker in a way that suggested that this was the first time he had ever thought of such of a thing, "other than observing the Sabbath with more a wink than a nod, we've never taken a day off."

"It is true," said Jan, shifting his weight, for the skinny rungs dug into his arches.

"They've got all those bloody fleshpots in town, and watering-holes, gaming joints and whatever else, yet ... " He was silent again, unmoving, but smacking his lips.

"Yet?" asked Jan.

"Ah, never mind. There's no money for such things." It was true: all their modest findings had gone back into supplies for their operation. But still he did not move.

"I have some money," began Jan.

"Oh no," interrupted Parker. "I couldn't, really. There was no ... well, you more than earn your keep, and I don't pay you wages, so ... " It seemed to Jan that there was an undercurrent of insincerity there. Nothing obvious, but there nonetheless.

"I cannot stand here any longer, Jon." He climbed to the surface; the sunlight was brilliant, and it took his eyes a moment to adjust. The other man followed, his head poking out like a gopher, sheepish.

"I will take enough for a jug of beer. You are right. We need some ... relaxing from the work. Let us go." And having stoked the fire under the steam kettle, they headed off among the drifts and torn earth of the denuded valley. It was as bleak a place as Jan had ever seen, for the hand of man had turned nearly every rock and gravel bar in sight. Nothing green showed, nor, Jan imagined, could anything grow here once the miners had left. He expressed this to his companion as they picked their way among the boulders and irregular heaps of dross.

"The Mount Morgan mine was the same. A bloody mess. But since there, like here, there's nothing but a bunch a bloody aborigines, nobody gives a damn. Just get the gold if it tears your trousers, and get out."

Jan mulled this over. "So you come here, all this way, to do the same thing? You have not enough gold from that other place?"

"I suppose there's never enough gold for some bloody folks, mate. I'm content enough. Back in Ozzie land I was working for a company. Missed the boat you might say, in America, and was working to save passage money when word of the Klondyke hit 'Frisco like a bloody copper's truncheon. So here I am."

"Seeking your fortune," finished Jan.

"I dunno. I've got no great dream I'm chasing, no boundless bloody glory that's out there or up here for me, somewhere, whatever. Just getting on. Oh, I'll go back to Australia when I get enough together, maybe get a little place up by the Barrier Reef where it's warm. Oh Jesus I'd like to get warm again, to be sure." It was odd that there was no passion in it, Jan thought, no real conviction.

Jan thought about his own great dream, his own land. It troubled him that it seemed so far away, and that he did not fret as much as he might have thought, for the leaving of it. Home and away were not opposites as much as they were two masks of human fate which chance might have anyone wear at any time. Perhaps yearning for one was really yearning for the other. For Jan now considered, for the moment at least, that the sorry shack on Claim number 580, was home.

# X

One jug of beer led to several, as is the way of beer and lonely men. The Golden Hill was a clamorous mass of shouting men and broken glass and choking smoke. Conversation was impossible without great effort and cupped hands, which suited Jan. He began to think of his pale companion as a member of his family, for beyond the work, Parker made no demands on him. They functioned as brothers united by need as strong as any blood tie. True, Parker's peculiar speech was difficult to understand, but as he tended to repeat himself, Jan knew that what he did not catch this time around, he would the next. By degrees he let his guard down, so that he was able to open himself to the man.

"Jan!" cried Parker in his reedy voice that carried above the general din. "This is a bloody beautiful place!" He was smiling broadly as the ale seduced him. "Life is one great, bloody monotony, broken only by periodic moments like this."

Jan grimaced. "Not so beautiful, I think!"

"Oh yes, mate! Nice and warm, good company, a glass of drink: what more can a man ask for?"

"A little more money perhaps? We are surrounded by rich men ... I have always been poor ... "

"Ah, yes. If only the rich could hire the poor to die for them, why, then we could make a bloody nice living."

This instantly struck Jan as hilarious; the beer sprayed from his mouth as he erupted in laughter. Settling down, he said, "You die first: I will hold the money for you."

Parker chuckled, "I'll bet you will you greedy bastard!" He sipped at his beer for a moment. "The three greatest inventions of the devil: impatience, hatred and greed. Every man's got one of 'em, and many got all three." He paused, and as Jan began to ask him which one was his, he spoke again, shouting across the table. "Hate's mine. I bloody hate impatience and greed. What's yours?"

"I think there is another one. Loss of hope; what is the word? ... despair."

"Ah, all despair is, is anger without passion. Which is the root of hate. So there you go. Hate's yours too."

Jan was puzzled by this logic, and the beer was not helping.

"Do you mind?"

The two of them looked up. A tall, well-dressed man with a waist coat ornamented with watch-chain and fob stood next to the table. There were only two chairs left in the entire room, and he had a hand on one of them. Next to him stood a lavishly dressed woman, a whore by the look and smell of her, and she was eyeing the other seat.

"Do you chaps mind if we share your table?"

"Not at all mate," cried Parker as he gawked at the strumpet. Under the paint and powder, she was a fine looking woman. The tops of her breasts threatened to spill out of her dress, which was tightly cinched at her narrow waist. Both pulled the chairs so that they faced each other, sitting knee to knee like school sweethearts. Parker feigned indifference, but Jan could see he strained to hear their conversation.

There was no great effort to hear what they were saying, for they needed to shout at each other to be heard. It all had to do with mutual admiration. A pitcher of beer arrived at the table, and the man lamented that the recent temperance drive had dried up the public houses, for the moment, of real drink. Beer, he complained, had a way of swelling up the insides so a body begged for relief. At this, he got up and went in search of the privy.

The girl toyed with the pendant she wore for a time, then suddenly looked up at Jan, meeting his gaze. She blushed and looked away. In that moment, Jan saw a young girl, unspoiled and pure. His sisters. His mother. Kinipi. Ervina. The women in his life that he had known but did not know.

"What is your name?" asked Jan.

"Belda," replied the woman, initially shy, then bolder, as if trying new skills for the first time. "What's yours, handsome?"

"Jan," he answered. "This is my friend, Jon."

"Jan and Jon, hey? You fellows find a pay streak, did you?"

"You might say that, sweetheart," said Parker with real enthusiasm, leering into her cleavage as if the gold had revealed itself. He winked at Jan. "When you've gold in your bloody poke, you are wise and handsome, and you can sing well too!" Chortling into his beer mug.

She ignored him, keeping her eyes on Jan. "Your accent: are you German?"

"No," began Jan, but he was interrupted by the suited one, freshly returned. "What the hell ... "

"It's all right Nathan. They're not bothering me."

"I should hope not," he said, blustering. To them: "I'm the god-damned sheriff of this town. Watch yourselves!"

For the balance of the time that they were there, Jan watched Belda surreptitiously, noticing that now and then, when she thought her companion was not watching, she would glance at him. Later, walking back to the shack, Parker was enthused.

"She's bloody *crazy* about you, man! No missing it. Couldn't take her eyes off you. I mean, why she wasn't taken with me, now, is a bit of a wonder. But you have to search her out. I mean, you can't afford not to. Chase her down. Soft as bloody butter, mate, and snug as they come. You must chase her down. I would."

Jan looked sideways at him. "In my country, there is a saying: when the fox gives the goose advice, the neck is in danger."

Parker looked pained. "What is that bloody well supposed to mean?"

"It means simple, that if you want her, then you be the one to chase her down, as you say. This is not something I can do. Nor do I want trouble from the sheriff."

That night, and many thereafter, he fell asleep with the thought of her. But the face of the woman was that of Ervina Cartwright.

# xi

Parker's health faded over the next year and into the following; but he clung precariously to life, in the same way that his claim yielded barely enough to make it worthwhile to continue to work it. The news of a strike at Nome, on the Alaskan coast, had drawn away men in the thousands, and the poorer claims were being bought up by syndicates which brought massive hydraulic methods to scour the hand-turned leavings, bought for a pittance. Parker sneered at them for leaving claims at least as potentially rich as the ones they sought. "Do they think it'll be any easier on the Alaskan beaches than it is here?

"It's one thing to look for something you can't see. Quite another to look at something and still not see it. What those chappies are seeking is right under their noses. These are fellows, Jan, most of them like you, that climbed mountains and risked rivers in leaky boats, froze near to death, got scurvy and blood blisters, only to run off questing at the first shout of treasure. What keeps *you* here? Lord knows, we haven't found much."

Jan thought on this for a time, listening to the green wood hiss and spit in the barrel stove. He was tired lately, and out of sorts. He resented the increasing share of the heavy labours. Gold had not brought him here in the first place. More than two years had passed since he had departed his homestead. Though he wrote home every two months, and enclosed small amounts of money when he could, he had not received a single letter back, for he was still anxious that he would be discovered. But that anxiety was a pale fear now, and the truth of it was, he felt anxious if not eager to leave. Parker had been good to him, and it seemed unlikely that he would last long. He would wait.

"It is a question that I ask of myself. What keeps me here. The gold? As you say it, we do not find much." He sighed. "Some times I think of *yedem stroi kryu*, which means, um, back to the old country, the good old days as you say it here. A wish. Yet I know that it was not good. But neither is this good. I eat, I work. I shit. That is all. I did not want to spend my life with a shovel in the pit, but it seems that is all that ever comes to me."

Parker coughed, and spat a gob of phlegm into the open door of the stove, where it sizzled. "Why did you and me meet up, then, mate? There's a purpose to it; has to be. Think on it: you and me are from opposite sides of the bloody globe, and here we are, together, in a God-forgotten shack on the poorest soil in the Klondyke. Why?" This last question was muttered, without passion, rhetorical. As if he did not expect an explanation for something he could not plumb by his own wit.

Jan pulled at his nose and scratched his beard. Lice. He would have to shave soon, and soak himself in kerosene. He sighed. "A priest once told me that there were certain people that are encountered in life, who are ... important?"

"Significant?"

"Yes, significant. They appear and re-appear, and even those who have goodness, still require a struggle. He spoke of Jacob's exertions with the angel, in the Book of Genesis I think; I forget it now exactly. He said that it was a good story of a man's struggle with the unknown in himself. This was a great battle, that goes on for days. But he does not let go of the angel until he knows him ... "

"I'm not much of a bloody bible-thumper mate. Didn't Jacob ... wasn't he the bloke who stole the inheritance away from his brother?"

"That is the one. And he is always afraid of his brother after this. In his fight with the angel, greatly tired, wounded, he say this, he say: 'I will not let thee go, except thou bless me'. I always remember this, for I do not understand it then, even when *popá* Kudryk explain it. I think I know it now."

"Well you've bloody well left me in the dark, mate. What are you saying?"

"I am saying only that we must face our fear. It is a struggle. Sometimes people who come into our lives assist this. Make possible to see what we cannot or will not see. Afraid to see."

Parker looked at Jan in the light of the open stove. Jan could not see his expression, for he felt awkward sharing this slender insight. Parker pulled through his nose and spat again into the flames. "Me partner's turned into a bloody philosopher," he said, but there was a slender tremor of awe in his voice. After a long moment of silence, he whispered, "I'm bloody frightened too, mate."

# xii

The fear which Parker disclosed was the fear of imminent death, which claimed him in the spring of 1901. The superficial fear which Jan withheld from Parker, but which he suspected that Parker knew all along, was his dread of authority. It was a timidity bred into him by a bold father who nevertheless doffed his hat to the *pahn*. An uncle who was tormented by police and killed by the rapacious greed of mine-owners. The smothering apprehension that his life was not his own, and that the only time that he was truly free was when he was voyaging. And what underlay all of this was the fear of losing his way.

The night Parker had died, he seemed to know it was upon him, though he was strangely effusive and alert. At the end, he had clutched Jan's tattered sleeve, and said, "I will not let thee go, except thou bless me."

He had meant it as a joke, the way he had said it, but tears started from Jan's eyes. Putting his hand on Parker's brow, he said simply, "I bless you, friend." Parker had slumped back on the stuffed dirty bag he used for a pillow, and faded, as if to sleep. He was stiff and cold in the morning.

There had been no partnership agreement, no will. The police who attended with the coroner to certify death had advised him that there was no longer any legal right to work the claim. No one expressed what was obvious: the abandoned claims all around suggested that there was no longer any point to working the diggings at all.

He walked to the door ahead of the others and threw it open. The day had changed to a milky white, and even the brightest stars had begun to diminish. There was no indication of what sort of day it was going to be; there was no sign that pointed the way for him. Overhead on heavy wings, a raven passed, croaking its mournful note; it seemed to symbolize his isolation more acutely than the corpse now being wrapped in a blanket by the coroner who muttered about paupers and municipal fees.

With a long sigh, Jan realized that once again he had been separated from what he had sought by events not of his own making. It was time to leave.

# Book Six

# HOME

# i

The platform had emptied before Byron summoned the courage to get up from his first class compartment and descend from the train. Track Number 4 of the Canadian National Station in Winnipeg was deserted, all passengers having fled down recessed steps from the cold to the warmth of the receiving hall and rotunda below the tracks. At the top of the stair railing, partially obscured from the steam that swirled from the brake lines under the Pullman cars, stood an old man. Much older and stooped, Byron thought with a pinch of alarm, than he remembered him. His father was swaddled in a buffalo coat, thick and warm. He had shown a preference for dapper woolen coats or the sheared furs that bankers or businessmen wore. A matter of appearances, he'd said. Very important. He seemed to stiffen as Byron approached. Gazing beyond the father Byron could see there was no one else there to greet him, and he felt a chill not entirely attributable to the Winnipeg winter. For a moment father and son regarded one another, silent, barely a yard apart.

"Father." He dropped his bags beside him. "Father, I ... " His eyes glistened.

Wordlessly, the old man stepped to him and embraced his son, awkwardly, for the coat was bulky. Then he stepped back, still holding the younger man by the shoulders. Byron could see the glow of the electric station lights reflected in the wetness of his father's eyes. It seemed difficult for him to speak. At length, his eyes fell to the two canvas bags.

"Is that it, then?" Without waiting for a reply, he nodded, as if Byron had spoken, "Let's be off, for I'm afraid the cold seems to pierce my very bones these days."

Actively seeking a neutral subject, they nattered about the weather, until they reached a hansom cab beyond the bronze portals of the new station. David Bloode addressed the driver, who was warming his hands over a sparking brazier of coal.

"Here we go, my good man. Away to the Palladium with us."

As they climbed into the cab, Byron asked: "Father — a hotel? We're going to a hotel?"

Sliding in beside the older man on the narrow seat, he repeated his question. His father turned to look at him. "I thought it best, just for tonight. There's ... there's ... well, there's been a lot of difficulty with ... your troubles." He grabbed for the loop at the sill as the vehicle lurched from the icy track. He hunched slightly and looked through the window, suggesting he was feeling

Byron's anxiety, but faintly impatient with it. "Look, let's leave it till we get to the Palladium. It's a small hotel, but a good one. You remember it, don't you, the one on McDermot? We can have something brought up to the room, and we can talk. I dare say we've a good deal to talk about." Cutting off Byron's attempt to press him, he gestured out of the glass that had not as yet frosted over from their breath, and continued to speak in a relentless way, forestalling any further comment.

"Look at it, will you!" he exclaimed. "Would you believe that the scrabble of huts that existed here in my own recent memory has become such a fine metropolis? Great buildings and grand roadways. Tram cars and steamships and railroads to rival anything the eastern cities could put up. Yes, indeed."

Byron knew his father loved this place: this city, the rivers that passed through it and the woodlands and plains beyond. There was an intensity to him surpassing proud as he identified the various businesses and structures they passed along the way. As if in some way he'd had a hand in the creation of each one. Which, Byron supposed, he had in a way. He was in a very real way, a part of it. But Byron felt no such affinity. The city seemed cold and forbidding: a far cry from the warmth of his last arrival.

After a short ride along Main Street, they entered the hotel where it was apparent they were expected. It seemed to Byron that the desk clerk was peering at him, but he shrugged it off. When they had settled into the room on the third floor overlooking the market, the sun was long gone. David glanced at his watch then snapped the cover and tucked it back into his waistcoat. He clucked. "Only a little after five, and already so dark. I wonder why I notice these things. Why they should irritate me after all these years." They were interrupted by the arrival of a meal which obviously had been pre-ordered. Again the curious stare from the bellboy, while David endorsed the slip. Byron looked away. He felt like a freak.

David settled on the bed, which groaned under him. Byron sat opposite on an over-stuffed chair, the food between them, untouched. There was a feeling in his guts akin to hunger, but wholly unconnected with appetite.

"As I started to say in the cab, there's been some, ah, notoriety around your activities in South Africa. The papers here were full of it. I've brought a copy of the *Manitoba Free Press*, front page, to give you an idea." He unfolded the paper, and Byron could see a headline which screamed across the top: Local Boy To Be Shot For Treason.

Byron gasped, and reached for it with a trembling hand. He stared at it, unseeing, feeling the fear like vomit rise into his mouth. Christ in Heaven.

David seemed calm, but his voice betrayed his own anguish. "You see, I'm not exaggerating. For weeks, we had this. And your mother." He shook his head. "I remember a woman who cared not a whit about what others thought, but living now as we do has changed her. Perhaps I have, I don't know. But the comments she overheard. The whisperings. Friends dropping us as if we carried the plague. It hurt her deeply, and though she wanted to believe there had been some terrible mistake, it ground her down. And what with the other ... "

There was a long pause. Byron still clutched the rag of paper, staring at it, silent.

"You see, I thought we needed to talk about this before you came home."

Byron sat as if in a trance. He heard his father, but it was as a voice coming from another room, disembodied. He had fretted about his reception all the way from South Africa, had expected the worst, but held a fatuous hope that perhaps the worst of it had blown over.

His father leaned back on the bed on one elbow. He sighed. "I don't suppose it's necessary to tell you how all-consuming our efforts were with the British Home Office and the War Office, our embassy in London, our Prime Minister and countless other sympathetic but utterly useless functionaries from this side of the water. Both your mother and I went to London to intercede on your behalf after a stay of execution had been obtained. The bleatings of the Canadian government were not unhelpful, but hardly worth the effort. It was only after retaining the services of a very well-connected Tory solicitor that I was able to get the attention of Whitehall. Like everywhere else, money speaks in trumpet tones. That, and a tide of euphoria as the war was slowly won seemed to help with the commutation of your sentence. To ten years imprisonment.

"Ten years! I was aghast." He paused and rubbed his eyes with one hand. "But I was assured you would serve no more than three, once the troops were home and the Empire got on with other things. And sure enough, here you are, and it is not yet three years passed since that dreadful time. But we have suffered in that time, make no mistake."

"But surely you received my letters explaining ... ?"

"Of course we did. Of course we did. But when the sentence was affirmed on appeal, and it seemed likely that ... well, your mother and I resigned ourselves that whatever we might think, the rest of the world thinks that you were a traitor to the cause."

"And Emma ... ?" Byron began.

It was the only time that he was to see a trace of hardness come into his father's eyes. "She has been sent away ... I would prefer that you not mention her. And I certainly forbid you to have anything to do with her. I may never come to terms with what happened there; these ... these unfortunate events have simply compounded the belief that you have behaved in a way unworthy of a son of mine. Your mother, I'm afraid, has the same view, though she's terribly angry with you in the bargain. It'll take time.

"You see, each man is where he is as an inevitable function of his being. His character. Things just don't 'happen' to you; as long as you believe that you'll always be subject to the next circumstance. Events do not make the man, they reveal the man to himself, if he cares to look. This is what your mother and I have struggled with. Do we know our own son?" He shook his head and looked away. "The truth is that a man doesn't attract what he wants, he attracts what he is."

He looked at his son. "So Byron, the time has come for you to take a long look at yourself."

Byron leaned forward, resting his elbows on his knees, his face in his hands. "Whatever shall I do?" he said softly, his voice tremulous. "I have disgraced you. Disgraced myself."

The old man sat up, the springs beneath him protesting gently. After a time he put his hand on the back of his son's bowed head. "I have given this a good deal of thought. I have something in mind."

Byron looked up, his eyes red and collar askew. The last time his father had rescued him, he had been delivered into the cauldron of South Africa. What did he have in mind for him now? He became aware that his breathing had almost stopped in anticipation. He sniffed loudly, for his nose was running, and wiped his eyes with the back of his hand. He stared at David expectantly, painfully aware that the other man's eyes reflected back a pitiful spectacle.

"This part of Canada is changing," David began. "Considerably. The immigration numbers are fantastic, and the majority of the newcomers are Galicians and Ruthenians from the Ukraine. Strong, determined men and women of the soil. They are opening up this province, taming it, and will create wealth in a very short time. I believe that much of what will be a prosperous future for Manitoba lies in the hands of these sturdy people - though I concede that not many at this point agree with me."

Byron looked mystified, but David continued. "Be patient, I will come to the point by and by. These immigrants need one thing which shall make the difference between success and failure, wealth and poverty: education.

"There are several areas in which they have chosen to settle, but the area which had the greatest density at the moment is around a town called Dauphin - you may recall it as 'Dog-Town'. I have learned, quite by accident from one of my better customers from the district, that the settlers there have just built a sort of boarding school for children during the winter, when they are not needed on the land. A *bursa*, they call it in their peculiar language. Their plans are well along, except for one thing ... "

Byron grasped what was coming. Oh no.

" ... a teacher. They have no proper teacher. I learned this last month, just after we received your last letter telling us you had been released on a general amnesty. The new school sits empty, though they have tried untrained instructors on permits from the Department of Education - with not very much success, I'm afraid."

"The children of these immigrants: they would not even speak the English language?"

"Precisely why an educated, English-speaking teacher is needed. Without the tongue of commerce, they will be relegated to the margins of society. And there are many, I know, that would prefer that. No, they must have the King's English, and their leaders know it."

Byron recoiled, though he tried to conceal it. "But I haven't the faintest notion of their language. How on earth will we communicate?"

"You will learn. Your Firsts at Oxford were no accident. You'll learn quick enough.

This is a perfect opportunity for you, though I know it is not quite what you may have had in mind. These people are our future, but they need our help ... "

"And you think that I ... " Byron faltered.

Fixing him with a direct look that answered the question, David shook his head dismissively as if he had already heard the reasons why the scheme might not work. "This is your chance for redemption, my boy. Like as not, the people there will not have heard of your troubles, and could care less if they have. I will not send you along penniless, your mother and I have no desire to see you suffer more than you have. But the condition of our assistance is that you take this task on. In time ... yes, in time, I think your mother will come to think of you as the angel you were as a young boy.

"Now listen: tomorrow morning, I have arranged a lunch at the Royal Alexandra. I'm going to introduce you to two people who are the drive behind the school in Dauphin. One is Ivan Khodororovsky, who is a bit unusual in that he came to this country two years ago with money. Has bought up a fair bit of land around the Dauphin area, and is something of an entrepreneur, rather than farmer. But he has philanthropic instincts as well. I think he understands the linkage between education and wealth.

"The other one is a bit more interesting. As I have it, she is the spinster daughter of a wealthy farmer in the Gilbert Plains area. I've not met her, but I hear she's rather extraordinary. She's taken on the role of patroness to the school not-withstanding - I gather - the objections of some of her own family. Apparently her father dotes on her, however, and indulges her. Her name is Ervina Cartwright."

# ii

The wooden platform bordering the track at Dauphin was covered with crates and sacks, around which men swarmed, calling and waving to others. Beyond this was the stationmaster's small cabin, with its tiny wicket opened into the side. Underneath the whitewashed awning stood a long line of passengers seeking tickets on Canadian Northern's sprawling network. Sifton, Gilbert Plains, Winnipegosis, Cowan, Swan River, and beyond. It was apparent to Jan that the town had grown in the nearly three years he had been away. There was an energy now that was palpable. He looked anxiously each way for a glimpse of Kinipi. He remembered, with a sudden realization that little did he know of this woman.

Then: there she was. Dark, silent, as he had remembered her. But dressed in poorer clothes. Beside her was a girl, two years of age perhaps, clutching a fold of her dress in her tiny fist. A child: strange business, this. He strode forward, a frown darkening his brow. Beyond was a wagon hitched to the most miserable nag he could ever recall seeing; even those wretched creatures in the Klondyke compared more favourably. It did not occur to him until he was nearly at the station that she might not be there, or his homestead long reassigned to another, for that matter. This was the purpose of the letters after all: to maintain things as they were. Here I am, they cried. Do not forget me. I will be back. But they were poor things, written on butcher's paper, two or three lines, 'I am doing good.' 'Hope the crops is in.'; more if the man who he'd asked to act as scribe suggested a better turn of phrase. Into each one, before sealing the envelope, he slipped three folded bills. Always three. All of the correspondence was addressed to his neighbour, Ahapii Boberski, whom he expected would pass on the notes. If he was still there, that is. A frustrating business, this. Twelve ounces of gold was sewn into the lining of his jacket. But the gold worried him. Though it had been won by the sweat of his labour, nevertheless, he had seen what happened to men who had been lucky in their finds. It was as often as not, a pitiful thing. In a place where everything was in short supply except gold, the highest bidder had what he wanted. Fine food, women and good clothes: men would pay absurd amounts. When a single egg fetched a dollar or more, one man was known to buy every single egg in Dawson, just to spite a woman who'd scorned him and who loved an egg for breakfast. Gold seemed to bring with it a sort of madness, and he worried about that.

He reached around the hem of his frock coat. It was still there, he felt with relief. He took off his hat, standing before Kinipi, unsure. She looked up at him, not moving. Her eyes searched his for some sign from this man in new clothes she could respond to. He put his hand on her shoulder, then after a moment drew her awkwardly to him. She felt stiff in his embrace.

She drew away shortly, and gestured to the girl, saying, "*Pitamá,*" just a minute. "Your daughter, *Mikinákos*, your daughter. I have called her '*Acimosis*'; it means 'puppy'. But she needs a name of your people, and it is for you to give her one."

Jan knelt before the child, grateful for the diversion. Her pet name for him, Turtle, had a calming effect; he had not heard it uttered in a long time. The child hid in the folds of her mother's skirts.

"But how ... " he began. Stefan's ribald story of the departed husband rang in his ears. He was conscious of reddening. "How is this possible?"

Kinipi drew him up, explaining that she did not want him to carry the additional burden of knowing she was with child. As he looked from her to the girl, it was obvious that this was his daughter. The colouring was darker, but the shape of him, the face: yes, this was his, all right. He looked back to the woman, and as he took hold of her, something in him released, and he wept. Not the damp eyes that fond or unhappy thought provoked, but those that accompany sorrow in all its threadbare, unadorned misery.

"*Tótem,*" friend, or more intimately, one who is always with me, she said huskily, holding him.

*.... it is not the sight of the dark world and all its grim events;*
*but a grey-headed man weeps and laments*
*because at times he had with grief been drunk*
*and now so deeply in the world has sunk ...*

# iii

Lunch at the Royal Alec, as locals referred to the grand new Canadian Pacific Hotel, had nearly overwhelmed Byron. First there were the persistent stares from nearly everyone in the plush dining room. They knew who he was, sure enough. His father was too well known in this city. David had stopped to speak to someone who had greeted him, and upon introduction, the man's gaze was withering. He had let his hand go limp and slipped away from Byron's grip as if he had felt something disgusting. The back of Byron's neck was damp; he had a nearly irresistible urge to flee. But he kept his face outwardly calm. They both rose to greet the couple who were brought by the headwaiter. The man was about fifty or so, nearly bald, but well proportioned and agreeably dressed in the style of gentlemen of the time. He had an engaging smile, and radiated confidence as he stepped forward, arm outstretched. Ivan Khodorovsky spoke excellent English, though with a sharp accent that belied his origins in Eastern Europe. His manners were impeccable.

It was the woman that intimidated Byron. He had been expecting a stereotype of what the word 'spinster' conjured for him: an older woman whose life revolved around church and good works, a tad shrewish and definitely asexual. But behind Khodorovsky was a beautiful woman whose presence turned most heads in the dining room. Her dress was in brighter, more avant garde material than was currently the fashion in Winnipeg, if the women in the restaurant were any indication, and over her shoulders was a pale silk shawl embroidered in a rich coloured floral pattern. Byron had seen such patterns favoured by the Ukrainian immigrants on the train, and nearly everywhere in the city that he had seen so far. He was not sure that the other diners would entirely approve of this fashion statement, but she seemed oblivious to such things. He felt a quick rush of inspirational courage from her. She took his hand firmly; as she was introduced by his father, she held David with her eyes, then turned to Byron, and closed her other hand over his. "A very great pleasure to meet you, sir. I have so been looking forward to this since your father mentioned the possibility of your help."

"Please," he said. "I cannot tolerate the 'sir'; you must call me 'Byron'."

"I would be delighted to call you 'Byron', Byron," she laughed, still holding his hand as he drew a chair for her with the other.

Suddenly, the appeal of a Ukrainian boarding school in Dauphin had increased immeasurably. "How did you get involved with this project?" asked David to both of their guests.

The couple looked at each other. Ervina spoke: "My father and Mr. Khodorovsky are friends, and have cooperated in a number of business ventures

240

together. Mr. Khodorovsky's great passion is for his people from the Ukraine, and he is determined to help them in any way that he can."

"That's quite right," Khodorovsky broke in. "And the best way I think to ensure the success of the people who now come to this country in great numbers, is to educate them."

While the man spoke, Byron could not keep his eyes off Ervina, who on a couple of occasions glanced at him, looking away quickly. Byron thought he saw her colour slightly, along the line of her jaw, but he could not be sure. Emotion roiled within him. Damn it, he reacted so poorly and inappropriately to women. He mustered all of his self-control so that he could focus on Khodorovsky's words, but at the next quick look she gave him, all that melted, and he was as flustered as before." ... this boarding school, really a converted grain warehouse, but quite satisfactory," the man was saying, sipping *vichyssoise* from a shallow bowl. "I'm quite convinced that the next leaders of this province, this country will spring from our little house of learning." The others laughed politely. He turned to Byron. "Your father has told me of your impressive educational credentials, and we are grateful of course for one of your calibre even considering the position. But do you know anything of our language, our culture?"

Byron opened his mouth to say something, then abruptly changed his mind, closed his eyes, and recited:

*remember brothers (how I yearn that this dark fate will ne'er return!)*
*how you and I in humble doubt,*
*between a window's bars peered out*
*and thought, perhaps:*
*'alas, and when on this bleak earth shall we again in gentle fellowship*
*convene for converse on the years between?*
*never my brothers! nevermore!*

At the last line, Khodorovsky chimed in, reciting in unison, delighted. "Bravo, Byron! I recognize quite a good translation from 'My Fellow Prisoners'. Well done!" He turned to Ervina: "Shevchenko."

Ervina was smiling. "Can you read the Cyrillic script, Byron?"

"Not at all," said Byron. "That is something I'll have to learn; presently it means nothing to me. The passage is something that engaged me, and I happen to remember."

"Well no matter," said Khodorosky. "No matter. The principal language of instruction is English, of course. But we are hoping that the cultural side of our heritage will not be ignored. I have friends at the university in Kiev, so I will be obtaining more volumes for our small library. But tell me: how came you by the poetry of our beloved Taras?"

Byron flushed. "I have a volume which was given to me. Fortunately, the translation of many pieces is written into the opposite pages. I have had a fair bit of time to read and reflect on the passages. The man clearly felt deeply and loved his homeland."

Ervina engaged him with her eyes. Byron fell into their olive-hazel depths, not really aware of what she was saying for the moment. Rather, he struggled with what he was coming to be aware was a weakness in him: he was prone to impulse, to infatuation. Not simply with women, he realized, but with ideas, well-turned phrases in poetry or speech, and what might be for other men the fancy of the moment. It was a pathetic thing, he thought, but perhaps the knowing of it, the naming of this dragon might be the way to its mastery. He blinked, and focused on what she was saying. Her voice was like lavender:

" ... unusual for a North American to acquire an interest in Eastern European poets. There must be a fascinating story there, I'd suppose?"

"Well, ah ... " he stammered, conscious of his cheeks warming. There was no real way of knowing just how much they knew of him, but it would be foolish to assume that his notoriety was hidden to these people. All the same, he had no desire to touch on it. He decided to say as little as possible. "Yes. Quite interesting, actually, and I'd like to take some time to tell you about it, when we have a little more of that commodity. Suffice it to say that I was given the book by an old Ruthenian mercenary. Quite a fellow. But let's talk about the school: when do you want me to start?" Then abruptly: "I'm sorry. Perhaps you want to consider my candidacy before committing." He searched Ervina's face for some clue. If her expression was any indication, he had the job.

Khodorovsky stood, clutching the crisp, oversized napkin in front of him. He reached his hand toward Byron, across the table. "Speak no more of that. Welcome. We look forward to having you at our little school in Dauphin." As he retook his seat, he added, "I wonder whether you would mind using the term, 'Ukrainian', as we take the terms 'Ruthenian' and 'Galician' to be rather pejorative now."

"Of course, sir. I meant no disrespect."

Ervina offered her hand, and he took it, taking in the firmness of her grasp, the suppleness of her touch. He held it rather longer than perhaps he thought he should have, reluctantly letting it go when he became aware of a quick, amused exchange of looks between his father and Khodorosky. His cheeks flamed again, and he cursed himself inwardly. Once the dragon is identified, then a different battle begins. But no less strenuous.

As they walked toward the cloakroom, Ervina slipped her arm in his, and said to Byron that she very much looked forward to seeing him the following month. Glowing with the pleasure of her contact and her intimacy, he was about to reply, when he came face to face with Major Botterill. Byron froze; the words died in his throat. The man gave him such a withering look of hatred that it was impossible not to notice it. He passed on without a word.

They continued in silence, Byron unable to say anything further. Ervina took account of the meeting, but decided to defer any comment. But this was what she had in mind for later. Looking back, having passed Botterill with a curt nod on the way in, David worried that there might be an exchange. The two men had not spoken since the event that had caused Byron's departure. He too resolved to speak to Byron later. The truth was that this was what his son could expect in the unforgiving society in which his parents now moved. Forgiveness was a slender reed in a slough of appearances.

All of them parted company, the exuberance of their meal considerably diminished. Khodorovsky was thinking that there might be an unknown price to pay for this teacher they were taking on. Well qualified, but ... ? He hoped they were not making a mistake. He resolved to speak to Ervina about it on the rail trip home. Holding back, Khodorovsky watched Ervina on Byron's arm at the curb; beyond, the churn of Higgins Avenue resonated with traffic. He turned to David, who smiled and said, "They seem to get on well together."

"Yes," said the other man. "I deliberately asked her to accompany me, for she is a great persuader, in addition to having a large enthusiasm for what we are trying to accomplish."

"Quite an extraordinary woman," mused David. "There's no one like her. Outspoken and free-thinking, which has earned her more than a little criticism. But she is very beautiful, and has a wealthy father, so most sins in such a creature are forgiven - at least for now, one supposes, given that wealth and beauty are transient."

David nodded absently. "Hmmm. Has she no suitors?" He was answered by a short laugh.

"Oh that *chaklunka*! Ah, one who casts spells. Many, many young men have sought her attentions, but I think she overwhelms them. Too independent, headstrong. I'm not sure they thought she would make a good, reliable farm wife. At any rate, she has found no one with whom she would be satisfied, as yet." He turned to face David. "I must confess that we accept him on the basis of your confidence in your son. This business in South Africa, well ... let me say only that ordinarily, such moral questions raised would end our consideration of such a candidate. But your reputation for integrity is so well-known that you would not compromise it, even for your own children. All the same, I have a small anxiety that ... " He did not finish.

David flushed. As he saw Byron turn; it must have been obvious to his son they were talking about him and that the subject was serious. He wondered what sort of compliment it was that a man would put his own reputation before the interests of his own offspring. Pursing his lips, he said only, "You have a well-qualified person to teach in Byron. Better than you could ever *hope* to attract. He is young, and has made mistakes. He will outgrow whatever foolishness led him to act in that way. I have spoken to him, and I am completely convinced he understands the error of his past ways. That is all behind him, now. I have *full* confidence that my son will never betray anyone ever again."

# iv

The house that Jan had built more than three years ago was there as he had left it, though shabbier in appearance. Beyond, the garden had been set in rows, and now, by late June, the greenery was thrusting upwards in the full glory of renewal. Unfortunately, Jan could see, there were plenty of weeds in the greenery as well. But that could be put right quickly enough. "You have had it hard, my woman?" he asked. It warmed her to be called so. She was indeed his woman, for she had given herself to him.

"Yes. I will not deny it."

"And my letters?" "Yes, Ahapii brought them to me. He has been helpful, even though his wife is dead now. It was hard for him in something of the same way as for me." He felt a twinge of jealousy. This man, recently widowed, sniffing around his woman during his absence. He struggled with the question. "He ... he is proper?" There was a thin smile on her lips. "He was very kind, and no wrongness happened, though I felt his eyes over me when he thought I was not looking." Jan's cheeks reddened. He said tightly, "I place great trust ... I take this up with him."

She put her hand on his arm. "Settle down, *Mikinákos*, it is the way of a man. No harm was done."

Jan chafed. "The money ... ?" he asked rather too quickly.

"Yes, it was there, as you said in the letters."

"You could read them?"

"I had many years in the mission school. I read well enough. But reading and having money and land is not ..." She bowed her head, and sighed.

As he turned the sagging pony into the yard, he glanced at her. The child was restless in her lap.

"What do you mean, woman?"

She looked at him. Her eyes were moist. "I have not been treated well. I have been pushed from the boarding, into the mud. Men have picked at my skirts and offered me money. Some stores will not serve me, and I have been accused of stealing even though I have nothing in my hand. I am a 'stinking Indian'." She put a visibly shaking hand to her brow, wiping each eye with the heel of her palm. She clutched the girl closer.

Jan was outraged, but words failed him. "In the new store of Joshua Slack," she continued, "it is called the General Merchant; he took the three dollars from me as I offered it up for payment. 'Where did you get this?' he say. 'Who did you rob this from?' he say. Then he pushed me from his store, *Acimosis* fell down and began to cry. It was a terrible thing."

Jan could barely contain himself. What manner of cruelty is this? "Why did you not tell him who you were, this land? The money I earn to keep it going? Why did ... "

"Because I am afraid," she said. "Afraid you will be caught, and be taken away again. At least you are free in Yukon, not locked up somewhere as Sergeant Jones said. I am so glad you come back to me - to us," she added. "Never leave again."

Jan was no stranger to this. He had suffered at the hands of many who thought him lesser than they. It was perplexing: it seemed to signal some fundamental estrangement of men from the nourishing aspirations of the human spirit. Good men were as capable of nasty words and deeds as were the men who were persistently caught in the net of their own weaknesses; he had seen it time and again in the frenzy that was the Klondyke. Doubt and fear were the enemies of understanding, and those who failed to deal with them undermined themselves at every turn, like as not erupting in the varied forms of antipathy toward other human beings. We use one another, he decided, which is why we hate one another. The diminishment of others served some deeply-rooted purpose in all men. It was a paradox that petty behaviours seemed to be those which were the most rewarded. He needed to get beyond that, but for now, he felt the dragon's teeth of those who had treated Kinipi with roughness and malice. What could he expect for his daughter, who bore the traits of her aboriginal ancestry as surely as she possessed the stamina and strength of the Cossack? Despite his family about him, Jan felt inexplicably alone.

*I am distracted. Where am I to go?*
*What shall I do, and where begins my woe?*
*To curse my destiny and men, by God - beggars the effort!*
*How am I to explain loneliness upon this foreign soil?*
*In this seclusion, what shall be my toil?*

It was toil that was called for, and Jan threw himself into it like a man possessed. Kinipi worried after him: "You will destroy yourself if you keep this pace!" she would cry after him. Yet abed, after more than twelve hours in the field, his need for her was constant. His lovemaking was a desperate thing, calling out in his completion like some night creature. She would draw him to her, and he would fall asleep instantly, the fatigue of the day overtaking like a narcotic. The living of a life with purpose was tonic to most ills, he discovered, when he paused to think about it.

And so the months passed. He restored his friendship with his neighbour, Boberski, who had taken for a second wife a child no more than fourteen, not half his age. Her belly was soon swollen with child, as indeed, was that of Kinipi.

One day, soon after his return, he went into the bustling town to buy a new horse to replace the sorry creature which Kinipi had obtained. Pausing in front of *J. Slack, General Merchant*, he got down from the wagon. Seeing his wife's pained expression, he knew that she would not come with him no matter what the persuasion. He walked inside, assailed by the good smells of new cloth, oiled wood, sacking and the varied odours of retail commerce. Slack, aproned and gaitered about the sleeves, turned and greeted Jan brightly: "Can I help you sir?"

Jan seized him by the front of his shirt, and pulled him, spluttering, toward the door. They attracted considerable attention as they crossed the boardwalk to the muddy street. Slack, red-faced and humiliated, put up a fine struggle, but

Jan drew him along as if he were a child. He stopped at the wagon, and gestured to Kinipi who was holding the girl against her face. "Mr. Slack," he said crisply; the sharp traces of accent had not left his voice, though his speech was much clearer than when he had left, "this is my wife. You owe her some money, and you need to pay it now."

Slack looked up uncomprehendingly, then to Jan. "Wh-what? What are you talking about? Let go of me, you peasant brute!"

Jan tightened his grip, lifting the hapless man slightly, so that he stood on his toes. "You steal money from her. Three dollars. Three dollars that *I* earn with my own hard labour." Something seemed to dawn in the man's eyes, though doubtless the number of such people he had abused in countless petty ways made the details of his crime uncertain.

"All right. All right! Let me go! I'll get the money." Grumbling and rearranging his clothes, he retreated into the store, returning a few moments later with the money, which he offered to Jan.

"No. To her." He was determined to make the revenge complete.

By now a small crowd had gathered; a good fight was always a draw. But bystanders were not on the side of the wronged woman. There were muttered comments of disapproval, most of which were aimed at Jan. When Kinipi snatched the money, they moved on, and when she looked back, Slack was angrily arguing his case to what appeared to be a sympathetic jury. Jan told her to put it out of her mind, for it was a finished matter. But Kinipi, with a last fearful look backward, did not look not so sure.

# V

Byron found to his intense pleasure, that he was a natural teacher. He had the ability to infuse a student with the natural joy of learning. Having grown up in a pedagogical environment which stressed memory and recitation, and the rote accumulation of disparate and meaningless facts, he was determined not to foist the same upon his charges. Rather he would treat them to the benefits of his Oxford education. In addition to fluency in the King's English, by God, he would teach them to *think*!

Now, his plans were somewhat blunted by the reality of his students. Ranging in ages from six to sixteen, and only attending classes desultorily when they were not otherwise needed on the farms, very few of them understood much of the English language. But Byron happily herded them together in what he called 'envelopes', according to age and ability. He was rewarded with enthusiasm and the near-fawning affection of his subjects.

He learned with the enthusiasm of an amateur sleuth about the *kobzars*, and the *dumy* they sang or recited. The living history of the vast reaches of the open steppes known as 'Ukraine'. He found that the *dumy* were differentiated from songs by their irregular verse and indifference to rhyme. He would scour the homesteads and the ranks of new arrivals to find those who could recite a *duma* to another who could translate. These he would repeat to his classes. He sought out those who could play the bandoura, so that performances of the *dumy* could be more accurately sung to that traditional instrument. He was struck with the tragedy of the Ukrainian people, and the way in which their songs and poetry were over-laden with the legacy of sadness:

*nema v sviti pravdy* / there is no truth / *ravai ne ziskaty* / truth cannot be found / *pochala ne pravda-* / iniquity has become-*v sviti panouvaty* / the ruler of the world...

Of all of his endeavours, he was the most gratified when Ervina visited him, but he kept his eagerness well hidden. He was determined to exercise the self-control which his father had underscored was the secret to a successful life: "There is no progress, no development as a man, without sacrifice, without abandonment of animal and unclean thoughts," papa had said. "Achievement is the crown of effort, but knowing yourself, and having a firm grip on your emotions is the only way to sustain it. See what you would have, and go after it. Be aware."

As always, Byron was confused about the often imponderable space that existed between the intellectual conception of an idea, and its translation to the real world — a world he had long been sheltered from by his father's wealth. But he decided that focus upon task would rectify what other weaknesses of character he had, and even the interventions of the lovely Ervina would not distract him.

Easier said than done. It was apparent that his studied indifference to her made manifest by scrupulous attention to the educational tasks he had set for himself, or the projects that various groups of children were working on, had only seemed to have heightened her interest in him. He declined several invitations to their farm in Gilbert Plains, pleading that the work was unforgiving. He was studying the language in the alien script in which it was written, and busy writing out the *dumy* he was learning. He needed to write out the Ukrainian in phonetic spellings, so that the teaching of the English would loosely but generally correspond. It was an effective pedagogical tool, he told her, and he could not spare efforts just now, even though everything within him cried out for more attention from her.

It was a visit from the woman's father, Henry Cartwright, that changed events for Byron. The man sat in the small classroom, looking quite out of place squeezed into the undersized desk with its attached chair. "You've been here near a year now, but my daughter tells me that you've declined a number of invitations to our home; I think she's a little, well, put out about it. You'd do me an honour, sir, if you would come out, even the once." There was something of a forced grin on his face. "My daughter is not used to *not* having her own way; you may have seen some of that."

It was certainly true. In the matter of curriculum and process, she had very definite ideas, and was not easily put off them without compelling reasons to the contrary. But intellectual sparring was what Byron loved, and she was no match for him. He worried that their debates were becoming eristic, in the sense that it was more important for him to win than for truth to prevail. He needed to remind himself that life was not an Oxford debate: that there were a thousand small acts of compromise and accommodation necessary for successful relationships, business or otherwise. He agreed at once, and was fulsomely apologetic. What had he been thinking of to create such a rudeness?

When Cartwright left, Byron was filled with unease. The attraction he felt for the woman simmered close to the surface, and he was afraid of himself. It should not come as a surprise, he decided: it is always ourselves that we meet. In this beautiful woman I see myself, and know the craving I have for her. In these children I teach, I know the hunger I have for knowledge. In this isolation I have imposed upon myself, I know the weaknesses of extremes of passion. He shook his head and sighed, sagging on the corner of a child's desk in the empty classroom. Choices were not avoided simply by declining to choose. But to make wise selections, that was the trick. I fear, he thought, that I am not strong enough.

# vi

One Spring day in 1904, Jan and Ahapii were at work stringing new barbed wire along their common boundary. It was good work, and both men were deeply absorbed in it. At once, Ahapii raised his head and called to Jan who was a fence length away. "Hey, *verisko*, person lazy as a snail, I forgot to tell you. You had a visitor when you both were away yesterday."

"Is that so?" Jan continued working, driving staples into the wood.

"Yes. The new school teacher, *Pahn* Bloode. He is searching for people who know the *dumy*. I told him you play the *bandoura*. He seemed quite excited by that. He had a woman with him who seemed along for the ride. She could not speak our language though the teacher was trying. She seemed interested in all that he was doing."

"How do you know I play the *bandoura*?"

"I see it hanging on your wall. Why else would it be there? Oh, I forget: perhaps Kinipi plays the instrument of our homeland." He was grinning.

Jan raised his fingers, spread, then cursed gently as a staple spun into the grass from want of proper attention. He would have to find it, for each one counted; such things did not grow on trees.

"Don't give me the *dula*, rude gesture, friend," shouted Ahapii gaily. "Either you play or you do not."

"Not in many years, neighbour." It pained him suddenly to think of Stefan. "I am not sure I remember. Perhaps it is just as well."

The strand was secured, and his companion walked over to him and hunkered down, mopping his forehead against the heat with his *khustra*, similar to the one Jan wore, save that Jan had taken to wearing a broad-brimmed hat over it. "It is a good thing that you should play the instrument for the children. Think of your own child, who must have a sense of where she comes from. Your wife does not neglect her roots in her people; you would do well to encourage her to understand the way of our old people."

"And you would do well to mind your own business, friend."

Gently rebuked, Ahapii fell silent, picked up the spool, and trudged to the next post they had driven into the soil. Jan pondered his own reaction for a few minutes. Memory has its own queer tricks, capable of reconstruction and modification. What was the profit in looking back? Only fools and cowards glanced over their shoulders. Such things as he had taken from the Old Country, such as the manner of building his home, gave comfort. Deep within a chest lay the handful of desiccated soil he had scooped up as he crossed the border into Austria. Why he kept it, he was not sure. The ties to Ukraine were frayed and evanescent, but bonds nonetheless. There was so much pain. Such recollections as he kept at bay with hard work had the fearful capacity to sneak in and torment him from time to time. Who was this man, this stranger who knew nothing of their ways, and what was his right to inquire into such things as comprised the soul of Ukraine?

He suddenly became aware of Ahapii calling him, grinning again; the man was irrepressible. "Jan! You should consider going to see this man, simply to see his woman, the one who accompanied him. I have never seen such a beauty - except of course my beautiful Lesia."

"You are an obsessed fellow. That is a poor reason to see a man, Ahapii. But I think he sounds well-intentioned. So I will go to him; I remember some of the *dumy* my *vuyko* Stefan told me. Perhaps they will help."

# vii

The dinner had gone much better than Byron had anticipated. Though they surely had some idea of the scandal three years before, no mention was made of it, and the focus of conversation was the years he had spent at Oxford. Byron did not know what to make of Ervina's brother, Henry, named after his father. He seemed a hard man, even arrogant. He'd met such men at Oxford, men who stood in the reflected influence of their father's money. Such coasted preferentially, all the while maintaining that their accomplishments were solely their own. Byron was fully aware of the irony of his thoughts; even the post he presently held a direct line could be drawn between the influence of his father and his attainment. At least I'm not smug about it, he thought.

Having told them of his affinity for poetry, they now called upon him for a recitation. Ervina would not be put off, he could see. A very determined woman, in all respects. She had taken to accompanying him in his research. Always cheerful, anticipating the need for an interpreter, and always dressed in a way that was not overwhelming to the peasant farmers from Europe, she won them over even when the labour of the fields had drawn their faces in scrabbled lines.

"Yes, recite for us. It is not often that we have such a luxury. Then mother can play some piano for us." At the older woman's gratified protestation, Byron looked at her and secured the bargain: he would recite if she would play - at the same time. Together they picked through the sheet music, and Byron chose one, a ballad titled *O Happy Time*. It was a slow, languorous tune, one that inspired a dreaminess of thought. Almost prayerful. Then standing in a corner, he waited for the initial bars of the melody to play, and with a quick glance at Ervina, he began to speak.

> *the lark begins its lay; its wings*
> *go soaring upward now*
> *the cuckoo has been heard to speak,*
> *perched on an oak-tree bow;*
> *the twitter of the nightingale*
> *throughout the woodland rings,*
> *beyond the hill the dawn appears;*
> *to it the ploughman sings ...*

He did not know all of Shevchenko's *Bewitched Woman* by heart. He recited those parts he had committed to memory, apologizing for the gaps, and the uncertainty of the translation. In the soft lamplight, the gentle background sounds from the muted piano, and the firmness of his well-disposed voice, he was aware that he had captured them. They were transported to the steppes of Ukraine as surely as if they had been on an Arabian magic carpet - and not a one of them versed in the language or the culture. It was a moment that Byron would recall all of his life. In the shining eyes of the woman opposite him, he knew that their destinies were irrevocably linked, and the thought frightened him. How was one to be sure?

> *...sometimes a cuckoo comes to grieve;*
> *each night a nightingale twitters its heart out*
> *as it sings their melancholy tale,*
> *until at last the moon appears ...*

Later, Ervina took him for a walk in the garden. "Your recital was marvelous," she said. "Wonderful. You have no idea how I miss such things living out here."

He puffed. "Thank you, Ervina." She took a quick step ahead of him, and sat on a rough bench, looking up at the stars. The light from the house barely reached them. She looked silvery, unreal.

"Sit by me, Byron." He sat on the bench, edgy. He could feel her eyes on him, and he shuffled his feet like a schoolboy in the gravel. She moved closer, and took his arm. He shivered. "You're cold! It's cool, but not that cold. Are you not feeling well?" She was playing with him. "Byron, why have you not ... well, why do you ... avoid me?"

He turned to her, startled. "Avoid you? Why I ... " She kissed him, forcefully, such that their teeth touched. The softness of her lips was a sensation he felt with every part of his body. He tried to speak, but she shook her head against him, forbidding it. Opening her mouth, she drew him in, the wetness of her dissolving his will. He held her awkwardly, his attraction for her held in perfect equipoise by his fear of her. She intimidated him. So certain was she of who she was and what she wanted. So confident. As she moved against him, he resisted an overwhelming and irrational impulse to flee. It came on him as a sudden thought that it was always this way: the beauty of a woman was a pale second to her strength and intelligence. But the boldness of her diminished him.

Shockingly, her hand moved lightly across his belly, tracing over his lap. Pressing gently against his trousers, she paused, and looked up at him: there was a question in her mind, he could see. She drew away in a nearly imperceptible shift of position. In the stillness, he could hear the shivery rustling of her dress.

"You are an attractive man, Mr. Bloode. Very attractive, if I may say so." She straightened his tie, patting the bows on either side of his collars in gentle but dismissive gestures. "But you seem not to find me so."

Byron protested. "Oh no. No. On the contrary." Blushing furiously. "I find you an *incredibly* beautiful woman ... lovely."

She wore a half smile, but there seemed to be little warmth in it. "There is no sign ... you seem not to be ... " Her eyes were cast down, but her hand remained on his shoulder, hot as a torch. He had no answer. He was aroused by her, but his fear stood in the way. He had always been taught that the paramount virtue of a woman was her modesty. Only in this way could a man's normal process and dominance be permitted their natural influence. It was a code understood and taken for granted, at least in the quiet halls of Oxford college, and the monied society in which his parents now moved. Upsetting such protocols threw him off. He tried to explain: "You are a very unusual woman. You are like a man, in some ways."

"I don't know whether I should be flattered or insulted by that," she said.

"Oh, I meant no slur, I assure you. It's just that ... that ... " His forehead was damp. This was going badly.

She had withdrawn her hand. "That what?" She stood up, glancing at the house.

"Please stay. Please." He took her arm and drew her back to the bench. She remained, but her arms were folded, a faint look of suspicion in her eyes. "I ... I ... " he stammered, unable to sort out the welter of thoughts that rushed at him. Suspicion seemed to have given way to amusement, for her look now was softened. "I want you to marry me," he blurted out.

The woman burst into laughter, clapping her hands to her mouth as she whooped. "Oh, I'm sorry," she said. "I didn't mean to react like that, but — did I *hear* you say you wanted to marry me? I mean, did I hear you say that? *Marry* me?" She uttered a short laugh again, but there was no hardness in it. "I have had such offers before, but never one so utterly unexpected."

She was suddenly serious, and something came over her, an intensity of the sort that characterized everything she set her mind to. Her brow furrowed and there was a determination at the corners of her mouth.

The truth was that she cared deeply for this man. His brooding handsomeness, sad eyes, longish coppery hair and thoughtful introspection were a combination of qualities she found irresistible. But he seemed to lack passion. True, she took joy in the things he did, but he seemed to lack fire. Other men upon such invitation as she had offered him, had seized her, and touched her in intimate ways. She had lost her virginity to such roughness, and the urgency of such a need thrilled her and underlay her pleasure at being handled so. Perhaps Byron would change, once they came to know each other well. Perhaps his ardour would grow if she were patient, for in all other respects, he would make a fine mate. And she had waited longer than most women.

She moved closer to him, putting her hands on his shoulders. "I will marry you, Byron Bloode. But you must learn to love me too, not in the distant way you do now. Now kiss me, and hold me, as if you *mean* to have me as a man would have a woman."

## viii

Though Jan had said that he would go to the school with his *bandoura*, the matter slipped from his mind, for his hands were full with the work required to put his farm in order, and clearing the land. Slowly, he and Kinipi reintegrated their lives, and it was not long before she was heavy with child again. Jan happily contemplated the prospect of a son who would work next to him in the fields, and who would take the land when it was time.

It was a joy to work the land; *his* land, to shape it in a way that matched his vision. The journey to reach this place had been hard, but as he reflected on it, it had seemed rich. The pilgrimage, in truth, occupied a considerable portion of his thoughts.

Jan stood and stretched. The extrication of stumps, even with oxen and the levers and pulleys he had arranged, was exhausting work. The team of oxen, which he had named Kudryk and Parker, shuffled and grumbled under the massive wooden yoke that Jan had fashioned from hard prairie oak. The poplar roots ran deep into the prairie soil, and were as stubborn as the people who had come here to sink their own ties in the earth. He did not notice Kinipi arrive with his midday meal, their daughter whom he had named Katya, after his sister, in tow, though the growling in his belly signaled their arrival well enough. She was consistent, never failing him, arriving each day when the sun was nearly overhead.

She stood silently, until he noticed her. She was showing large now, the dome of her impending birth swelling the rough dress she wore. Her face was wreathed in a smile of pride, for she loved to watch her man at work, never tiring of taking in his muscled leanness with her eyes, possessing him. He was not too tired at the end of day to pleasure her, though the roundness of her now required that he take her from behind, in the manner of the four-leggeds. Thus enfolded, his callused hands around her belly and heavy breasts, she reached new levels of intensity that she had not thought possible. She loved him, and had given herself completely to him from the start.

But it was not easy, this pairing, nor would it much improve. Their daughter was of them, yet not like either. She had the strong features of his Slavic forebears, and the deep colouring of her people. The disapproval of the townsfolk was palpable; their neighbours marginally better, with the exception of Ahapii Boberski, whom she was certain had more than friendship in mind until he had married the child of an impoverished newcomer. Even then, he stole sly glances at her body as it moved in the simple shifts she preferred. Beyond those who would use her or revile her, there was no one to whom she could turn, which had made the absence of her man that much harder. To imagine the same contempt visited upon her as yet unknowing child was a burden almost too much to bear. The drudgery of maintaining the place, so that the homestead improvements that were a condition of the grant could be met, was a balm. And the few letters that came were treasured far beyond the handful of folded bills they contained. Now he was home, she had scant need to go to town. She could spend the rest of her life on this farm, and never venture past its boundaries: that would suit her fine enough.

He grinned as he waved at her, mopping his brow with his *khustra.* "What need has a man of a clock, when he has a woman such as you?"

She felt a sudden rush of warmth at his use of the possessive. She cast her eyes down in modesty. "You work hard; you need to eat. Come, the cheese is still cool, and the soup I have brought is yet warm." She sat on a felled tree, and spread out her offerings. The girl fluttered around beside her and settled on a limb like a thrush. She was a miniature of her mother.

Jan took his wife's face in his hands for a moment, then ruffled the hair of the child, bowed his head and gave thanks briefly. The girl was still shy around him, even though he had been back more than two months, and her silence annoyed him. She seemed afraid of him. Girls were all like that, he decided, and deep within himself, he felt the disappointment that the first child he had fathered was not a boy. Perhaps the next one: a strong young lad, surely.

As he ate, she watched him, then spoke. He nearly jumped, for usually they took meals in silence.

"That man comes once again to see you."

"What man?"

"The school teacher. He tells me he is now our neighbour. He buys the two quarter sections abandoned by Urbanoski, and the one beyond, where the soil is rough with stones."

"What need has a school teacher of land?" asked Jan, mopping the last of the gruel with a slab of bread. "Does he not earn enough at the desk without dirtying his hands with heavy labour?" He was conscious of a curious tension in equal parts of snobbery and resentment here. "What did he want of me?"

"Oh, he has many things to say, and says them prettily. He will build a house, a grand one, to hear him say it." She took hold of the girl and cradled her awkwardly, for her belly protruded. The child cooed contentedly. "He say also that you must come to the school soon with your *bandoura*. Ahapii has told him. He want your songs and stories to write down. For the pupils. He wants Katya to go to that school when it is her time."

"This is quite a conversation with our neighbour, the school teacher." He emptied the chipped ceramic jug of cool water down his throat, saving a few drops to mop his face.

She detected something in his tone, though she was uncertain what.

Defensively, she replied, "He shows me respect. He seems kind. Why would you not do these things for him, as he asks?"

He looked at her sharply, not really understanding why he was annoyed. Was it the woman? Or an intrusive neighbour? "I do not say that I refuse to do these things. It is only that the work takes my time. Perhaps in the winter, I do these things. Perhaps then."

# ix

Henry Cartwright poured the treacle-coloured brandy into two glasses, and supported them in one generous hand. With the other, he beckoned Byron to walk with him to the verandah. The sun was not yet down, and the coolness of the east side of the house was welcome. It had been dry that summer of 1908, and there were very few mosquitoes to bother them. In a gesture of uncharacteristic warmth, he put his arm on Byron's shoulders, and escorted him to the chairs that awaited them.

"I think you're going to like this brand of sipping liquor, Beamish's, very expensive. I got it in Winnipeg the last time I was there. Special occasion." He settled into the wooden chair, squirming on the thick horsehair cushions. Byron wondered. Something had been on the old man's mind ever since he had arrived unannounced with his obnoxious son, for dinner.

Cartwright settled back, and propped his heels on the rail, and lighted an over-large cigar. "Ahhh," he sighed, looking over the yard to a thin screen of poplars beyond. "You've built a fine place here for my daughter. Looks like an English garden out there. Far cry from that little teacherage in town, I'd say."

"Ervina likes it out here," said Byron. "I do too. It's home." The house had been two years in the building, and the garden a further seven months. In all, it had nearly depleted the trust his father had established for him, but the old man had approved. It seemed clear that Byron would not return to assume the family business, at least not in the foreseeable future, so this seemed a wise thing to do: get established in the community in a tangible way. And what better evidence than property? Before a man could claim to be of consequence, current thinking held, he needed to possess land.

He did not work the half-section he owned, but rented out the cleared space to others for one-third the harvest. On the less arable quarter, where the bedrock in an unusual formation had pushed up through the prairie soil, he found an attractive site to put up his two-storey half-log and fieldstone house, the biggest private dwelling at that time in or anywhere near Dauphin. Embroidered with Victorian tracery at the eaves, and ornate fretwork bordering the broad verandah, it was as stylish as it was functional. Soon there would be imitations on holdings by the more well-to-do farmers and merchants in the region. The Ukrainians which far outnumbered them chose to build replicas of homes they had known in the mother country.

Cartwright turned to Byron, sipping the brandy noisily. His red face had aged since Byron had first met him, and he seemed to have gotten broader about the girth. "Byron my boy," he said expansively, "I want to engage you in a proposition."

Byron was curious, but said nothing. "Have you ever taken an interest in politics?"

"Not really, sir. It has always seemed to me the dullest pursuit imaginable." He wondered where this was going.

"Oh quite the contrary, son. Quite the contrary. Listen here: there's a young fellow, name of Nathaniel Clement, school teacher like yourself, who's creating quite a stir."

Byron listened without hearing. At one time he had considered that a career in politics was an attractive pursuit for a man of his talents. Discounting for vanity, he had an agile mind, was well-spoken, presentable in appearance, and possessed of a fine voice for oratory. All talents, he reckoned, suited for successful leadership. But the business in South Africa had ended all that. A long time ago, but his opponents would be sure to dig it out. There was no shortage of newspapers these days, and they were forever digging for scandal so that broadsheets could be flogged by shrill boys on street corners. He shuddered at the thought of it. Ervina had listened patiently to his version of events, and seemed to have accepted them, but a doubt gnawed at him.

It was the way she had put it: "I care not a whit for the man you were, only the man you are," that left the tiny prickle. But she had never raised the subject again. For him, it was a murky secret, scabbed over with time, but easily disturbed. The pain of its recollection was as presently keen as it had been at the time. Perhaps more so with the effort of its repression. The thought of entering an arena in which events would be unearthed and slurried about in the newspapers sent a deep and pervasive shudder through him. The papers were ready to feed on such things as would surely be provided by his opponents.

Cartwright was nattering on; he and his son seemed to be having a conversation oblivious to Byron. Ervina was nowhere to be seen, and Byron thought this a little unusual. With some reluctance, he decided to interrupt: "Pardon me, but I must say, I really have no interest in standing for office."

They both turned to look at him as if he had joined in a private conversation. With a quick look at his son. Cartwright laughed dryly, saying, "Oh, it's not a candidacy we're after. As I've been saying, our man is Clement. Nat Clement. Fellow's an invalid, but has more fire in his belly than four men with all their limbs. No, we see your participation as more of a ... well, a support for our candidate."

Byron mused over this for a moment, sipping the aromatic brandy. He held it in his mouth briefly, swallowing its pungency by degrees, then spoke. "I'm a little embarrassed to be saying this, but most of the money I had has gone into the building of this house, and ... "

The younger Cartwright spoke. "It's not money we're after; our fellow is well set-up with backers. We need your contacts and influence in the Ukrainian community. That's where you can help us. These are new voters. It would be an easy thing ... "

His father cut him off. "Look Byron, it's simply a matter of good citizenship. The franchise has to be respected; people must vote. Why not get out there and persuade people to vote for the right candidate?"

Byron's brows knotted as he pondered the discomfort he was having with this. He had no particular loyalty to a man he had never met, simply on the basis of an endorsement from Cartwright — even if the man was his father-in-law. Moreover, there was an ethical issue here that had to do with subornation. He was not sure he could — or wanted — to do it. A demurrer formed on his lips, but it seemed as if the old man could read his mind.

"I know what you're about to say, my boy. You might think that there's an issue of trust here, that supporting one candidate over another is a private choice that you have no business interfering with.

"Well, I'm here to tell you that politics is not that simple. Not so cut and dried. Getting elected is a damned difficult business, and all the stops need to be pulled out to get the job done — within proper bounds, of course. We simply have to get the right man sent to the legislature, and Nat Clement is the man for the riding of Dauphin-Turtle Mountain."

His voice had raised a little, as he did when the least objection was raised to what he might be saying, though Byron put it down to drink. The younger man was scowling, but that seemed to be a natural reflection of the son's disposition.

"Let me think on it," Byron said, smiling.

It was as a slap. "What? I come here, cap in hand to ask a favour from a member of my own family, and I'm told, well, 'I'll *think* about it?'" He bobbed his head. "I never would have expected this from you. It won't do. It simply won't do."

Byron was discomfited, and he gulped the remainder of his drink. The hotness seemed to gather at the base of his skull, making him seem reckless. "Look, all I'm asking for is a little time to ... "

Cartwright's voice grew cold. "You look. When you came to me asking for my daughter's hand in marriage, I knew full well what sort of sorriness was in your background. Oh yes indeed. Don't think for a minute I make decisions that are not well thought out. Oh no."

Byron was aghast. What manner of man would speak to his daughter's husband in this way? What was he about to bring up? His war record? Worse? Drink had fogged his thoughts, allowing fear to assume its sovereignty. He dared not order the man and his wretched son out. Dared not defend his dignity. Dared not assert his right to respectful treatment. Instead, he looked at Cartwright, his mouth flopping, an apology of sorts forming on his lips.

Again it was as if the man had read his mind, and nodded, his face losing its sudden tightness. "Good. You're with us then." Then softer: "I want you to put your trust in me the same way I have trusted you with my daughter. And let's leave past what's past."

But Byron knew that past was never past. Its grip on the future was as certain as the mistakes men seemed destined to keep repeating. He shuddered inwardly at the thought.

# X

The trestle tables having been scrabbled to the sides of the room, and the benches arranged in rows, the children began to settle down, jostling for position next to favourites, further back, or close to the door.

Byron watched Jan setting up his *bandoura*, twisting the keys and plucking the strings so that the chords were resonant and distinct. Jan wore a splendid white shirt, startlingly embroidered with a fabulous floral pattern surrounding his broad shoulders, and the bell-shaped sleeve of his left hand was rolled out of the way of the fingering. It revealed a powerful, deeply tanned forearm, fanned over with fine golden hair. The high forehead suited him, thought Byron, for it emphasized a strong nose, set between eyes the shade of robin's eggs; a handsome man, by any standard.

The introductory chords stilled the children's shuffling. The board walls of the classroom reflected each note, so that it was like a living thing set free from the instrument. If the listener were to anticipate it, the music rose and fell in a way designed to gather attention, then lowering as Jan's thumb picked out a parallel tune that led to the main event. This melody fell against gentle, clear chord arrangements that cut off diversion like soft velvet curtains.

When Jan sang, it was in Ukrainian. Though Byron was passably competent in that tongue by now, this was a dialect which gave him trouble in the precise following of it, but no difficulty at all in its understanding; a paradox he would later puzzle over. Jan had a deep voice, and he had trouble following the instrument in its higher reaches. He had developed a way of tracking these notes at a distance, drawing abreast of them in a different key. It should have been discordant, but it was not.

Byron stole a glance at Ervina. She was transfixed, her eyes had a sheen to them, and her fingers were locked together tightly in her lap. One of the children had braided prairie daisies into a ringlet, twisted into her hair, so that with the light streaming through the window behind her she looked like a faerie queen. Byron was pulled away from her, by the textured voice that pleaded:

*Suppose I light a fire here on the open steppe,*
*Fling wide the ashes, flying down the wind?*
*I'll lay thee on the mound!*
*And when the boisterous wind shall*
*Fly along the steppes,*
*O let him touch thee!*
*Let him play and gambol, pitiful with sorrow!*
*Maybe some wandering Cossacks a-gallop, will ride near -*
*And they will hear, perchance*
*Thy piteous music -*
*Turn them to this mound,*
*And bury me.*

Byron looked back at his wife. She was lost among the notes now filling the room like gaily-feathered birds flitting over one another, then back upon themselves. Perhaps this is the way of it, he thought. No woman ever really belonged to a man completely.

As the dying notes of the *duma* faded and Jan's hand dropped from the strings, he looked up with the aspect of a man surprised that there were others in the room. Their expressions were rapt.

Suddenly Ervina clapped her hands lightly. The others broke into applause. What was it, Byron wondered about the spoken recitative or sung verse that captured the human imagination? He had seen the magic, for his own talents at recitation were not ordinary. Yet he presently stood in the shadow of another's performance feeling oddly inadequate and irrelevant, and not a little jealous. Who was this peasant's son who so roundly had captivated his class, his wife, and won his own begrudging admiration?

Such thoughts disturbed him, for this was not what he was about, he told himself. He had thrown all of his efforts into the making of this school, and the learning of a new culture and language quite alien to his own. No one could challenge his commitment and dedication to a benighted people in need of both introduction to the ways of the new world they had entered, and the preservation of a cultural identity which serves all peoples in the search for what is good and necessary in their treatment of each other - in that order of priority, of course.

But behind all that, well down below the horizon of his regular thoughts, lay the anxiety that he was hiding. Lurking like phantoms were the memories of his disgrace and the ways in which such events might be refreshed to current attention. He fretted over the possibility that Ervina would wake up one day and find him unworthy. She was strong-minded and deliberate, often flaunting convention and tossing off gossip as trifling inconsequentialities; she was like no other woman he had ever known, for few of the ordinary protocols of the day restrained her. Yet fear hung over him, a sword suspended by his own hand. He smothered these thoughts in the deliberate act of standing up and shouting, "Bravo!" Clapping loudly. But his heart was not in it, and he believed it showed.

Later, when the children called to Ervina to come outside, and she had shooed them to the door, flapping at them, smiling broadly, Byron poured Jan a glass of cider from a cold jug. Its sweating sides left a wet circle on the hard-used surface of the table.

"I should like to get your *duma* — translated of course — onto paper, written down for the children."

"I am proud to do this."

For a time they sat by the window and watched the children and Ervina outside, ring-a-rosy, laughing as they tumbled on the flattened prairie sod. The warps in the cheap glass played a trick on the eye, so that their movements appeared sticklike and sudden as their images passed through the defects.

Jan spoke: "She is well with the children."

"Yes. She has a special gift. She has some capacity in the language, too."

Jan addressed him in Ukrainian. "To speak in a man's mother tongue is to do him a great honour."

Byron looked out of the window, yet, and smiled warily; his thoughts seemed elsewhere. "Ah, honour. Exactly what is that? A matter of courtesy?"

Jan was unsure whether this was a theatrical question, the kind that a man simply pronounces, only to answer himself, having set the stage for some profundity or other declamation. He was silent, choosing to cross his legs and fold his arms. The cider had fuzzed his thoughts in a gentle way, so he felt no compelling need to contribute.

"Honour," Byron repeated, as if hefting the idea to determine its real weight and balance. "I cannot say I take the full meaning of the word. If one tells a lie to a dying child to instill hope or banish fear, do I honour the child, or dishonour the truth?"

Jan tried to get his mind around the question, but it slithered out of reach. "A riddle," he responded at length.

"And if a man does a thing for a selfish reason, but clothes it in another, perhaps high-sounding purpose, and all are pleased with the results, does he act honourably?" He seemed ill at ease with the topic, though his voice was calm and his hand sturdy as he brought cup to lip. He looked at Jan quizzically over the rim. Outside the shrill squeals of children at play pierced the thin walls like distant birdcalls, random and muted in their arrangement.

Jan thought back to his meagre teachings in the Old Country. Honour for his father had meant all that was necessary in the service of his family. For *pópa* Kudryk the idea had meant service to God, and the engagement of others to the same view. For his *vuyko*, Stefan, honour was the unguent quality which bound his service to Jan, even to his dying moments. Honour, in sum, seemed to be what a man attended to in the ministry of his fellows. He opened his mouth to frame these ideas before they tumbled away from him, but Byron spoke again, setting his glass firmly on the table.

"Fact is, I think it's all context."

Jan had trouble with the word, and he said so.

"Situational, you know: all depends. Depends on the facts, what they are at the time, and so on. There was a case we studied at college, law. Dudley versus Stephens, it was called; funny how I never forgot it." He poured another glass and started to add to Jan's but Jan drew away the vessel, for liquor even as light as this went straight to his head. Byron nodded, and topped his own drink.

"What happened there was three shipwrecked fellows fetched up in a lifeboat. No food, no water, all destined to die sure as cats see in the dark."

This put Jan in mind of Sergeant Jones' story of the shipwrecked cats. Memory was the strangest thing: what imbedded itself there a man had no way of knowing for certain. Then years later, a recollection popped out, often unbidden. Perhaps everything stored itself thus, the sum total of a man's life randomly recalled, which would account for most men being so generally unhappy and mean-spirited. He drifted back to Byron, whose relating of the case was animating him as the teacher and expositor took over.

"So they conclude: all perish eventually, or one die in the cause of the others. They drew lots and the youngest, a plump-red cheeked cabin boy, wouldn't you know, unhappily lost, so he was bludgeoned and bled and eaten. I must confess to a nagging doubt that the boy's fate was something less than a coincidence, but there were only the two stories at trial — for they were rescued and prosecuted -- and the law adjudged that this was irrelevant anyway. Necessity was pleaded and rejected. Wrong to kill, and that's the end of it. But look you: suppose a band of marauders was attacking you — still wrong?"

Jan was getting uncomfortable with this. The law was no friend of the ordinary man. Besides, his mind was not as agile as that of the teacher, who was plainly conflicted about something. He struggled for something to say that would calm him, yet not give away his own anxiety at such high questions.

"It seems to me, at the end of it, that we are obliged to do what is right, no more."

Byron opened his arms dramatically, as if he had just stumbled upon a hitherto undiscovered truth. "There, you see? This is my point: how do you know what is right?"

Jan stood up, nodding. He took his hat from a row of pegs by the door with an easy reach, and held it in front of him like a shield to further interrogation.

"I do not have the answer. It is a matter of instinct, of our parents' instruction perhaps. It is inside." He gestured with a thumb to his chest. Byron looked near disconsolate, but seemed to pull himself together as he rose and reached for Jan's hand.

"Forgive me. I tend to rattle on about things that don't matter, I suppose. I hope you will come again soon, and we can write down your song."

Outside, Ervina saw him walk to his wagon, and she extricated herself from the group of noisy, clinging students. Holding her skirts, she came swiftly to him as he was about to step at the set-brake. Putting both hands on his forearm, she complimented him extravagantly again on his music, then asked with uncharacteristic coyness: "Do you remember when you nearly crippled me?"

He looked into her gaze and was profoundly discomfited. These were eyes into which a man might disappear. He trembled, and he was not sure that she had missed it.

"I remember." Her hands were light upon him, yet heavy as anvils.

"I never forgot it either. You were so gentle with me, coaxing the soreness from my foot." Her mouth was slightly parted. The smell of her was lilac and fire smoke. The steel-rimmed wheel pressed against the back of his thigh; there was no further retreat.

"I must go," he said abruptly, tearing his arm away. He turned to put his foot on the hub; she stepped back, folding her arms. He could not see her expression, nor could he sense what she was thinking. As for his own thoughts, Jan was experiencing something close to delirium.

Through the imperfect panes, Byron watched.

# xi

Henry Cartwright Junior could be a man of considerable charm; one only had to see him at a gathering. Many had asked him to consider trying for the new federal seat in the forthcoming elections, but it had no appeal for him. Though he spoke often of "the right man", and the importance of "getting the best man for the job", he relished the politics of the backroom arrangement and the parlour chat. His father's wealth enabled him to have influence. There was something about the man that Byron found at once irresistible and repugnant.

The meeting that the younger man's father had called in late October of 1912 was one to consider the strategy for the provincial election. Guest of honour was Nathaniel Clement, Liberal candidate for the constituency. Byron had met the man on two prior occasions, but this was the first time where he would hear him speak at length. Through the haze of tobacco smoke, sherry and the warmth cast by a blazing hearth and more than two dozen bodies in the same room, he studied the man he had pledged to support.

The first thing that one noticed about the candidate was, curiously, not the crutch that he kept fitted under his arm. Much was made of his war wound, of course, that he had given a limb for his country, and that by implication, no sacrifice was too great. Rather, it was the man's intensity. His eyes seemed to blaze with passion not only when he spoke, but when he listened, fulsomely nodding his head and agreeing: "Yes! *Yes!* My thoughts *exactly.*"

He wore a trimmed beard, cut without a moustache, perhaps to offset the sparseness of his straw-coloured hair. The effect of this particular vanity gave him a benign appearance, like a pastor or a headmaster.

Not far off stood Cartwright, glass in hand, eyeing the candidate as a man might appreciate fine livestock. Turning back to Clement, Byron noticed that his conversation partner had moved on, and Clement stood alone for a moment. He wore a sheen of perspiration on his forehead, and he took out a handkerchief, and patted his brow. He looked about and for a moment, Byron saw the facade drop, and the man's eyes narrowed sharply, and his ears seemed to lay back in the way of a feral cat. Had Byron recollected only that moment to describe the evening, he would have thought the man had nothing but contempt for those around him. He shuddered at the sensation, but when he looked again, Cartwright had steered someone else in front of him, and Clement's face had brightened again, drawing in the newcomer.

Tapping his ring finger against his glass, the senior Cartwright brought silence to the room as men turned to him expectantly. The firelight was reflected in their flushed faces; several had taken off their jackets. One, the storekeeper named Slack, had great moons of sweat under his arms, and a generous belly insisted against a waistcoat that no longer fit.

"Friends," said Cartwright, "you all know my son Henry. I'm going to call on him to do the introduction of our guest, whom by now you will all have met informally. Henry?"

His son spoke from where he stood. Confident, assured, projecting a witty, engaging personality, he spoke of Clement's brief career as a school teacher, and of course, his war effort that "secured the Northwest Territories for Canada and glorious opportunity," pointing out that he had chosen to go, "not shrunk from duty as so many do in this age."

He spoke well, worthy of any candidate. There was almost a stirring quality to his words, but Byron felt unconvinced. He wondered whether that was because he was a reluctant participant to begin with.

To a round of polite applause, Clement raised his right arm, and shifted his weight from the wooden prosthesis that had been fitted to his thigh. "Friends," he said. "Thank you."

He looked around, as if to satisfy himself that this was a friendly audience. His face hardened for a moment as an unrevealed thought scudded behind his eyes, then he spoke.

"Last spring, May 15, nineteen and twelve, to be precise, was the birthday of a new Manitoba. Our boundaries extended north of fifty-three, creating a jurisdiction of such fabulous vastness and untapped wealth as will surely make the twentieth century ours.

"The Roblin government for which I shall oppose as a candidate in this riding, has been four times returned to power because they claim to offer sound management and prudent husbandry of our God-given resources. The proof is in the pudding; this is empty rhetoric. Manitoba has enjoyed prolonged growth in wealth, by whatever measure you may care to choose, be it wheat, livestock dairy products or industrial fabrications. A new legislative building is about to rise at a cost in excess of two million dollars. Two million dollars!" He looked about conspiratorially, "The government has benefited from a tide of economic prosperity that has worked to their advantage. It may not last."

"If we are to continue on this course, it hardly need be said, a new government is required. This is my first bid for office, but I have no doubt as I look about the room, I see the sustaining confidence of men who know what they are about, men with vision. Powerful men who will reap with me the fruits of power and leadership."

The gentle tug of inclusion and promise.

Clement smiled a fleet expression of engagement, and put the cuff of his jacket to his shining forehead. Then he slipped his jacket off and tossed it to Cartwright. His voice lowered slightly, a note of concern inserting itself like a child's hand.

"We face threats, it's true." He slapped his leg lightly to emphasize his artificial limb. "And I know something of threats." His face tightened, and the corners of his mouth drew down.

"Our greatest threat is the Tories. That man who leads them is dangerous, mark me. This coming election, when it is finally called sometime early in 'fourteen, will be the dirtiest on record. He will pander to the coarse element and the rabble-rousers. And there are plenty of them in the gutters and back alleys of our burgeoning cities. We may even see a challenge from the socialists who take their lead from such stock. Mountains heave in childbirth and a mouse is born said the poet. But we will need every vote that can be turned out against such vermin, which means special efforts to ensure the newcomers' vote."

He seemed to sag against the crutch he had wedged under his arm. "Make no mistake: those who prey on these gullible and uneducated immigrants, especially the ones who are landless, will be a factor. The Socialists and the labour groups. The General Federation of Trade Unions and their ilk threaten to destroy the British way of life by their endorsement of violence and corrupt practices — we only have to look back to the streetcar strike five years ago. Troops in the streets again? Is that what we want? These people thrive on unrest."

Slack raised his hand, and Byron thought he saw a slight annoyance in the interruption.

"That sort of thing is all very far away in Winnipeg and the larger places. Do we not need to worry more about local matt- ?"

"Hold it there, friend," said Clement. "We're looking at the big picture here. Dauphin is growing as fast if not faster than the surrounding area. Gilbert Plains, Grandview, Ukraina, Neepawa — heavens man, we take a back seat to no one in this province!"

There was a smattering of applause and other sounds of approval. The draw of local pride.

"There are rumours of war, fed by the troubles in the Balkans. Can anyone sit still and pretend that we are solely concerned with local matters when the world stage is taken with events that could easily overtake us? Surely you - " and here he looked directly at Slack, "as others surely, are conscious of the socialist threat? The rantings of followers of Marx, and the idea that a man's hard-won wealth might be taken from him by the state?"

Now his face took a grimace to it as the topic suggested its repulsive nature: "If there is war — and mark me, friends — it seems likely, decent men will rise to the occasion. This is something I know of, believe me. We will not have the time for the pacifist grovelling we hear from the Trades and Labour Congress. Class division and struggle!" His voice had risen, and the threat he hinted at was palpable. One could not envision a safe future when the very things taken for granted might be snatched away.

He smiled suddenly. Opening his arms slightly, he said, "But let us not talk of such things at length. We will triumph, *whatever* it takes." The sharpness in his tone bespoke determination, and more. Just what he would do to defeat his opponents was something that caught Byron's imagination as he stood with the others, applauding. The man would stop at nothing.

# xii

The spring of 1912 was the best for planting that Jan could remember since his return from the north. Warm, dry conditions together with light after-noon rain to hasten germination, allowed for quick seeding, and an earlier start to the endless round of chores called into being by a new farm.

One afternoon, he was at work clearing stones from land he had stripped of poplars and willow. The soil was rich, and the ash from burning felled timber would increase its fertility, but there were many stones ranging in size from a walnut to the size of a man's chest. His team of oxen pulled a rough flat sledge, a 'stoneboat', upon which Jan piled the rocks. He had devised a way to drive one runner over an embankment, so that the load tipped of its own weight. In the process of righting the sledge, he heard a light trap pull up in the roadway opposite. Some premonition made him shake.

Getting out of the Democrat was Ervina. She had a small basket in the crook of her arm, and wore a flat straw hat with a wide brim against the sun. It was uncommonly warm, and Jan had stripped to the waist. A fact which sud-denly made him self conscious.

"Helloa," she called brightly, as if the meeting had been prearranged, and nothing could be more natural than this friendly visit.

He nodded.

She walked at an angle to where he stood, stopping in the high grass at the edge of the field. "Come over here, Jan. I don't wish to drag my skirts through all that charred wood and dust."

The space which separated them was no more than twelve paces, but it seemed to span different worlds. With her expensive clothes and stylish hat, she stood among the greenery like an advertisement for fancy soap he had once seen in a shop window.

He, on the other hand, wore a *khustra* tightly around his head, which was wet with perspiration, and rough canvas trousers reef-knotted with a double turn of hemp at the waist. His blouse was hung on a bough at the other end of the field, and he was acutely conscious of his rough nakedness. Standing in the blackened filth, he must have seemed like a pirate to her, yet she spoke to him as if they were on a street corner in town. He walked toward her, emotions strangely tumbling within him. He became aware of his own filth, the dark smudges of soot and patina of dust. The musk of labour under his arms.

"If you permit, I will go to the water and wash," he mumbled, and walked past her without waiting for a reply.

Down at the torpid creek which wound back upon itself twice before it formed the eastern limit of his property, Jan was glad of the moment to calm himself. He knelt at the stream's edge and threw water over his body, scrubbing with a fistful of swamp grass. His heart thumped within its cage, and he wondered at the depth of his present anxiety.

He had gone several times now to see her husband in the matter of the *dumy* he wished to share. It was, he realized, a matter of considerable pride, though his culture was something he had not given much thought to since leaving the Old Country. Once awakened, it seemed not to be denied. Each time, she had been there. And her husband's annoyance was barely perceptible, but there nonetheless.

She was an unusual woman, as bold and as forthright as he had ever known. Jan fought the unreasoned influence of her, the planetary pull of her passing. Since he had first laid eyes on her, many years earlier, she had tormented his private thoughts at various times as unexpected as an ambush. All through his absence and his return, over the years, her image and his frequent preoccupation with it, floated never far from his consciousness. Gradually, by sheer force of will and determination, he had compressed his prurience to the point where the imagining of her was a manageable matter, as a man might learn to live with a disability. Part of this process was aided by simple guilt, for his woman had suffered long, maintaining the property in his absence, and over nearly a decade, had borne him two daughters, if one excepted the stillborn child — a girl — of whom neither spoke.

Faithful, constant, and an attentive mother to Katya and Kristina, his wife felt his disappointment at not having a son to follow him into the fields. Though Jan repressed this feeling, the effort of it provoked other prickling thoughts: her silence was an irritant to him, where once he had found it merely curious. Her compliance in all matters, where once it had pleased him, now seemed servile.

The other matter that ate at him was the increasing inability to differentiate between the years. They were all very much of a sameness. And he could see the future all too clearly, a fact which hitherto had comforted him, but now which was a source of some ill-configured uneasiness. The thought began to lurk within him that he was not suited for the land, that the urge to throw off his boots and set off in search of fortune ought not be denied. But hard work and routine had its own pallaitives for the uneasy mind, and he managed.

His break with the church had come two years previously when the new pastor, *pópa* Semeniuk, had visited, taking him outside for a chat.

"Son," he had said unctuously in Ukrainian, "perhaps it is time for you to take a wife ... "

"I have a wife," came the curt reply.

"No, I mean a real wife. One of our own people. Look at your neighbour, Ahapii: now on his third wife. A bit young, perhaps, but she is a sturdy thing, quite unlike the frail child he ... "

Jan cut him off. "And what would you have me do with my woman?"

"Well, she has her people, surely. I would think she belongs with them."

"And the children?" A rage was beginning to build. He had barely contained himself, but Semeniuk seemed not to notice, in the way of the self-righteous.

"Well, again, they seem more of the mother than of the ... well, that would be up to you, but perhaps it would be best if they left with her."

Jan had seized him by the collar, and nearly lifting him, he marched the spluttering man to the roadway, where his cart awaited. Throwing him physically into the road, Jan spoke through clenched teeth. "I think it would be best if *you* left. I do not expect to see you again." Yet even here, there was a creeping sense that his reaction had more to do with guilt than with outrage.

The result had been an increasing isolation, which he increasingly and unreasonably felt had to do with Kinipi.

Jan shook away these thoughts and finished drying himself. He returned to the field, but it was empty. For a moment, Jan felt both relief and disappointment tumble in his chest. Ervina's horse drooped in his traces and cropped idly at the tasselled grasses at the edge of the roadway. But she had disappeared. He wandered about, confused. A strange thing, this.

He heard a giggle. Then her voice. "Come here you silly."

She had lain in the grass, on the blue and white checked cloth she had draped over the wicker basket that was opened beside her. He gasped as he saw that she had drawn up her dress and rolled down her hose, exposing pale white legs to the sun. "I beg your pardon," he said, averting his gaze. He had never seen such limbs, slender as a fawn.

"Oh, one would think you had never seen legs before. The sun feels wonderful on my skin. Oh, to be a man, and walk about as you, stripped to the waist with the heat of the day full upon one's body!" She shaded her eyes and looked up at him. "Well, aren't you going to sit down? If not, at least move over a bit so you can provide some shade."

He sank beside her, and she sat up. To his consternation, she kept her dress over her knees, and sat as a man might, leaning backward against her arms. She passed him the small bottle she took from the basket. "Try this. Blueberry wine, of all things." From the wetness on her lip, he could see she had taken from it already. "I'm afraid I have nothing to sip it from ... "

He drank a deep draft from the dark vessel, and instantly felt the sweetness and the lightness of it rise to the back of his head, adding to his befuddlement. The world had become telescoped into this tiny space ringed by prairie greenery, the pale primroses and the last of the butter-hued crocuses. Where the birds had been in full-throated song, there was now only silence as he awaited her next utterance; some explanation, he hoped, of this adventure. She said nothing, simply looked at him, taking him in, as one might examine a curiosity.

"Your husband ... " he faltered.

She laughed, a small sound empty of mirth. "His father died a week ago in Winnipeg, and he remains there yet. I can't abide the city much, though I suppose we'll end up there one day. All dust and noise, and now automobiles to add to the clamour. He is thinking of assuming his father's business, which I'm afraid I'm not very happy about. Bloode and Bell Hardware. Can you imagine how I'll fit in with that?"

"I know this place," said Jan, unable to tear his eyes away from her. "I was there once, a very long time ago. I buy a broken cart there. I still have this cart." He paused, recalling, glad of the neutral topic. "A kind man, I remember. Gentle. Perhaps it was this man. It is a long time."

"Perhaps. He was a gentle man. I cared for him very much. Once the funeral was over, though, I wanted to come home. Here."

She reached with a fleet movement and touched him on the chest, just above his brown nipple. Her fingers barely moved against the firmness of muscle, but the skin puckered and trembled under it. She took her hand away.

"You are a well-favoured man, Jan Dalmynyshyn." Her face was a mask of seriousness, and the quickness of her changed mood frightened him. "A prince."

"Prince?" he asked stupidly.

She smiled, but the cause of it was not obvious to him. In truth, not much was clear at all, for this was as a dream. His movements were slow and disconnected. His voice seemed to come from another. He heard her voice, but not her words.

"My husband calls you a 'lord of the sod'. And though I think he initially meant some funning of you in that expression, it is clear to me that there is some grudging admiration."

Jan's breath had shallowed, the place on his flesh where she had touched him felt like a brand, and he longed to bring his own hand to it, but his anxiety kept him still. She lifted a foot, and placed it in his lap. It was a shockingly wanton thing to do, but he was past understanding, past any sense of what he ought to do beyond follow where this was to lead.

"Rub my foot again, Jan, as you did once. I have never forgotten it." Her own breath was audible now, from her mouth, like someone whose lungs touched with the coughing sickness. He fumbled clumsily, aware of the blushing stain that warmed his jaw and chin, and now which reddened his chest.

"No," she whispered, "take off the boot. And the stocking." This last was barely audible.

He took the shoe away, and removed the sweet smelling hose. His hands were shaking so violently, that she sat up and placed both hands on his. "Be calm, gentle Jan. I will do you no harm." She took his face in her hands, and after searching his eyes for something, she put her mouth against his, her lips at the last moment parting so that he felt drawn into her. It was a evanescent sensation, as one might have upon casting wealth for a wish into a dark well. She pulled away for a moment, then lowered her hands to his shoulders; now her breath was ragged. Under her touch, a stirring in his belly began, and he felt the claw of lust, so that everything else but his need fled his mind.

He rose on his knees, and tore away the knot that held his trousers, and pulled them away to his knees. She cried out at the sight of him, tumescent, saying small words of no coherency.

She flung herself back, eyes shut. She moaned, drawing up her clothes so that the fork of her body was exposed to him. He tore away her under-clothes and entered her with a single minded urgency he could not remember ever experiencing before. Her cries now became rhythmic with his thrusting, and he felt his completion building and then releasing in a searing sensation that made him call out in a prolonged groan that mingled with her sounds. He collapsed beside her, rolling her with him so that they remained joined.

As the flesh ebbed, the world came back into focus; the twittering finches in the woods nearby filled his ears. The sharp smell of the burned wood filled his nostrils. He looked over to the woman, and it startled him that she was weeping quietly. He drew away from her.

"Have I hurt you?"

The back of her hand was over her eyes, so he could not read them. But she shook her head from side to side. She sat up, and took a handkerchief from the basket, and blew her nose. It was a loud sound, incongruous in the smallness of her. "I'm sorry," she said, "give me a moment, here."

A confounding thing, this, he thought. He would have his own misgivings about this later, but for the moment the fire of lust had burned too close, and he was disconcerted by this reaction to their coupling.

She smoothed her hair, and picked the bits of grass from it that had become entangled, and picked up her torn underclothes. "These won't be much good anymore," she laughed jerkily, making a small diversion of it.

This upset him. "My sorrow is great," he began, but she shushed him, her palm up.

"I only wish my husband would want me in that way. I have not lain with him in nearly two months."

The reminder that he was an adulterer, a fornicator, came as a blow. For though he had become estranged from the very church he had helped to build, he had not broken with his faith. He struggled with his trousers to cover himself, clutching shame like a tattered cloak. "I have wronged your husband," he said quietly, with the subdued pride of confession. "I have done a great wrong - "

"There is two in this wrongness," she replied quietly. "I was the planner and the schemer. It is I that cannot get you out of my thoughts. How often have I imagined this, the sight of you, the hardness of you. Oh, it is I that ... " She wept silently, without the sobbing or heaving that sometimes accompanies grief. It seemed to Jan that she wept not for herself, but perhaps her husband. How true it is sometimes that the apparent source of woe is not its root. He reached for her awkwardly, but she warded him off. He stood up, as did she.

"Do I look so wretched as I feel?" she asked. "This was not in any of my thinking ... "

"You are beautiful," he said simply.

She touched his face for a moment, then turned to go. Hesitating, she faced him again and said, "I shall come again tomorrow. If you are not here, I shall understand."

But he was there the following day, and the next. And the one after that. Five days without missing, they lay together in the same place, the grass crushed down by the weight of their movements, the petals torn from the fragile prairie flowers, and the fieldwork undone.

Her eyes were fathomless. It was disturbing that he discerned nothing of her save the glitter of passion, yet beyond that was reflected a world he had thought he could never be a part of. As she desired him, so he craved participation in a life she represented that was far below the curve of his peasant's world. She was the means by which he would pass through to something better, he now believed, better than what he presently had. It was a powerful aphrodisiac, imbuing his connection with her with something more far beyond the fleeting ecstasy of possession. He was becoming part of her, as he was sure she was becoming one with him. Their coupling was a passage, as most such unions are, but this one held portents that intoxicated him; his fevered mind could not take its compass. And nothing in the way her gaze held him yielded any clue to whether these tumultuous feelings were being reciprocated.

That afternoon of the fifth day, twice had he taken her, even more violently than before, and his need for her now was far beyond the fleeting ecstasy of possession. Later, as they lay still in the cooling of their ardour, he sought to make some sense of this, why she would betray her husband. He knew his questions held great risk, but he sought the answers recklessly.

There was the faintest tremour of annoyance in her voice, but he chose to ignore it. Her gaze was over the grasses that formed their private space, distant, unconnected. "My husband is in many ways a quite remarkable man. The people who leave their children in his care call him an angel. And indeed, he *is* an angel to me. A tortured, damaged angel, who perhaps ... " She seemed to catch herself, and turned to look at him, as if seeing him for the first time. She scrambled to get her clothes in order, and would not be restrained in her leaving. She ran to the Democrat, leaving him naked in the field.

On the sixth day, when he drove his team to the same corner of the field, they stopped of their own accord, their great heads swinging around to look at him in seeming silent reproach. Jan took notice of this as a portent of something; what, he did not know, any more than any of these recent events made sense. He addressed the beasts as if they were human, speaking in Ukrainian:

"Ah my friends Kudryk and Parker, you might well look at me, the fornicator and the cuckolder. What has become of me that I forsake all labour and normal thoughts, and dwell upon her, and think only of the next moment I can be with her?"

He looked at the sky. It was mid-afternoon; she should be here soon, he thought. He wandered to the road and looked in both directions, furtively, then anxiously, but there was no movement at all. Only the grasshoppers made their mechanical sounds, and far away, a dove called its mournful note. He sat fretting at the end of his empty stoneboat. Exhausted from his feverish imaginings over the woman who had now claimed him, he fell asleep.

# xiii

Byron Bloode contemplated the officer in front of him. Closely cropped gray hair was the only concession to the military tidiness that he was accustomed to seeing in members of the Royal Northwest Mounted Police. Indeed, the man seemed past retirement age, and perhaps that accounted for the sloppiness of dress. The tunic was worn open, and the woolen shirt beneath seemed as worn and rumpled as the serge. He sighed. The war had taken off the best of the young men, and he supposed that this was what had kept officers like this around.

"Inspector ... Jones, was it?" he asked, looking at the obscure document in front of him. "I'm not really sure what you're after here. This is an Order-in-Council from the federal government, but you're here on behalf of Attorney General Nathaniel Clement?"

Rishton Jones shifted in his chair. He was tired, and he had no appetite for this business. Still these were times of war, and the government believed that if they moved swiftly, it would assist in the swift resolution of the fighting in Europe. At least, that was the thinking, but Jones had little faith in it. Fighting and bloodshed and hatred was inherent to mankind, not at the margins as some might like to think, and he expected that an effort like this would continue for some years. Now this.

He leaned forward and reached across the desk, taking the papers from Byron. Looking at them, he took the Meerschaum pipe from between his teeth, and spoke, using small stabbing motions to punctuate his clipped British accent.

"The Attorney General advised my Commanding Officer that you were a man whose loyalty and trustworthiness is unquestioned, and one ideally situated within the Ukrainian community to let us know who the potential risks might be."

"Risks?"

"Oh, I daresay there are plenty of risks in the minds of those paid to consider such things. They'll take an event and magnify it: one of the Ukrainian bishops, Budka — Nykyta Budka — rather stupidly sent around a letter in which he exhorted his fellow Ukrainians to return home to serve in the Austro-Hungarian Army. Fight for the enemy! Imagine.

"There are still fears left over from the streetcar strike of ought-six. You may remember that the army was called up, and we had machine-guns and sand-bags along Main Street. It was militant labourites, true, but a lot of the Ukrainian element there too."

"What are your orders?" asked Byron, intrigued.

"I am to compile a list of suspected collaborators, traitors and other undesirables. Persons who would put the war effort at risk, or sap the will of the Canadian public to sustain our fighting men overseas. These papers are really quite plain, you see ... "

Byron took the papers back, and looked at them without seeing. His mind was elsewhere. The profits at Bloode & Bell were better than ever, for the war had brought increased business, rather than what he might have expected. But the role of merchant palled on him. He had been happy when Ervina had rejoined him that summer, but alternatively joyous and suspicious to discover she was pregnant.

As the fact of her condition had taken hold, he had become increasingly wary, then withdrawn. It was difficult for him to broach the matter with her: she was so strong-willed, and tended to sweep aside his faltering doubts on any subject. Tormented by a persistent anxiety, he had taken the opportunity which presented when she spoke of her morning sickness.

"We have not been, you know, together that ... often. The pressures of the school at term's end, the deaths of mother and father so close together. The back and forth between Dauphin and Winnipeg ... Your news surprised me." The statement with its implicit accusation hung like a threat between them, but she seemed oblivious, though there was nothing in her manner that allayed his fear.

"Look, Byron, dearest. I am getting on, as I hardly need tell you. I think I wanted a baby more than anything in the whole world. I wanted it so much, I think I could have willed it into being. But I didn't have to: we *have* been together. It hurts me to think that it was so unmemorable that you scarce recall it. Really, it is a matter of good luck, that's all."

But his suspicions stayed with him nonetheless, lingering like an unpleasant smell. Nonetheless, he might have managed, but for an unexpected visit.

One early afternoon, a Monday, when he ordinarily should have been at his desk at the warehouse, he answered the door. It was Jan Dalmynyshyn. For a long moment, the two of them stared at one another in mild astonishment. Holding the door, Byron at last found his tongue.

"Jan. It's ... it's a pleasant surprise. What on earth are you ... doing in Winnipeg, and how ... did you ... "

Jan coughed. "I came to see ... Ervina. And you."

There was a voice, behind Byron. "Who is it?" The question stalled on her lips as she saw Jan standing on the stoop. "Oh. Jan." She seemed uncharacteristically flustered. "Ah, hello." The awkwardness between them was palpable, and it was apparent to Byron. My God, he thought. This man has cuckolded me! And he comes, like a cur that has buried a bone, in search of another morsel. The urge to strike him had been as powerful as would have seemed ridiculous at the time. Pleading preoccupation with woman's business, she fled, leaving the two men facing each other. They had not moved. Byron still clutched the edge of the door in such a manner as to block entry. But Jan made no effort to engage the woman, though his gaze followed her retreat.

"You will not ask me in, then?" A difficult situation this, calling for neither wit nor strength, merely grace.

Byron's face hardened. "Another time, perhaps. It is difficult at the moment ... "

Jan allowed his temper to edge past his usual wall of reserve. "What can a man such as you know of difficulty? All things have come to your hand with ease. How can you know of the contempt of other men when you have not had the experience of it, as I? Such contempt as you show me now?"

Byron had nearly shouted, but he would not, could not lay bare his own pain to anyone, let alone this man.

He dismissed him, curtly, saying that he really had to get to work. Jan if he wished, might make an appointment. His wife bedded by a sod-breaking peasant. My God. The humiliation was too much.

The Inspector was speaking again, and Byron's focus returned to the moment.

"I have my own misgivings about all this. It seems an unfairness to put a man away on suspicion, but we live in difficult times. The black clouds of war cast shadows far from the fighting, and who are we ordinary folk to challenge the judgement of our elected officials?" He smiled thinly, betraying precisely what he thought of such judgements, setting his pipe firmly back between his teeth. It had gone out. His eyebrows raised slightly.

"Enemy aliens might throw all precautions aside to attempt something. The fact is that there *are* German sympathizers about, who actively support the enemy cause. The question is: are there those about who hold a similar view?"

Byron cleared his throat self-consciously. "If I am to inform, what of my own protection? By definition, these are dangerous people. One assumes they will stop at nothing ... "

"You will have your anonymity if you wish it, sir." Jones stiffened, sudden formality suggesting to Byron's mind a faint disgust with the idea. "I am obliged by the nature of my orders to protect the confidentiality of my sources."

Byron took a deep breath to steady himself. What he was about to do was such a leap across the steps of his imagination that the enormity of it filled his consciousness. That it was a wretched thing he knew to be true. Yet he could not stop himself. It was as if temptation in him had a life of its own, and clamoured after him like a hungry beast which must be fed. Justifications, rationalizations, intuitions and punitive thoughts blended as stirred in a bowl, in a matter of moments coming to this: he had been powerfully wronged, and it must be avenged. Byron had stood for nothing in his life, of this he was certain, but he would stand now. He would not be abused further; he would not turn the other cheek.

"There is one name that comes to mind," he said. "A man who is capable of treachery."

Inspector Jones took a short pencil and notebook from his chest pocket, and looked at Byron expectantly.

# xiv

Jan had fled Armstrong's Point, walking the city streets blindly, overcome with humiliation and despair. When he had gone in search of Ervina, first to the school in Dauphin, then to the house, and had found all locked and silent, he realized that she had returned to Winnipeg. Abandoned him, after a week of such intensity that his heart had been torn from its moorings with such force that he had known that nothing would ever be the same. He had loved the soil of Manitoba that was his to work with every fibre of his being. His family; the faithful woman who had sustained him in his relationship with the land: these were all as chaff now, as he was driven by a force greater than all of these.

When he had announced a trip to the city, Kinipi had been profoundly upset. The crops were nearing harvest, for it was late summer, and the Defense Department had already committed to buy whatever they could deliver to the Pool Elevators in Dauphin. There was no reason for this travel, nor was one offered. And the train fare seemed a squandering. She had driven him to the station, a grand, newly constructed affair of gables and cornices that declared the prosperity of the growing town.

As he had taken his bags down from the bed of the wagon, she said, barely above a whisper, "It is that woman, is it not?"

Jan had no answer. For he could not add further lies to the edifice of his sins. His turmoil was such that he boarded the train without further word or look back.

He had not taken much money, not thinking beyond the immediate matter of transportation. He looked for inexpensive lodging, and was directed to the north end of Winnipeg where poverty was evident and money scarce. Here, many of his countrymen lived in squalor that rivaled anything he could recall in the Old Country. Tenements, hovels and even ragged tents held families which suffered terrible rates of infant mortality and disease. The anger simmered on street corners and in the beer shops. A current case in the courts was being hotly debated. A sleeping man — a Ukrainian immigrant who held a job at night — had been poisoned by an exterminator, quite by accident. He was survived by five children and a wife of no means. While the trial judge had awarded reasonable damages for the time, the Court of Appeal, staffed by unsmiling representatives of the elite classes, had reduced the amount to a niggardly sum which was an affront.

Jan had been drawn into these debates, and he followed them easily, for injustice was a full meal for any man, and Jan had the taste of it on his tongue already. Bad enough that a man could not live decently on what was paid for his labour.

He had gone to Armstrong's Point impulsively, feeling suddenly that he could not lurk about forever. He had put on his best shirt, and blindly hoping that Byron had gone to his father's warehouse, he approached the door and pulled at the large brass knocker. And then – rejection. It seemed a bitter thing that nothing in his life ever seemed to work out the way he imagined it. To be dismissed like a vagrant had been humiliating. His despair was all-consuming.

For several days, he had not left the poor room that he had rented, until, one afternoon, as he lay listless on his vermin-infested pallet, members of the Royal Northwest Mounted Police came for him.

# XV

Jan opened his eyes. It was yet the half-dark that precedes the dawn. Snow had fallen. He could always tell, for the silence and the altered light of the coming day gave him a different sense of the morning. It was cold in barracks number twelve, for the rough board structure which he and seventy-two other prisoners had helped build was poorly fitted, owing to the quality of the timber, and the promised rolls of tar paper having not arrived. He lay still under his single blanket, feeling the chill invade his shoulders and knees where they poked past the limits of his meagre covering, thinking.

*The saucy wench was so unprincipled,*
*She placed a pretty price upon herself;*
*And her lord-husband was a puny thing!*
*At last he spied me with her, as you know,*
*And had me taken to Kaluga Barracks ...*

Even the poetry of his beloved Shevchenko was conscripted in the service of his melancholy.

Living now was a function of blind progress, for he was being propelled by something beyond a simple exercise of will. Like his flight to the gold fields, driven by fear, his present thoughts were as unfocussed and evanescent as an idle daydream. His misery was an alloy of worry and memory and loss, confined by shouted order, barbed wire, and heavy labour. His time in the Klondyke had been sustained by the thought of home; now he was uncertain of anything except his betrayal. This was no mere injustice, for such a yoke he had worn many times; this was evil. He began to experience the thin nourishment of hatred, and by degrees, it became the beacon by which he plotted his deliverance.

Under the War Measures Act of 1914, on August 4 of that year, the Canadian government issued an order-in-council which permitted, among other things, the internment of aliens of 'enemy nationality'. Those who had come from the Austrian crownlands of Galicia and Bukovyna, as had Jan, were subject to arbitrary arrest — often on the basis of informants and 'police intelligence' — and confined to what some newspapers referred to as 'concentration camps', for that is indeed what they were. A total of twenty-six camps or 'receiving stations' were established, including the one to which Jan had been sent, just outside the City of Brandon, about one hundred and forty miles west of Winnipeg. Detainees were compelled to work at road-building, park development and wood-cutting, in addition to all of the maintenance that their imprisonment required.

Perversely, time passed quickly. Perhaps it was a form of protection. Men were beaten for insolence. They were put on half-ration for lesser crimes. Visits from relatives occurred at a pair of fences which kept them apart from the prisoner by a distance of six feet. Though Jan had heard that the misuse of prisoners was not officially tolerated, it seemed to him that those with command authority turned a blind eye to what was happening. Two men committed suicide, others simply died from having given up. Disease and depression took their toll.

Yet Jan bore it all until the spring of 1916, when Kinipi arrived unexpectedly. Called to the visitor's gate, he wept upon seeing her, sinking to the ground on his knees, clutching at the wire which separated them. The intensity of the emotion in him surprised him, for she and the children had drifted from his thoughts, thoughts too crowded by resentment and longing, and were a distant memory.

She shed no tears. Her face was stiff, cold, unlike any expression he had seen before. He stood up, sniffling through a running nose. He was ridden with lice, his clothes were foul, and his hair stood up at one side, matted, as he had slept. His beard was lank, unkempt. He could not see what was in her eyes, but he was conscious of his wretched appearance for the first time since he had been brought to the camp. There was a parcel at her feet. Beyond, there was a wagon he recognized, and in the bed, a tool chest, bound in brass, much worn so that it had a dull gleam to the wood.

She shrugged. "Why did you not tell me where you were?"

"I am in hell."

"Boris Louka, who lives at Ukraina, has an uncle here. When visiting last, he was told of you. He spoke to Ahapii, who told me. Too late, of course."

Jan felt an uneasy stab of fear, though it seemed instantly ridiculous in his present circumstances. "Too late?"

"The farm has been taken from me."

The farm gone? This was impossible. "Who did such a thing?"

"The government. They took the children four months after you went away. Orphan, they said." Her voice trembled. "Am I not their mother? Then it was said that there was no taxes paid at the end of the next year. I was without money. There was nothing I could do. Last week I was put off the land, as it was to be sold. No one came to my aid. The man Slack bought the land, and he was nasty to me."

This was as a hammer-blow to Jan. He raised his head, and cried aloud, a long moan of grief.

*Why does the Lord afflict you; why so harshly*
*lay punishment upon you?*
*... he is intent to devastate your fields*
*And punish you till not a trace remains.*

"Slack took my land?" he faltered, disbelieving. "He took my property? They have taken my *children*? It is not possible."

"They took nothing from you. You threw it all away."

He looked over to the horse and wagon. "The rig ... ? How ... "

"It was hidden at the house of Ahapii, for I knew of their coming." Her head was down, and she paused. "But even he took from me in payment."

"What?" There was a current of feeble anger. "What price? What 'price' is this?"

"Nothing more than he has always wanted. He is only a man."

She had in her hand a package. "This contains the pouch of soil you brought here from your country," she said. "I must hand it 'round through the guards."

"Keep it," he cried. "Scatter it!"

She shrugged, the faintest of all possible gestures. "You may believe differently one day. You always say to me that you want soil from your homeland with you in your grave. I will leave it in the tool box. Do with it as you will ... you know, once I considered you *okesikoo*, an angel, *okemasis*, close to God. But ... "

She turned to go, but he cried out, a wordless sound of imploement. "Where will you go?"

She faced him, gathering her shawl about her, for it was a cool spring day. "To my people," she said simply, barely audible.

"You have been gone so long. Will they know you? Will they take you in? Better it seems to me to ... to ... " His tortured mind searched for what it was he wanted to say, but there was nothing. He had long ago wearied of his dreams.

"As long as there is one left, I shall be taken in. I am *Anishinaabe*. That part of me does not die." She walked back to the restless animal. "I leave the tools at the guard room," she called, without looking back again. She climbed to the seat and clucked the horse into motion. The steel rims bit into the near-frozen earth, leaving pronounced scars that a man might, had he liberty and inclination to do so, easily follow.

# xvi

Two soldiers of the 23rd Light Infantry were commiserating in the time-worn way of idle warriors. The war had ended, and it looked as if overseas service was no longer an option. Though both protested loudly, only one was sincerely regretful. The other moaned, but there was no passion in it.

"At least we'll be out of this lot," Insincerity said. "Guarding a bunch of lice-infested foreign trash is not my idea of military service."

"You have problems with the Bohunk Brigade, mate? Easier service you won't find. This bunch is sure to be deported if I know anything about it."

Jan shuddered. These men spoke of him and the others as if they were cut stove lengths. As if they did not exist as men. The camp was closing, and as a final indignity, they had been required to pull the buildings down and the wood separated and stacked, free for the taking. Already there was a line of vehicles of all sorts waiting to take their turn at the salvaging. Soon nothing would remain of this site, once the prairie grasses and purple thistles had reclaimed what was theirs before. All of them now were waiting, unknowing, for the will of the Government of the Dominion of Canada to be expressed in one more insidious form or another. Rumours were rampant, and men — at least such men who had not surrendered to their circumstances — lived in terror of gossip.

At last they were addressed by the Commanding Officer, a pale, slight man with a ruined shoulder. "I have my orders from General Otter. The camp is to be closed permanently." He waited for this to sink in, though that much was obvious to even the most disheartened man.

"Moreover, I have an order for the immediate release of all prisoners, save the following." With a pause, as he shuffled through a sheaf of papers in his hand, then selected one and handed it to the Sergeant-Major. This one-armed officer called off names in a stentorian voice, which fell like hammer blows on those called. Finally, it was done, and Jan was not among those mustered to one side, near an awaiting fleet of three trucks. Oddly, he felt no relief, only a continuing emptiness which had allowed him to suffer the years in captivity. Though the conditions of his confinement had been harsh, there was nevertheless sufficient food, and some of the guards had been tolerable. It was as if the vastness of the unjust detention was the subject of an unspoken truce. In any event, it was no worse than he had suffered at the hands of the Austrians and the Poles back home. It was a common sentiment.

The men were mustered at the remaining building, the guardhouse, where personal property was returned amid considerable dismay. Poor records had been maintained, for no administrative regime accompanied the policy decision to intern enemy aliens. Much was missing and both objection and entreaty were met with ill-temper. Jan recovered his tool box only because he was able to identify its inner construction without lifting the lid. Mercifully, all of the tools were still there. Viewing its contents, he felt something faintly stir within him, the ghost of a yearning to bring focus and meaning to his life. But it was distant, and it might be some time before hope was born of it.

# xvii

Nathaniel Clement, Attorney General for Manitoba, paced back and forth in his new office, situated importantly in the grand legislative building at the upper end of Broadway. From either of the ten-foot windows, he had a view of the magnificent grounds being prepared; even now workmen struggled with a pedestal which would accommodate a large bronze of Queen Victoria. For several minutes, Byron watched him. Over the few years that he had known him, Byron saw that his disability was nearly imperceptible, so adept had he become at walking with his prosthetic leg. Yet in public, he walked with a pronounced limp, and favoured a crutch, for he trumpeted his war injury as a reminder to his personal courage. As he vaingloriously wore the evidence of his wounds, so did Byron fearfully shield his own. Finally Clement turned and faced his guest.

"I hardly need tell you that in the last election, the previous government was barely returned to office. The Premier has acknowledged that it was largely the immigrant vote that did it for us, this time, that made the difference. Oh, we were so close in 'fourteen. The foul bog of corruption which caught up with Roblin and his gang certainly helped us along. As you know, he was very appreciative of your support in the Dauphin-Grandview area. Grateful for your, ah, other support as well, as I think you saw in some of the war department's supply office contracts we were able to steer in your direction."

Byron looked at him, expectant. There was something coming. The yawning maw of politics was never sated. Once into the Faustian bed, there was no out of it.

"The war is over. We must start planning for the next election call. I'm aware of course that you make your home in the city now, attending as you are to your father's business. It is our hope that your ties to the Ukrainian community are ... will enable you to be of further use to us."

Use to us. Byron cringed inwardly. "The business has preoccupied me of late, with the war and everything."

It was Clement's turn to stare, waiting.

"My connections with ... that community, here in the city, are not strong. Perhaps I could return to Dauphin during the next campaign?"

Clement shook his head, puffing slightly. "I do not fear that my seat is much in jeopardy. I won by quite a handsome margin as you no doubt recall, and, ah, as the incumbent this time ... well, you are needed here, is the point."

Byron thought for a moment. "I have a number of Ukrainians in my pay. Perhaps through them ... ?"

Clement nodded. He had taken his seat at his massive desk, where he contemplated Byron as a sculptor might regard a block of stone which he had only just begun to hew. "Of course. There is no influence like the pay packet," he smiled thinly, adding quickly: "Not that you would need to resort to such leverage at all: I have heard that they refer to you in Dauphin as an angel."

Byron looked down. "It is an extravagance."

"But nevertheless a measure of the esteem in which you are held." Again, the flattering smile, the voice a fraction higher, unctuous. "Still, it may be difficult for you even for that, given recent events."

Byron looked at him quizzically.

"Oh all this nonsense inspired by socialist agitators. This puerile fascination with Bolshevism. Activities that were designed to impair the war effort. Riling up the working classes, threatening our way of life. It's sickening. Sickening, I say. I fear we may not continue to enjoy the support of even the most reasonable of them, if this ferment continues to spread. I mean, the last election saw four Socialists, two Labourites, and the one Ukrainian Nationalist. Oh sure, they were all defeated, but they could have been spoilers for us, had the Liberal vote not held."

He lighted a cigar with a flourish of exaggerated motions, offering one to Byron, who declined. "I mean, even the Conservatives introduced progressive legislation to mollify this lot. Workers Compensation in ought-ten, a Bureau of Labour in '16, but at the end they were abandoned by the fickle newcomer."

He blew a cloud of smoke, leaning back in his leather-trimmed chair. "Well Byron, my good fellow, do you think you can do something for us?"

Byron nodded instinctively, knowing this was not a request.

The same feeling came over him the following day as he approached Leo Dudyck, the foreman on his loading dock. Dudyck straightened and snatched off his hat at Byron approached. "Good morning, *pahn* Bloode," he said in a thick accent. Byron liked Dudyck: he was a good worker, industrious and reliable.

"Good morning, Leo," he replied with a forced cheeriness. Politicking was not to his liking; he doubted whether he would ever warm to it. To be open and courteous was one thing, but always having to maintain relationships on different levels was complicated and difficult. "How goes the work?"

The other man grinned with genuine warmth. "Slow, oh it is slow. The Ferguson ploughs are far heavier than the Deere. More of us to having it lifted, but we will get it done, sure enough, sure enough."

Byron nodded. If Leo said it would be done, then it would. "I say, Leo, what was the name again of that reading club you belong to?"

"*Robotchy Narod*. Why do you ask this?" There was a trace of a frown on his damp brow.

"Would you take me along, next time you go?"

"Sure, *pahn* Bloode. But the language, it is not your language. You might ... "

"I might surprise you, Leo. I might surprise you."

The Reading Club known as *Robotchy Narod* was an extension of the newspaper by the same name, which had been suppressed the year before on the basis of its anti-war sympathies, bluntly expressed. Orders-in-council banning strikes, the public use of 'enemy alien languages', 'idleness' in healthy males, and so on, had provided a focus for reading club discussions that sometimes verged on incitement to riot. Informers were everywhere, and though the war had ended, many of the extraordinary powers government had reserved to itself remained.

The economic downturn of 1913 was starting to recover by the end of the war, but it had eaten away any gains that had been made by organized labour. On the streets of Winnipeg as elsewhere, there was an anger among the labouring classes that was palpable. Presently it was given voice in the union halls and reading clubs and street corners where workers gathered in the evenings. Politics was a natural outlet for this mounting frustration, and socialists recognized that their lack of dominance meant that they needed the support of moderates and conservatives. It was into this fragile alliance that Byron hoped to insinuate himself.

Dudyck stood up and called in Ukrainian for recognition, holding his thumb up. "I wish to introduce my employer, *pahn* Bloode. He would speak to us."

In another time, there might have been polite applause for a guest, but there was none. Some grumbling, which Byron's understanding of the language led him to believe that there was general disapproval of the use of the honour.

"There are no *pahns* here. This is not the Old Country. We bow to no one."

"Hold friends," called Dudyck. "You know me. I am no grovelling toad. But I think we should not forget our old expressions of respect. This man is responsible for the success of the *Taras Shevchenko* day school in Dauphin. Many years has he spent in the education of our brothers' children, and in the recording of our songs and stories. Mention his name in Dauphin, and they speak of an angel." He smiled at Byron, who was surprised that Dudyck knew so much. Looking around, he could see that the attitude toward him had changed considerably by these few words. When the foreman extended his hand to Byron, he took it, rising, and addressed the room.

The faces upturned toward him all wore the creases of hard toil and frustration. They were hard faces, showing a pallor and a fierceness borne of the most common heroism: getting by in difficult times. Byron was suddenly conscious of his fine clothes, and wished that he had dressed less finely. He tugged self-consciously at his waistcoat.

"Friends," he began in English, for he was not so confident of his Ukrainian expressions. "Thank you for allowing me to come here and speak to you today. I bring greetings from the government of Premier T.C. Norris." More grumbling, muted this time, but Byron spoke over it.

"I will make no rose-cake out of my message. I have come to ask your support for Premier Norris. I bring greetings on behalf of Taras Ferley, your countryman representing the constituency of Gimli. First Ukrainian in the House! I come not empty-handed. This government has given the vote to women, has introduced Bills in the House to provide for a Public Service Commission to clean up the business of getting government jobs, and has plans for election reform - "

"Where does he stand on matters that concern the working man?" came a voice.

"There are improvements planned to the Workman's Compensation laws. The Shops Regulation Act is intended to permit greater school attendance ... " Byron began.

"All baby steps where giant strides are called for," cried another. "What about limiting the hours a man has to work, or requiring proper pensions for our widows?"

The bitterness from one: "Tell us of your own war-supply contracts!"

Others took up the cry, darting questions at him so that it was impossible to speak.

"How has your law against liquor helped us, the working men of this city? The chemists are the only ones who can sell spirits, and they grow fat off our sweat!"

"Why has the government closed our Ukrainian-language schools?"

"Why has there been no response to our pleas to limit the price of coal?"

Byron felt overwhelmed. He was not here as an apologist for what the Norris government had not done. He was here to pledge his credentials as a friend of the immigrant, in order that they may be persuaded to support the government. There was time yet for the usual cat's paw promises, the disingenuous engagements that marked an election campaign. He was heartily sick of it, and he bitterly resented the continuing influence of his father-in-law; he was in no mood for dissimulation. He shouted:

"Wait! I have not come with answers to all your questions. I have come only to say this: if you have any hope of changing your lot, it lies in your access to power. Powerful people. I am not one of them, but I know them. They want your votes. In return, they will make the changes that you demand, within reason. You cannot expect a wholesale difference, as the recent revolution in Russia. It will be incremental. Step-by-step. Small changes, one after the other. Heed me on this."

This brought no obvious diminution of the fractious mood. He looked at Dudyck, who shrugged. "Thank you gentlemen," he called, the edge of his words lightly feathered with sarcasm. "Good day."

To another man it might have been apparent that the sufferings of the ordinary worker, the newcomer and the poor, could not be easily mollified with a pledge of friendship, or past acts of kindness. Byron's understanding of empathy occurred at the intellectual level; he had yet to internalize a capacity to appreciate the joys and sorrows of other men, because he was largely insulated from the consequences of his indifference. For that to change would take an event so horrific that it would shake him to the core of his being. He had no idea that such an occurrence was nearly upon him.

# xviii

Jan had no difficulty finding work. Carpenters were in demand, as the post-war economy started to shift gears to accommodate the thousands of returning servicemen. Competent tradesmen easily commanded five dollars a day or more, but the hours were long and the work hard. Strikes and disruptions to protest conditions of labour were constant, and they frequently interrupted Jan's work. He had some sympathy with men who worked twelve hours a day, six days a week, for the long years of detention had drained him of his former robustness. Still strong, he nevertheless found that by end of day, he had little strength for anything but food and bed. He joined a carpenters' union because there was little choice. Had he chosen to go it alone, his tools would have been stolen or broken, his work dismantled, and other petty intimidations. He had seen it happen to others. He had no will to resist, nor was he enthusiastically supportive.

Jan had been three times to the Bloode home at Armstrong's Point, and had twice been intercepted by police. There was an unrest in the city, a fear, that mystified him. Each time he had pleaded that, as a former labourer from the Dauphin district, he was unfamiliar with the city. He knew such a tale would not hold should the same team of officers question him again. He had to be careful. Though he tried to keep watch at the Bloode & Bell warehouse, he caught no glimpse of Byron. He had no plan, save that he intended a revenge upon the man and woman he was certain had set out to destroy him. There was no other explanation for his imprisonment. Members of his union had written to the Borden government demanding answers, but the responses came cloaked in the gibberish of bureaucrats, citing Orders-in-Council, national security and the common weal as reasons why Jan's arrest must go without further explanation. There would be a time for confrontation and atonement, and Jan was patient. His boots were off, and he would walk across the continent should it be necessary. There would be a reckoning.

Luck was to intervene. Jan worked for a company, Brigden Woodworks Limited, which specialized in the framing of homes that were to be constructed of other than brick or stone. A house in Armstrong's point was having a large covered verandah added to it, one which would entirely surround the dwelling, enabling the family to enjoy the coolness of shade during the day, without the attendant nuisance of mosquitoes. This placed Jan on a daily basis three houses down and across the street from the Bloode mansion. He took it to be an omen, a portent of a final calculation yet to be made.

When he first saw Ervina, his heart surged, so great was the pull she still possessed in him. Byron seemed the same, though his coppery hair seemed paler now. But what dismayed Jan was the tiny blonde boy that trotted between them. There was no mistaking it: that boy was his. A son. And he belonged to someone else. Jan became obsessed to the point where it attracted the attention of the foreman, Begley.

"Dalmynyshyn. I've been watching you. I've noticed you can't seem to take your eyes off that woman down the street. If we get a complaint, you're gone. Understand me. I'll have no more of it, hear?"

Jan looked at him. Without thinking, he said, "I knew her once."

Begley laughed, a snort without humour. "*Knew* her? I should say! How in hell would a ruffian like you have to do with a creature like that?" He paused, admiring the woman as she played with the child in the garden. "Yeah, and I know the Queen of England!" He walked away in obvious contempt, tossing over his shoulder, "And get back to work. We don't pay for gawking."

Moments later, one of the stewards sidled up to Jan. "Fuck him. Work us near to death and then berate us for a moment of rest. Never fear, Jan. You go, we all go, and *no one* works this project." He paused, looking in the direction of Jan's gaze. "She *is* a beauty, I'll give you that." Smirking, he withdrew.

Jan was unable to look away. He watched for a few more minutes, then stiffened as Byron came out and handed something to the boy. The child ran off with whatever it was, and Byron put his arm around his wife. Jan felt sick as the enormity of their duplicity settled over him, mocking him like a witch's laughter. His hand tightened around the claw hammer he was holding. He had no plan. He could go over there now and confront them, and ... what? Beat the two of them to death? Tell the boy he was his father? What would he do then? His impotency galled.

"This is your last warning, fella. Back to work, or you can pick up your last pay packet in the morning."

Slowly, Jan turned back to the framing he was completing, lowering his head as if in deference. But his mind was in that yard, where she was, and he; his hate a living thing, eager for possession of his nocturnal as well as his waking mind.

Late that night, hands clasped behind his head, his thoughts were tortured by the recollection. What had happened to him starkly contrasted in the balance.

*Such evil in this sorry world*
*Do men on men inflict!*
*For one they chain, and one they wound,*
*And one to death is kicked ...*
*And why? God knows the cause!*

He knew he would have no peace until this matter was put behind him. By and by, he determined that the only choice open to him was to take the boy. That would hurt them, right enough, and it would place the child where he rightfully belonged: with the one that sired him.

It was not much of a plan, and the obstacles were significant. Police patrols were everywhere, and this spring of 1919 brought a heat to the city that was not simply of the unusual dryness of weather. Labour unrest was festering in pockets of anger and disruption among metal workers and coal carriers, tram drivers and electrical utility workers. Men on street corners used gimmicks to catch the attention of passers-by, then launched into tirades against the monied classes. Meetings, even sermons were interrupted, and Winnipeg became known as 'injunction city' for the number of court orders sought and obtained against striking workers. Time and again, the courts sided with business interests, for every institution was drenched with the same established mindset, the same prejudices.

Jan had little time for these quarrels, but he found himself drawn into them all the same. It was hard not to be engaged, for the calls to join One Big Union were everywhere among people of influence in the labour movement. A general strike in Seattle had paralyzed that city, and the popular view expressed in the *Tribune* and the *Free Press* was that the 'Red Menace' was real. In May, all the construction trades walked off the job to back wage demands. Jan was put out of work. Two weeks later, as momentum built among the umbrella labour groups, the entire city was closed down. Nothing moved except by permission of the core labour group, the Strike Committee, which permitted some essential services.

The business interests established a 'Committee of 1000' which required the presence of every well-to-do merchant in the city, including Byron Bloode, which then set about linking the strikers with the 'foreign element', the 'enemy alien', and the 'undesirable'. Though it was a canard, it nevertheless built on the prejudices and fears of the day. For six long weeks the city simmered under the tensions thus created, and movement abroad was impossible. Jan stayed in the single room flat he rented in the north end, not far from the Higgins Bridge. It was barely a fifteen minute walk to the Bloode & Bell warehouse, and it was there that he spent his days.

He had developed his plan carefully. Since there was no possibility of going to Armstrong's point now that work was stopped, he volunteered for placard duty with the Labour Council. This gave him relative freedom to march up and down Bannatyne, around the block to the rear of the warehouse. It was quiet, for not a single workman was in evidence. That there were armed guards on the premises was obvious, for every now and then, one would emerge, shotgun in hand, to change shifts, or to take delivery of bread and sausage brought by a colleague. Byron came frequently, to Jan's surprise. He took no notice of Jan, for the placard-bearers were everywhere, and Jan's message was relatively benign. On one occasion, Byron's automobile stopped beside him, and he could have touched the man as he stepped out of the car. But Jan waited.

Sooner or later, he expected, he would bring the boy with him. Then Jan would act. He would move as decisively as he had more than twenty years ago, when he had been threatened, not far from where he now stood. He basked in the haze of that little-recalled event, which had so profoundly re-directed the course of his life. Now he was on the verge of another such significant event. But many weeks passed, and there was no sign of the boy. And circumstances were conspiring to defeat Jan again.

On June 10th, not far from the warehouse, at the junction of Winnipeg's principal arteries, Portage Avenue and Main Street, anti-strike 'specials', no more than thugs in the employ of the business interests, replaced the fired police force and charged assembled strikers on borrowed milk horses. The shrieking tumult flooded away from the intersection under the blows of the specials' batons, and dozens of strikers fled past Jan on the sidewalk pavement, some of them with blood streaming from their heads. Jan had not seen what had precipitated the commotion, and he struggled against the flow of bodies to determine the cause. Byron had not arrived as yet, and he worried that this uproar may forestall that event altogether.

As he did so, his eyes locked on a familiar face. For a moment, the two men stared at one another, recognition distant but unconnected. Then a cry:

"Jan! Jan Damination! By God! I'd recognize that beak of yours after a hunnert years, even though it's been no more'n twenty!"

Jan looked dumbfounded, for the voice was familiar as well, yet ... then there it was even as the other announced himself.

"Snow. Whyteas C. Snow! The 'C' don't stand fer nuthin', remember? Now don't tell me you don't remember me?"

Jan smiled in spite of himself. He had little cause to feel cheerful these many years, yet here before him was an apparition from his past, chatting as if the chaos around them did not exist. He remembered that the man had stolen off in the night when it looked as if the wounded police officer might not survive, or the desperate Indians return. The excitement now was lost on him, and Jan took his sleeve. "Come with me. There is a coal cellar not far from here where we hide. Trouble will find us soon enough if we stay here."

"Yer English's a hell of a lot better than I recall it," said Snow as he was tugged along by his sleeve. "But youse just as strong, dammit." He looked up admiringly. "Jesus Lord, man. Have yer grown? Big as a ruddy house! Hey: slow down, this samples case is heavy! Where you going, anyway?" He strained at the leather bag.

Once inside the coal cellar, they relaxed, for it could be secured from the inside. The white light at the sides of the ill-fitting door provided enough illumination to limn the two men perched opposite one another on the burlap sacks of Souris anthracite.

"So these many long years ... " began Jan.

"Seems like twenty minutes, don't it. I don't know where the time has gone. Can't even lay claim to anything great. 'Fraid I ain't done much with my life. Still pushin' pills fer a living, though. People still want to live forever." He cackled. "Or fuck forever. Two of three rings thet's set in a man's nose. The other's wealth, a course, and thet's my ring. Only it's seemed ta elude me, don't ya know?"

Jan nodded, as if in agreement. But there were many rings in a man's nose when it came to that. Pride, vanity, lust, avarice, cowardice: how many were there?

He looked at the cheerful peddler, his threadbare clothes forgotten in the chiaroscuro of the coal bin. "Still you sell medicines?" As the other nodded, he asked, "Do you have anything for hope?"

"Hope? I should say so!" He drew a long finger toward Jan. "Do you realize that ninety-nine out of every one hundred men have some form of sexual weakness? Is there hope? You bet there is! The habits of self abuse, running riot in a body young and but partially developed, acting over a period of years upon a nervous system as soft and susceptible to impressions as potter's clay, must of necessity leave its marks behind. In ninety-nine cases out of a hundred, it is the effects of the slimy serpent of ignorance and passion that drags its repellent lengths through a whole lifetime, that lead to lack of ambition, consumption, failure, lassitude, sterility, divorce, and a thousand and one other ills.

"This vampire of youth can be vanquished ... "

"Hist!" shushed Jan. "We can be discovered. Lower the voice." Shouting men ran by, then horses clattered on cobblestones. More shouts. In the distance, the din of confrontation was muffled, ebbing and flowing like water on a distant shore.

" ... by the simple topical application of *Singleton's Medicated Electricity*."

He was smiling broadly; Jan could see the dull gleam of his coated teeth in the gloom.

"This I remember ... "

"Quite impossible. This a new product. Very effective, a brand new battery inside each bottle, but the electrolyte is much refined, like treacle, almost. Just spread it on your ... "

"Hold, Whyteford C. Snow! I remember saying, 'do you have anything for hope?'"

Snow examined his face closely, as if the near-darkness was hiding something more than was apparent. He saw that Jan was not mocking him. "Oh, *hope*. For the man who has all but given up?" Jan said nothing.

Snow rummaged in his bag. His voice became conspiratorial. "There is something new, but it is very expensive. In spite of its salutary effect, I have to limit myself, for even at my cost, it is a rich man's tonic."

"What is it?" asked Jan, mildly curious. They both shrank back suddenly as someone beyond tried the door. "It's locked tight!" came the cry, and footsteps ran off.

"The newest thing. Radium water. I also carry the suppositories — them things you sticks up yer ass — and the Testone Radium Energizer to be worn at night, all I tried, but listen Jan, my friend: this radium water really works. It really does! I been takin' this stuff for eighteen months, and I tell you, I feel like a new man! I feel like I'm literally bursting! Now if I could only stop my teeth from falling out, an' get rid of these big red sores I got on my chest an' arms ...

"But oh Jesus Lord, it's expensive. Buck a bottle. But listen, why don't I give you a free sample, sorta, well, ta even things out. I know I run off on ya all them years ago, shouldna done it, but ... there was other stuff."

Jan held the bottle in his hand. It was green, dark, and mysterious. The idea that a small drink could change a man's life seemed ludicrous, unless it was poison. He held the vial up to the crack of light at the jamb. The fluid inside drifted magically, withholding its secrets like a charm that can only work if believed in. But Jan had lost faith in all things, and he handed the bottle back. "It is no good. Hope has never served me well before: why should it now?"

"Aw, go on. Drink up. It can only kill ya!" Again the rough cackle. "For old times' sake. A man without hope might as well be dead."

Jan unstopped the cork, and upended the contents into his mouth. It had a curious, metallic taste that was neither pleasant nor offensive. He waited for something to happen, but after a time, handed the empty container to Snow. The peddler seemed disappointed.

"I don't remember the first time I started takin' the stuff, but I remember that the reaction was strong. Felt like I had two hearts pumpin' blood. Felt like I was ready to sow the wind an' reap the whirlwind. You'll see." He stood, hunched over from the lowness of the ceiling, and pressed his eye against the door.

After a time, he spoke: "Looks like it's quieting down a tad. Never been in a place where there was more fuss and commotion than this city. Seems like nobody's happy here, and they want ta share it with yer. If it ain't the money people givin ya what fer, it's the cops. Then it's the socialists and Methodists an' Communists, Bolshevists and God-knows-what-elsivists carping after yer. An all I want ta do is flog a little medicine — a little do-it-yerself, feel-good, starch-in-yer laundry vitality — an' get by. Is that too much ta ask?" He pulled open the bolt, and peering this way and that, stepped into the sunshine.

He turned and peered in at Jan, who remained on the coal sacks. "You don't seem like you got much ta be content with, friend. Not that ya had a lot ta say twenty years ago, but you was content then, I recall, knew what ya wanted, was goin' after it. Did ya ever get that land you was lookin fer?"

Jan's silence seemed to give him all the answer he needed, and he shook his head. "Well, too bad. If yer peg yer hope to a thing that yer got no control over, well, you'll always be blue. It's the truth of it." He reached in and took Jan's hand. Shaking it, he said, "Well, you haven't contributed a whole lot ta this conversation, but that's the nature of our friendship." He cackled. "See ya in another twenty years."

He strode away whistling to the foot of Bannatyne, rounded the edge of the docks, and was gone. His thin notes hung in the air like a fool's prophecy. The notes were telling Jan something, but he could make no sense of it. There was no sense in anything anymore. He lay back on the sacks and slept. In his tormented sleep, Whyteas C. Snow pitched potions that changed the world, reassembled lost dreams and restored love. He had an impression of arguing with him, debating in his native tongue. What was wrong with pinning your hopes on things past command? Wasn't all that really mattered always beyond your control?

And what of the folly of becoming captive to the very things once scornfully sold to the gullible?

To which the peddler replied: "Where you going, anyway?"

# xix

These committee meetings were the last word in boring, Byron thought, as the speeches droned on. The so-called 'Committee of One Thousand', touted as the 'cream of the Winnipeg business and professional community', was organized to respond to the threat of domination of all civic activities by the Strike Committee of the Winnipeg Trades and Labour Council. The tactics they chose to employ would seize the offensive, by labelling the strikers as the 'alien enemy', and the 'refuse of Europe', and other epithets that had been around since the first waves of eastern European immigration.

Byron found this sort of hyperbolic rhetoric quite unuseful. All of the strike leaders save one was British born, and that one an Orangeman from Ontario. But the rage seemed to feed itself, and if a helping of epithets moved it along, there was none to object.

"Listen to me now," cried a prominent lawyer. He was holding aloft a copy of the *Liberal Voice*. "'Canada did not give her sons to die in order that the old rag of anarchy might float over the country'. As well-written a statement of my exact sentiments as you'll find."

There were general noises of approval.

"These bastards have sent greetings to the new Soviet government in Russia, to add to the grossly insulting campaign designed to undermine the war efforts. All this clap-trap about One Big Union, boys, I tell you, will lead to anarchy. Sure as sin. Damned foreign scum.

"The question before us is really quite simple: will we allow ourselves to be driven by events, or as men of honour, shall we rise above them, and act according to principle?"

This struck Byron as sheer hypocrisy. How facile it was to invoke high moral tones to justify a course of action. Yet the rhetoric stung: all his life he felt he had been driven by forces beyond himself. He shuffled impatiently as the florid-faced man droned on.

Byron knew that the lawyer had long since ceased the practice of law, only maintaining a place on the letterhead of his firm for the sake of prestige. Having won his King's Counsel appointment through his political connections, he was content to dabble in the halls of power, funding his influence with his considerable wealth. However, he had invested heavily in the metal trades; these workers were among the first to go out. He was co-owner, among other things, of Pritchard Metal Works, which was one of Byron's suppliers. Each day that passed in this seemingly endless strike was costing him more now than he could hope to recover. His anger was deep and personally held. Demonizing the strikers in this way gave vent to his frustration, his rage, his greed and his vanity. Byron felt disgusted.

It was not as if his own business was escaping the effects of the work stoppage. He had been compelled to go in on his own to do paperwork and inventory, tasks which he abhorred. While there were plenty of hard men to retain as guards, skilled or experienced men dared not be seen going to work. He was unused to such a heavy schedule: there was a catalogue to get ready, there were invoices to record, billings to prepare, a Spring inventory to complete, light maintenance, and winter orders to get ready for delivery to the border for mailing. Though it was quiet, no telephones ringing, no customers on the floor, no staff bustling back and forth, the work was torture for Byron. As the shutdown dragged into its sixth week, he was increasingly impatient with his wife, who saw no role for herself in the business. His requests of her were constant.

"Ervina, why can't you see your way to giving me even a single day? You were marvellous at the school. Your handwriting is superb, and your head for figures far better than mine. I just *have* to have some help."

She had objected, pleading the need to attend to Michael, for the nanny was not working either. The school was something she enjoyed. Toiling in a dusty warehouse seemed not to her a labour of love.

"Then bring him along," he had said. "There is no one about. He'll have the run of the place. He should have the time of his life."

She had looked doubtful.

"Come on," he had said. "What could possibly happen to him?"

# XX

Inspector Rishton Jones tugged at his too-tight collar. His wind-beaten face didn't look much older than during his days patrolling the Dauphin region, but he felt old as dust. Since the war, everything was changing, changing too fast for an aging horseman.

Looking up at the sky, Jones could see moisture-laden clouds piled like dirty pillows, and it was not yet mid-afternoon. She'll be a cat-screamer of a storm coming, boys, he thought. A little rain might be of some use now, and he willed it to happen. His mount shifted under him; it was soaked from withers to fetlock with sweat after the run down from Fort Osborne Barracks to Main Street.

As broad as Main Street was, it seemed confining to the crush of bodies. Demonstrators, strikers, activists, idlers and the curious were gathered; the mischief had already started. Unable to topple a northbound streetcar, they snatched the electric cables away from a car headed in the opposite direction, and being unsuccessful at tipping it, they smashed out windows and set the interior ablaze. Black smoke drifted southward in their direction, lazy in the summer heat, stinking, ominous.

A mob is a funny thing, Jones thought. You never know if it will dissipate without real harm, or explode with single-minded ferocity. No sense provoking it, he thought, just let the rabbit run, and see what he does.

But the Mounties had already been instructed to make one pass up the street, as far north as the Canadian Pacific Railway underpass at Higgins, then around and back through the crowd. Initially, the mob folded back against itself like a snarling beast before chair and whip. It was a resentful yielding, with a surliness to it that the stony-faced men on horseback tried to ignore: eyes fixed straight ahead, cudgels at the ready in silent threat. But the horses sensed it, and skittered at a shouted curse or flashed hat, eyes rolling.

Jones would not have deployed in this way so quickly, but there were so many damned fingers in the pie that it was impossible to know who was in charge, or where the ultimate orders were coming from.

He was not much aware of the efforts of strike leaders, anti-labour activists, civic officials including Mayor Gray — and even his own boss, Commissioner Perry — to end the parade that had been planned this day. The bare fact of it was that the strike had festered on far too long, and there seemed no will on either side to resolve it. Jones had an overwhelming sense that no one was in control, and it worried him. The strikers were surly over recent arrests of strike leaders and street car service had been resumed in spite of the Strike Committee's contrary instruction. All he knew for certain was that the three levels of government were firmly on the side of the anti-strikers, and there would be order, or damn the cost. He cursed under his breath.

Command had been given to the junior inspector, a fussy, blustering man named Mead. It was not surprising since Jones was well aware that his superiors regarded his own performance with some suspicion for his 'untidy ways', and unconventional policing practices. But his rank was an acknowledgement of genuine ability in law enforcement, even if that talent yielded in the end to more subtle politics and gamesmanship.

Jones had objected to the ostentatious show of force: it was sure to provoke men who sought provocation. Not far off were four Maxim-Vickers machine guns mounted in the back of motor lorries. Mead had threatened him with replacement if there "were further outbursts of insubordination."

"You will do as you are told, sir. Take the platoon and parade to the underpass. Divide the mob and disperse it," he had said.

It was difficult to return now, for the Mounties had become targets of bottles and stones, and attempts were made to unhorse them. They swung their batons like grain swiples, and men fell back before them, or fell, some frightfully injured. Jones sensed the mob's dim brain becoming galvanized as one, and stood in his stirrups, signaling with a gauntleted hand the request to withdraw.

Angrily, Mead shook his head, and the Staff-Sergeant with him made the circular motion for another pass. In the past, Jones had winked at or outright ignored so many orders that sidestepping this command might have been in the end inconsequential. However, the tension was so great, that in his hesitation, and upon men seeing the signal having already begun to wheel in the direction of the crowd without his order, he cursed again, and drove forward, calling, "Be careful boys, they're a mean lot." But his words were lost in the hiss of angry men.

# xxi

"It looks to me as if they're having another one of those blessed parades," said Byron as he pulled the Whippet to the curb in front of his warehouse. They had passed considerable numbers of men and picketers streaming north along Main Street. Ervina waited while he pulled up the convertible roof. Michael ran towards the side of the building where the packing crates were stored, whooping like an Indian. "It looks as if it might pour buckets soon," Byron said.

Ervina looked anxious. "Listen to that racket! There must be a thousand people over at City Hall." Byron turned in the direction she was facing. Voices could be heard on megaphones, and cheers every now and then sounded to punctuate particularly approved remarks, though at this distance of several blocks, the din was largely unintelligible. There seemed to be smoke in the air.

"Never fear," Byron said. "They don't bring their silly marches along the warehouse district. They'll head out by and by for Victoria Park and listen to more clap-trap. Blast it! Don't these people realize that we've got costs too? Maintaining a payroll is no picnic at the beach. Everything's going up. Where does the tradesman turn when we're out of business?"

He stopped himself, blushing. Ervina was giving him that look again. He had been listening to too many speeches at the Empire Club. That a man who lived in a mansion along Armstrong's Point, or the fashionable crescent along the river could claim the same level of grievances as the hourly-wage employee might seem indecent, were it not for the prevailing view that a man wrought of himself what his wit and energy would. The lower classes were predestined their lot, Byron mused. The privileged community had taken him in on the coattails of his father's wealth. It annoyed him that he was having to put in so much time in this building. Shouting out to the guard, he unlocked the massive door. Turning to see where his wife was, he called to her. She was nervously glancing up the street, arms folded.

"I don't like it," she said. "I don't think we should stay long."

Ervina looked around suddenly. She could no longer hear Michael scruffling about on the packing crates stacked beside the building.

"What's wrong?" asked Byron.

He looked suddenly old to her, with his spectacles perched on the end of his nose. Could this man protect his family, if it came to that? "I'm going to check on Michael," she said. "I don't hear him anymore. I'll just check. There's a lot of commotion down the street... "

"Oh don't worry about that," Byron replied breezily. "We've got a man with a shotgun out there, should it come to any sort of trouble, with the Committee's sanction, of course." He turned back to the door, already anticipating the day's work. "Call me if you need me."

# xxii

The police rode in pairs, disciplined and practiced. The redcoats in full dress led the way, and the others in 'falling out' uniforms, khaki, brought up the rear. Jones kept to a canter pace, and he swept though the mob like an arrow through smoke. But behind him, the missiles became heavier and more frequent. Paving stones, bottles, trash and stripped branches from shade trees all were flung at the riders. The khakis got the worst of it.

On the return run, the column began to waver, unsteady under the press of men who could unseat them. Some were wild now, oblivious to the blows of the police batons, and struggled with the horses, as if to pull them down. Then a mounted policeman rode his horse over a length of sheet metal torn from a tram. The animal stumbled badly, and went down. Staggering to its feet, it bolted, dragging the unfortunate man with him, his foot firmly lodged in the stirrups. They were quickly stopped by the crowd, who set upon the hapless policeman.

Jones made for him, but was brought nearly to a standstill by a swarm of angry men. Above them, incongruously, Mayor Gray was reading the Riot Act through a brass horn. His voice sounded tinny and distant. "His Majesty the King charges and commands all persons being assembled immediately to disperse and peaceably depart to their habitations or lawful business upon the pain of being ..." The mayor ducked a splinter of paving stone as it clattered off the parapet at City Hall, and hurriedly finished a shortened version, " ... sentenced to imprisonment for life!" He ran inside.

At the sight of the fallen rider surrounded by a jam of attackers, some of whom were swinging batons seized from other riders, Mead panicked and gave the order to fire, just as the Mayor was completing his recitement. Officers drew their .38 revolvers and began to shoot into the crowd, at first concentrating their fire near where their fallen comrade had gone down. One man collapsed immediately, shot through the head, dead before he struck the roadway. Others set up a fearful keening that sounded high above the general din as they were struck by the slow-moving bullets. For several minutes, the police emptied their revolvers at the swaying mass of men, until its distant, collective brain realized that a mortal danger was upon them.

Hemmed in by the streets, plugged by blockades thrown up by the special constables who stood waiting with clubs and blackjacks, and the arrival of the militia and mobile guns from the barracks, hundreds of men dashed back and forth in frantic attempts to escape. It was bedlam at all points. There were knots of struggling combatants, others pleading for mercy as they were beaten to the ground, groups being chased, and others hiding in pathetic attempts to avoid the vengeful bloodlust that was upon the police and their reinforcements.

Jones cantered back and forth attempting to bring some order back to his men, but they were wild with the fear that had so recently possessed them, and he would not be heard. Coming upon two anti-strike 'specials' thrashing a screaming man with cudgels of their own making, he dismounted and shouted at them to desist. As he seized one of them by the shoulder, he was struck from behind, then again. Blackness took him, and he did not feel the embrace of the cool street.

At the foot of Bannatyne stood the Botterill Bag Company warehouse. Its single attractive feature was a trio of bold archways through which carts or motor-trucks could be driven to loading docks that were built into the sides. At the street side of these docks were hinged platforms that could be dropped to the beds of vehicles for ease of loading. Drawn up, they were a perfect place to hide, while having a complete view of either direction of the street, according to which side one chose. On the afternoon of June 21, 1919, this was where Jan had been lying, dozing.

The sound of the Whippet's wheezing engine, and its pop-popping at having its spark retarded, drew Jan's attention. He started, knocking stiff knees against the catwalk. There, at the nearby Bloode & Bell warehouse, was Ervina with that fawn-like gait of hers, her head casting about, obviously looking for someone. On the other side of the building stood the boy, his hand over his eyes, staring down the street.

Jan's heart pounded; whether from the sight of her, or the boy, or the enormity of what he had decided he must do, he was not sure. He walked slowly toward the Bloode & Bell warehouse. Cries and distant shouting, and a clattering din coming from the direction of Main Street a block and a half away had distracted the guard, and the man had walked off a distance, for Bannatyne Avenue angled slightly as it came away from Main. His shotgun was laid carelessly upside down over his shoulder, pointing backwards, as he craned his neck to see what the fuss was about.

Singly, then in small groups, panicked men fled toward and past the guard, the soles of their boots slapping noisily against the paving stones, echoing flatly in the silent street. Jan saw them only as a welcome screen for himself. There had been so many disturbances associated with the work stoppages that he took no particular notice of this latest flurry.

He edged his way to the loading docks behind the warehouse, just off the street. He was now out of sight of the security man. That the uproar seemed to be intensifying mattered not in the least to him, for he was fixed upon what he was ready to do. It struck him again that across the laneway was the same yard in which he had restored his cart, more than twenty years ago. It was disconcerting; time seemed to freeze. He was a young man again.

The small access trap that was let into the larger freight doors was left open; beside it was the rail-back chair that the guard had been slumped upon, tilted back against the wall. He made for this door like a panther, all of his being focused upon gaining access to the building. As he came abreast of the platform, which was about the level of his lower chest, he stopped short. The boy was stepping carefully over the high sill of the access port.

He was dressed in short pants with a matching blue blouse. He wore white knee socks, one of which had drooped to his ankle. Dampness glistened on his forehead; his face was smudged.

"Hullo," the boy said.

It took Jan a moment to catch his breath, for he was taken by surprise.

"Hello." A grimace more than a smile crossed Jan's face. "What is your name?" His heart thumped a tattoo in his ears, and the world ceased to exist beyond what was happening to him. He and the child were the universe; beyond the rough stage where the boy stood, there were only blurred edges.

"My name is Michael, but my mama calls me 'Mikey'."

Jan tried smiling again. "Can I call you Mikey?"

"Sure." The boy walked over to him. He stood within arm's reach, looking down at Jan from his ledge, amused, his arms crossed. The sun, high overhead, framed his curly head like a halo. My little *unhalum*, angel, Jan thought. You are so beautiful.

"This is my papa's work building, don't you know. We're closed. You can't come in here. 'Cause my mama said."

"Oh ho!" Jan replied, "So you are the boss of the place are you?" Here was his boy, there was no doubt of it. Tall, blonde, precocious. Here stood a Dalmynyshyn, no one could seriously dispute this. It seemed improbable that Byron Bloode himself could not see it, for the reason that his life had been destroyed stood before him now, smirking, as young boys will do.

There is no loyalty like the loyalty of blood, the blood of tribe. Jan felt a powerful bond, an unreasoning love for this small creature. With it, there was an instinct that this was a love stronger than death. He could never have expressed or verified or even made coherent what he felt, for the thin roots of what he was experiencing stretched all the way back to the sun-splashed village of Kameneta-Podolak. He had become Stefan; the boy become him.

Michael looked toward the street. "Why are all those men running?" he asked.

"They play a game," replied Jan. "Would you like to play?"

A smile creased Michael's sweaty face, for he was bored. His parents were no doubt scribbling numbers in books. "Yes sir. I would, too!"

Jan raised his hands to him, and the child leapt into his arms. At the crush of this tiny, warm body against him, Jan felt wetness start from his eyes. His voice shook, and it was suddenly difficult to speak. He kissed the boy on the top of his head, and whispered. "Are you ready to play the game?"

There was a vigorous nodding of the head.

"Good," said Jan. "Now we are going to run, too, so do not be afraid. No one will catch us now." And he began to run toward the street. The boy shrieked with delight, and behind them, from the loading dock door, came a harrowing scream of denial.

# ⋮ XXiii

Jones shook his head, for the pain was sharp and his perceptions still dull. All around was chaos. He gripped the edge of a window ledge, and pulled himself to his feet. He slapped his holster; his pistol was there, thanks be to God. He looked about, shaking off the last of his dizziness, though the pain still stabbed at the back of his head.

A half dozen men were swarming over a Ford military truck stalled nearby. In the back, bolted down, was a Vickers water-cooled .303 calibre machine gun. No uniformed officers were in sight. Good God, he thought. If the strikers or anti-strikers, or whoever the hell they were, managed to figure out how to use that thing, we're in for a lot more trouble. To his dismay, the truck started, only to move jerkily away, for the driver seemed inexperienced. Several others pulled at the weapon, but not a one seemed to have any understanding of how it worked. Jones could see that it was primed with a belt of ammunition fed into the chamber; it was only a matter of time. The truck gathered speed down William, headed for Main.

A riderless horse cantered by, coming up against an abandoned barricade near Jones. Momentarily confused, the mare whinnied her frustration and fear; Jones seized the mount by the bridle, snatched the reins from the pommel, and swung himself up. Digging his spurs into its flanks, he turned the startled animal in the direction of the motor truck as it careened south on Main. The sparks flew from the mare's hooves as she galloped over the foot pavement, scattering people in her wake. He yanked the whistle from his breast pocket, and sounded three sharp blasts, the police call for help. Within moments, three other police riders were at his side, for the object of the pursuit was obvious to all.

Squealing tires protested the sharp turn onto Bannatyne, and the vehicle nearly lost its passengers as they frantically scrambled about for better purchase. Cutting at an angle, Jones closed the distance, and he began to worry that the two men who struggled with the Vickers might actually stumble upon the safety lever, which was awkwardly situated under the chamber, forward of the left grip. He dug his spurs in again, and fumbled for his revolver. It was secured about his neck by a braided lanyard, so that he could let it hang until it was needed. Up ahead, he could see that his quarry would soon fetch up at the docks.

Suddenly a hunched-over figure dashed into the street in front of the truck. A big man, by the look of him. There seemed to be a bundle clutched to his chest. Jones cried out a warning, though his shout was lost to the other sounds of chaos. There was a terrible scream of rubber against pavement, and the figure disappeared from view under the charging vehicle.


Jan heard and saw nothing. His body was immobile, as if he had somehow left it, and now contemplated his condition from afar. He was only aware that he was lying on his back, numb, as if in a dream; the sort of fantasy that comes to a man in the false light of dawn, and there is no window to gaze upon. In his vision, his boots were slung about his neck, and he was striding a great flat plain, sun at his back. There was a small lad, his son, at his side.

"Where are we going father?" asked the boy. It seemed to Jan there was a tremble of worry in his voice. "Are we going home?"

*Weep not, my little son, my grief -*
*Let all be for the best!*
*I will go on - I can endure ...*
*Perhaps I'll meet her yet;*
*Then, dear, I'll place you in her hands,*
*Though death my path beset*

Jan thrilled to the sound of his son addressing him thus: there could be no title more grand or honourable than 'father', for it carried the implication of a sacred trust. How to answer properly? How to know that the chosen direction was correct, and the object clear? And how to convey that in an assured way, inspiring confidence?

"Yes, my son, we go home."

Since times of deepest antiquity, *pópa* Kudryk had taught him, men were sent by their hearts upon pilgrimages. Some men are guided to what they seek by the polestar, the visible world of roads and landmarks. Others pursue their dreams depending upon faith or the teachings of ancestors. For a few, a blessed few, the journey is itself enough.

# ACKNOWLEDGEMENTS

*Why do we live? What is our will?*
*Why do we die with wistful mind?*
*And leave unfinished deeds behind?*

— *Shevchenko*

Taras Shevchenko, poet prince of Ukraine, died in 1861 at the age of 47, one week before the abolition of serfdom in the Russian Empire. His poetry is a paean to the freedom of individuals to choose, to pursue their dreams, and to triumph or fail as their choices may compel. Unfortunately, he is not well-known in Canada outside the Ukrainian community, and much of his work has been translated by unknown scholars at the University of Kiev, in undated volumes not widely available. There is one fine anthology by C.H. Andrusyshen and W. Kirkconnell published in 1964. All the poetical references in this book, save the two related by Byron to his family, are excerpts from Shevchenko's work.

Many hands have contributed an abundance of technical detail to this story, and I would like to record my debt of gratitude to the following persons: Donnie Malano of South Africa; Judge Mary Ellen Turpel-Lafonde; Christina Kopynsky; Robert Stefaniuk; the helpful staff of the Museum of Medical Quackery in Minneapolis; Dave Neufeld; Trevor Anderson, QC; the kind staff of the Elizabeth Dafoe Library at the University of Manitoba; Phil Gatensby, whose Tlingit name appears in this volume with his permission; the staff of the Ukrainian Museum in Saskatoon; Neil Whitley, for constant and undisclosed sources for Ukrainian idioms; Glenn Wright, staff historian for the RCMP; Jacqueline Nelson; Kevin Lalo; Major Bell March of Air Force Public Affairs; Reverend Rob Oliphant; Glen and Don Lewis; and Pat Porth.

I also want to express my gratitude to my family at home for the past five years who have tolerated the innumerable drafts and research material all over the house: my wife Christie, children Jenny, Ashleigh, Ted and Scott, Amy, Jennifer and Morgan, and my parents Ted and Peggy, who are always supportive of my incessant scribbling.

Finally, my thanks to Great Plains Publications, in particular publisher Gregg Shilliday and his staff — Charmagne de Veer and Jewls Dengl — who had confidence that this was a tale worth telling.